The
Berlin
Zookeeper

The
Berlin
Zookeeper

ANNA STUART

bookouture

Published by Bookouture in 2021

An imprint of Storyfire Ltd.
Carmelite House
50 Victoria Embankment
London EC4Y 0DZ

www.bookouture.com

ISBN: 978-1-80019-432-8
eBook ISBN: 978-1-80019-431-1

For Mum – I hope you know how precious you are to me.

Prologue

Katharina Heinroth
Ursula Franke
Gisela Schultz
Sasha Eberhard
Countess Sylvie
Anke?

Bethan's hands shook as she looked at the strange list, written years ago in her mother's precious hand. Clipped to the top of it was a small silver brooch in the shape of a chubby hippo and, unfastening it carefully, she pinned it to the lapel of her coat. Her hand shook and she stabbed her finger with the pin but she almost welcomed the pain. It reminded her of the terrible day she'd found the now yellowing piece of paper.

She'd been eleven and raw with grief. Her mother's funeral had been awful and afterwards, when she'd just wanted to curl up in her dad's arms to resist the grief that threatened to drown her, there had been what felt like hundreds of people in their house, drinking and crying and endlessly telling her how much Jana had loved her.

Bethan hadn't wanted their assurances, she'd just wanted her mother's love alive and well, scolding her for not eating her crusts, nagging her to do her homework, making her pancakes on a Saturday morning. She hadn't wanted all those heavy arms around her, just her mum's tickles and easy cuddles, so when the food had been served, she'd snuck away to hide upstairs under her parents' bed. At eleven she'd been almost too big to fit but it had still felt right. So had grabbing her mum's jewellery box to take under with her, as if the contents might give her a key back to the past.

And in a way they had – just not to her own past. For there, beneath the pretty necklaces and bracelets of happier times, had been the hippo brooch. She'd been instantly caught by the cute animal, and with it had come the small sheet of paper she was gazing on now, filled, in her mother's distinctively rounded European hand, with women's names.

Bethan had stared at it until her tear-red eyes had swum with more than just sorrow. She'd always been fascinated by her mum's German roots and the language that had been their own little code. She'd loved visiting the country and staying with her Oma Erika and had missed it once Oma had died three years ago. And now this – a suggestion that there had been things going on in Jana's life that Bethan hadn't known about, people that had been important to her, questions she had wanted answers to. It had been a special link to her mum just when it had felt as if all connection had been lost.

Later that night, when it had finally just been her and Dad, she'd asked him about it. His reaction had hit her like a thunderbolt.

'Where on earth did you get that, Beth?'

He'd snatched it out of her fingers, jolting her.

'I found it. It was in Mum's jewellery box and you said everything in her jewellery box was mine now, so that means it's mine.'

He'd made a strange noise in the back of his throat, then fought to control himself.

'I did, sweetheart, I did. But this is just a silly thing. Just a, a shopping list.'

'Who are they?'

'I'm not sure. Just people in Germany. Friends, I think, from when Mum was young.'

'Friends? Are you sure? This one's a countess, see.' She'd tried to take it from him but he'd pulled it away, tearing the edge, and she hadn't dared fight for it in case it ripped totally.

'Please, Daddy. I like it. It's in her writing.'

'So is this.'

He'd plucked the card off her bedside table. It had a picture of two elephants with their trunks entwined and, inside, a long message of love from her mum. It had been Bethan's most treasured possession but that hadn't stopped her wanting the list.

'What's so secret about it?' she'd demanded.

He had backtracked then, insisting, again, that it was just a 'silly thing', before sweeping it off downstairs. She'd heard the slam of the kitchen bin and lain there, the hippo brooch clutched tightly in her hand, picturing the list rotting amongst the tea bags and potato peelings and trying not to hear her father crying quietly in front of the TV. Later, when he'd finally trudged up to bed, she'd crept back down, opened the bin and dug amongst all the sludgy mess until she'd found the paper, stained and damp but whole. She'd hated deceiving her dad but had been convinced there was something important about the list. It had felt as if it were a little part of her mum, still alive and contained on the paper, and Bethan had clung to it.

Now her fingers went to the brooch, tracing the indented letters on the silver hippo's chunky feet: BZ. She'd had no idea what they signified until Google had been invented years later and given her some basic information about the top name on the list: Katharina Heinroth – director of Berlin Zoo after the Second World War. Somehow, it seemed, the zoo had been important to her mother, so that had made it important to Bethan, even before she'd landed a job there.

Carefully, she placed the fragile list into her leather vet's bag. It was time to head for her new workplace, a new chapter in her life and a chance to try and find out more about the mystery list. Both, she knew, would be a challenge but it was one she was finally ready for.

Chapter One

'Wilkommen!'

Bethan stared happily up at the word, scrolled across an ornate archway supported by two huge marble elephants. Was this really the entrance to her new home? All around her, crowds were filing in, pointing at the monkeys playing in the cages to their left and running across to see the pandas lounging in their bamboo grove ahead. Bethan's fingers went to the hippo brooch and she almost skipped with excitement.

'I'm so pleased to be here,' she said in German to Ella, the young vet who'd kindly picked her up from the airport.

Ella was twenty-five with silky copper skin, a shock of dark curls in a bouncy ponytail, and a seemingly unfaltering smile. She was very chatty and already Bethan could feel the language coming more easily to her. She'd worked hard over the years to keep her German fluent, but without her mum to chat to it had inevitably become a little rusty. It felt special to hear their 'code' in action again.

'We're delighted to have you,' Ella said. 'We've been run off our feet recently. So many animals seem to be breeding that we can hardly keep up. Last week fifteen turtles hatched, yesterday we had two baby chimps, and Reina is due to give birth soon.'

'Reina?'

'One of the lionesses. Don't worry – you'll soon to get to know all the names. Come on, let's take you to the vet centre and then we can show you around.'

The queue of visitors parted at the sight of her dark green uniform and she waved at the young lad in the ticket booth and headed off past the monkeys, threading her way around a rocky compound from which baboons shrieked and chattered. She blew them a kiss and led Bethan round the back and up to a low, modern building. Big doors blocked their way but Ella's pass let them straight through and, as Bethan saw a few of the visitors eyeing them curiously, she felt a surge of pride. She was an employee of the zoo with access to all the private areas, and she felt like a kid in a sweetshop. It was everything she had dreamed of and more.

'Are you sure this is a good idea?' Callum had questioned her this morning, as she'd taken her medical bag through to their room to get the rest of her luggage.

She could see her boyfriend now, his chocolatey eyes shadowed by a frown as he'd sat on their bed, plucking at a loose thread on the Leicester City duvet cover that had been about his only contribution to the decor of the flat.

'You know how much I've been wanting to work in a zoo, Callum.'

'What's wrong with Twycross?'

She'd blinked, wondering why on earth he'd waited until now to express his doubts.

'Nothing, really. It just hasn't got a research department as big as Berlin. This is a huge opportunity for me, Cal, you know that. You've read my PhD on animals in captivity. You said it was interesting.'

'It *was* interesting. I just didn't realise it was going to, you know, consume you.'

'Consume me?'

Callum had plucked again at the duvet, puckering Jamie Vardy's face.

'Are you sure this is about the zoo, Beth?'

'What else would it be about?'

'Your mum,' he'd said. 'And that stupid list you're so obsessed with.'

Bethan had gasped.

'How dare you? It's not a stupid list and it's not the main reason I've taken this job. If you can't see that then maybe it's a good job we're having some time apart.'

He'd jumped.

'What d'you mean by that? Are you leaving me, Bethan?'

For a moment she'd been tempted to say yes. Things had been rocky between them since Callum had turned thirty-five at the back end of last year and started partying hard, trying to ward off impending middle age. Bethan didn't like it – she'd invited him to move into her flat a year ago to share their future, not to save him beer money – but friends had told her it was just a male-crisis thing and a few weeks without her would soon sort out his priorities. She hoped they were right, but for now she had to focus on her career.

An athletic older lady came striding towards them and she rushed forward to shake her hand.

'Hi, Tanya.'

'Bethan – welcome to Berlin Zoo.'

'It's fantastic to be here. Thank you so much for taking me on.'

Tanya, the head vet who'd video-interviewed her last month, was tall with sharp grey eyes and a long plait of hair far blonder than Bethan's own strawberry locks. She shook her hand enthusiastically.

'You were the best candidate by far so I'd have been mad not to. Let's show you around. Ella, could you…'

But at that moment Ella's phone bleeped and a highly realistic meerkat avatar peeped out of the screen. Bethan squinted at it and Ella laughed.

'It's our bleeper system. I'm a meerkat and I'm needed at the hippo house. Sorry, Tanya, can you show Bethan around?'

'Of course,' Tanya agreed, but then her phone bleeped as well, displaying a picture of a giraffe. 'Hang on – me too. Come on, Bethan, straight into the heart of the action!'

Bethan followed the other two women as they headed up past the elephants doing tricks for their keepers, and two rhinos digging in the dirt, and made for a futuristic glass dome. They moved fast and Bethan, encumbered by her bags, was soon panting. She fought to keep up as they laced their way through a large group of visitors and past a statue of a hippo, startlingly realistic save that it was wrought in rich bronze that sparkled in the spring sunshine. Something about it seemed curiously familiar and Bethan paused to look.

'Knautschke,' Ella told her. 'Father, grandfather and great-grandfather to most of the hippos in here, bless him.'

'Is he still alive?'

'Lord no. He was born in the war. Nearly died in it too by all accounts, but was saved from a burning building just in time. This way.'

A keeper was waving to them from the edge of the water, and Bethan again felt the thrill of being part of the team as Tanya's pass opened up the gate. Two of the younger hippos had been fighting and one, Klumpig, had a nasty gash in his side.

'It'll need stitching up,' Tanya said straight away. 'We'll have to get him somewhere more private.'

She nodded to the growing crowd beyond the barrier and the keeper, Sonya, fondly patted the head of the hippo who looked up at her forlornly. Bethan's already laboured breathing caught. Klumpig was clearly a juvenile, but he was a big lad with a huge mouth and long teeth. She had to remind herself that he was a herbivore. This was a far cry from the parade of dogs, cats and hamsters that she'd been used to in the practice back home, and she bent down to touch the animal's leathery back to be sure that it was real. Behind her another hippo let out a furious bellow and she jumped.

'Don't worry – Mummy hippo's behind the gates.'

Bethan looked over and saw that the other hippos had been locked off by a metal barrier, both above and below the blue pool. Within moments Sonya was fetching a sling-device and they were able to winch up Klumpig and carry him into the sleeping area at the back. A disappointed sigh rippled around the crowd and Tanya laughed.

'Did they think I was going to whip out my needle in front of them?'

'They certainly hoped it,' Ella said. 'Sorry, Bethan, we threw you in at the deep end there. Let's see if we can find someone to show you around.'

'No rush,' Bethan said, as Tanya began swabbing the hippo's thick skin.

'It's best. No offence, but the more of us in here, the more agitated Mum will get.' She nodded in the direction of the bellows still sounding out from the pool. 'I'll bleep Max.'

Before Bethan could protest further, Ella pulled out her phone, opened the zoo app and selected a picture of a cheeky chimp.

'Max, hi! We've got an incident in the hippo house. Have you got time to come and show the new vet around? The English one, yes.'

'Half German,' Bethan corrected her self-consciously, but Ella was talking again.

'Course you can, Max. It's good for you to get away from your precious monkeys and talk to something a little more evolved.' She laughed merrily at whatever poor Max replied. 'She won't bite you. She's nice. And very pretty.'

'Ella!' Bethan objected. Already the younger vet was feeling like a sort of mischievous little sister. 'I'll just wait somewhere till you're done, really.'

Ella waved her quiet.

'Thank you, Max,' she trilled. 'See you in a minute.' She clicked off the phone. 'He's coming to get you. Leave your bags here and head back out to the entrance. He'll see you there.'

'But…' Bethan started, before she saw that Tanya and Sonya urgently needed Ella's help and she was only getting in the way.

Shyly she edged back round the pool, very aware of myriad visitors' eyes on her. Outside, she rested a hand on the broad, bronze back of the Knautschke statue to steady herself. But something about the smooth feel of it triggered a memory that sent her already strained senses reeling.

She was ten and dressed in shorts and her favourite penguin T-shirt, her strawberry blonde hair in two little pigtails and a rucksack on her back containing a camera, a notebook and pink pencil with which she intended to record all she saw at the zoo. Her mother was with her, and suddenly Bethan could imagine herself back in time and reached out a hand to try and touch the hem of Jana's sky-blue dress. It met only thin air and she snatched it back, worried she looked insane.

'This is Knautschke, Bethie,' her mum's voice said in her head. 'That means Crumples in English. Cute, isn't he?' Bethan could remember looking into the big mouth of the bronze creature and not being sure that 'cute' was quite the right word for him, but her mum had looked so eager that she'd nodded. 'Want to ride on his back?' Before Bethan could answer, Jana had hoiked her up to sit astride the hippo. 'Isn't that great? Isn't he cool?'

Bethan closed her eyes, trying to capture the moment, and was relieved when her phone pinged, pulling her back into the present. It was her dad.

Are you there safe, sweetheart?

She grinned and typed back.

I'm here and it's fab.

The little dots squiggled as her father typed an answer.

Send me lots of pictures. Can't wait to see it. Tickets booked for Easter weekend. Missing you already. x

Missing you too, Dad. xxxxx

She added a couple more kisses for luck and pressed send. Callum thought her close relationship with her dad was 'weird'. He never understood why she popped in to see him every few days, or how often she liked to invite him over to eat with them. He and Paul shared a love of sport which gave them plenty to talk about, but he still insisted it was strange to be this attached to a parent at thirty-three. Maybe it was, but it was *her* strange and she liked it that way.

'Bethan Taylor?'

Bethan jumped and looked up to see a tall man with dark, floppy hair, intense blue eyes and impatience written across every line of his slim body.

'That's me. Max?'

He nodded.

'Max Femer, head primate keeper and assistant manager here at the zoo. I hear you need a guide.'

His voice was low and warm but he had a very clipped way of speaking, as if there wasn't enough time for more words. Bethan leaped to answer.

'That's very kind of you, but I'm sure you're busy and I wouldn't want to hold you up.'

'No trouble. I have half an hour before feeding time so if we're quick we can just about fit everything in.'

'Really, I—'

'If we're quick,' he said sternly, and she clamped her mouth shut and hurried after him as he made off up the path.

His legs were long and his strides as purposeful as his speech, and within moments Bethan was out of breath again. Thank God she'd packed her running shoes; she *had* to get into shape.

'Eagle canyon,' Max was saying, waving to the heavily netted area to their right. 'Over there, our bears. Everyone loves the polar bears but I think they're over-rated. I like the brown ones far better. Much more unassuming. And they're the symbol of Berlin, you know.'

Bethan, almost jogging to keep up, couldn't think of anything to say but Max was already striding onwards. He took her round the large zoo at speed, ducking expertly around dawdling visitors and throwing animal names at her – 'penguins, zebras, storks, pandas'. Bethan stopped to stare at the gorgeous black-and-white creatures lazily chewing on bamboo cane beneath an elegant Chinese-style pagoda but Max tutted quietly and, suspecting he found this another over-rated creature, she forced herself on. She was here for a year, after all, so there'd be all the time in the world to drink in every one of the beautiful animals. She hugged herself at the thought and ran after him.

'And here are the monkeys.'

He stopped so suddenly that she almost ran into him. She put out a hand to steady herself and it met with a surprisingly muscular back. Hastily she stepped away.

'Sorry.'

'No problem.' The look in his dark eyes suggested otherwise, but just then a chimp came swinging across the ropes and he softened instantly. 'Binky!'

He swiped his pass to open the door and stepped inside, arms held out to the chimp who leaped into them with a chatter of delight. Bethan was so mesmerised that she forgot to catch the door before it locked behind him, and it was only Binky leaping and pointing at her that reminded Max she was there at all. Wordlessly he swiped his pass again and she slid inside. Binky, at least, seemed pleased to see her and reached out to twine her slim fingers into Bethan's fair hair. She laughed and, to her surprise, Max did too.

'She likes you.'

'I'm honoured.' Beth stood very still as Binky's fingers went up to her skull and started plucking at her roots. 'What's she doing?'

'Grooming you for fleas.'

'I hope she doesn't find any!'

'Me too. We usually de-bug new arrivals but I'm guessing there hasn't been time to catch you yet.'

'I'll have you know…' she started, and then saw a twinkle in his dark eyes and stopped. 'Very funny.'

He grinned.

'Come on, you can help feed this lot.'

Binky obviously knew the word 'feed' as she let go of Bethan's hair and flung herself around the cage, whooping. Other monkeys appeared instantly, heading their way in loops and somersaults. Bethan watched, transfixed, and was startled when Max's hand closed around hers and pulled her sideways.

'Come on, before they get over-excited.'

'They're not over-excited now?' she asked incredulously, but he was heading for a door at the side, and with his hand still holding hers there was little she could do but follow.

His grip was firm, his skin warm and work-callused so that it tickled against her own, sending a strange tingle across her body. It was just tiredness, she told herself, tiredness and a fierce awareness of this exotic world into which she had been so swiftly plunged. Max paused in the side room and looked down at their hands as if he, too, was surprised by the touch.

'Sorry,' he said, snatching his fingers away. 'The monkeys can be a bit frisky with newcomers.'

'Frisky?'

'Lively,' he corrected hastily. 'I meant lively. Playful. Mischievous, you know.'

He turned to a young man who'd just come in with buckets of fruit and Bethan finally had time to study her impromptu guide. Max looked to be in his early thirties, like her, but he had a wiry energy that stopped him from standing still for even a minute. She watched him checking through the feed, one eye on the clock that was counting down to the hour. Outside the monkeys were shrieking greedily and a large crowd was gathering, pointing and laughing at their antics.

'Little show-offs,' Max said, coming back to her side. 'Fancy a go?'

'Yes, please!'

'Follow me then. Make sure you throw well so they have to go and fetch their food. It makes it last a bit longer for the visitors.'

Bethan nodded and looked uneasily at the tangle of ropes and vines through which she would have to aim her fruity missiles, wishing she'd paid more attention in rounders lessons at school. But the chimps were banging their chests in excitement as she and Max reached the feeding platform above them, and there was nothing to do but go for it. Taking a juicy orange half, she pulled back her arm and flung it. It flew across to right near the big windows and two chimps leaped for it instantly.

'Nice shot.'

She smiled at Max's praise and she threw again. The second piece landed on one of the platforms and more monkeys dived. She relaxed a little. This was fun. Through the glass she could see the eager faces of all the spectators and felt anew the privilege of her position. Just this morning she'd been with Callum in her Leicester flat, and now here she was in soft German sunshine feeding semi-wild monkeys. She threw fruit with all her might and was shocked when she reached into the bucket to find it empty.

'Oh!' she gasped out, and Max gave a throaty laugh.

'Did you enjoy that?'

'Very much. Thank you.'

He seemed more relaxed with this duty performed.

'You did a good job. Now, let me finish your tour and get you back to Tanya.'

'No rush.'

'Ah-ha – you like chimps better than hippos.'

'I don't, I…' She stopped herself just in time. Max's delivery was so dry that she kept missing him teasing her. 'I definitely like hippos best,' she said, touching her fingers to her brooch. He shook his head in mock displeasure.

'Then the tour is cancelled.'

She laughed and handed him back the bucket.

'I'll have to ask Binky to show me round.'

'She would as well. I swear that one thinks she's human.'

'She almost is.'

'True. Far more so than an ugly old hippo.'

'Or an over-rated polar bear?'

He grimaced.

'Sorry. We keepers get a little protective of our own animals. I love them all, really, even the vultures. Now come on, let's go.'

He reached for the door and showed her out of the monkey house and down towards the predators' enclosure. The big cats were stunning, and Bethan was so busy staring at the muscled movements of a tiger as it paced through the grass that she almost tripped over something.

Looking down, she was horrified to see it was an old woman. She was sitting on a bench, drowned by a huge puffa jacket and with a bobble hat pulled low over long silver hair. Her legs were outstretched beneath a tartan blanket from which the feet that had almost sent Bethan flying protruded in scuffed purple DMs.

'I'm so, so sorry,' Bethan said. Goodness, she was clumsy today.

The old woman, however, didn't even seem to have noticed her. She was staring dead ahead and muttering quietly to herself and, with another apology, Bethan edged around her.

'I nearly hurt that poor lady,' she said to Max.

He glanced back.

'Ada? Oh, you won't hurt her. She's as tough as those old boots she's wearing.'

'You know her?'

'Everyone knows Ada. That's her bench. She comes in first thing and heads straight for it. If anyone ever has the cheek to get there before her, she just stands next to them until they get the hint and move on. Then she settles in with her flask and her sandwiches until the bell sounds out for closing time.'

'Every day?'

'More or less.'

'But what does she do?'

'Just watches the world go by. And talks to Katharina.'

'To who?'

Max pointed to a statue – the bust of a woman on a white plinth, one of a run of eight sitting quietly amongst the bushes. Bethan edged over and read the plaque:

Katharina Heinroth
Zoodirektorin
1945–56

She jumped, recognising the first woman on her mum's list.

'I know about her!' she cried.

Max grunted.

'I should hope so, if you've done any research into your new workplace. She was a heroine.'

His voice had taken on a new edge and Bethan looked nervously at him.

'In what way?'

'In every way. She worked tirelessly for this zoo. Without her, I don't believe we'd have survived the war, let alone become the pioneering animal centre we are now.'

'I see. It was, er, hard here during the war then, was it?'

'Hard?' Max looked down at her. 'It was a living nightmare. Berlin was almost totally eradicated by the Allies, and the zoo with it.'

'Right. Sorry.'

He looked down at her for a moment longer, his eyes ablaze with blue fire, and then visibly shook himself.

'Bethan, it wasn't your fault. Or mine for that matter. It's in the past and thank heavens for that. Now look – there's Tanya come to find you.'

Sure enough, the senior vet was hurrying towards them with Bethan's rucksack over her shoulder.

'Beth! What must you think of me? I'm so sorry.'

'It's fine, really. How's Klumpig?'

'All sewn up and resting. And hopefully musing on the wisdom of fighting bigger hippos! But come on, we need to show you to your apartment and find you a uniform, then Kaffee und Kuchen are on me.'

Bethan's stomach grumbled obligingly, and Tanya laughed and took her arm to lead her across the zoo. They passed Ada, deep in conversation with the statue of a woman from the past, and Bethan wondered what she had to say that felt so vital and longed to know more of the one-time Zoodirektorin. For now, her new home beckoned and the past, however fascinating, would have to wait for another day.

Chapter Two

November 1943

Katharina Heinroth pushed her small frame tentatively against the heavy door of the underground shelter and edged out into the heart of her beloved zoo. Or rather, what had previously been her beloved zoo. She looked around her, horrified. All night long the bombs had rained down, splitting the air apart with the squeal of their descent and shaking the earth as they pounded holes into what had once been homes and lives. She supposed she should have expected the wreckage but it was still a shock to see it with her own eyes.

The zoo was all but destroyed.

As the other keepers and staff came blearily out of the bunker into the sharp November air, she fought to take it all in. Ahead of her, the magnificent Elephant Gate was in tatters. Miraculously the two stone elephants were still crouching either side, but the ornate archway was blown into pieces, as was the beautiful aquarium building just past it. She heard a choked cry behind her, and turned to see Oskar scrambling through the ruined gate and out into the street.

'No!'

She ran after her husband, her feet skidding and crunching on the rubble, the acrid taste of smoke filling her lungs and there, to the left of the gate, was a vision that could have been straight from a Hieronymus Bosch painting. She felt bile rise in her throat and put up her hands to her mouth as Oskar made for the bodies of their four giant crocodiles, apparently flung out of the gash in the roof of the aquarium and splatted across the pavement like stark sacrifices to the heartless god of war.

They, along with so many of the exotic aquarium creatures, had been Oskar's life's work, and as Katharina watched, helpless, he threw himself down next to the wily old matriarch. His slim hands stroked her broken spine again and again as if he might will her back to life, but her long mouth gaped loosely and her ferocious teeth would never bite again. Katharina ran forward to pull him away.

'It's no use, Oskar, she's gone.'

He turned desolate eyes up to hers.

'Why, Kätsche? Why would they bomb innocent animals?'

There was no answer to that, any more than there was an answer to why they were bombing innocent civilians, but they, too, lay dead in the street. Just across the way a woman was cradling a child's body and crooning pitifully into the smoke-filled morning, whilst behind them what must once have been their house burned fiercely. A team of firemen were battling with the flames but the water main was ripped open and gushing water into the street, where it could do little but send the mud running over those fighting through the carnage.

As Katharina watched, a dark stream welled up over her feet and around myriad exotic fish, also blown out of the aquarium, though it was too late to be of any use to them. Every fish was dead and already hungry Berliners were snatching them up to take home for dinner. Oskar scrambled to stop a thin hausfrau from grabbing a gleaming manta ray, but Katharina put out a hand to hold him back.

'Let her – it might as well be of use to someone.'

'I suppose so, meine kindl.'

She felt him go limp beneath her grasp and held on to him tightly, her heart tearing apart with his. A fiercely proud scientist, Katharina had insisted romantic love was a myth conjured up by storytellers until, aged thirty-five, she'd been introduced to

Oskar Heinroth at a conference in her native town of Breslau. Twenty-six years older than her, Oskar had been small and neat with a snow-white circlet of hair, warm, wise eyes and an irresistible passion for life. Despite being self-taught, he had been every inch her intellectual match and academic discussion had swiftly turned to something deeper for Katharina. To her delight – and secret astonishment – he'd felt the same way and she'd come north to marry him just a few months later in 1933. Every day spent with him only made her more certain of her choice, and she hated to see him so sad.

'Kätsche – look at the zoo. Our baby. Our poor baby.'

She pressed herself in tight against him and together they looked back through the ruptured gates into the broken zoo. Ever since she'd joined him here, she'd thrown herself into the preservation of the many wonderful animals. The sad absence of their own children had made the creatures they cared for that little bit more important, and with Katharina now forty-six and Oskar a dignified seventy-three it seemed they were going to have to be enough for them both. But now so many of their precious animals were dead.

'Lion on the loose!'

A scream ripped through the people on the street and all was instantly chaos. Katharina looked round fearfully but could see none of the pride.

'There!'

Someone pointed and Katharina squinted into the smoke to see a creature limping towards them. She shook her head and ran forward.

'That's no lion,' she shouted, 'that's a dingo.'

As she drew close, she slowed her steps and held out her hand to soothe the creature. It was staggering and its honey-coloured eyes fixed onto hers with relief, so that she was able to step up and grasp the matted, dusty hair at the back of its neck.

'She's tamed the lion!' the hysterical crowd shrieked, and Katharina rolled her eyes at Oskar.

'Come on, let's get this poor thing back into the zoo and see what else needs doing.'

'What doesn't, more like,' Oskar said, throwing a bereft look at the aquarium he had run with such pride for three decades. But, pulling off his belt as a makeshift lead for the dingo, he followed her inside.

The zoo was a parade of desolation. The primates' cages were thankfully intact but several of the community had been hit by shrapnel, and Katharina felt the bile rise in her throat again as she saw one of the cheeky chimps lying in a pool of his own blood whilst his fellows plucked heartbreakingly at his arms to try and bring him back to life. Pongo, the silverback gorilla, was pounding at his bars in fury, clearly desperate to take his revenge on whoever was threatening his kingdom, but he was at least alive and well.

Over in the pools, Roland, the gargantuan elephant seal, was lying dead on his favourite rock and two pygmy hippos, nurtured for years, were piled against each other, spilling blood into the murky water as it drained out of a wide fissure to one side. Walter Knaus, the hippo keeper, was frantically shovelling the remaining water onto the large bodies of gentle Rosa and her six-month-old baby, Knautschke.

'Is Knautschke all right?' Katharina called to him.

'He's not dead,' Walter said darkly, 'if that counts as all right? But he needs to stay wet or his poor skin will crack apart.'

He shovelled more water onto the confused-looking hippos as Katharina moved past them towards the dingo enclosure. The wild dogs were looked after with the zebra and deer by Robert Eberhard and his wife Sasha, and Katharina was hugely relieved to see both them and their ten-year-old daughter Adelaide unharmed.

'Isn't it awful?' she cried, running forward to hug them all.

'It breaks my heart, Kätsche,' Sasha agreed. 'Of all the horrors of the war, this one is the worst yet.'

Katharina squeezed her friend tight. Sasha had been heavily pregnant when she'd come to the zoo just a couple of months after Katharina in 1933 and, with her mother down in Bavaria, had asked her to attend Adelaide's birth. Seeing the child placed into her mother's arms was still a memory that brought joyful tears to Katharina's eyes, and the two had been close ever since. Now they watched together as Oskar released the dingo into his run. The bewildered dog made a dash for the bedding hut and they were delighted to hear happy howls of welcome from the rest of the pack – a relief from the wails of pain of so many other animals.

Everywhere keepers were running around, trying to repair broken fences and soothe distressed animals. It was no time to linger, so Oskar and Katharina left their friends securing their enclosure and moved through the zoo. Reike the giraffe peered over the wall of her enclosure, her eyes seeming to seek Katharina's as if to say, 'What on earth is going on?', but she was calm enough. Siam, the stately bull elephant, however, was up on his hind legs, bellowing fury into the treacherous skies. As they drew close to the smashed elephant house, they could see why – the bodies of all seven of his harem were crushed beneath fallen bars. Tears sprang to Katharina's eyes but what use were tears now? She brushed them fiercely away and turned to where Ursula and Gisela, two of the zoo's most dedicated cleaners, were energetically sweeping the paths to provide access for carts to carry the dead.

'Thank you so much, ladies,' she said, rushing up to them.

Slim-built Gisela turned and threw her arms around Katharina. 'Oh Kätsche, it's so awful. Our poor animals.'

Katharina hugged her tight, welcoming her gazelle-like friend's quiet strength. Gisela had come to the zoo as a cleaner seven years ago when she was just eighteen, and thrown herself into her work from the first moment. She clearly loved animals and had confided in Katharina that she had longed to study them, but her father had been most insistent that education was not for women. Katharina's own parents, both dedicated biologists, had been enlightened enough to let her pursue her passion with a doctorate – one of only two women in her year – and she had taken Gisela under her wing and started to teach her on the job. These days the young woman was every bit as expert in animal care as any of the keepers, and with so many men called up to fight, she was worth her weight in gold. Today, though, there was nothing for it but to pick up a broom again.

'Come on, the pair of you – less hugging, more working!'

Ursula poked them both with her broom and they came apart, protesting.

'There's so much to do,' Katharina said, pushing her hair out of her eyes to get a good look at the mess, and noticing streaks of grey amongst the fiery red that had always marked her out. She felt suddenly weary before the younger woman's energy.

'We'll sort it,' Ursula said brightly.

'How can we sort *that*?' Gisela asked, pointing towards the bellowing Siam.

Ursula grimaced.

'I've no idea but we have to try. There's no point just standing in the rubble weeping.'

That much was true and Katharina looked round for another broom to help, but Ursula suddenly stepped across her, a big smile on her pretty face and her voluptuous body set at its finest advantage.

'Oooh – where did you find that cart, Pierre? It's beautiful.'

Pierre Dubois was coming towards them with one of the pretty little carts that had sold cakes and sweets around the zoo in more plentiful times.

'It's far too beautiful for this grisly job,' he said in halting German, 'but we cannot just let the animals rot.'

He hastened forward with the cart as two of his fellow Frenchmen came out of the antelope house with a dead deer between them. Together they hefted it onto the cream-and-blue cart, and with difficulty Pierre turned it round to wheel the animal away.

'Let me help,' Ursula offered, pushing her broom into Katharina's hands and hurrying to his side.

'This is no job for a lady,' he objected, but she tossed back her glossy black hair and smiled up at him.

'None of this is a job for a lady, or a gentleman besides, but it still needs doing and I'd be happy to help.'

Pierre did not object further and no wonder. Ursula was a lively young woman who'd come to the zoo to work with her best friend, Gisela, but unlike Gisela, whose husband Dieter was fighting on the Eastern front, she was still single – and not keen on staying that way. With few able-bodied Germans to hand in the capital, her eye had swiftly turned to the six Frenchmen who had been recruited to help the zoo as part of the Service du Travail Obligatoire.

Thousands of young Frenchmen had been brought to Germany last March in exchange for prisoners of war. As far as Katharina was aware, shamefully few POWs had been released, but she was very glad of the programme. The six that they had been assigned were all hard workers and kind men, and had made a huge difference to the tricky job of keeping the zoo running during the hard war years. Last month, she and Oskar had managed to get them moved out of their rough camp on the other side of Berlin and into rooms above the zebra house. They were part of the Zoofamilie now and thank heavens, she thought, as they hefted the large animals as easily as if they were mere bunnies.

'Where are you taking them?' she asked.

'To honourable rest,' Pierre said, then threw her a swift wink and added, 'in the kitchens.'

'Pierre!'

'What? This is finest venison, Frau Heinroth. It will feed us all in style for weeks. And half of Berlin as well. Marcel is sharpening his knives as we speak.'

Katharina looked to the poor deer draped across the cake cart and sighed. Pierre was right of course, just as the women on the street had been right to snatch up the aquarium's fish for the table. Meat was meat, whatever its exotic provenance, and it was at a premium these days. She had no doubt that Marcel, the burly French butcher who usually sorted the meat for the carnivores, would do an excellent job, and despite herself her tummy rumbled at the thought of venison stew. Hunger, it seemed, was her near-constant companion these days and the thought of a full meal was tantalising.

'Make sure the animals eat first,' she managed.

'Of course, but after that, some for us too. We will need it by the end of today.'

He gestured sadly around the battered zoo and Katharina nodded. The thought of a communal meal at the end of all this sorrowful cleaning up certainly spurred her on and she began to sweep as Ursula sauntered off with Pierre, hips swaying in a way he could not fail to notice.

'She's impossible, that one,' she said to Gisela with a smile.

'She's in love.'

'Love? You think so?'

Gisela shrugged.

'*She* thinks so, which comes to much the same thing.'

Katharina watched the pair go with new interest.

'But he's French.'

Gisela giggled.

'I'd noticed.'

'I mean, she won't be allowed to marry him. Liaisons with foreigners are against the law.'

Gisela's smile faded.

'Yes, well, last time I looked killing innocent people and animals was against the law too, but no one seems to pay much attention any more.'

Katharina shivered.

'The Gestapo do.'

'Then we must make sure the Gestapo don't know,' Gisela said firmly.

'Don't know what?'

Both women leaped out of their skin as Lutz Heck, the zoo manager, came out of the elephant enclosure, moving silently under the cover of Siam's bellows. Katharina looked around for Oskar, but he'd gone to help the other Frenchmen shift the prostrate body of the zoo's only black rhino.

'That we are cooking the animals,' she said hastily.

Heck grimaced.

'Oh, they know that all right, and they'll be first in the queue when we serve up.'

'That'll be nice for you.'

Lutz looked at her, his thin face as sharp as that of the dingo she'd just saved. She forced herself to smile back. Heck was a signed-up Nazi and a good friend of a number of the 'Golden Pheasants' at the top of the party. He'd worked closely with Göring in his capacity as Reichsjägermeister – Chief of Hunting – and a number of their animals, including two recently born lion cubs, Sultan and Bussy, had come from the big man's personal estate on the Schorf Moor just outside the city. Lutz's political leanings were a source of constant tension for Katharina, who hated so much of what the Nazis stood for, and she could rarely resist needling him.

'Always good to have support from the top,' she said sweetly.

Lutz narrowed his eyes.

'Running a zoo is about more than just keeping the animals safe, Katharina, as you should know by now.'

She did know it and she couldn't deny that Lutz was a good manager, as passionate about the animals as she and Oskar, or perhaps even more so as he had personally brought many of them back from his extensive travels. His father had been manager before him, and he and his brother had grown up in the zoo. He'd been part of the many innovative programmes to make the enclosures mimic natural habitats and to breed struggling species back into the world – at least before humans started blowing them up. All that, Katharina admired, but there were other aspects of his work that she hated.

She'd been furious, for example, when he'd put up a Juden Unerwünscht – Jews Not Welcome – notice on the Elephant Gate back in 1938. At least that dark piece of art had been obliterated with the rest of the archway. Not that it mattered any more. Goebbels had declared Berlin 'Judenfrei' some months ago, and although Katharina knew, in ways she should not, that plenty were still tucked into the city's nooks and crannies, they lived in fear for their lives and would certainly not be trying to visit the zoo.

It was all wrong. How could an intelligent man, who'd devoted his life to promoting diversity of species in the animal kingdom, be so set on honing humans down to one narrow set of characteristics? It dangerously eroded her respect for her boss and often set her sparky redhead's temper alight. Oskar was always cautioning her to be careful – falling out with Nazis was very, very dangerous – but Oskar wasn't here.

'Göring will be sorry to see so many of his animals destroyed,' she said.

'Katharina,' Gisela hissed, tugging on her arms. 'Come and sweep.'

Katharina stood her ground.

'He will,' Heck agreed tightly. 'But this terrible suffering isn't Göring's fault. It's the British who dropped the bombs last night.'

'Yes, but only because—'

This time Gisela's hiss was more urgent.

'Katharina, come and sweep!'

Katharina glared at Lutz a little longer but then let herself be pulled aside. There'd been enough trouble at the zoo without her looking for more. Still, as she took her broom to the detritus of the elephant house, her heart burned with fury at the senseless waste of so many lives. Even the simplest chimp could learn to modify his behaviour to keep himself safe, but humans, it seemed, were doomed to repeat their very worst mistakes. When would this hideous war ever end?

Chapter Three

Bethan threw herself down on the sofa of her apartment and looked longingly across at the fridge, as if it might obligingly open up and pour her a glass of wine. Even German efficiency, however, had not got that far yet and, in the end, she hefted herself back up and went over to fetch it. Riesling in hand, she moved to the window and took a long, slow sip as she stared out across her new home. She smiled. She'd been at the zoo for two weeks now but had not yet tired of this view, and suspected she never would.

She had a neat little apartment on the same floor as Ella and Max above the veterinary centre. It looked out onto the baboon rocks and, beyond that, Max's precious primates. With dusk falling, she could see the chimps swinging themselves around in a final burst of energy and laughed out loud at their antics. Behind them the antelopes were grazing sedately, and past them she could just make out the black-and-white pandas beneath the striking red roofs of their pagoda lair.

The zoo was closing and the last visitors were being reluctantly herded out of the Elephant Gate, leaving the wide avenues deliciously empty. Bethan took another sip of her wine, letting the crisp flavours sink through her as the place settled down for the night. Lord, she was tired. Happy but tired. The last two weeks had been a whirl of activity and already she'd learned so much. Every evening she'd been at her books, brushing up her knowledge of all the new species she was having to deal with, and her brain felt full to bursting.

She knew the names of almost all the animals around the zoo now and was becoming familiar with their routines and preferences.

She'd become an expert with a tranquiliser gun and yesterday she'd done her first operation. Cutting into a tiger had been the most nerve-racking moment of her career, but it had been a simple enough procedure and the inside of the gorgeous creature had been much like your average family moggy, only on a grander scale. The patient was doing well and Tanya had praised her work, but Beth was certainly ready for a rest. Tomorrow, thank heavens, was her day off and she intended to make the most of it to see some of Berlin. For now, though, it was Friday night.

Suddenly restless, Bethan returned to the fridge to see what she had to eat. There were lovely food shops in the giant Bikini Haus mall right behind the zoo, but she'd not been for days and a sorry collection of leftovers met her eyes. What on earth could she cook with a carrot, some bratwurst and a tub of strawberry yoghurt? She reached for the wine. She'd go out and buy something soon, she promised herself, although for perhaps the first time since she'd arrived, she felt a twinge of loneliness. Back home, she'd most likely be meeting Callum and a few friends for beers after work, before going on for a bite to eat or grabbing a takeaway in front of a film. Callum had been sending gratifyingly loving messages this last week and right now she was missing him.

Gulping at her wine, she reached for her phone and pulled up his number. Perhaps they could have a FaceTime drink together? And perhaps his project would be nearly done and he could come out and see her. In the two years since they'd met at a mutual friend's New Year party, she couldn't remember being away from him for more than a week. No wonder it all felt a bit weird.

'Beth! Hey, darling, how are you?'

Callum was bare-chested and the sight of him made her body stir pleasurably.

'Better for seeing you. You look good.'

'What? Oh. Thanks.' He patted his flat stomach. 'Been down the gym a lot with you not here to come home to.'

'Nice. I can't wait to get my hands on you.'

'Same, darling. On you, that is. I can get my hands on myself any time. Often have to.'

He winked lewdly.

'Callum!'

'What? I miss you.'

She softened.

'I miss you too. How's the project?'

His reply was muffled by the T-shirt he was pulling over his head – her favourite one, in a chestnut brown that brought out the rich colour of his eyes.

'So,' he said, appearing again, 'that's why we're going out for drinks tonight.'

'Because the project is finished?'

'As I just said.'

'I couldn't hear… Never mind. That's great, Callum. Where are you going?'

'Just to the pub with a few of the lads. Josh says there's a new microbrewery on the marketplace so we might try that.'

'And then a curry?'

He laughed.

'You know me too well.'

Bethan felt tears brim pathetically.

'I wish I was there with you, Cal.'

'Me too, darling, really.' He smiled at her. 'How are the lions?'

'Good. I operated on a tiger yesterday actually.'

'Nice one. Get any photos?'

'Erm, no. I was a bit busy.'

'Shame. People keep asking where you've gone and if I could show them you cutting into big cats they might, you know, get it.'

'Get what, Cal?'

'Why you've left me.'

'I haven't left you.'

'You know what I mean.'

'Not really. I'm working away. I did ask you to come with me.'

'And I did tell you I couldn't.' He shook himself. 'Look, Beth, let's not go round that. Taxi's due any minute and I'm not ready yet.'

'You look pretty good to me.'

He winked at her, then the phone hit a strange angle as he bent to pull on his best trainers.

'Are you going out, Beth?'

'No one to go out with.'

'Poor baby. Don't worry, I'll be there very soon and we'll hit the town together.'

'Next weekend?'

He grimaced.

'Bit early.'

'You said the project was finished.'

'It is, but there's a few things to wrap up. And, to be honest, Johnno's got tickets to the rugby. They're like gold dust, Beth.'

Her heart sank.

'I'm sure they are,' she agreed dully.

'What about the weekend after?'

'Easter? That's when Dad's coming, you know that.'

He stiffened.

'Oh, well if your dad's coming…'

'Don't be like that.'

'No, no. I know my place. Daddy comes first.'

'Like rugby does?'

'Oooh! Touché.' He suddenly looked round. 'That's the doorbell, Beth. I've got to go.'

'Now? Callum, don't, please. Not yet.'

'Taxi's here, darling.'

'Can't we talk in the cab?'

'Johnno's in it already. You know the rules on talking to girl-friends on a lads' night out.'

'Callum, you're thirty-five. Surely those sorts of silly rules are long gone?'

'If only, hey?!' The screen wobbled nauseatingly as he ran down the stairs, then his face suddenly filled the screen as he blew her a kiss. 'Love you, Beth. Let's talk properly tomorrow, hey?'

'OK. Love you too, Callum. Have a—'

But he was gone, off out to the pubs of Leicester without a glance back. She put her phone slowly down on the table and gulped at her wine. So what? He could have a night out, couldn't he? It was good that he had friends, even if being thrown over for the Leicester Tigers was a little galling.

You've got your own tigers, she reminded herself, *and they're far better than rugby ones.* Mainly that was true but right now, with Friday evening stretching out before her, long and empty, it was a little hard to believe. Ah well, perhaps it was a chance to grab a takeaway and start work on the list. With so much work to get a handle on, she'd not had a moment to think about it and she suddenly felt guilty.

'Sorry, Mum,' she whispered, touching her fingers to the hippo brooch she'd pinned to her smart green uniform on her first full day.

She went through to fetch the little piece of paper from her rucksack, but a knock on the door made her jump in fright.

'Beth? It's me, Ella.'

'Ella!' Bethan yanked the door open. 'Hi. Is everything OK?'

She looked back to her phone. She'd been assigned a seal as her bleep avatar – on the grounds that they were the only creatures in the zoo you might find in the UK – but she was sure its beady-eyed face hadn't come up on her screen.

'Everything's fine,' the younger girl assured her. 'I'm not here for work.'

She tossed her crazy curls, let free for the evening, and Bethan noticed that she was wearing make-up and a sparkly top over skin-tight jeans.

'You're going out?'

Ella laughed. '*We're* going out. Get yourself changed, Bethan Taylor, because I'm taking you to Helter Skelter.'

'The jazz club?'

'The very same. There's a great band on tonight and loads of people are going.'

Bethan looked around, flustered.

'I've not eaten.'

'Good. Their gumbo is to die for. Now come on – you must have something cute to wear.'

It was clear Ella wasn't going to take no for an answer and Bethan felt her heart rise. Friday night was suddenly looking a whole lot more fun, and she obligingly dived for her bedroom to hunt down something appropriate for the Berlin nightlife she'd heard so much about.

Hours later and Bethan was exhausted again. She'd been dancing far too energetically for her already weary body and was grateful when the band called a break. Helter Skelter was a fabulous cellar bar, all brick walls, low lights and funky photos of acts. Various people from the zoo were here, and Bethan had been introduced to other friends and partners as they danced the night away. Her body might be struggling to keep up but her soul was loving it.

'They're brilliant,' she said, waving to the band.

'Aren't they just,' Ella agreed. 'Especially the drummer. He's hot!'

Bethan laughed.

'I like the saxophonist. So talented. I wish I could play like that.'

'That's Peter – Max's brother.'

'Your brother?'

Bethan spun round to Max who shrugged.

'What can I say – talent runs in the family.'

'You can play?'

'Not the saxophone. I'm nowhere near cool enough for that.'

'What then?'

Max looked shy and Ella leaned across with the answer. 'Max is brilliant on the piano. You wait, he might treat you to a tune or two when we've got a couple more beers down him.'

'Not tonight,' Max said firmly. 'I'm on my best behaviour.'

'Not on my account, I hope,' Bethan said, horrified.

'You heard the girl,' Ella cried. 'Tequilas all round.'

She bounced off towards the bar and Max groaned.

'Ella has more energy than Binky! But I guess she's young. Here.' He pulled out two chairs.

'I wouldn't call myself ancient,' Bethan protested. 'I'm only thirty-three.'

'Me too,' Max said, 'but the monkeys have aged me terribly. Still, at least in here my grey hair doesn't stand out.'

He tugged at the vaguely charcoal flecks above his ears and Bethan shook her head at him.

'You'd be right at home with those guys, hey?' she said, pointing to a group of old men sitting chatting in the corner with a bottle of Wild Turkey on the table between them.

'I would actually,' Max agreed easily. 'Detlev there used to be the monkey keeper. I went to Tanzania with him when I first came to work at the zoo.'

'Really? What was it like?'

'Fantastic. I was fresh out of university and thought I knew it all. Travelling through the jungle with Detlev showed me exactly how much I still had to learn. He was amazing. He could track anything and he had the patience of a saint. We spent hours hidden away just watching the communities interacting with one another, and then he took me to the rescue centres and my eyes were well and truly opened. The things that people do to wild animals, Beth!'

His blue eyes pooled and he closed them a moment. 'Sorry. It was hard. I saw some terrible injuries from shootings and trappings gone wrong. I saw tiny babies with limbs missing and youngsters clinging to their dead mothers and this poor creature that would only sit in the corner, curled into a ball for weeks on end and—' He cut himself off. 'God, listen to me! We're meant to be having fun. Where's Ella got to with those tequilas?'

He looked self-consciously around, and Bethan reached out and put her hand over his.

'It's OK, Max. I'm interested. You must have seen hope too, though, right?'

Max looked at her for a long moment, as if checking she really wanted to hear, and then he smiled.

'So much hope, yes. We fed the babies and, if we were lucky, paired them with other mothers. We mended the injuries and nursed the chimps back to full health.'

'And the one curled up in the corner?'

His smile widened.

'That one is Binky. We restored her confidence bit by bit and then we brought her to the zoo.'

'That's why you love her so much?'

'I love them all,' he said, 'but, yes, I suppose Binky has a special place in my heart.'

'That's incredible, Max.'

'Is it?' He looked surprised. 'Thanks. Ah – here we go.'

He pulled his hand out from under hers as Ella appeared with a tray of shots. Tanya, her partner Maria, and several of the other keepers all drew round, and they solemnly dusted salt onto their hands and raised their glasses. Comforted to see a familiar ritual from home, Beth joined in.

'Prost!'

She licked the salt, chucked the tequila down her throat and grabbed at a slice of lime to chase the burning spirit on its way. Everyone was spluttering and laughing, and now the band were coming back and it was time to dance again.

The rest of the night seemed to disappear in a swirl of music and laughter. The tequila turned Bethan's tiredness into wired-up energy and she threw herself into dancing, glad to let go of the responsibilities of the last two busy weeks. At some point pictures flashed up on her Instagram of Callum with a gurning group. Judging by the spangly background it was no microbrewery and the curvy girls either side of him were most certainly not 'the lads', but so what? If anyone posted a picture of her right now, she'd look pretty wild. They didn't have to live like monks and nuns just because they were apart, and it was healthy to allow each other space, wasn't it?

Finally, her feet gave way and she collapsed onto a velvet-covered bench at one side. Settling back, she felt herself sliding blissfully into sleep, but then someone grabbed her hands and she forced her eyes open to see Ella on one side and Max on the other.

'Come on, sleepyhead.'

'No more dancing,' she mumbled.

'No more dancing,' Max agreed. 'Let's get back to the zoo.'

The zoo! Her heart thrilled that she could call the zoo her home, and it gave her just about enough of a rush to stand up again. She followed the others up the steps, out into the street and gasped.

'It's light.'

'Almost,' Ella agreed, as they all looked to the line of candyfloss pink over the buildings to the east.

'We've danced all night,' Max said, sounding nearly as surprised as Bethan.

She nudged him.

'Not so old yet, hey?'

'Nope,' he agreed, looping her arm into his. 'Not so old yet. Come on now – what is it you Brits say – home, James!'

Bethan giggled and looped her other arm through Ella's, and together they staggered back towards the zoo in the growing light. Bethan had a horrible feeling she wasn't going to see much of Berlin today but she didn't care; she'd had a wonderful night. They turned down Budapester Strasse and cheered to see the gold, red and green archway of the Elephant Gate. Bethan marvelled again that such a magnificent structure marked the entrance to her home.

'It must be so old,' she said, gazing up at it.

'Not *so* old actually,' Ella said, digging her pass out of her jeans pocket. 'That's to say, the elephants are – 1899, I think – but the rest is a reconstruction. The original archway was—'

'Destroyed in the war,' cut in a wavering voice, and they all spun round to see Ada, sitting on the pavement below the ticket booth. She gave them her curiously straight-toothed grin. 'First in the queue,' she said. 'I get up early.' She pointed a gnarled finger at the three of them and added with a chuckle, 'Earlier than you get to bed.'

'Only tonight,' Bethan said primly.

Ada waved her hand.

'Where've you been?'

'Helter Skelter,' Max said. Ella had stepped back a little, unsure of the old lady, but Max went over to crouch down next to her. 'Do you know it?'

Ada shook her head.

'Lordy no, I'm not one for dancing. Fancy, is it?'

'Not fancy, no. Just an old cellar with good music and good beer.'

She seemed to consider this, then suddenly grabbed Max's hand.

'Back in my day,' she said intently, 'cellars were for hiding, not dancing. Bombs were our music. Bombs and shells and Katyushas.'

'Katyushas?'

'Rockets, boy. Nasty, squealing rockets. You don't forget one of those in a hurry.'

'I can imagine.'

She shook her head violently.

'I really hope you can't, young man. It was hell. All you could do was try to keep yourself alive and the babies safe.'

'Babies?' Bethan asked, going over to join them.

'Babies!' Ada repeated, suddenly animated. 'Lots and lots of babies. You had to keep them safe. The babies, you know. They had to be safe.'

Her cheeks had flushed and she was squirming alarmingly. Max held tight on to her hand and ran his other one gently across the top of it until she stilled a little.

'You did an amazing job, Ada.'

She huffed and threw herself back against the wall.

'I had to. We all had to. We were a family. We were the Zoofamilie.'

'That's nice,' Max said, but Ada had retreated into herself and there seemed little to do but move away and leave her to whatever pictures ran around in her head.

Ella opened up the side gate and they slid through. Bethan paused to glance back at Ada, who was staring up at the sky with a look of curious contentment in her cloudy blue eyes.

'The Zoofamilie,' Bethan repeated under her breath. 'How lovely.'

'Come on, Beth,' Ella called and, with a smile on her face, Bethan ran after her new friends.

It seemed that she had a Zoofamilie too now, and it was a wonderful feeling.

Chapter Four

25 December 1943

Katharina looked around the concert hall dining room and sighed with rare contentment. It was Christmas Day and, for once, all seemed well with the world. The long dining table had been set with the best tableware, polished to a high enough shine to hide any chips, and someone had found a couple of white tablecloths that had not yet been torn up for bandages. The huge room had once echoed with chatter from hundreds of diners and felt a little empty with just the small group of festive revellers, but with the far end boarded off to hide the recent bomb damage and the lights on low, it was cosy enough.

'Grace,' Lutz Heck announced from the head of the table. 'Father Jörg – would you be so kind?'

Father Jörg, a white-haired old priest from the Kaiser Wilhelm church just outside the zoo, rose slowly. The poor man had aged a great deal in the last two months as night after night of raids had taken their toll. His once beautiful old church was a shell of its former self, but this morning's service had been defiantly held within its broken walls, with bricks for kneelers and all eyes turned up to God's scarred heavens as they prayed with all their hearts for a year without more planes. It had been a surprisingly beautiful experience, if thankfully short, for the weather was bitterly cold and the Zoofamilie had rushed home to warm up with higher fires than they normally allowed themselves in these times of shortage.

In Katharina and Oskar's apartment to the side of the shattered aquarium building they had more coal than usual, because Gisela had brought supplies with her when she'd had to move out of her bombed home at the start of December. She'd arrived at the zoo in rare tears that morning and Katharina had not hesitated to offer her their spare room. When they'd first moved in, they'd intended it as a nursery, but with no children it was free for the young woman and Katharina loved having her around.

Gisela was still eager to learn and many an evening had been happily spent with her and Oskar sharing their animal knowledge. At first Katharina had felt self-conscious and mainly let Oskar talk – his experience, after all, was so much greater than hers. But then news had come in that Gisela's husband, Dieter, had been injured and sent to a field hospital, and she'd seen how focusing on the animals had helped her houseguest to forget her worries for an hour or two, so had thrown herself into the discussions. Besides, Gisela asked very interesting questions and recently their sessions had become less teaching and more debate – a welcome distraction from the Allied bombings for them all.

Today was Christmas Day; surely even the Tommies would not break the peace of this sacred occasion? As Father Jörg raised his hands and asked for God's blessing on all people caught in this bitter conflict, Katharina found herself wondering what Christmas tables looked like in England. Were there women like her, fretting over whether their rations had gone far enough to make this special meal feel somewhere near normal, and praying that the Luftwaffe planes wouldn't break their festive family time? Were there women like Gisela, who didn't care about the political jostling that had brought them all to war and were just praying for their husbands to come home safely? Of course there were, she thought, and screwed her eyes up tight as if that might help her pray even harder.

'Amen,' the old priest finished, and they all fervently echoed him. 'Now,' he said, rubbing his hands, 'dinner!'

Lutz stood and lifted the carving knife above the giant bird, glowing succulently golden in the candlelight before him. Katharina felt her mouth water and tried not to remember the sight of the poor ostriches lying dead beneath the broken columns of their Egyptian-style house two weeks ago. Those that had not been hit by the bomb seemed to have died of heart attacks, as if the shock of having their home blown sky-high had been just too much for their elegant bodies. Katharina could still see them lying in a pile of dusty plumage and, for a moment, she felt too sick to eat. But war left no space for the luxury of queasiness, so she took her plate and swiftly covered the meat with potatoes as if that might somehow block out the memories too.

'Wine, meine kindl.'

Oskar leaned over and poured her a large glassful, and she took a sip. Lutz's father had kept a very good cellar and there were still enough bottles at the back of the bunker to mark the season in style. Katharina reminded herself that it was generous of the manager to share so freely and raised her glass in a quiet toast to him. He raised his back and gave her an awkward smile. It was sad, really, that politics should divide them when they were so united in their love of the zoo, and she vowed to try, in the year ahead, to work with him as best she could.

'Eat up whilst it's hot,' Lutz urged, as he kept on carving for those further down the table.

Across from Katharina, Sasha picked up her knife and fork eagerly. She'd been sick recently and Katharina was glad to see her tucking in.

'You look well, Sasha.'

'I feel well,' her friend agreed. 'In fact, I *am* well. Very well.' She glanced to Robert and when he gave her a little nod, she turned back to Katharina. 'I'm pregnant.'

'Oh!'

Katharina's hands flew to her mouth and Sasha looked worried.

'I wasn't sure whether to tell you,' she said anxiously, 'because of, you know…'

Katharina did know, but her own lack of children did not diminish her joy at this blessing for her friend. It had been hard for Sasha too as she'd struggled to conceive again after Adelaide, and this seemed like a welcome miracle – new life amidst so much death.

'I'm so pleased you did,' she assured her. 'It's wonderful news, Sash.'

'You'll be his or her auntie, Katharina, like you are to Adelaide.'

Katharina looked guiltily to the young girl at her side.

'I'm a rubbish auntie. I never take Adelaide out on any trips or buy her any treats.'

Adelaide laughed.

'Don't be silly, Auntie Kätsche. There's nowhere to go on a trip, save to the workcamps and who wants to go there?'

'Adelaide…' Katharina started, chilled by her easy acceptance, but the girl was still talking.

'I don't need treats, really, save to work with you and the animals. Especially the baby animals. I love the baby animals.'

Her eyes glowed and Katharina smiled fondly at her.

'Soon you will have your own baby animal.'

Adelaide's nose wrinkled.

'I suppose so, though it will be noisy I think.'

'Not as noisy as a chimp baby.'

'But at least I can leave those in their cages at night.'

Robert laughed and rubbed her hair affectionately.

'You're wise beyond your years, sweetheart. Fret not, Baby Eberhard won't be here till summertime so you can enjoy your sleep a while longer.'

'Not when the bombs fall.'

Robert stopped laughing.

'No. Not then.'

There was an awkward pause, filled by a dirty chuckle from Walter and Gustav the cattle keeper, who were making enthusiastic inroads into Lutz's wine. Katharina looked down the table to the rest of their party. Beyond the old men, Gisela and Ursula were chattering away to Pierre and his five French friends. Gisela was animated. She'd received a letter from Dieter yesterday, assuring her that he was well and safe – the best possible present she could ever have had. Ursula, in her best dress and silk stockings she'd procured from who knows where, was sparkling too, mainly up at Pierre, who had eyes for no one else in the room.

Opposite, wide-eyed and quiet, were two young Hitler Youth, Hans and Mark, who Gisela had taken under her wing. Their father was away fighting and their mother had been senselessly killed in a crush at the entrance of one of the big public bunkers. They were being looked after by a cousin, but she had several children of her own and the burden was high. Gisela had come across the lads staggering around the park just beyond the zoo, trying to master the Panzerfaust that would, in theory, destroy any enemy tanks trying to enter the city.

'Ridiculous!' Gisela had ranted to Katharina, when she'd brought them in for a hot drink and a rest. 'The damn thing's bigger than they are.'

They'd brought the weapon with them and Katharina had eyed it fearfully. It was a simple enough device – a long tube attached to a conical warhead that, at the pull of a lever, you could fire wherever you chose. It looked almost like a toy, especially in the hands of these two brothers, the oldest of whom was only fourteen, and she hadn't been able to believe they might be asked to fire it for real. The boys had put it down thankfully enough, far keener to see the monkeys and throw balls for the seals, and in the last few weeks Gisela had taken to inviting them in regularly. It was good to have them here today, and Katharina noted that they had no qualms about eating ostrich and were wolfing down all they could get onto their plates. She smiled. Some things didn't change.

At the far end of the table sat Dennis Hartmann, once Lutz's personal driver and now a general dogsbody like the rest of them

– though unlike the rest of them, very unwilling to muck in with the tough tasks the raids had imposed on the daily life of the zoo. At his side was Kurt Müller, a seventeen-year-old lad who'd been working as an underchef in the restaurant before the war and, with the rest of the staff called up, had found himself running the place. He was as lazy as his friend Dennis, however, and had happily let Marcel and the other Frenchmen take over the cooking duties. Both had wine glasses but were drinking something clear out of a bottle they kept to themselves beneath the table. Katharina's eyes narrowed.

'Is that schnapps, Dennis?' she called loudly down the table.

Dennis jumped and glared at her.

'Water,' he slurred. 'I don't like wine, especially this nasty French stuff.'

Marcel bristled but Pierre put a hand on his arm and leaned towards Dennis.

'Quite right. I'd love some water too, thanks, Dennis.'

He held his glass out, and Dennis shifted in his seat and looked to Kurt for help. The younger man leaped up and fetched a carafe from the side to fill Pierre's glass, and Dennis relaxed. Marcel half rose to challenge him further, and Katharina was glad when Oskar rose and proposed a toast.

'To the zoo!' he cried, his eyes alight and his white hair making him look like Father Christmas himself. 'And its continued survival.'

That, at least, was something they could all drink to, and the table settled down again and began eating. For a little time, all that could be heard was the chink of cutlery on china and the happy murmurings of stomachs being filled.

'I reckon this is the best meal I've had all year,' Robert said happily.

'Apart from the crocodile tails,' Ursula suggested.

'True,' he conceded. 'They were amazing. Who knew those scaly beasts would be so tender?'

Oskar flinched and Katharina took his hand under the table, lacing her fingers tightly into his. Berliners had a macabre sense of humour. Oskar was from Mainz in western Germany, Katharina from Breslau in the east, and the dark wit of the capital often caught them both out. The other day Katharina had gone past a jaunty Christmas poster with a picture of a family opening a large present and the slogan: 'Be practical; give a coffin.' She'd actually laughed out loud and had felt that maybe she was finally settling into the capital – or what was left of it.

'The crocs were by far and away the most popular dish at the canteen,' Marcel said. 'Victor even sold some into the Reichstag. Made a fortune.' Everyone looked up sharply but he smiled. 'Bought us forty tonnes of hay – that should see the herbivores through to spring.'

They all cheered, save Gustav, who said bitterly, 'If we still have any herbivores by spring.'

'What d'you mean?' Katharina asked.

The old man looked mutinous and Robert answered for him.

'We're losing stock. Two of Gustav's wisent went missing when we were all down the bunker last week.'

'Bombed?'

Robert shook his head.

'Stolen. With half the walls and fences down, it's hard to keep people out if they're willing to risk the bombs to grab themselves a ropeful of prime steak.' He sighed. 'We can hardly blame them – they're hungry – but we need to do something to up security.'

'Perhaps we can ask the flak tower to keep an eye out?' Sasha suggested.

Robert put his arm around his wife.

'Nice idea, my love, but it seems unlikely. They're meant to be shooting planes from the skies, not civilians out of the cattle pens.'

'They can do both,' Gustav said stoutly. 'If we have to have that concrete behemoth on our doorstep at least it can help us out.'

Up and down the table people nodded. The gigantic zoo flak tower had been built two years ago after the initial spurt of raids. It stood, six storeys high and almost a block wide, a solid concrete tower with medieval turrets at all four corners topped with huge anti-aircraft guns. There was room inside for 15,000 civilians and when the sirens went, the sound of them all running for shelter was almost as loud as the thunder of the fast-arriving planes. The tower even had a fully functioning hospital and an air-conditioned room to house the finest treasures of Berlin's museums. It was a wonder of engineering but also a chilling representation of the perpetual threat to them all, and Katharina hated it. If, however, it could help protect the animals it might be worth it.

'Would they do that?' she asked. She turned to Lutz. 'Could you ask them?'

He shrugged.

'I could try,' he said, 'but I doubt they'd see cattle-rustling as a high priority.'

Gustav gave a heavy sigh but then suddenly Hans, the older of the two Hitler Youth boys, jumped up.

'I could ask them, sir,' he said. 'Mark and I have been assigned duties on the flak tower in the New Year so we might have some influence.'

Everyone around the table looked down, not wanting to pour cold water on the lad's eager suggestion. Surely no one would listen to a boy? But on the other hand, with precious few men still here, perhaps they'd soon have no choice.

'That would be very kind, Hans,' Oskar said. 'The zoo would appreciate it.'

The boy glowed.

'Don't you worry,' he assured them, his thin chest puffing out. 'Mark and I will do our very best to protect both the animals and the people of Berlin. It will be different next year, you'll see.'

'In what way?' Victor asked him.

'In every way. Germany will turn the tide of the war.'

'How?' Katharina dared to ask.

'With the WuWas, of course.'

Everyone tightened at the mention of the Wunderwaffen – the wonder weapons. Rumours had abounded about them for what felt like forever but they simply hadn't materialised. The boy looked nervously up and down the table, then over to Gisela for reassurance.

'Oh, Hans,' she said quietly, 'I don't think there are any Wunderwaffen.'

'There are,' he insisted. 'They told us about them at Sunday training, didn't they, Mark?'

His younger brother nodded keenly.

'Great big rockets,' he confirmed, 'that will blow all our enemies out of the way.'

His enthusiasm was chilling but Katharina could hardly blame him. The child must have been born not long before Hitler came to power so this sort of rhetoric was all he'd ever heard.

'Is it good to blow people up?' she asked him gently.

'Not all people,' he said, as if she were stupid, 'just the bad ones.'

Katharina could think of nothing to say to that, but Ursula leaned forward.

'I see. Are the French bad?'

She cocked an eyebrow to Pierre, sat tight up at her side. Pierre smiled at Mark who looked petrified.

'I don't know,' he whispered. Then, after thinking a moment, he looked straight at Pierre and said, 'You aren't bad, sir.'

'Thank you,' Pierre said. 'Most people aren't, I think you'll find. We're all just doing our best to survive.'

The boy squinted, trying so hard to take it in that he almost went cross-eyed. Katharina passed him down the potato dish and he snatched at it, grateful for something simpler to consider. Just then, however, Lutz spoke up.

'I'm told there *is* a Wunderwaffe.'

All heads swung his way.

'By who?' Hans asked.

Lutz gave a modest shrug.

'Lutz has friends in high places,' Katharina said, twisting a strand of red hair around her fingers.

Oskar reached up to take her hand, pressing it in warning, but the boy was eager for more.

'Like who?' he demanded.

'Like Hermann Göring,' little Adelaide told him, keen to impress.

She succeeded. The boys turned their wide eyes on Lutz as if he were a Hollywood star.

'Truly, sir? You know the Reichsmarschall?'

'I do,' Lutz agreed, throwing a sideways glance at Katharina as if to say: *see – some people appreciate me.* 'He and I worked very closely together before the war in the development of many of the animals you see here today.'

'Including half the dead ones,' Katharina said under her breath. Oskar's grip tightened around her fingers.

'Hermann has some of our cattle up on his personal estate for safekeeping, and our two lion cubs, Sultan and Bussy, were his pets before they grew too large.'

'As they were always going to,' Katharina grumbled.

'Hermann is very concerned about preserving Germany's wildlife,' Lutz preached on to his eager audience. 'He was especially involved in our attempts to bring the pure-blood auroch back to life.'

Katharina groaned and drank more wine. She wasn't sure how she felt about the auroch, a long-extinct German oxen that the scientists at the zoo had been trying to genetically engineer back into existence. In some ways it was exciting to explore the possibilities, but in others it scared her. Recently, the animal had been held up as an example of the Blut und Boden policy that was seeing the poor Jews sent into the workcamps, and she'd come to hate it. What made one animal any better than another just because of where it came from?

'Shame Hermann isn't so keen on preserving Germany's human population,' she said sharply.

'Is it the party's fault that Britain chose to attack us?' Lutz retorted.

Katharina leaped to her feet.

'Well of course it is, because *they* attacked Poland.'

The table sucked in a collective breath. To speak against the party was treason of the highest order and you never knew who was listening.

'Katharina!' Oskar was up and pulling her tight in against him immediately. 'Don't pay her any heed. It's the wine, that's all. She's not used to it.'

'And why's that?' Katharina demanded. 'Because we're at war, that's why!'

'Kätsche,' he hissed into her ear. 'Please. Think of the zoo, meine kindl. Who will look after the zoo if the Gestapo take you away? Who will look after me?'

Katharina took in deep breaths and looked into Oskar's eyes.

'I'm sorry.' He nodded towards Lutz and, gritting her teeth, Katharina forced herself to turn to her boss. 'I'm sorry, Lutz. Oskar is right. I'm a little… giddy. Of course we Germans must defend ourselves.' Lutz was still glaring at her and, much as it pained her, she went on. 'I'm just a weak woman who wants it all to be over.'

To her surprise, Lutz's usually quiet wife, Rita, came to her aid.

'It's so hard for us females,' she said, simpering up at her husband. 'We don't really understand the machinations of war as you men do.'

It worked. Lutz's skinny chest swelled again.

'Then stay out of it,' he said to Katharina, adding with a patronising smile, 'and try not to worry. I really think the WuWas will be the answer. You'll see – by this time next year we'll be celebrating Christmas at peace, and with the Third Reich back on the road to prosperity.'

Katharina wasn't convinced and was relieved when Gisela fetched the plum pudding and Ursula, so close to Pierre now that she was almost openly on his knee, declared that she had games for them all. Half an hour later and everyone was doing wheelbarrow races up and down the great hall as if there were no tensions, no bombs and no damned Wunderwaffen – just love and laughter and silliness.

Katharina focused on running her hands across the floor as fast as she could as Oskar steered her past Ursula and Pierre, trying to preserve this simple happiness as they'd preserved the fruit for the pudding. But as she reached the end of the hall and tumbled, laughing, to one side, she saw Lutz's eyes following her intently and her rich meal curdled in her stomach. She had to make the most of this brief happiness, she knew, for the enemies were coming and there would be hard months ahead.

Chapter Five

Bethan grabbed her flask of coffee and made a dash for her favourite spot in the zoo, to snatch ten minutes' rest before her bleeper inevitably sounded out again and her little seal avatar summoned her to another job. Ada was there on the bench beneath her tartan blanket, but with the late March sun shining brightly, Bethan was quite happy on the grass behind. Settling down, she reached into her pocket and drew out her mother's list, blinking at how white it looked in the German sunshine. She studied the names, written in Jana's distinctive hand:

> *Katharina Heinroth*
> *Ursula Franke*
> *Gisela Schultz*
> *Sasha Eberhard*
> *Countess Sylvie*
> *Anke?*

Bethan looked from the words on the little sheet of paper to the same words on the bronze plaque. Katharina Heinroth had to be the key to properly starting her search. But how? She edged closer to Ada.

'Lovely day,' she said casually. The old woman ignored her. 'The animals are all out sunbathing.'

At that, Ada looked around.

'Nothing like the sun on your face.' She edged her blanket down a little, as if registering the spring warmth herself for the first time, and stared at Bethan. 'You work here?'

'I do. I've been here three weeks now.'

'It's good working here. Better now, of course. Better now than then.'

'Then?' Bethan asked tentatively.

'*Then*,' the old woman repeated impatiently. 'In the war.'

'Of course. You mentioned that before, at the gate the other morning?'

'The gate? I didn't work at the gate.'

'No, you were sitting at the gate.'

'I wasn't. No time to sit, there wasn't. Always something to do. Always some creature to help. Always the babies to look after.'

'Babies, Ada?'

'Babies, yes. Lots of babies. I was good with them, everyone said it. I could calm them. Even when the bombs were falling, I could calm them.'

'The babies?'

'Yes! Are you stupid?'

She stomped one purple boot crossly on the floor and Bethan put up her hands to calm her. 'No. Sorry. So, you used to care for the babies?'

'Exactly. Cuddle them and change them and feed them. It was important. But the Russians were coming. We had to get them out.'

'The babies?' Ada rolled her eyes and tapped her purple boots faster on the pavement, making a group of visitors jump and scurry around them. Bethan pushed herself up and hastened to Ada's side. 'Sorry, Ada. The babies, of course. You must have done very well to get them out.'

'I did. We all did. We had to. It was important. The Russians did things to babies, that's what they said. They did things to babies and they did things to women. Bad things.'

Bethan swallowed. She hadn't studied the period but she could imagine what Ada was referring to. Had this poor woman been raped in the war? Had others?

'Whose babies were they, Ada?' she asked, but at that, the woman's feet tapped even harder and she suddenly clapped her hands over her ears and began wailing incoherently. Only a few clear words spurted out of the tumble of distress: 'bombs' and 'Russians' and, again and again, 'babies'. Her arms were flailing around now and people were looking over in alarm. Bethan reached out to try and calm her, but the old lady jerked violently away and began a high-pitched keening that penetrated right under her skin.

'Ada, I'm sorry. It's OK. You're safe. The war's over. Long over.'

'The babies!' Ada wailed.

'The babies are safe too, I promise.'

Ada seemed to listen to her, but only for a moment before she set off wailing again. Bethan scrambled for her bleeper, though she had no idea who to summon for a human emergency and stared helplessly at the screen.

'Beth! Are you OK?'

She spun round to see, to her huge relief, Max coming striding down the path towards them.

'It's Ada, Max. She's having some sort of fit.'

'Here. Let me.'

She stood up gratefully as he slid onto the bench and took Ada's shoulders in a firm grip.

'Ada,' he said, his voice gentle but assertive. 'Ada, it's me. It's Max. I'm here for you. I'm here to take you for cake.'

'Cake?'

Ada's head snapped up and, miraculously, she stopped wailing. Bethan held her breath.

'Lots of cake, yes. I hear they have all sorts of lovely new ones in the cafe and I thought you might like some.'

'Some cake?' she asked, childlike now.

'As much as you'd like.'

'Really?'

'Of course. Shall we go?'

He offered her his arm, like an old-fashioned gentleman, and she took it, gazing trustingly up at him.

'Real cake? Made with real eggs?'

'And real butter and real sugar.'

'Yummy!'

She let him lead her, meek as a lamb, down the long avenue towards the canteen. It was bustling with people, but at a nod from Max the staff ran out and cleared space at a small table towards the rear. He eased Ada onto a chair and sat down opposite her, as if this were nothing more than a pleasant afternoon treat. Bethan hovered, watching with admiration as he kept talking quietly and reassuringly to the old lady, barely breaking eye contact with her as he arranged for a large slice of chocolate gateau to be brought over. It was only when Ada bent over to fork the first bit into her mouth that he finally looked up at Bethan.

'Thank you,' she murmured.

He grinned.

'No bother. It happens sometimes.'

'And cake is the answer?'

'Always.'

'I'll remember that.'

Ada was totally engrossed in her cake now, eating it almost a crumb at a time as if she might make it last all afternoon. Bethan slid into the third chair at the table.

'What set her off?' Max asked.

She glanced at Ada, but as far as the old lady was concerned there was nothing around her but chocolate frosting.

'I asked her about the war. She kept talking about bombs and Russians – and babies. Above all, babies.'

'Babies? Wasn't she muttering about them the other morning?'

'She was and it… interests me. I pushed her a bit, I'm afraid.'

Max tipped his head on one side, looking at her curiously.

'Why does it interest you, Beth?'

Bethan's fingers went instinctively to the list in her pocket. She'd told few people about it, but Max was looking at her with unjudgmental curiosity and suddenly she longed to confide in him. She pulled the little sheet out before she lost her nerve and smoothed it open on the table between them.

'Katharina Heinroth,' he said, homing in on the first name. 'She was—'

'The zoo manager after the war. I know.'

Bethan had googled her last night to remind herself about her history. She'd found out all about her doctorate in animal studies – unusual for a woman back then – her marriage to Oskar Heinroth, another passionate animal scientist much older than she was, and her time at the zoo, both during the war and afterwards. She sounded fascinating so it was little wonder her mum had been interested in her, but what she couldn't figure out was how she fitted with the other women on the list and why they'd ever come to Jana's attention.

'Do you recognise any of the other names?' she asked Max, but he shook his head.

'Sorry. No. Have you tried Google?'

'Of course.'

'I guess records are a bit sparse from the forties, especially from Berlin. The war turned everything to chaos.'

'You sound like you know a lot about it?'

'Oh, we get taught it at school. It's important. We don't want anything like that to happen again.' He flushed, lines of colour that made his cheekbones look more pronounced and his eyes a brighter blue. It was unusual, Bethan thought, blue eyes and dark hair. 'What's up?' Max asked when she didn't reply. 'Is it because you're English?'

'No! Oh sorry, God no. It was nothing to do with history. I was just, er…' Now it was her turn to flush; she could hardly say she'd been admiring his eyes. 'Thinking about my mum,' she finished lamely.

'Why haven't you asked her about the list?' Max asked.

'She died.' He gasped and she hurried on. 'Don't worry, it was ages ago. I was eleven. I'm not going to say I'm over it or anything, but it's not so raw these days.'

'Still awful though. I'm so sorry, Beth.'

Sympathy radiated from his eyes, making them look even more damned blue.

'It's fine. It just means that, you know…'

'The list feels important?'

'Exactly.'

'I can understand that. Well, perhaps we can have a dig in the zoo records and see if we can turn anything up. There's a dusty old set of files at the back of the main offices that goes back years. People often mutter about computerising them but there always seem to be better things to do.'

Bethan felt hope stir.

'That would be fantastic. Maybe we'll find a few skeletons in there?'

'Skeletons?' Ada, cake finished, suddenly leaped back into life. 'Where are the skeletons? Who found them? They're not the babies, are they? Not my babies?'

'No, no, no,' Max hastened to soothe her. 'Definitely not the babies.'

She looked at him and nodded.

'We got the babies out. Got them out before the Russians came.'

'Well done. More cake?'

Her eyes gleamed and Max made for the counter, beckoning Bethan to join him.

'You know,' he said, as he picked out a gooey piece of carrot cake for Ada, 'when I first worked here there was an old caretaker, a great bloke called Hans. I remember him telling me that they smuggled babies out of the zoo towards the end of the war. I thought he was talking nonsense at the time, but…'

'Baby smuggling?' Bethan looked back to Ada, who had now picked up her plate and was carefully licking every last bit of icing off it. 'Really?'

She looked around the canteen, seeking sense amidst the normality of the happy families. The doors were flung open to let in the sunshine and she could see across to the hippo house where the bronze Knautschke was gleaming handsomely. She squinted and suddenly the memory was back – she and her mum here in the zoo. She'd been so happy playing on the big hippo's back until suddenly she'd noticed Jana was gone. Panicking, she'd scrambled down, catching her precious pink pencil and blunting it in the process. Now she moved towards the door, drawn by the statue as if it might reveal the scene from her past right there before her.

'Mum!' she'd shouted, cross at first and then a little panicked. A large school group had come out of the hippo house, crowding her. Bethan put a hand to the doorframe, feeling her heart flutter as if she were back there again. It had been OK, she told herself. Jana hadn't left her, not at that point at any rate. She fought to remember and suddenly she could picture her, round the side of the hippo house, deep in conversation with a lady in brightly coloured boots with a large shawl – or maybe a blanket – slung around her shoulders. Had that been Ada? She'd have been far younger then, of course, but perhaps still as eccentric, and hadn't Max said she'd been coming here forever?

She swung round to look back across at Ada, who was cooing with delight over her carrot cake. Max caught her eye.

'OK?' he mouthed.

She nodded. She was OK, if perhaps even more confused than before. Her fingers went to the hippo brooch and she pictured it stashed at the bottom of her mum's jewellery box with the precious list. Had Jana bought the brooch that day, or was it the brooch that had brought her to the zoo? Clearly she had been certain that there were answers to be found here, and that strengthened Bethan's resolve to find them now. But twenty years had passed since then.

What had Jana hoped to find here in the zoo? And had she succeeded? If so, she'd told Bethan nothing of it, and neither had Paul. Bethan narrowed her eyes, looking at Knautschke through the slits so that he became a haze of bronze. There was something very odd going on here. Thank heavens her dad was coming out next weekend. He might not have wanted to talk about the list when she was small but, if Bethan had anything to do with it, he'd definitely tell her the truth now.

Chapter Six

January 1944

Katharina crept out of the bunker and looked fearfully around the snow-encrusted zoo, sparkling deceptively prettily in the moonlight. It hadn't taken long for the raids to start up again after Christmas, but this one had been the worst since the terrible November attacks, with bombs crashing down for hours. The all-clear had not yet sounded, but the wail of the animals had been too much to bear and she'd decided to risk a look. Most of the others were asleep in the makeshift bunks, worn out by the noise and fear, but Katharina was restless and hated being stuck underground so was glad to escape into the zoo.

The sky was clear and the stars like shards of ice in a dark pool. She pulled her old sheepskin coat around herself and headed warily towards the source of the noise. It was like Siam's bellows of last autumn, but Siam had retreated into himself without his harem and rarely uttered any sound at all these days. Besides, it seemed to be coming from the hippo house. Katharina gasped and started to run.

'Rosa!' The noise was coming from the female hippo standing in the outdoor pool, and Katharina rushed up to the bars but she didn't seem to be hurt. 'What's up, old girl? What's wrong?'

Rosa glanced her way a moment, then turned back towards the doorway into the indoor area and bellowed louder. Katharina followed her anguished gaze and saw, to her horror, the face of young Knautschke, twisted in pain as he fought to try and get to his mother. He seemed to be wedged in the doorway whilst, behind him, the house was on fire.

Instantly she was running again, round to the side door which was skewed in its hinges. Katharina pushed it aside and stumbled in to see fallen bricks and caved-in rafters and, on the far side, Knautschke's large rump squirming around as little bits of burning wood fell mercilessly on his hide. Either side of him, two small figures were battling to pull away the collapsed doorframe, and as Katharina went to them she realised it was Hans and Mark.

'What are you doing here, lads?'

'We were sent to fetch coffee for the soldiers on the flak tower.'

'Coffee?' Katharina queried incredulously. Who would send two young lads into a bombsite for coffee? But that was not the key issue right now. Knautschke's squirming was slowing, suggesting the youngster was losing his strength, and the rafters above were creaking perilously as the fire crept up them. If they didn't hurry this might be the end for them all. 'Let me help. Here, Hans, come round next to Mark and me. If we all pull on this side of the frame, we might just get it free.'

Hans nodded, clearly relieved to have an adult in charge, and came obediently to her side. His hands, she noticed, were horribly charred, but he grasped the wood without flinching and she and Mark joined him.

'Pull!' Katharina yelled.

They all pulled. The wood shifted and Knautschke's wriggles started up again. Outside, Rosa bellowed encouragement. Katharina planted her feet against the lower part of the frame and strained with all her might. At just five foot tall she was no bigger than the two lads and it was hard going. The fire above them was horribly hot and the smoke burned her lungs. A piece of rafter fell, bouncing off poor Knautschke and landing inches from their feet, and she looked fearfully to the boys. Should she be getting them to safety, instead of keeping them trapped in here trying to help a hippo?

'Hans…' she started.

'It's working!' he shot back, and suddenly Katharina heard the wood of the frame give a loud crack.

She was just in time to yank the lads backwards as it gave and, with a roar of triumph, Knautschke sprang forward and threw himself into the pool with his mother. A cloud of steam rose up from his poor, hot body, enveloping mother and son, and the boys burst out laughing. It *was* funny but the danger wasn't over yet, and Katharina took them each by the hand and pulled them after the hippo just before the whole frame collapsed, taking half the building with it.

The boys turned to stare at the pile of rubble where they had been standing just moments ago and both went white. Katharina wasn't surprised. Her own body was shaking and she felt dangerously close to tears.

'It's all right,' she told them. 'We're all right. We're safe. We made it.'

She was babbling, she knew, so she closed her lips and gave the boys a hug instead.

'Knautschke is still steaming,' little Mark pointed out.

'We need to cool him down,' Katharina agreed, grateful for something practical to focus on. 'Let's throw snow on him.'

The boys took this instruction gleefully and began pelting the hippo with snowballs. It evidently felt good for Knautschke came closer, Rosa tight at his side, and Katharina formed her own ball and flung it. It hit the side of the hippo with a hiss, turning almost instantly into water and running down his poor hide and into the pool below. She threw another and another, and her arm was aching by the time someone grabbed it and she looked round to see Oskar.

'Enough, meine kindl. Enough. Knautschke is well.'

That wasn't strictly true, she knew, but he was alive and he looked as if he would heal, so she let herself collapse into her husband's arms, sending up a prayer of thanks that, for once, she'd helped save a life instead of having to help end it.

'It was Hans and Mark,' she said, waving at them as others came running up. 'They saved Knautschke. They're heroes.'

The boys blustered a rebuttal but Katharina was having none of it.

'These boys deserve medals,' she told Lutz.

He looked to Knautschke and then to Hans and Mark.

'I'm not sure we have medals, but I could offer you a slap-up breakfast and lifelong membership of the zoo?'

'Yes please, sir,' they both said, beaming, and went happily off with him to his villa.

Katharina watched them go, praying that their lives were long enough to make the most of the offer – and that the zoo survived to let them. Neither, right now, looked very certain.

Later that day the keepers met in Lutz's villa, their faces pale and weary from another heartbreaking clean-up. Not all the animals had been as lucky as Knautschke and there was more meat for Marcel's makeshift kitchen. The people of Berlin would, at least, be thankful. A line was already forming as tantalising smells began to waft out of the Lion Gate at the rear of the zoo, watched over by Reike the giraffe, still miraculously calm as she stretched her long neck curiously over the bars. People brought hay, vegetables and peelings for the animals in return for a bowl of Marcel's best stew, and all brought their prayers and love as well.

Every time anyone – usually Dennis – muttered about closing the zoo, Katharina pointed to the affection with which the people of the city held it. In a time that sometimes felt devoid of hope, the continued presence of Berlin's zoo animals was something many clung to, and every day there were visitors seeking a little escapism from the hard grind of day-to-day life. For Katharina, at least, that was enough. She looked to Lutz as they all gathered, but he refused to meet her eye. He had things to say he knew she wouldn't like, then, and she steeled herself for an argument.

'Thank you all for coming,' he started formally.

They were a group of less than forty these days, a ridiculously skeleton staff compared to the two hundred who had looked after the zoo in the happy times before the war had taken them off to face enemy guns instead. Those qualified keepers who remained were either over sixty or with medical conditions that precluded them from fighting. Robert, for example, had lopsided legs from a bad bout of childhood polio. ('First time I've been glad of that,' he'd joked with dark Berliner humour.) They were all, however, experienced and dedicated and were ably helped by the many determined women, like Gisela, who had stepped into the departed men's shoes.

'As you all know,' Lutz was continuing, 'we suffered another bad raid last night and we have no idea how many more may come. The anti-aircraft teams on the flak tower are fighting hard, but the Tommies seem to have endless planes and they love nothing more than bombing our helpless animals.'

Katharina flinched. She wasn't sure the British pilots were picking out the animals specifically, but they were hitting them all the same and she didn't interrupt the manager.

'I've been keen to keep them here, where we experts can care for them,' Lutz went on, 'but I am starting to fear that the centre of Berlin is no longer the best place for our programmes.'

Katharina drew in a deep breath.

'You would close the zoo, Lutz?'

He looked at her.

'Not close it, Katharina, no, but I think we should start shipping some of our more valuable animals elsewhere.'

'How will they cope with the journey?' Walter demanded. 'And where is safe for them anyway?'

Lutz gave a little sigh.

'It's hard to tell, Walter. As you know, I brought a number of animals here to Berlin earlier in the war, believing our expertise would keep them safe, but that was before the Tommies developed their longer-range planes. Nowadays I cannot help but feel that if we can manage to find secure transports, rural destinations must give them a better chance. No one is bombing fields.'

Walter frowned.

'We cannot release zoo animals into Germany's fields, Lutz.'

'Of course not. Well, perhaps some of the cattle.'

'They will be eaten within days,' Gustav cried.

'Not on Schorf Moor. No one would dare steal the Reichsmarschall's goods.'

Gustav gave a begrudging nod but still looked pained.

'What of the lions though? Or the polar bears? Who else can take care of them?'

'A fair point,' Lutz conceded. 'And they, I think, will need to stay with us and take their chances. But I have contacts in a number of zoos and, perhaps more crucially, with private collectors who could safely house our remaining reptiles, smaller mammals and primates.'

'Kalifa?' Katharina asked sharply, and Lutz looked pained.

Kalifa was the alpha male of the baboon tribe. Lutz had brought him back from Cameroon on his first ever expedition with his father, and was often to be found talking to him in his spare moments.

'Not Kalifa,' he said.

'Then not the chimps either, Lutz, please. At least not the pregnant ones.'

She had increasingly taken on the care of the chimpanzees and had grown very fond of them. Several of the mothers were due to give birth in the spring, and she hated the thought of someone else being in charge of them when that happy time came around.

Lutz tipped his head, dog-like.

'Perhaps not. The details can be finalised on an individual basis. My brother at Munich zoo thinks he can help, and I have a good friend at Mülhausen in East Prussia. It is quieter there and they have strong cages and qualified people.' He set his jaw and seemed to look straight at Katharina. 'I will send no animal anywhere I do not believe they will be cared for.'

That she did not doubt and she forced herself to smile her agreement. No one wanted to have to clear corpses every morning, but she had a terrible fear that shipping the animals out would be the end of the zoo, the end of her baby. She reached for Oskar's hand and he squeezed it tight.

'Don't worry, meine kindl,' he murmured. 'It is for the best. When the war is over, we can bring them all back and start again.'

'When will that be, O?'

He gave a sad little shrug.

'Who knows, but it surely cannot go on forever.'

'Oskar!'

They both jumped guiltily as Lutz rapped out his name.

'Lutz?' he asked.

'I would like to put you in charge of this. With the aquarium sadly gone you have no direct responsibilities at the moment, and I think you would do a fine job.'

'Thank you, Lutz.'

'Perhaps you can stay for coffee and I can give you what contacts I have?'

'Of course.'

'Good. The rest of you are free to return to your duties. Remember, we are in this together. And we will get out of it together.'

It was the closest Katharina had ever heard him get to admitting that all was not going well with the war but, in many ways, that chilled her more than his bullish nonsense about WuWas and 'turning the tide'. If Lutz Heck was losing hope for Berlin, then things must be dire indeed. She gave Oskar a quick kiss, then got up and reached for Sasha's arm as they all filed out of the villa.

'Things sound bad,' she said cautiously.

Sasha nodded and looked round for Adelaide, but her daughter was bouncing off to the zebras with Robert and was not in earshot.

'I hear the Russians are driving the Eastern front back every day. When does that turn from them chasing us out of their country into invading ours?'

A chill ran down Katharina's spine greater than the January cold.

'You think they are coming for us?'

'Why would they not? And the Americans on the Western side too. Robert says they are preparing for an invasion of Europe this summer.'

'Really? How does he know?'

Sasha drew Katharina round the back of the baboon rocks. Kalifa came bounding over to look down on them and his tribe chattered excitedly at their approach, offering natural cover for their conversation.

'He listens to the BBC.'

Katharina gasped.

'That's a crime, Sasha. Men have been strung up for it.'

'I know! But he says that not knowing what's going on is worse than death.'

'Nonsense! You have a child on the way. Nothing is worth jeopardising that.'

Sasha shrugged sadly.

'True, Kätsche, but Goebbels's pet radio tells us nothing but lies. If you listen to him, Germany are winning the war but we can see that isn't true. Yesterday I was in the bread queue and a string of women and children went past, bundles in their arms and their faces like those of wild things. I spoke to one and she told me they were refugees from the east, fleeing the Red Army. They are monsters, she said. They do unspeakable things to civilians. *Unspeakable.*'

Her hand went instinctively to her belly and Katharina threw her arms around her.

'Perhaps it's not just the animals that we should be evacuating, Sasha. Perhaps we should be thinking of getting you out too.'

Sasha pulled back.

'Why me, Kätsche?'

'Because of the baby, of course. And Adelaide. This is no place for a young girl any more.'

'Adelaide loves it here.'

'She won't if the Russians arrive.'

They stared at each other. A tear welled in Sasha's eye and Katharina reached up and wiped it gently away.

'I don't want to go,' Sasha whispered. 'I don't want to leave Robert. I don't want to leave you. I don't want to leave the zoo…'

Another tear welled and Katharina sighed.

'I don't want you to go either, Sash, but promise me you'll think about it. If Oskar is arranging the transports, we'll have some control over what – or who – goes with them. It wouldn't hurt, surely, to make plans in case?'

'In case of what?' Sasha asked, but even as she spoke the words, she shook them away. It wasn't a question that either of them wanted to answer out loud.

Chapter Seven

'Dad! Dad, over here!'

Bethan waved excitedly as her father came through the arrivals door and looked around. He caught sight of her and a broad grin broke out across his face.

'Beth!'

He rushed forward, his little suitcase banging against his legs, and she flung herself into his arms. His hug was tight and warm and gorgeously familiar, and she stood there as other travellers flowed around them, just soaking him in.

'I've missed you,' they said at the same time, and then they laughed and hugged each other again.

'Come on,' Bethan said, grabbing his case. 'Let's get you to the zoo.'

All the way into the city, in the zoo van that Tanya had lent her, Bethan kept glancing at her father, checking that he was really here. Perhaps Callum was right and her dependence on him was 'weird', but it didn't feel that way to her. Throughout her teenage years it had been just the two of them battling on together and, despite a few inevitable arguments, they'd got on well. They'd understood each other's grief but, more than that, had been joined in their determination to enjoy their lives as Jana would have wanted.

Paul had done an amazing job of being both father and mother to her. He'd moved his army career over to a desk job to be around for her every evening, and done his best to help her with homework. He'd watched tutorials on how to do make-up so he could have discussions with her about gloss vs matt lipsticks, or this season's eyeshadow colours. He'd taken her shopping, standing patiently outside the changing rooms in New Look as she'd tried on outfit after outfit – though she suspected he'd been very relieved when she'd started doing that with friends instead. He'd taken her out for afternoon tea and on holidays. He'd bought her tampons and brought her hot-water bottles when she'd got cramps, and unflinchingly talked to her about contraception when she'd started seriously dating in sixth form.

She'd done her best to reciprocate, especially as she got older. She'd tried to take up golf so she could go out and play with him, but had been useless at it – though at least it had meant he'd met the blokes in the 'old farts' group he now played with. She'd been more successful at cultivating an interest in real ale, and they'd gone on a fantastic tour of the pubs of Ireland after her A-levels.

She'd worried about how her dad would cope without her and considered going to university from home, but Paul had put his foot down. She was his daughter, he'd said, not his wife or his housekeeper or even his friend. She had to go out into the world and live life her own way – and he had to get on and live his too. She'd hoped he was considering dating again but he'd shown no sign of inviting anyone into his life. His heart, he always said, still belonged to the laughing woman he'd met back in the mid-eighties when his platoon had been stationed in Berlin as part of the peace-keeping force along the hated wall. Both her parents had been in their thirties – late to love for the times but quick to snatch it up – and Paul had told Bethan more times than she could count about the night he'd walked into a bar and found Jana doing an impression of a British officer on the snooker table.

'She was so funny, Beth – so spot on. I just went straight up and saluted her, then asked if I could buy her a drink. The rest, as they say, is history.'

Sadly, it had become the worst sort of history and, with the woman he loved gone, Paul had shown no interest in finding another. Instead, he had taken up carpentry, pouring himself into beautiful creations in wood. Then, once he'd retired, he'd thrown himself into it even more, joining up with other artists at a local craft barn. He had plenty of friends there and was content, and nowadays she only worried about him maybe every second day, but these last four weeks had been the longest time she'd gone without seeing him since university and she hadn't realised until now how strange that had been.

'How's the craft barn?' she asked.

'Great. We're planning this huge show next month and everyone's working really hard. I've been there till all hours finalising my pieces.'

She glanced over at him.

'You're not wearing yourself out, are you?'

He laughed.

'Probably.'

'Dad…'

'Don't worry, Beth – the barn doesn't open until midday so I take my time getting up. I'm quite the hippy these days.'

Bethan giggled; her ex-military father was as straight as they came.

'We'll have to get you some baggy trousers and tie-dye shirts then, hey? They have some great markets in Berlin – we'll soon get you kitted out.'

'Not *that* hippy,' Paul said. 'Though I have to say those trousers do look comfy. And d'you know, most of them don't wear any pants underneath.'

The laugh jerked out of Bethan and she had to concentrate hard not to pull the van out of their lane. Luckily they were turning into Budapester Strasse and she pulled up at the Elephant Gate, gratified when Mikey, the lad in the ticket booth, gave her a cheery wave, and pressed the button to open it up for her.

'I feel like royalty,' Paul said, leaning out of the window as they passed through the beautiful archway. 'This is so lovely, Beth. You did so well to get the job here.'

'I'm very lucky,' Bethan agreed.

'No luck about it, sweetheart. You've worked hard all your life even after we, you know, lost your mother. You deserve every bit of success you get.'

Bethan smiled at him but a chill ran down her spine at the mention of Jana. She eased the van into a parking space and drew in a deep breath. She had to ask her dad about the list and she wasn't looking forward to it.

Not yet, she told herself. Paul was here for four whole days across the Easter weekend so there was time enough. For now, there was a whole zoo to show him. She leaped out of the van.

'Come on, Dad. Let's get some food and then I'll give you the full tour.'

The sun was shining and many of the animals were out enjoying it, meaning the Easter crowds were happy. The zoo buzzed with laughter and chatter and Bethan revelled in taking her dad around, swiping her pass like a pro to let him into the back areas and the 'staff only' zones. Everywhere she went people said hello and, as she saw Paul taking it all in, she could hardly believe she'd only been here four weeks. The zoo, she realised, was now her home and, as they paused in the space-age hippo house to watch the giant creatures swimming in the blue waters, she tried to picture her flat in England and realised that it was a struggle. The only image that truly came to mind was Callum's damned Leicester City duvet, and she sure as hell didn't miss that.

Suddenly she felt a little sad and turned away, glad her dad was engrossed by the hippos. She'd bought that flat when she left university and got her first job back home in Leicestershire. Her mum had arranged for her to receive a large payment on her twenty-first birthday and the flat had been like a gift from her. She'd loved it and spent every spare hour making it perfect, so letting Callum move in a year ago had been a big deal for her. Looking back, she wasn't sure he'd seen it that way. If she recalled, his words had been 'not much point us both paying rent, is there?' By which, she thought, a little cruelly, he'd meant 'not much point in me paying rent'. Certainly, he hadn't volunteered to pay any more than his nominal contribution now that he was living there alone, apparently preferring to spend his money in the pubs and clubs of Leicester.

'OK, Beth?'

She spun back to see her dad looking at her with concern.

'Fine, fine. Just, er, checking Klumpig there is healed. We had to stitch him up the day I arrived and I thought maybe the wound was oozing a little, but it's not.'

'Klumpig?'

'The little fat one turning somersaults over there.'

They both looked to Klumpig, who was indeed performing acrobatics for a crowd of squealing children.

'He looks good to me,' Paul said.

'Me too. Right – rhinos?'

Her father came after her happily enough but a couple of times she caught him looking sideways at her, and when they finally got back to her apartment and she made them coffees, he put his hand over hers.

'All well, Bethan? You like it here?'

'I love it, Dad. Really. It's fantastic. The place is so cool and the research programmes are amazing and the people are so welcoming. Wait till you meet Tanya and Ella, the other vets, oh, and Max.'

'Max?'

'He's the chimp keeper and the assistant manager. He lives on this floor and he's a good laugh. You'll see.'

'My German's pretty rusty, Beth. I hope I don't show you up.'

She laughed.

'It'll come back to you in no time, I promise, and they can all speak English anyway. It'll be great.'

'I believe you. How's Callum got on?'

Bethan tensed.

'He's not been out yet.'

'Really?'

'He's in the middle of a big project at work. All the hours. You know what it's like.'

'Not really. I wouldn't let work stop me visiting my girl.'

'Dad! It's not his fault I chose to come out here, and he'll be coming very soon.'

'Good. That's good. Is that good?'

'It's good, Dad.'

'Good.' They both sipped awkwardly at their coffees. Paul ran a hand through his salt-and-pepper hair and sighed. 'I'm not so good at this, Beth, not like your mum would have—'

'Don't, Dad! You've been a brilliant parent.'

'Thanks, love. But mums know how to talk about emotional stuff, don't they? It's a knack, right?'

'Judging by the way some of my mates talk about their mums, it's more just inherent nosiness. Don't sweat it, Dad, I'm fine. Really.'

'Nothing else is bothering you?' Bethan drew in a breath but he saw her hesitation and pressed her hand again. 'What is it, Beth? Tell me.'

She bit her lip.

'It's the list.'

'What list?'

Slowly she got up and went through to retrieve the tiny piece of paper from her bedside drawer. She placed it down on the table in front of Paul, who leaped up as if it was a spitting snake.

'Where on earth did you get that?' he demanded, almost an exact echo of his reaction all those years ago when she'd first shown it to him.

'I kept it.'

He screwed up his face, clearly fighting to remember.

'Didn't I throw it out?'

'I dug it back out of the bin that night.'

'You…?'

He stared at her, rare anger in his eyes.

'I had to, Dad. It was hers. It obviously meant something to her and therefore it meant something to me. I dug it out and I hid it, and when I got the job at the zoo I remembered it and thought it might be worth bringing it with me. And it was, wasn't it?'

'What on earth d'you mean?'

'It's important, isn't it?'

'No, it—'

'I can see it is, Dad. Don't mess around with me, please. I'm a grown woman now, not a scared little girl. You can tell me what it was about.'

He shook his head violently.

'I can't.'

'Why?'

'Because it's not my secret to tell.'

'It's Mum's secret?' He flinched but nodded. 'And it affects me?' This time he just closed his eyes. Bethan hated seeing him hurt but she had to know more. 'Then you owe it to me to tell me what it is. Mum would have done, I'm sure she would. Mum would have known that I was strong enough to cope with whatever that list is hiding.'

'Bethan, that's not fair.'

'Maybe not, but you're not being fair either, Dad. Please – tell me.' Paul got up and went over to the window, looking out not into the zoo below but across to the roofs of the city. Every line of his body was taut and Bethan longed to go over and hug him, but not yet. 'Is it to do with babies?'

He gasped and spun back, staring at her.

'You know?'

'No!' she all but yelled. 'But I will do, Dad. If you don't tell me then I'll dig and dig until I find out, and surely it – whatever the hell "it" is – is better coming from you?'

Paul put a hand to the window glass and stared up into the sky. Bethan had the distinct impression he was talking to Jana in his mind and forced herself to sit down again. She sipped at her coffee but it had gone cold and tasted disgusting. Frankly, right now she fancied a glass of wine but that, too, would have to wait, for now Paul was coming back to her, his lined, familiar face racked with pain.

'Do you remember your grandmother dying, Beth?'

'Oma Erika? Of course. It was awful.'

She thought back to the time when they'd all crept around her Oma's Berlin house, hushed and scared, as she'd fought for life for three days after a sudden heart attack. It had felt like the worst thing that could ever happen to Bethan at the time – but of course it hadn't been. Three years later, she'd found herself at her mother's deathbed and the loss of eighty-year-old Erika had paled in comparison. Now, she forced herself to think back to it and remember how sad she'd been to lose the lively, funny, irreverent old lady with whom she and Jana had spent every summer she could remember.

'It was more awful for your mum.'

'Well of course, she—'

'Just let me speak, Bethan.' His voice was strained, and she nodded and clamped her lips shut. 'On the last day, when Erika was fighting for every breath, she asked Jana to come into her room. She had to speak to her, she said. She had to tell her something important. She had to tell her that she wasn't her mother.'

'What?'

Bethan battled to take it in. She'd imagined all sorts of possibilities but not this. Never this.

'It was a shock,' Paul said flatly. Bethan stared at him.

'I bet! Poor Mum. But how...? I mean, what happened?'

'It was at the end of the war, Erika told her. A woman gave a baby to her. As a gift.'

'A gift? Wow, Dad, it's not your average gift.'

'I know! Don't you think I don't know that, Bethan? Don't you think your mum didn't know that? She begged for more but Erika was fast running out of breath. I was furious with her for that. I know she was dying and I shouldn't have been angry, but I was. God, I was. Why wait until she hadn't enough breaths left to explain? Why say anything at all if you couldn't give the whole story? It didn't make any sense.

'Jana had her birth certificate, legitimately signed at a Berlin registry office – signed months after her birth, true, but it was 1945. Berlin was wrecked in the final weeks of the war so a bit of delayed paperwork was the least of the city's problems. Erika had always said how lovely it had been to be able to wait until Opa Georg was back from fighting to register the baby together. Jana had never questioned it before – but there were holes for sure. Just enough holes to make what Erika was saying possible.'

'That a woman gave her a baby as a gift?'

'A woman called Anke. That's all she'd say. I heard Jana cry out and sneaked into the room so I was there, Beth. I heard her. Erika was babbling by then, and her breaths were rasping out of her lungs like nettle stings. It was horrible. I think she tried. I think she thought she had enough strength to tell Jana more, but, but...'

'But she was wrong?'

He nodded, his eyes moist.

'All she managed after that was to repeat "gift". She clutched at Jana's hand and just said "gift" and "wonderful, wonderful gift" over and over until she breathed her last. Then she was gone, and Jana was left with no mother. Literally, no mother – neither the one who had brought her up nor the one who had apparently birthed her. It was terrible.'

Bethan fought to imagine. Her Oma had died in the night, she knew that much. She'd got up in the morning to find her mum and dad asleep against each other on the sofa, their skin white and their eyes red-rimmed. She'd crept into her Oma's room and found the body laid out peacefully, with not a sign of the battle of the last hours that she was now hearing about for the first time. It felt as if someone had taken her past and turned it inside out. But then, of course, that must have been how her mum had felt too – and fifty times worse.

'So,' she said slowly, 'Oma Erika wasn't my real grandma?'

'I'm afraid not, biologically speaking. But, Bethan, she loved you dearly and—'

Bethan brushed this away.

'I know that. But her blood was not my blood?'

'No. Does that matter?'

'Does it matter?' Bethan's brain spun. 'Of course it matters. What if my real grandmother had a history of, of…'

She stopped. The first words that came to mind were breast cancer but, of course, Jana had died of breast cancer so it was a pointless argument. Except that…

'If Mum had known, if her own mum – her real mum – had had a medical history of cancer, then she'd have been on a testing list sooner, wouldn't she? Wouldn't she, Dad?'

'Probably not, Bethan. We didn't know so much about the genetics of it in the eighties and nineties.'

'But she'd have been on alert. Oh my God…' A new thought came to her. 'Was it the stress of this that brought it on? Is that possible?'

'No! Come on, Beth, you're the medical one. It doesn't work like that. Although I admit…'

'What? You admit what, Dad?'

'I sometimes felt that because Jana became rather, well, obsessed with trying to find her real mother, she maybe… maybe…'

'Maybe what?'

'Maybe didn't pay as much attention to her own health as she might otherwise have done. Maybe didn't pick up the, you know, the lump until later than she should have.'

Bethan screwed her fists into her eyes where tears were stinging painfully, spiking her with sorrow and disbelief and anger. Far, far too much anger.

'Why did no one tell me?' she demanded.

'You were little, Beth. You were only eight when Oma Erika died.'

'And eleven when Mum died, I know. God, I know. But Mum went through all that for three whole years without me even realising? I could have helped her. I could, at least, have comforted her.' She heard Paul sit down opposite and felt his hands trying to pull hers away but yanked back. 'You lied to me, Dad.'

'I didn't lie. I just didn't tell you everything. Because she didn't want me to. You were still a child. Truly, Beth, she begged me not to tell you. She begged me to spare you what she was going through.'

'I wouldn't have minded. She was my mum, wherever she came from.'

'I know. I'm sorry.'

Paul's voice shook. His head was down and he was wringing his hands round and round in his lap. She felt terrible. He'd only been here for a few hours and she was shouting at him, but Lord knows he deserved it. How could he have kept this from her for all these years?

'So,' she said, fighting for control, 'Oma Erika was gifted a baby at the end of the war and, at some point, took Opa Georg – who must, by the way, have struggled with that story – and registered her as Jana Weber, their own child.'

'Yes,' Paul said on an outbreath.

'Somehow Mum made a list of women that she, what, believed might be her real mother?'

He nodded.

'How?'

'Sorry?'

'How did she make the list? How did she get the names?'

'Bethan—'

'How, Dad?'

'OK, OK.' He looked distressed, and every fibre of Bethan's body wanted to go to him and hug him and tell him it was all right. But it wasn't. She forced herself to sit still and listen, and after a moment, Paul spoke.

'She had no idea for ages. She had one name – Anke. Do you know how many Ankes there are in Germany, Beth? It seemed like we'd never find anything out at all. Erika and Georg both lost their siblings in the war so there was no one to talk to, or so it seemed. But then one day, when we were finally clearing out your grandma's house, we found something under the floorboards.'

Bethan leaned eagerly forward.

'What, Dad?'

'Jana's birth certificate. The original. We'd only had copies up until then but there it was, with some money and some jewellery – people of that era liked to keep a few things close, in case. It was the war, I think.'

'I imagine so. And…?'

'Pinned to the top of your mum's birth certificate was a brooch.' Bethan's fingers went to the little hippo on her chest and he nodded. 'That was Oma Erika's brooch. Or, perhaps Jana's mother's. That's what we had to assume. On the back of it were two letters.'

'BZ,' Bethan said, feeling for them. 'Berlin Zoo.'

'Right, though of course we didn't know that at the time. Your mother spent ages trying to find someone with the initials BZ, until finally a jeweller told her it was a cheap piece and suggested it might have come from the zoo. That was something of a breakthrough.' He sighed deeply. 'Your mum was off to Berlin the moment you broke up for school.'

So the brooch *had* brought her mum here, just as she'd suspected.

'I remember,' she told her dad. 'We came here together.'

'You did. She spoke to an old caretaker who was convinced babies had been smuggled out of the zoo in the war, and that was enough for her. He helped her compile the list of women who'd lived at the zoo during the war, but by then...'

Tears clogged his words and now Bethan did go to him. She saw, again, her mum talking intently with the lady in the colourful boots when she left her stranded on the back of bronze Knautschke, and knew now what she'd been asking. She took her dad's hand and he looked at her, his distress raw in his dear eyes.

'By then we'd had the diagnosis,' he managed. 'After that, as you know, Beth, it was hard to focus on anything else. If it helps, she died at peace with it. She knew how much Erika loved her. Georg too. A womb is just a receptacle, that's what she said to me. Love is what makes parents – love and care and support.'

'And truth,' Bethan said.

Paul groaned.

'I'm so sorry, Beth. Can you forgive us? Can you forgive me?'

'I hope so.'

It wasn't enough, she could see that from the pain in his eyes, but at the moment it was all she had to give, and suddenly the happy Easter weekend seemed horribly tainted. Slowly she picked up the list:

Katharina Heinroth
Ursula Franke
Gisela Schultz
Sasha Eberhard

Countess Sylvie
Anke?

Who were these women? Bethan had no idea but she could see one thing very clearly. Her mum had died without completing the search for her real mother; now Bethan was going to complete it for her.

Chapter Eight

May 1944

'Ursula – you look beautiful!' Gisela stepped back from adjusting the hem of her friend's dress, her eyes filled with tears. 'Oh, I so want to hug you but we mustn't rumple the bride.'

'Nonsense,' Ursula retorted. 'It's only a dress. Come here!'

She pulled her friend in for a hug, and Katharina looked to Sasha and smiled at the sight of poor Gisela trying not to crush herself against the gorgeous cream silk of Ursula's gown. At their side Ursula's mother, Hetti, clapped delightedly. She was very like her daughter, and it had taken few adjustments to her own wedding gown to get it right. Wartime had made even voluptuous Ursula too thin but taking in a dress wasn't so hard and, with the aid of a silver brooch to hide some stitching, the fit was perfect. She looked every inch the bride, and Katharina had to admit to tears tickling her own eyes as she looped her arm through Sasha's.

'She looks wonderful,' Sasha said. 'Which is more than can be said of me. I'm a lump.'

'That's not true, Sash – you just *have* a lump.'

Sasha nudged at her but laughed. She was seven months pregnant and her belly was growing fast. With the rest of her as thin as everyone else, however, it looked like someone had pushed one of the seal's big balls down her dress and it had taken rather more adjusting than Ursula's. With clothing coupons far too short to buy a new one, they'd had to be inventive, and her floral frock now had two plain panels down the sides. It wasn't ideal but it would do, and they were all just delighted for a chance to spruce up and have some fun.

It had been a long hard run into spring with little let-up from the air raids, but now Berlin's resilient trees were bursting into blossom and the skies – when they weren't filled with smoke or fire – were blue once more. The other day Katharina had been out shopping and, passing a deep crater where the General Staff building had been blown to bits last year, had found it filled with surprisingly clear water. Reeds had been growing around the edges, lilies budding, and ducks quacking happily across its surface. Nature, she'd seen, was ever-resilient and it had given her hope for them all. And now, a wedding. She looked at her watch – a pretty silver band Oskar had given her on their fifth wedding anniversary.

'We'd better hurry up, ladies. Pierre will be waiting at the altar.'

This announcement was met with squeals of excitement, not least from Adelaide, whom Ursula had asked to be her flower girl. Sasha had made her dress from some pretty fabric that had been exchanged for a large bowl of Marcel's antelope stew, and she looked radiant. She was turning into a young woman and Katharina wasn't sure whether to be happy to see her blossom with the rest of nature, or scared of what it might mean if the Red Army came.

Oskar had been busy arranging the first transportations of the animals out of the zoo. He had a smart red notebook to record all his contacts and plans, and every day that she watched him working, she was tempted to ask him to arrange to get some of their friends out too. She shook the thought away. Enemy troops were miles off yet and today was not a day for fear but for happiness – albeit in a clandestine manner, as Germans were most certainly not allowed to marry foreigners. Not that that had stopped Ursula proposing to Pierre at Easter.

'*You* proposed to *him*?' Gisela had gasped when Ursula had come to them with the happy news.

'Why on earth not? I had to, didn't I, as he's more or less powerless here, poor lamb.'

The idea of big, handsome Pierre as a lamb had made everyone laugh, but Ursula had had a point and Katharina had been proud of her for standing up for what she wanted. Pierre was a wonderful man – kind, strong and caring. He was also, they'd discovered recently, surprisingly poetic. One night in freezing February, when the raids had been especially bad and they'd all been cowering in the bunker, eyes fixed on the shaking ceiling, he had started talking about his home in Provence.

His voice had been calm and melodious, a strangely soothing mixture of German and French, lulling them all into forgetting the bombs and the cold and the dirt. He'd taken them with him to pretty villages rising up on the soft hills, with rolling fields of purple lavender and yellow sunflowers below, and the church bells ringing out to call the workers in for lunch beneath vine-laden pagodas. Almost every night since, someone had begged Pierre to 'take us to Provence' and they all ached to see it for real.

'After the war,' Pierre would always end. 'After the war I will make a home there for Ursula, and you will all come and visit and we will be happy.'

It was something to cling on to and today it felt more possible than ever before. Katharina placed her own cloak around Ursula's shoulders to hide her white dress, and hustled her out of her apartment and along to the underground bunker. Her heart raced and she had to force herself to walk normally so as not to attract any attention. Once the zoo walls would have hidden them from prying eyes, but bombs had torn great gashes in them and they had to take care. Even if they avoided any passing Gestapo, you could never tell who might inform on you for a party bribe, and Katharina was relieved when they reached the bunker safely.

She peered in and was glad to see the curtain had been drawn inside the entrance, leaving them a form of porch in which to compose themselves. She could hear the buzz of voices beyond and, imagining Pierre waiting eagerly for his bride, her heart steadied and she turned back to Ursula with a smile.

'Ready?'

'Never been readier!'

It was not, sadly, a church, but there was little they could do about that without giving away their lethal secret and they were lucky, at least, that Father Jörg had agreed to conduct the ceremony. It was very good of the old man, as he would be shot along with Pierre if he was found out, but he had not hesitated for a moment when Katharina had approached him.

'Of course, of course.'

'It will be dangerous, Father.'

He'd shrugged.

'It will be worth it.' She'd hugged him then, overcome by his simple goodness, and he'd laughed and patted her back. 'I worship a God of love, Liebchen, and that God would want this man and this woman joined in holy matrimony. And see the need of it, besides.'

He'd winked at her as she'd pulled back, shocked. 'Come, Katharina – I may not have a wife of my own but I know the ways of the world. Those two are going to be together, and better it is with God's blessing.'

Katharina had smiled her agreement. In truth, she suspected Ursula and Pierre were 'together' already. War was making people reckless. When a bomb could fall on you at any time, the scruples of civilised society ceased to have as much meaning. Besides, with rumours of the Red Army's atrocities growing at an alarming rate, many a girl in the city was choosing to give herself to a German boy whilst there was time. If you were foolish enough to head out after dark, there were myriad rustles to be heard in the remaining foliage of the Tiergarten, or amongst the rubble heaps of the city. The only consolation, Katharina supposed, was that love-making was better than thieving, for which there was little need now that so many houses were cracked open for the taking.

She shook the thought away. She was distracted and it was a foolish waste of a rare celebration amongst the drudgery of their days. Gisela and Sasha had taken the cloak off Ursula and were arranging her gown and checking her dark hair. Adelaide handed over her flowers – a bouquet of May blossom collected in the park earlier – and Hetti stepped up at her side to give her away. Her father was stuck on the Eastern front. They had sent letters hinting at happy news but had no idea if they had reached him or if he had divined the content.

'Men can be obtuse,' Hetti had said easily. 'He will find out when he returns and he will be so happy, but for now it is up to us women.'

Katharina looked at her, tall and proud as she offered her daughter her arm, and knew the truth of that statement. Aside from Pierre and his French compatriots, most of the men in this secret wedding were under sixteen or over sixty. The city was bereft of male youth and everywhere you went things were being kept going by women. They ran the shops, drove the buses, worked the factories and tirelessly tidied up the rubble of people's homes. Lines of Trümmerfrauen – aproned women passing buckets of bricks off the roads and pavements – were as common a sight these days as the same women elegantly sipping coffee in smart hats and gloves before the war. That was sad, but today Katharina felt proud of them all for keeping some semblance of normality going, and she took her place behind the others as Adelaide skipped forward and pulled back the curtain with a flourish.

There was a gasp, all eyes turned their way, and Katharina forgot that they weren't in a church and just drank in the scene. Last week the Frenchmen had given the bunker – all sixty metres of it – a new coat of whitewash and everyone had spent as much of yesterday as they could spare from zoo duties decorating it with vines, spring flowers and bunting made, ironically, from cut-up party news-sheets. This morning the men had arranged the smart chairs from the once-elegant concert-hall dining room in church-style rows to create an aisle, and Father Jörg had smuggled in a beautiful altar cloth and two silver candlesticks to transform the table at the top. As Hetti and Ursula took their first steps into the makeshift church, Pierre stepped out and smiled a smile of such perfect joy that Katharina's heart filled, pushing tears into her green eyes. Honestly, she was weeping all the time these days. It must be her age.

Ursula's French groom looked very handsome. His suit, bor-rowed from Gustav, was old-fashioned and a little tight across his shoulders, but that only served to highlight their breadth. His shirt gleamed as white as the flower in his lapel and he had new shoes, made for him by Walter from the hide of a bison. The cattle keeper was proving to be a talented cobbler and everyone in the zoo was well-shod this year, but Pierre's wedding brogues were particularly fine.

Ursula picked up pace and Katharina smiled to see her mother pull her back into line. They reached the front and Katharina slipped into her place beside Oskar, with Sasha joining Robert in front of them. Gisela, as Ursula's matron of honour, stayed standing at her side, one arm around Adelaide, but her eyes crept to her left where her husband was miraculously sitting.

Dieter's injuries had turned gangrenous in the field and his left leg, sadly, had had to be amputated below the knee, but that had at least meant he could no longer fight and so he'd been returned to her last month. The Frenchmen had been labouring to repair some of the residential buildings and had managed to make two apartments safe so far. One had been intended for Ursula and Pierre once they were joined in matrimony, but the other had been free for Gisela and Dieter. Gisela had been a little less diligent in fulfilling her duties around the zoo in the two weeks since he'd been back but everyone had forgiven her that and, besides, now Dieter was here to help too, so no one begrudged them an extra hour in their bed every morning. Not all of Dieter had been amputated, as Gisela had told them, giggling wildly, and these days she glowed with love.

'Welcome, all,' Father Jörg said, his soft voice echoing around the bunker, drawing them all in. 'We are gathered here today in God's *very clear* sight to join this man and this woman in holy matrimony.'

A few eyes went to the bunker ceiling at Jörg's added words, and a little sigh of something like relief rippled through the congregation at the reassurance. Sometimes these days it felt as if God had turned His back on Germany and, whilst Katharina couldn't really blame Him, she hoped He could still see the innocents like Ursula and Pierre amongst the carnage of this vicious war.

Surely, she thought as she watched Father Jörg take the young pair through the wedding ceremony, it couldn't go on much longer. Dieter had brought back horrific tales from the Eastern front which had now got as far as Odessa. That was still a long way from Germany, but Dieter said the Red Army were crushing German battalions wherever they encountered them and it was only a matter of time. The party, he had said in hushed tones, needed to make peace with the Soviets, but all of Goebbels's rhetoric was of defiance and Katharina feared that Hitler did not understand reconciliation. He would let Germany be destroyed rather than hand it over, which left all her citizens at the mercy of their enemies.

At least a lot of the animals were out of Berlin. Oskar had been working hard on the export programme, spending hours on unreliable phone lines to all of Lutz's contacts to work out the best places to send their myriad species. Most of the animals had been packed into trucks heading west, to Halle near Leipzig and further afield to Königsberg, Frankfurt and Cologne. They, at least, would be in the path of the Amis – if they came – rather than the Soviets. But a few had been sent east to Warsaw, Vienna and Mülhausen, and Katharina worried for them. Reike the giraffe had gone to Prussia. She missed him peeking over her wall to say hello every morning and prayed that even the Soviets would not be stupid enough to shoot giraffes.

'Katharina?' Oskar nudged her out of her reverie and back to the front, where Father Jörg was joining Ursula and Pierre's hands and lifting them high.

'I now pronounce you man and wife,' he proclaimed, and everyone in the bunker cheered.

The little door shook with their joy but stayed firmly closed and Katharina just prayed that down here, shut away from prying eyes and falling bombs, they could celebrate all night long. Lord knows, they deserved it.

Chapter Nine

'Callum?'

Callum's dark head emerged from under the duvet and he peered blearily out at Bethan. The miracles of technology, she thought – she could almost be there next to him, apart from the fact she couldn't roll over and cuddle up to him. It was like having an avatar boyfriend, although if she'd programmed him herself, he'd wake up quicker.

'Callum, can you hear me?'

He gave her a lazy smile.

'Hiya, gorgeous. You're a sight for sore eyes.'

Her heart filled. She'd never have dared ask her avatar boyfriend to say that.

'Good to see you too. Big night?'

He rubbed his hand over his eyes, tousling his already messy hair, and she longed to run her own fingers through it.

'Bit of a session with the lads.'

Bethan felt herself clam up instantly. She opened her mouth to ask if it was the same 'lads' she'd seen on his Instagram last time he'd been out, but thought better of it. If touching wasn't yet possible over FaceTime, arguing certainly was and she couldn't face that right now.

'That's good,' she said instead.

Callum hefted himself up and yawned.

'Excuse me a minute, Beth. I have to pee.'

'Course.'

He put the phone down on the bed as he headed off to the bathroom and Bethan noticed that he'd changed the duvet cover.

Leicester City had been replaced by her own cover – pale blue with little grey elephants dancing across it. She was pleased to see it and then caught herself wondering why he'd changed it; who was he trying to impress? She was already telling herself off for being ridiculous when he returned.

'Where've Leicester City gone?'

'What? Oh! I spilled red wine on them when I fell asleep in bed the other night. Had to take them off and this was all I could find. To be fair, it's quite nice. I like elephants.'

'If you come out here, you can see real ones. I can even get you in the actual cage with them.'

'Check you out, big shot!'

She drew back a little.

'I was just saying—'

'I know, I know. Don't listen to me. My head's banging. Charlie's mate was DJ-ing at this new club in town so we all had to go and check him out, but he wasn't on till 1 a.m. I'm knackered, Beth. I think maybe I'm getting too old for clubbing.'

Bethan hid a smile. She'd accepted that of herself years ago but Callum had been battling to stay young and cool.

'Maybe just *those* sorts of clubs,' she suggested.

'What – the lively, cool, fun ones?'

'I guess. There are other things to do.'

'Like what? And don't say theatre. You know how I feel about theatre. It costs a fortune and I never understand it.'

'I wasn't going to say theatre. I was thinking more of other music venues. There's this really cool jazz club here that—'

He cut her off with a yelp of horror.

'Jazz club? Beth, I may be too old to rave but I've not been out and got myself a pipe yet.'

'It's not... Oh, just come and see, Callum. Please. It might surprise you. All of it – the elephants, Berlin, the jazz. And above all else, me.'

'You'd surprise me?'

He raised an eyebrow and Bethan groaned.

'I'd certainly like to see you.'

Her voice shook a little, or perhaps a lot – certainly enough for Callum to pick it up even with his hangover. He leaned in.

'Are you all right, Beth?'

'Sorry. I…' She fought for the words. Her dad had left four days ago and she'd been wanting to talk to Callum about it ever since, but they'd been snowed under at the zoo after the hectic Easter weekend and she'd got in late and exhausted every single night. This morning, she'd finally had the space to think about Paul's revelations again, but speaking them out loud still felt hard. 'I had some news at the weekend, Cal. Some rather strange news.'

'Really? What about?

'Mum.'

He sucked in his breath. He didn't like her talking about Jana. He said death made him uncomfortable. He had once told her a story about being forced to go and see his grandad laid out in the undertaker's and his mum getting them there too early, before the poor man's features had been coaxed out of rigor mortis. It had sounded rather traumatic for an eleven-year-old, but then, she'd sat at her own mum's death bed at that age.

'What about her?' Callum asked stiffly.

Bethan composed herself.

'Apparently she found out just before Oma Erika – her mother – died, that she wasn't her real mother at all.'

'Wow! Your mum was adopted?'

'Gifted.'

'What? You can't gift babies.'

'Apparently at the back end of the war, with a country overrun by enemy armies, you can do pretty much anything.'

'This was in the war? Cool. So, what's the problem?'

Bethan stared down the phone at him.

'What's the problem, Cal? Mum's mum wasn't her real mum. She wasn't my real grandma. And we have no idea who was.'

'Ah. Right. Course. Sorry. I'm on go-slow still.' He clicked his fingers suddenly. 'Your list, Beth – it must be a list of your possible grannies.'

'I know that.'

'Oh. OK. Well, that's quite cool, isn't it? You've got a… a quest.'

That was true, but the way Callum said it made it sound somehow Monty Python-esque. Bethan scratched her temple.

'Don't you think it's kind of unsettling?'

'Unsettling? I suppose so. But some people never know who their parents are, and some just, you know, have slightly crap ones, like me. The other day I called my mum, feeling a bit lonely, and d'you know what she said? She said, "Can you call later, I'm watching *EastEnders*." How rubbish is that?'

Bethan gawped down the phone at him.

'It doesn't sound that bad.'

'Not that bad?' He looked at her and his eyes narrowed. 'Sorry, I forgot – nothing trumps the dead-mum card, does it?'

His words hit her like a punch in the stomach.

'Callum – that's horrible!'

'Don't be so melodramatic.'

'Melodramatic?'

'Yes! Listen to yourself. Poor me, with my dead mum and my mystery granny. Boo hoo.'

The pain in Bethan's stomach grew. She looked at Callum, seeing the cold light in the brown eyes she thought she loved, and the petulant frown on his handsome face.

'Fine. Forget it. I'm going now. I won't bother you again.'

'Beth…'

'And perhaps you should think about flat-hunting, Callum. I'd hate you to be stuck in the home of someone so melodramatic.'

His eyes widened in horror.

'Bethan, no! You're being silly.' He caught himself. 'That is, not silly. Emotional.'

'I'm being logical, Callum. I think it's time—'

'I'll come out.' He was pulling on a dressing gown now, heading for his computer. 'I'll get flights for next weekend. I'll get them now – look.'

He clicked on the computer and typed 'flights to berlin' into the search bar. Bethan watched, unsure if she wanted him to find any.

'Callum…'

'I want to see you, Beth. It'll be easier, once we're together. We can talk properly. I'm not doing this right, I can see that now. I was half asleep, hungover. Look – there's a flight on Friday. I'll book it, yes? I'll come and see you.'

He peered into the camera, the coldness all gone and only a sort of desperate longing remaining. Bethan softened. She hated arguing and it would certainly be easier face to face.

'OK. That would be good.'

'Course it would. Really good. What you need is a whole lot of loving. So I'll be there. Next weekend.'

'You will? Really?'

She'd forgotten how swiftly his moods could change; she was never sure how to deal with him when he was like this.

'I will, Bethie. I'll make it all better, you wait and see.'

Weary now, she desperately hoped that was true. Coping with the new job was hard enough without fighting with her boyfriend too.

'That would be great, Callum.'

'Anything for you, gorgeous. Really. I'd better get off and book this in case the price goes up.'

He blew her a kiss and then he was gone. Bethan stared at the empty screen, a little stunned at the speed of his departure, but he was coming to see her. Hopefully they could sort everything out once he was actually here.

*

All morning long, Bethan felt restless and unable to settle to anything. She'd promised herself a proper visit to some of the sights of the city so set out determinedly to see them, but her mind couldn't focus on the Wall or the Jewish memorial and, in the end, she slouched back to the zoo. Everything seemed to be going wrong. She'd argued with her dad, and although they'd patched things up and done their best to have a nice weekend, their usual happy ease had been missing and she'd almost been glad when he'd left. That niggled at her.

Ever since she'd lost her mum, she'd hated falling out with anyone, fearing that, somehow, they would die without the argument patched up. Now, with Paul in another country, that fear was stronger than ever, yet she couldn't quite bring herself to forgive him. Maybe he'd been right to withhold the news when she was younger, but she'd been an adult for years now and she couldn't help feeling he should have trusted her with it. As for Callum – he just didn't get it and that hurt.

Honestly, she told herself, she was getting her knickers in a twist. She probably just needed some lunch. She turned past the elephant house to head for her flat and Bobo, the big matriarch, trumpeted out a hello, making her jump. She stared at the beautiful beast.

'Was that for me?'

'Reckon it was,' the keeper said. 'She knows you now.'

A family hanging over the railings looked at her with respect, and Bethan blushed and gave Bobo a self-conscious wave. The elephant responded with another trumpet and she felt her steps lighten instantly. Things weren't that awful; she just had a bit to sort out, that's all.

She spun away to head home and bumped straight into a tall, broad figure carrying two buckets of vegetables.

'Max! Sorry, I—'

'No problem.'

A cabbage had fallen off the top of one of the buckets and they both bent to pick it up. Their fingers touched and Bethan jumped back.

'Sorry,' she said again, her Bobo-bounce draining from her as quickly as it had arrived. 'I'm so clumsy. Honestly! I'll get out of your way before—'

'Beth, are you OK?' Max's hand was on her arm and, when she dared to look, his blue eyes were soft with concern. She opened her mouth to say that of course she was fine, but all that came out was a sort of pathetic, strangled sob. 'You're not! Poor you. Here, let me get these to the elephants – they came to the monkey house by mistake – and then we're going for a coffee.'

'No, Max, you're busy. You—'

'Not too busy for you. And, actually, it's lunchtime. You need lunch, right?' She nodded. 'Me too. So, stay there and I'll be straight back.'

He rushed off, handed the buckets over the fence and was back before she'd even had time to think, let alone scarper.

'I won't be much company,' she warned.

'As long as the Kartoffelsuppe is on, I won't mind.'

He winked at her and, despite herself, she laughed and let him lead her to the canteen, where he fetched two big bowls of the potato and sausage soup with delicious crusty rolls. She picked up her spoon and ate eagerly. She was right about one thing at least – she'd needed lunch and could feel her strength returning with every mouthful. Max was easy company, applying himself to his food and not pressing her with conversation, but after a while she looked up to find him gazing questioningly at her and offered him a shy smile.

'It's to do with the list.'

'Right. You spoke to your dad about it?' She nodded. 'It didn't go well?'

'It was... strange. The list, it seems, is of women who might be my grandmother.' Max's eyes widened but he just sat there waiting for her to go on. 'Before my Oma Erika died, she told Mum that she'd been a "gift", handed to her by someone called Anke at the end of the war. That's it. That's all she had breath left to say. Then Mum found her brooch.'

She reached automatically for the brooch but, as she wasn't in uniform, it was missing.

'The hippo one?'

'You noticed it?'

'Yup. I remember thinking I'd better get you a decent monkey one instead.'

Bethan smiled.

'Well, this hippo brought my mum to the zoo. I remember her asking questions here when I was young, but she never got to the bottom of the mystery. She died without finding out who her biological mother was.'

'Wow!' Max stirred the remainder of his soup around thoughtfully. 'That must have been very hard for her.'

Bethan felt her shoulders soften and only then realised how tightly she'd been holding herself.

'I think it was. I have this memory of her bringing me here when I was about ten. She sat me on Knautschke – the statue, obviously, not the actual hippo – and then rushed off. I found her talking really intently to someone, someone who I think might have been Ada.'

'Our Ada?'

She smiled at the possessive.

'Maybe. I don't know and I don't dare push her in case I upset her again.'

'Perhaps we can try together sometime. For now, could I see the list again?'

'Of course. I don't have it with me, but I took a photo.'

She pulled it up on her phone and handed it across to Max, who studied it carefully.

'Could I have a copy, Beth? I could do some digging in those files in the office. I'd forgotten about them, to be honest, but I can see how important it is now.' Bethan stared at him, touched by his ready interest. 'What?' he asked self-consciously. 'Am I interfering? My mother says I'm terrible at interfering.'

'No! God, no, Max, you're helping. So much.'

'OK. Thank you. I know it must be hard for you. It's unsettling, isn't it, finding out you're not quite who you thought you were?'

Again she couldn't help but stare; his reaction was so simple, so honest.

'How do you know?'

He flushed a little.

'I don't have any direct experience, nothing like you, so this probably sounds ridiculous in comparison...'

'I doubt it, Max.'

'OK. It's Binky. We thought we knew who her mother was when we rescued her, and we took DNA from the corpse to help us with Binky's care down the line if needed. About a year later Binky had this strange growth, so we tested the DNA and...'

'It wasn't a match?'

He shook his head.

'I told you it was ridiculous, Beth, but it threw me all the same, so I can't begin to imagine what it must be like when it's your own family.'

Bethan concentrated for a moment on finishing her lunch, drawing Max's words into her with the warmth of the soup.

'Thank you,' she said eventually.

'For what?'

'For understanding.'

He gave a little laugh.

'Understanding is easy. The question is, what are we going to do about it? Do you want to find her – your grandmother?'

'I do, Max. I really do, but it's hard. The internet doesn't even seem to know the women on the list exist.'

'Then let's put our minds to old-fashioned ways, shall we?'

'You don't have to—'

'I want to,' he said firmly. 'Now, the files are one thing but they'll take ages to go through. What you need first is a way to access these people, whoever they were – to get under their skin, yes?'

Bethan hadn't thought of it that way before but she nodded keenly.

'Is that possible?'

Max thought.

'There's only one place I know of in the zoo that's still the same as it was during the war – the underground bunker. Part of it has been turned into the nocturnal animals exhibit, but I'm told that at the back there's a secret door.'

His eyes twinkled and Bethan felt her hopes lift. She'd always been a sucker for a secret door.

'What are we waiting for then?' she asked, pushing back her chair, but Max grimaced.

'My shift to end, I'm afraid.'

Bethan blushed.

'Of course, yes. Sorry, Max. Binky would be furious with me.'

He put up a hand.

'Binky, of all creatures, would understand. Give me two hours and I'm all yours.' She glanced at her watch; two hours felt like forever. 'Want to come and help? Then I'll be done quicker.'

She beamed.

'Too right I do. Let's go!'

*

They had the monkeys fed and cleaned out in record time and, after Max had retrieved the key to the secret door from the main office, he led her down the side of the darkened nocturnal animals' house. The door was not quite the arched wooden one Bethan had been imagining – rather, a utilitarian grey rectangle – but she felt a thrill rush through her all the same as Max turned the key in its lock. It opened with a metallic grunt and she took two hesitant steps inside. It was dark and cold but, as she found her phone torch, light flooded the room and she moved into its centre.

The remaining portion of the bunker was quite small, with a low, curved brick ceiling, reinforced with several concrete posts that had obviously been put up when it had been converted from a wine cellar into a bomb shelter. Along the walls, the frames of makeshift bunk beds were still standing and there were even a few blankets folded at the bottom. Bethan reached for one. It was scratchy and damp but she picked it up all the same, wondering if it had once provided warmth for her grandmother, hiding down here from British and American bombs.

'It must have been so scary,' Max said, his low voice echoing around the little room. 'And so uncomfortable. This bunker was sixty metres long back in the forties. It took a hundred people if needed – and it often was. Imagine sleeping down here with ninety-nine other people night after night.'

Bethan shook her head.

'We don't know how lucky we are.'

She turned just as he moved past her and found herself pressed up against him. She wanted to say sorry but the word wouldn't form in her throat. She stepped hastily back.

'Horrid blankets,' she spluttered foolishly, patting the one sandwiched between them.

'Horrid,' he agreed, moving hastily round her.

He made for the rear of the room and she bent to place the blanket back on the bed, taking a moment to gather herself. When she dared to look at him again, he was peering at a gap in the wall and, intrigued, she moved to join him.

'Is there something in there?' Her voice came out rather squeaky; clearly she hadn't gathered herself very effectively.

'It looks like a chest,' Max said, and she noted that he, too, sounded rather hoarse. 'There's a couple of bricks fallen away here, see.' He kicked some rubble at their feet. 'And it's opened up this little alcove. Let me just…'

He slid his hands inside and drew out a small wooden box. He looked at her, then down at the chest. Bethan laughed nervously.

'Treasure?'

'Maybe.'

He tried to lift the lid but it was locked. He pulled and rattled but it stayed firmly clasped. Eventually he looked to Bethan again.

'We could break it.'

'Should we?'

'No. But what use is it like this?'

'True.' Bethan stared at the mini chest; it reminded her of her mum's jewellery box that fateful day of her funeral. She drew in a deep breath. 'Do it!'

Max gave a little nod then pulled a penknife from the pocket of his uniform. Opening up the largest blade, he inserted it carefully alongside the lock and pulled upwards. The wood creaked in protest then, with a splintering sound, yielded and the lid flew up. Bethan leaned forward, telling herself to banish the ridiculous childish images of gold coins and fancy necklaces that sprang irresistibly to mind, but what was in there was, if anything, better – a sheaf of documents, tied up with a ribbon.

Bethan moved even closer, training her phone torch on the contents. Her body brushed against Max's, sending strange shivers up inside her, and she tried to move back again but the space was tight and the light low.

'It might be nothing,' he warned.

'It might,' she agreed, not taking her eyes off the papers.

They were clearly not nothing. The first one seemed to be a will, the second a set of deeds for a house in the city, and the third… Bethan stared as Max gently unrolled it on the table. Before them was a wedding certificate.

'Ursula Franke,' she whispered, tracing the curve of the bride's name. 'That's the second name on Mum's list.'

'Look,' Max said, indicating the witness signature below: Gisela Schultz – the third name.

'The groom?' Bethan stuttered, scanning the precious document. Ursula seemed to have married a man called Pierre Dubois. 'She'd have been Ursula Dubois then. Perhaps Google will have something on her?'

'Perhaps,' Max agreed. They both glanced to their phones but down here they were sealed from the wonders of 4G, so Google would have to wait. That was fine by Bethan; she wanted time just to let this sink in. The certificate was dated May 1944 and she marvelled that something so old had stayed intact down here all this time.

'When did the Allies invade Europe?' she asked.

'The sixth of June 1944,' Max said promptly.

Bethan looked curiously at him. She was pretty sure British kids didn't get taught the dates of their historical defeats and she admired his openness about a tricky time in his nation's history, but that was hardly the point right now.

'So poor Ursula and Pierre would hardly have had a honeymoon, would they?'

'Not immediately, certainly. Let's hope they survived the war and had a long and happy life afterwards. Not to mention lots of children.'

'Children? Why?'

'Because if they did, surely at least one of them is still alive. If we could find them, we could talk to them.'

Hope flared in Bethan, almost dizzying in its intensity. A week ago she hadn't even known that she was on this – what had Callum called it? – quest. But already they were making progress. If Ursula did have children and they could find them to talk to, it might just unlock some of the mystery of what had happened at the zoo. Then again, if Ursula had given birth and died without leaving a trace of that child, they might have their answer right there and then. So many possibilities were opening up. It was a heady thought and, as the room rocked a little, she leaned into Max and was grateful for his quiet strength at her side.

A thought occurred to her and she scrabbled through the rest of the documents, but they were all dusty deeds and legal contracts. No more marriage certificates and no birth ones either. She was going to have to keep searching for answers, but at least she had a few questions now: Did Ursula Franke have a baby before the war ended? If she did, was the child smuggled out of the zoo, perhaps by someone called Anke, and gifted somehow to her Oma Erika? She had no idea, but she was determined to find out.

Chapter Ten

July 1944

'Who'd bring a baby into this?'

Katharina looked despairingly around the bunker as it shook with yet another bomb, dropped so close that already she was trying to calculate which animal enclosure it might have hit. But that was hardly their main concern right now. Sasha had been in labour for almost twenty-four hours and the baby was showing no signs of coming out. Katharina didn't blame it, but she was getting worried.

'Here, Sash – try and drink.'

She pressed the glass of water on her friend, who lifted her head weakly to sip at it. Her hair was wet with sweat in the thick summer air and there were dark circles under her eyes. The midwife was trying to keep everyone calm but Katharina could see that even she was faltering and, on top of all that, the bombs were now falling too. She glanced at her watch – they were early today. It was only half past nine; it must barely be dark. Had something happened? Was this going to be a huge attack?

Ever since the Amis had invaded Normandy last month, the air raids had been building and the possibility of defeat seemed to hang heavy over the city. She looked to the low ceiling, glimmering mystically with the phosphorescent paint that was daubed on everything these days to give a semblance of light in the darkness, and wondered if one day it would just fall in on them all. The war, at least, would then be over.

She shook the foolish thought away. Here was Sasha battling to bring new life into the world and she was contemplating their deaths. Her perspectives were becoming ridiculously skewed. She glanced at the candles – one placed at foot height, one at waist height and one at shoulder height – to monitor the air quality, and was relieved to see that they were all still alight. Only the other day the pump had failed and the foot-height ones had gone out. They'd had to lift up the children to keep them out of the danger zone until Gustav had been able to fix it, and they could do without that sort of problem now.

'Owww!'

Sasha rocked forward in the bed as another contraction ripped through her and Ursula, who had recently admitted to being pregnant herself, rubbed her back desperately. Katharina felt her cries vibrate through her own skin and wondered suddenly if God had, in fact, been being kind to her when he'd kept her from childbirth. She glanced to the curtain they'd rigged up to offer Sasha a little privacy from the others sheltering in the big bunker, wishing she had Oskar at her side, but this was no place for men.

Not that such considerations had stopped Robert. He'd paced outside at first, his uneven legs making a strange thud, clunk, thud, clunk on the concrete floor, but as night had ground into day and then agonisingly slowly back into night again, he'd thrust the curtain aside and come in to cradle his wife's head and offer her tender encouragement. The midwife had sucked in a shocked breath but said nothing. If women could drive buses, why could men not deliver babies? The war, at least, was breaking down barriers as well as houses.

'The contractions are getting closer together, Sasha,' Katharina assured her friend. 'You must be nearly there. Right, nurse?'

'Well on the way,' was all she would offer. Then, with a glance at Sasha, panting in Robert's arms, she drew Katharina aside. 'Progress is very slow, Frau Heinroth. I think perhaps baby is breech.'

'Breech?'

'Head up, instead of—'

'I know what breech is. I had it the other day.'

'With whom?'

'Kiki.' She saw the lady's face and almost laughed. 'She's a chimp. It was hard but we got the baby out in the end.'

The midwife pursed her lips.

'Frau Eberhard is not a chimp.'

'Well no, obviously. I just—'

'And humans are not good at delivering breech babies. The pelvis is not designed for it.' She came close and added on a hiss, 'I tell you – if God was a woman, we'd have been configured so much better.'

'Quite right,' Ursula agreed. 'The big cats have a much better time of it, and you should see the giraffes – just drop them out into the hay with barely a moment's effort.'

The midwife gave a dramatic sigh.

'Would that we were giraffes then, but we are not. I think it might be as well if we had a doctor here. It's possible we will need to transfer your friend to the flak tower to be operated on.'

'In this?'

Katharina looked to the ceiling again as yet another bomb fell.

'If we have to,' the midwife said grimly. 'Will someone go and find medical help?'

Katharina looked back to Sasha, who seemed to be fading into ghost-like colours.

'I will,' she said decisively. 'I'll go.'

'Thank you, Frau Heinroth. Oh, and…' She put out a hand to pat her arm. 'Take care out there.'

Katharina raised an eyebrow at the nurse. She wasn't sure how she was meant to take care with enemy planes filling the skies, but she appreciated the sentiment all the same. She considered going to kiss Sasha before she left – just in case – but quickly dismissed the idea. It would only scare her. Instead, she slipped quietly around the curtain and thought she'd got away before she was stopped by Adelaide, her young eyes filled with fear.

'What's happening to Mummy, Kätsche?'

Katharina took the girl's trembling hands.

'She's giving birth to your little brother or sister, sweetie. It can take a long time but she's doing very well.'

'Can I go in?'

'Best not.'

'But can I?'

Katharina glanced to the curtain. It didn't provide much of a screen, certainly not from the sound of Sasha's distress, and she knew that if she was in Adelaide's place she'd hate being stuck behind it.

'If you're good and stay out of the way.'

'Of course.'

Adelaide was gone before Katharina could question the wisdom of her decision and there was no time to delay. She had to get a doctor and fast.

'Kätsche – where are you going?'

This time it was Oskar who stepped in front of her as she made for the door.

'The flak tower.'

'The hospital?'

'Yes.'

'Is it bad?'

'It could be. She needs a doctor, O.'

He nodded.

'Then I'm coming with you.'

'So we can both be killed?'

'If it comes to that, yes.'

He pulled her to the door before she could protest further and she felt his fingers warm and firm around her own. He was not a big man, but she was a tiny woman and his solid presence at her side was reassuring. She hadn't been out at the height of a raid before and paused for a moment to take in the sight.

The Berlin skyline was lit up by the great, sweeping lines of searchlights, seeking out the planes which crossed them in dark, predatory shapes. The firework sparkle of flak fire, both from the planes and their own anti-aircraft guns, criss-crossed above them like a thousand shooting stars, and Katharina could not help but stare. It was starkly beautiful and for a moment she was pleased to be out defying them all instead of cowering underground, but then a bomb flew over, so low it blew the hair on the top of her head. It exploded a mere block away, sending bricks and glass spurting into the air, and she cursed her own foolishness.

'Run!' Oskar urged, and they both dashed down the zoo's avenues towards the Lion Gate at the rear and, beyond that, the flak tower. Katharina had always hated its looming bulk but tonight it looked like safety personified. She made for it at speed, head low – as if that would help – and had rarely been more thankful than when they arrived at its vast doors. Hundreds of empty prams were lined up outside, there being no room for them within, and a shell had blasted several of them into tiny pieces. Katharina shivered and tried not to look as Oskar hammered on the door.

It was opened by a cross-looking guard in full uniform.

'What?' he demanded.

'We need to get to the hospital,' Oskar told him. 'We have a woman in trouble in the zoo.'

'Bombed?'

'No – giving birth.'

The guard curled up his nose as if such everyday traumas were beneath his notice, but he waved them through.

'Bad night for it,' Oskar said conversationally, nodding to the skies, now thankfully shut out by the iron door of the tower.

'Maybe they've heard.'

'Heard what?'

The guard looked at him.

'You haven't?' His eyes gleamed with dark pleasure as Katharina and Oskar shook their heads. 'They're saying Hitler's been assassinated.'

'What?!'

The guard gave a scathing laugh.

'Where on earth have you two been all day?'

'In the zoo,' Oskar told him.

He looked at him as if he'd said on the moon, despite the fact that his duties in the tower surely involved him looking into the zoo every single day, but then he remembered his news and rubbed his hands at the chance to tell it afresh.

'It's been a huge plot, they're saying. Loads of the top brass in on it. Well, the second-top brass at least. Some bloke called Stauffenberg let off a time bomb in the Wolfsschanze over in East Prussia.'

'Hitler is in East Prussia?'

'Not any more! Or is he? The radio's been playing the Baden-whatsit Marsch all day long – you know, that tune they always bang out when the Führer's about to speak – and Goebbels has been on saying that Hitler will address the nation later. But then, Goebbels will say anything, won't he?'

Oskar looked the man up and down.

'Will he, soldier? What are you suggesting? Because that sounds like treason to me.'

The man paled instantly.

'It doesn't. I mean, it isn't. I'm praying the Führer isn't dead. Praying every moment of the day. I'm on tenterhooks to hear him speak. I just meant—'

Oskar clapped him on the back.

'Don't worry, lad, I'm not going to tell on you. Just watch yourself, hey? If there's a plot afoot then the Gestapo will be all over us.'

'Right. Yes. Er…'

'The hospital?'

'Of course. Fifth floor. Straight up the steps.'

'Thank you.'

Oskar pulled Katharina forward and together they started up the stark spiral of concrete steps.

'Heil Hitler!' the guard called, but they didn't pause to return the salute.

'What would it mean, if he truly were dead?' Katharina whispered to Oskar once they'd turned the first bend.

'I don't know, meine kindl. I daren't even dream about it. Come.'

They pushed on upwards, glancing into the vast rooms where thousands of people seemed to be camped out for the duration of the raid. Babies were wailing, people were shouting, and lovers were grunting beneath thin covers. The whole thing felt like Babel itself and suddenly the zoo bunker looked cosy in comparison.

Hold on, Sasha, Katharina willed her friend, as they edged past a gaggle of young women sitting on the stairs. At the fourth floor, everything opened up a little. Guards stood stiffly at the doors and Katharina could see past them to an extraordinary treasure trove. The rooms were stuffed with statues and paintings, vases and trophies, and an Egyptian king winked at her, golden in the low stair lights from the eternal glory of his sarcophagus.

'What's he doing here?' she gasped.

'Sheltering from the bombs, like the rest of us. The party emptied out the museums when the raids started – first sensible thing they've ever done.'

'Oskar – hush!'

They were rounding another bend now and suddenly came out into a room painted bright white, welcome after the dark greys and greens of the rest of the building. Row after row of trolley beds were set up, and doctors and nurses were bustling around. It was a reassuring sight, and Katharina hastened forward to grab the first nurse she could find.

'Can I help you?'

'I really hope so. My friend is giving birth in the bunker beneath the zoo and she's in trouble. The midwife fears the baby is breech.'

'Oh no!' The nurse looked around. 'Let me find Dr Heiman for you. He's best with babies. Wasted stitching up wounds, he is, so he'll be glad of a proper case.'

The clinical reaction was further reassurance, and Katharina watched eagerly as the nurse hurried down the makeshift ward and collared a white-coated man. He was old, Katharina noticed, his hair as white as Oskar's, but he walked with purpose as he came towards them and she felt sure he knew what he was doing. If anyone could help Sasha, it was this man.

'A breech birth, you say? Show me the way.'

They made it back to the zoo bunker in a lull in the air attacks, the searchlights above them finding only empty air, though this time Katharina did notice a lot of activity through the Tiergarten and into the city. She had no idea what was usual during a raid but was pretty sure no one, not even the Gestapo, chose to be out with planes overhead, so perhaps what the guard had said about an assassination attempt was true. She felt a flicker of hope in her heart but told herself not to let it grow; Hitler was probably coated in something indestructible. Besides, there were plenty more where he came from so it would make little difference. Right now, all that mattered was Sasha.

Dr Heiman took charge the moment he came into the bunker, the midwife almost melting with relief at his arrival. Sasha looked paler than ever, her eyes struggling to focus and her brow beaded with sweat.

'It's all right, Sash,' Katharina told her, 'the doctor's here now. He's going to look after you. He's going to make sure you're safe.'

'And baby,' Sasha panted. 'Make sure baby is safe.'

'Of course,' Dr Heiman said smoothly. 'Baby will be absolutely fine, I promise.'

He did not, Katharina noted, make the same promise about Sasha, but perhaps he was just busy. She looked around for Adelaide but the girl seemed to have made herself scarce, and it was probably better that way. She prayed all would be well, but feared it was going to be a hard, bloody slog and, in an attempt to distract everyone, she told them the news.

'Hitler? Assassinated?' Even Robert was temporarily caught off guard. 'Is that possible?'

'It seems not. They say he escaped harm. They say he's going to address the nation once he's secure.'

'Turn the radio on then.'

Gisela went to the radio, rigged up via wires through the bricks to an aerial above. It only got Deutschlandfunk, the Nazi-controlled channel, but that would be Hitler's network of choice if he were still alive and everyone crowded round to listen, leaving the doctor and Robert to tend Sasha in peace. As the guard had said, the station was playing Hitler's personal theme tune, the 'Badenweiler Marsch', but there was as yet no sign of the man himself.

The night ground on. Dr Heiman confirmed that Sasha's baby was breech, but that he believed he would be able to deliver it without surgery. Sasha was clearly too weak to be moved, especially across a bombsite, and as the doctor called for hot water and clean towels – neither easy to come by in the bunker – Father Jörg led those beyond the curtain in prayers for her safety as the Führer's strident march played on.

On the stroke of midnight, the march came to an abrupt halt and there, as if conjured up out of thin air, was the voice of the Führer. He sounded shaken but alive, and unmistakably himself.

Katharina felt a rush of disappointment so great she had to cover her face to hide it. The bunker froze in utter silence as Hitler spoke on, spitting fury against the plotters and promising the direst consequences for all those caught. The warm July air in the bunker seemed to drop several degrees. Katharina saw Ursula curl herself onto Pierre's lap and Gisela twine her arms around Dieter, and she wondered what they'd all been hoping – that with Hitler dead someone sensible would take command and negotiate peace before they were all exterminated? Well, there was fat chance of that now.

'Ooowww!'

Sasha's piercing cry brought them all crashing back to the far more immediate danger within their own little world.

'Sash!' Katharina dashed through to the bed and flinched at the sight of the doctor wrestling between her legs, blood already soaking the sheets. 'What the hell are you doing to her?' she shouted, but Gisela grabbed her before she could pull the doctor away.

'You know what he's doing, Kätsche. You've seen it before – you've taught me all about it, remember? He has to help pull the baby out.'

'But it's splitting her apart.'

'She will mend,' Ursula assured her, coming round on her other side. 'Surely it must only be a little time more.'

Sasha's screams strangled in her throat and morphed into a rasping, animalistic pant.

'Push, Frau Eberhard!' the doctor urged. 'Push now.'

The veins seemed to stand out across poor Sasha's pale face as she tried to do the doctor's bidding, but it was clear she had little strength left.

'One more!' the midwife called from the doctor's side, and suddenly, like fifty times the miracle of hearing Hitler bark out from the radio, came the thin but determined cry of a newborn.

'You've done it!' Katharina cried. 'Sasha, my love, you've done it. You have a baby.' She leaned forward as the doctor handed the baby to the midwife, who wiped it gently free of blood – so much blood. But it was done now. The baby was here. 'You have a baby daughter.'

Sasha's eyes flickered and she held up her arms. The midwife passed the little girl into them and she held her close up against her breast. The baby rooted for the nipple then found it and latched on, and at last Sasha smiled. She looked up at Robert.

'A baby.'

'A miracle. You did so well, my beautiful one. You were so brave. So strong.'

'It's another girl,' she said tentatively, but Robert didn't hesitate.

'A girl as beautiful as her mother and her sister, and who I will cherish as much as I cherish both of them.'

Sasha burst into tears, and Robert leaned over and tenderly kissed them away.

'Where's Adelaide?' she asked. 'I want Adelaide to meet her sister – to meet Hanna.'

Ursula made a move towards the curtain but the doctor put up his hand.

'Wait a little longer, Frau Eberhard. Rest a little longer. We need to be sure that you are well before we invite others in.'

Sasha seemed to accept this, but Katharina saw the looks that passed between Dr Heiman and the midwife. The amount of blood on the bed seemed to be growing, and Katharina gripped Ursula and Gisela's hands tightly in her own as the medics worked to stem the flow. Robert, lost in the feeding child, didn't seem to notice anything amiss, and he was still kissing his wife's brow as she quietly lost consciousness.

'Sasha!' Katharina screamed. 'Sasha, don't go.'

'She's not going,' Robert said. 'She's resting. She's just resting.'

'Herr Eberhard,' the doctor said, approaching him as Katharina might a frightened lion, 'you need to take the baby.'

'But she's feeding her. Sasha is feeding her.'

'Herr Eberhard!' Dr Heiman's voice took on new urgency. 'We must tend to your wife – now.'

Robert blinked, dazed, but did not seem to be able to take his arms from around Sasha's limp form, so Katharina stepped forward and detached the little girl from her nipple. Thankfully, baby Hanna had already stopped feeding, and nuzzled in against Katharina as her head lolled in doubtless much-needed sleep.

'Poor little mite,' Gisela murmured, stroking her downy head.

Katharina held her close, feeling the soft weight of her new body, and prayed with everything she had for her mother. But everything she had did not seem like it was going to be enough. Ursula ran to ease Robert away from Sasha as the doctor produced needle and thread and tried frantically to sew her up, but it looked hopeless and Gisela slipped away and returned with Father Jörg, who crossed himself and went quietly to the top of the bed to murmur the Last Rites.

'No!' Robert wailed, the sight of the cleric finally penetrating his mind. 'Sasha – no!'

None of them could save her now and, as a new run of bombs fell mercilessly on the city above, Sasha Eberhard slipped quietly from unconsciousness into death, a soft smile still on her now frozen features. The doctor stepped back, tears in his old eyes, and Robert pulled his wife into his arms, kissing her again and again as he had done just minutes before, though this time she could not respond. Katharina, her heart breaking open beneath the flutter of the new life in her arms, looked desperately around for Oskar but instead saw Adelaide, bursting up from the dark corner of a bunk to fling herself, wailing, on her mother's body.

'Addie,' Robert gasped, pulling the child close. 'Oh Addie, we've lost her.'

As Katharina stood there looking down on the bloodbath of the worst night of her war – a night when death had come right into the very bunker that was meant to keep them safe – she knew that they had all lost her, and a little piece of themselves besides.

'Why,' she growled furiously, holding the precious newborn close, 'could God not have taken bloody Hitler instead. Why did He snatch Sasha, dear, good, kind Sasha?'

'Because,' Gisela said through tears, leaning close in against her, 'Hitler would have made a crap angel.'

It was typical Berliner humour and Katharina was strangely grateful for it, but there was nothing funny about this situation. It had been a bloody night and it would be a dark, dark dawn.

Chapter Eleven

Bethan stood in the airport arrivals lounge feeling a disturbing sense of déjà vu. Just two weeks ago she'd been here waiting excitedly for her dad, but the visit had soured rapidly and she was terrified the same would happen again this time. Callum's attitude to Oma Erika's revelation still nagged at her, and she had to admit she was oddly nervous about seeing her boyfriend.

'Beth?'

She blinked.

'Callum! Oh my God, Callum, you're here. You're really here.'

'Course I am, silly. I texted you I was on the plane.'

She threw her arms around him.

'I know, I know. I just…' She looked up into his smiling face, and it was so wonderfully familiar that she felt instantly stupid for having doubted their relationship. 'Oh, I've missed you.'

She reached up for a kiss and he covered her lips with his own, drawing her in against him and running his hands down her back in a way that made her feel pleasingly weak all over.

'I've missed you too,' he murmured when they finally drew back. 'So, come on – take me to this zoo of yours.'

She laughed and laced her fingers in his to lead him out to the van, then laughed again at the sight of his face as he spotted the gorilla emblem on the side.

'Stylish motor, Bethie.'

'Isn't it! Hop in.'

He took a quick look around, as if afraid someone might see him getting into a gorilla van, but settled as she drove him out of the airport and towards the city.

'I've been reading up about Berlin, Beth. It sounds like a great place. This guy at the office came here on his stag do last year and said it was wild. He's told me all these top bars to go to.'

'Great,' Beth said, focusing on the road. 'And I know a few places I want—'

'He gave me the name of this amazing restaurant too. It has a champagne fountain, apparently. You can buy an "all you can drink" ticket and refill from it whenever you want to. Imagine that!'

Bethan imagined hundreds of sticky, drunken hands putting their dirty glasses under the same fountain and shivered, but simply offered another 'great'. At least Callum was enthusiastic about the city she was rapidly growing to love.

'I bought a bottle of bubbly for us to have tonight, actually,' she said.

'Fantastic.' He put a hand on her knee and squeezed it. 'It's so good to be with you again, Beth. Friday night drinks without you just aren't the same.' Bethan glanced across and smiled at him, then he added, 'It's not German bubbly, is it?' and her heart sank just a little.

Two hours later and Bethan was remembering exactly what was good about having a boyfriend in the flesh. She curled up against Callum, a little sweaty, a little breathless, but fizzing with their lovemaking. She'd been upset when Callum had rejected her offer to show him round the zoo, saying that it was her he wanted showing around, but he'd been right. They'd needed to get close, to reconnect. There had been far too many gaps between them recently for doubts and concerns to worm their way in, but right now everything felt rosy.

'You lie there, gorgeous,' Callum said, kissing her forehead. 'I'll get the bubbly.'

'Lovely.'

She was drifting off again when the loud pop of the cork made her jump. Callum laughed.

'No sleeping. It's Friday night.'

She reached out for her glass.

'So? Bed seems like a very nice place to spend it.'

He grinned lasciviously.

'OK, OK, but not *all* night. I want to see this city of yours.' He climbed back under the duvet, put his arm around her and chinked his glass against hers. 'Cheers!'

'Cheers, Cal.'

'Tomorrow you can show me round the zoo, yeah?'

She swallowed.

'Sort of, yes. I have to work tomorrow.'

'What?'

'I'm sorry. I used up my afternoon off coming to collect you so I'm on call tomorrow. I won't be needed all the time and you can come with me, but we won't be totally free.'

Callum set his glass down.

'I came all the way out here because you begged me to—'

'Because you wanted to, I hope?'

'Yeah, yeah, that too. But you aren't even off work? You can't even be with me?'

'I can, Cal. I'll just be on duty too. I thought that might be good though – you can see what I do.'

'I know what you do, Beth. You're a vet. You mend sick animals. It's one of the most obvious professions out there. I don't need to see it in action.'

Bethan swallowed some of her wine but it tasted sickly and the bubbles went up her nose.

'I'm sorry. It was a bit last-minute and we're on tight rotas. You don't want the animals to suffer, do you?'

He shrugged.

'I don't really care, to be honest.'

'Callum!'

'What? I came here to be with you, not the bloody meerkats.'

'I know and I'm sorry, but it's only eight till four. Then we'll be free. I'm off on Sunday.'

'Lucky me! Hang on – 8 a.m.?'

'Yes. But you can have a lie-in and join me when you're ready. It's only just out there.'

'I noticed. Some big cat roared while I was getting the bubbly from the fridge – made me jump out of my skin.'

Bethan hid a smile.

'Cool though, right?'

He sighed.

'Kind of, I guess. OK, well, we'll make the most of it, I suppose. But if you have to put your hand up anything's bum, I'm not watching.'

'Callum!' she protested again, but he had at least picked up his glass and she made an effort to smile at him. 'Thanks.'

'No problem. Now, drink up, lass, and let's hit the town. Maybe you can show me this jazz club of yours, hey?'

'Great. Let's go.'

Helter Skelter was lively, Bethan was glad to see, and a young band were just setting up which boded well. Callum looked around with something like approval and ordered them two large beers. Bethan wanted to warn him quite how large a 'large beer' could be in Germany but was too slow, and when the steins appeared on the table, Callum's brown eyes widened in surprise – and pleasure.

'This city's all right, you know, Beth. Cheers!'

Bethan tried to go slowly with her own beer, but it was hard to sip out of a glass that was so heavy you almost needed two hands to pick it up. She reminded herself she was on duty at 8 a.m. and hoped that when Callum went to the loo she could tip a little of her own beer into his without him noticing. The band stepped onto the stage and Callum looked with approval at the very funky female saxophonist, then leaned in to Beth.

'Looks like you're right about jazz – it's not all men with pipes.'

It was a concession, and she pulled her chair next to his so they could both see the stage. He dropped a kiss on her forehead.

'I've been thinking,' he said, 'about this stuff with your mum.'

She spluttered her beer in surprise.

'You have?'

'Yeah. Well, actually, your dad came to see me the other day.'

'Dad did?!'

'I was a bit surprised too, but he took me out for a nice beer. Good man, your dad. Crap taste in footie teams, mind you – who supports Forest these days?'

'No idea, Cal. What did he say?'

'What? Oh, yeah. He said you'd been upset when he told you about the stuff with your grandma and he was worried about you. He was very relieved to hear I was coming out to see you. Said I was to take good care of you, which I'm doing, right?'

'Right.'

'Oh, and he gave me something for you. It's back at your place. I'll give you it later.'

'Thanks.' Bethan rubbed at his hand where it sat on her knee. 'How did he seem, Cal? I'm a bit worried about him too. We've never really fallen out before.'

Callum laughed bitterly.

'Lucky you. I fell out with my parents every second day when I was growing up. You get used to it.'

Bethan pulled back.

'I don't want to get used to it. I want to sort it out with him but I still feel a bit, you know, betrayed.'

'Betrayed, Beth? Because he was protecting you from something he thought would hurt you – *is* hurting you? Because he was doing what he'd promised your dying mother he'd do?'

'Because he didn't trust me enough to give me critical information about my own family.'

'Or loved you too much to do so?'

It was certainly a different way of looking at it and she supposed Callum had a point. She knew her dad loved her and she could only assume he'd been acting in what he thought were her best interests.

'You're right, Cal.'

'Course I am. Look, it's easy, Beth – if you let it be. He made a mistake, but an honest one. Call him up next week and have a proper chat about it, and things will all be fine.'

'Maybe.' Bethan thought about the bunker and the marriage certificate. She thought about Ursula Franke and Pierre Dubois. Sadly, Dubois was an exceptionally common name in France and Google had not yet turned up anything useful, but she was still trying. 'Even if Dad and I sort things out though, the fact still remains that I don't know who my grandmother was.'

'Don't know who the spurious person who provided your biology was,' Callum corrected. 'Your grandma was your Oma Erika. Why Oma, by the way? Odd word.'

She squinted at him.

'It's German, Callum.'

'Oh. Right, yeah. German. Fair enough. Well, anyway, I'm sure your "Oma" thought of you as her proper family, didn't she?'

'Yes,' Bethan conceded.

'So that's what counts. More beer?'

Bethan led the way into the railway station on Sunday evening, praying the train would come on time and whisk Callum away to the airport. Somehow the weekend had flashed past and her boyfriend was heading home. He had pronounced his visit a big success and, frankly, she was too tired to disagree.

'I've had a great time, Bethan,' he said now. 'Berlin's cool.'

'That's good.'

'Even that jazz club was OK, though I think we were right to move on when they got to the moody stuff.'

Bethan had rather liked the 'moody stuff', and had certainly preferred it to the banging dance music at the venue of Callum's choice, or the champagne bar he'd insisted on the following night. She'd been worn out, having dragged herself up to work at 8 a.m. after only getting in at four, and had wanted nothing more than to curl up with a nice takeaway but Callum, bored from following her around for the last two hours of her shift, had called her dull and insisted she'd 'soon perk up' once she got out again. She had, for a while, but when she'd fallen asleep in a corner at midnight, Callum hadn't been impressed.

'Take me to bed or lose me forever,' she'd tried, but he hadn't been fooled and had left her to sleep in the corner while he danced with his new-found German friends.

Sunday morning had been more peaceful. To Callum's credit he'd got up and made her breakfast in bed, but he'd been reluctant to come to lunch with the others from the zoo and, despite everyone making an effort to speak in English, he hadn't really bothered to engage. He'd only come to life when Max had asked him about Leicester City's historic league win.

'I didn't know you were into football?' Bethan had asked the chimp keeper when Callum had eventually run out of superlatives for his team.

'Oh, everyone knows about Leicester City,' Callum had said before Max could answer, adding, 'Crap teams in Berlin, aren't there, mate?'

Bethan had seen Max tighten.

'It depends what you are looking for,' he'd said stiffly. 'I've been a Union fan since I was a boy.'

'Union? Never heard of it.'

'It's a small club, originally in the east of the city.'

'A commie club?'

'Callum!' Bethan had cried, mortified, but Max had been calm.

'A club for fans,' he'd said quietly. 'It has a very, how do you say – positive atmosphere.'

'Sounds great,' Bethan had said, and Max had turned to her.

'I can take you to a game if you'd like?'

'I would, thanks Max.'

'You're going to take *my* girl to watch *your* football team?' Callum had blurted out, though even he had realised quite how ridiculously possessive that sounded and added a lame, 'I guess that'd be good. Won't be like Leicester though, Beth.'

In Bethan's book that could only be a good thing. She'd found her few trips to the hallowed King Power stadium noisy, coarse and borderline violent, and she loved the sound of a 'positive atmosphere'. Now, she looked up at the departures board, relieved to see that Callum's train to the airport was on time.

'Five minutes,' she told him.

'It'll take me straight to the airport?'

'That's right. It's not far. About ten minutes, I think.'

'Couldn't you get the gorilla van this time?'

'I could, but there's roadworks around the airport so you'll be far quicker on the train. I can come with you if you want?'

'Nah. No point. I'll only have to go through customs when I get there.'

He looked up the line and Bethan found herself wondering if he was as ready to get away from her as she was to have him gone. What did that mean? She was too tired to think about it right now and just wanted to curl up in bed and sleep off the excesses of the weekend. Plus, she really had to call her dad. Which reminded her…

'Didn't you say you had something to give me from Dad, Callum?'

'Oh yeah! Hang on.' The announcement system bonged and a strident voice announced the arrival of his train. He set his bag down on the platform and scrabbled through it. 'It's here somewhere.'

Bethan glanced up the line. The train was coming. She wanted to grab Callum's bag and wrench it open to find whatever Paul had sent her, but she didn't even know what she was looking for.

'Hang on a minute.' The train came into the station, slowing with a hiss of brakes. Bethan felt panic rush through her but just then Callum stood up again, a small leather book held triumphantly before him. 'Here you go.'

'What is it?'

'Not sure. Paul said something about a scrapbook.'

She stared at the little treasure, then to the train as the doors slid open.

'Can I have it then, Cal?'

'For a kiss.'

'Of course.'

She reached up and touched her lips to his. He crushed her against him and kissed her, hard and deep. She struggled a little.

'Callum, your train.'

'It's fine.'

The doors were closing.

'It's not. This isn't Britain. Trains here stick to time. Go, Cal – go!'

He looked round, panicked and, grabbing his bag, leaped onto the train just in time. But the book was still in his hand. 'The scrapbook, Cal.'

He looked down and tossed it to her just before the doors closed on him. It was a poor throw and she scrambled to snatch it up just before it hit the platform. By the time she'd stood up again, the train was pulling away and Callum was gone. She gave a little wave but doubted he could see it. Damn. That had hardly been the romantic parting of the century. She waited until the train was gone and then, feeling forlorn, trudged out of the station and back into the zoo.

'Evening, Mikey,' she said to the lad in the booth.

'Evening, Beth. What's that you've got there?'

She looked down at the leather book and a small smile crept onto her lips.

'Treasure!'

'Lucky you.'

She nodded and, as the evening was still warm, walked around to sit on a bench near the elephant enclosure. It was almost closing time but a few determined visitors were clinging on, and she watched a little girl leaping delightedly up and down as Bobo pushed herself onto her hind legs to show off to her.

'Nice one, Bobo,' she called, and got a proud trumpet in return.

She smiled again and, smoothing out the book on her lap, carefully untied the leather cord and opened it up. A piece of paper fell out, crisp and fresh, and when she opened it, she found a letter from Paul.

Bethan,

I'm so sorry I didn't tell you about Oma Erika's secret before. It was wrong of me. I did promise your mother that I wouldn't but, let's face it, that was when you were eleven. Jana would have had the sense to see that you'd developed and moved on from that point and that you could cope with the information. She would have admired the amazingly strong, resilient, caring woman you've turned into and trusted you with what happened to her.

I guess I was angry – angry that Jana had to go through all that hurt, and angry that she was so drawn into it that she missed the cancer until it was too late to make it go away. Angry with myself that I missed it too. The identity of her 'real' mother seemed so important to us both that we were distracted from what was truly important – her health and wellbeing. I didn't want that to happen again.

I hope you know how much I love you. I hope you know how important you are to me and that I'd never do anything to hurt you. But I know too that, without thinking – indeed, because I didn't think – I have hurt you. Please forgive me, my beautiful girl.

This is Oma Erika's scrapbook from the early years of her life. Your mother went through it again and again but found nothing to help her, but maybe you can. I hope so. If there is anything else I can do to help, please just let me know. The identity of your grandmother may be impossible to find and I hope you can make your peace with that if it turns out to be the case, but if anyone can find her, Beth, you can.

All my love, Dad.

Tears in her eyes, Bethan picked up her phone and texted him.

Thank you for the letter, Dad. And the scrapbook. Of course I forgive you. I love you. Xxx

He came back straight away.

Thank you, Bethan. I've been an idiot. No more secrets. Can't wait to hear if you find anything out. Xxx

*I'm on it, Dad. I've got help here at the zoo so we might
just get somewhere. X*

She stared at her own message for a moment then pressed send.
She felt a sudden urge to take the scrapbook to show Max, but that
was foolish. This was *her* family puzzle. She opened up the book
and leafed slowly through it. There were pictures of Oma Erika as
a child; some pieces of ribbon that must have been important to
her; a label from a cereal packet; a school prize certificate; a ticket
to a music concert. Then suddenly there was a picture of a young
Erika with a handsome man in a suit – presumably Opa Georg,
though Bethan had only ever seen him hunched and bald so it
was hard to tell. Her Oma, sadly, did not seem to have favoured
labelling her keepsakes. She pushed on and there was the same
man, standing at Erika's side in the door of a church, both of them
beaming. Definitely Opa Georg then. Erika was in a white dress,
cut daringly to the knee, and Georg was in a soldier's uniform.
Bethan's heart contracted and she turned the page.

Another photo – Erika again, but this time in a rough house
dress and apron, holding a bucket and standing knee-deep in rubble.
A glimpse of the Brandenburg Gate in the background told Bethan
it had to be Berlin. The rubble surely meant it was wartime. Erika
was smiling but God knows how, because the street behind her
was ruined. Not just a little bit broken up but blown totally apart.
Bethan shivered. How many times in history class had they been
taught about the poor Londoners caught in the Blitz? No one had
ever mentioned that the civilians of Berlin had gone through the
same and, by the looks of it, much, much worse.

Bethan stroked a hand across the celluloid face of her grandma
– or, it seemed, her adoptive grandma – and saw that Callum had
been right. This new information didn't make any difference to
how she felt about her, but all the same, she couldn't help a burning
curiosity about how she had been 'gifted' little Jana. She looked

keenly to the next page and found Erika again, not much older but this time standing to the left of two other women in a landscape that could not have been more different. Gone were the buildings and the rubble, and in their place were green, rolling fields. As with everything else in the scrapbook, the photo remained infuriatingly unlabelled and Bethan held the book to the light, desperately trying to look into the eyes of the three women as if they might somehow tell her who they were.

They did not and when she turned the page again, the war was miraculously ended and Erika and Georg were holding a baby dressed in a beautiful christening gown – Jana. She was here, arrived with her 'parents' with nothing but the turn of a page to indicate how she had come into the world. Bethan banged the book in frustration. It was wonderful to have this glimpse into the past, but all it had done was to open up even more questions about what on earth happened at the end of the war.

Chapter Twelve

August 1944

Katharina took Ursula's arm and guided her closer up against the wall of the bakery. Recently, with the Amis advancing across France and the liberation of Paris expected at any moment, the Americans had started bombing in the daytime. It was bold, reckless and horribly dangerous for those on the ground, who could be caught out with only minutes of warning. The other day Katharina had been with Oskar negotiating hay prices with a supplier south of the zoo when the sirens had rung out. They'd been forced to scramble, with thousands of other people, into the huge public bunker near the Anhalter Bahnhof, and it had been so cramped and unpleasant that Katharina had considered facing the planes instead.

The day raids were not just dangerous but exhausting. No one could rest easy any more. Every moment of both day and night was fraught with potential danger, and it was making the people of Berlin as reckless as the pilots shooting them down. Only last night Ursula had been forced to stopper Pierre with a long kiss as he told the bunker that he longed for the Amis to win. It was only natural that the Frenchman would crave the liberation of his country, but there was no point in that liberation if he had been strung up from a Berlin lamppost by the Gestapo. And there was, of course, another very good reason for him to stay alive.

'Are you well?' Katharina asked Ursula anxiously.

They'd been standing in the bakery queue for ages and it wasn't good for Ursula to be on her feet for so long in her condition. The midwives believed her baby would be born in January, making her around four months pregnant. No one had commented on the fact that she'd only married three months ago. Really, what did it matter when they might all be dead at the drop of an Allied bomb?

'I'm very well, Kätsche,' Ursula insisted with her usual ready smile. 'Honestly, I don't know what everyone complains about – the baby's giving me no trouble at all. Well, he or she has taken away my appetite, but with so little food around these days that's a blessing.'

Katharina put her arm around Ursula's still slim waist and gave her a hug. Over the last dark month she'd been hugely thankful for the young woman's optimism and positivity. Without it, she might have slipped with Robert and Adelaide into the dark hole that Sasha had left behind. Robert, to his huge credit, was looking after baby Hanna with the attentive tenderness he always gave to his precious zebras and deer, feeding her with goat's milk and carrying her around with him in a papoose. It took almost all his strength, and in the bunker at night he would curl up with both his daughters and sleep through any noise, bar that of his baby crying. Every day that Katharina watched his brave battle to care for his girls, she felt like screaming out loud at the pity of it, but what use would that be? No one, it seemed, was listening to the inhabitants of Berlin any more.

She did her best to help, especially with Adelaide. The only thing, bar her tiny sister, that seemed to bring the poor girl out of brooding silence was the chimps, especially the five babies that had recently been born to the community. Katharina encouraged her to help with them for as much of every day as she thought the girl had the energy to do so.

'We're almost in!'

Ursula pointed happily to the door of the bakery as a larger lady (she must have good access to the black market, Katharina thought unkindly) left and the queue shuffled up, allowing them inside at last. Barely moments later, the sirens sounded and chaos broke out in the queue on the pavement. Some, with cries of frustration, left to make for the safety of nearby bunkers. Others, however, simply huddled in against the wall, producing tin hats, or makeshift versions fashioned from pots and baking dishes, as meagre protection. The daytime planes flew in low and though they rarely dropped big bombs, they fired indiscriminately and Katharina looked, aghast, at the desperate women who were prepared to chance their lives for a loaf of bread for their family.

'Down,' she cried to Ursula, dragging her into the shop as everyone dropped to the floor. The baker had long since boarded up her windows and the shop was as safe a place as any with no time to get back to the zoo. Barely had they huddled in against the counter than a plane shrieked down the street, so low they could surely have looked into the pilot's eyes had they been outside. There was a scream from the tin-hat women the other side of the wall and Katharina clutched at Ursula and tried to pray for them, save that prayers just seemed to echo hollowly around in her brain these days, as trapped as the Berliners in their precious city.

'How long can this go on?' she asked Ursula under her breath.

'Not long, surely? The Amis are closing on Paris, the Russians are on the border of Poland, and Pierre says that the people of Warsaw are rising against us. All must surely be lost? We just need the bloody Golden Pheasants to realise it.'

'Ursula, hush!' Any one of the huddled hausfraus in the bakery could be a party informer so they couldn't afford to let their guard down. 'Think of the baby.'

'It's not me you need to shut up,' Ursula hissed, as another plane whined past outside. 'It's Pierre. He's so upset, Kätsche, that I swear he doesn't care what he says any more.'

Katharina nodded. She couldn't really blame Pierre for being angry. In the weeks since Stauffenberg and his cronies had tried to assassinate Hitler, the Gestapo had been more active than ever, stalking the streets and yanking anyone with so much as a suspicious set of eyebrows in for questioning. Some made it out but not many, and people were living in as much fear of their own police as the American planes. Then last week the Gestapo had come to the zoo and bundled away self-appointed chefs Marcel and Victor, on the spurious reason that they 'cooked crocodiles'. Every time Katharina thought of burly, cheerful Marcel being tortured in some dark cell, her skin crawled, so she had no idea what it was doing to Pierre.

'He cries at night,' Ursula whispered. 'It breaks my heart, Kätsche.'

'At least you have a heart left to break.'

Ursula gave a dark laugh.

'Careful – you are in danger of becoming a true Berliner with remarks like that.'

Katharina gave a little huff and wormed further into the shop. It seemed, from what they had been able to glean from the information underground, that the plot to kill Hitler had come tantalisingly close to success. Stauffenberg's bomb had killed three people, and it was only because someone had inadvertently moved the rigged briefcase that Hitler had not been one of them. An old-fashioned officer, Stauffenberg had long been key to German resistance to the Nazis and, although far from liberal, had moved with an intention to try and negotiate peace. His failure had condemned Germany to further war – and Berlin to persecution.

Katharina squeezed her friend and they lay there, with all the other women who just wanted food for their families, as the flashy American pilots cut their way through their city. It did not last long. Within half an hour, the all-clear sounded and everyone in the bakery could pick themselves up off the floor, dust the flour from their dresses and resume their queue, almost as if nothing had happened. Outside, people were crying for help and a glance out of the doorway showed two women splayed across the pavement, their place in the queue held for eternity.

'What a waste,' Ursula muttered, but she faced back in to wait patiently for her turn at the front all the same.

'Guten tag,' the baker greeted them politely, but when Katharina handed over the collective bread coupons from the zoo, she shook her head. 'If I give you all this, meine Damen, I will have nothing left for anyone else.'

Katharina looked to Ursula, then back to the frowning queue.

'But if you don't, then our Zoofamilie will starve.'

She shrugged.

'Very well then. It is not up to me to control who gets what, simply to take the coupons.' She leaned in. 'But I don't fancy your chances of getting out of the shop with it all still in your hands.'

Katharina sighed. The woman was right. They'd be set upon if they took all that was left of her precious stock and probably rightly so. Reluctantly she took back half the coupons, and stood bullishly as the baker gave her three loaves and two small raisin breads for the rest. It would barely last the day and someone would have to chance the queue again tomorrow, but what could they do?

'Bleib übrig,' she said to the baker as she made for the door and was pleased to hear her respond in kind.

'Bleib übrig.' The simple phrase – 'may we survive' – had replaced the official greeting of 'Heil Hitler' for many of the disillusioned population, a small rebellion that felt strangely empowering. They may not have much bread, but they still had their pride.

She was glad to get back to the zoo, and left Ursula to take the bread to the kitchens as she headed for the chimp house. The monkeys squealed excitedly, calling to her and swinging through those ropes and branches still standing, as if this happy moment was all they needed. Katharina admired their ability to live in the present and vowed to try and copy their example. She let herself into the cage, drawing their ready joy into her like a balm.

'Kätsche!' Adelaide came running up to the bars, Gisela and Dieter in tow. 'Can we come in too?'

'Of course, sweetheart.'

Katharina unlatched the door and little Adelaide came in. She went, as she always did, straight to the young monkeys. They were a month old now and growing brave enough to leave their mothers for short periods. They liked and trusted Adelaide, and one of them launched itself onto her shoulder and clung tightly on to her hair, as it might to its mother.

'Look, Kätsche! Look at me!'

'I see. She loves you.'

'She does. She really does!'

The girl beamed, perhaps the first true smile Katharina had seen from her since her mother's terrible death, and she looked to Gisela and Dieter to share the joy of it.

'We could learn a lot from animals,' Gisela said, laughing as one of the other babies played with her silver brooch, turning it to watch the light flash.

'Perhaps all political meetings from here on in should be held in zoos,' Katharina suggested. 'Surely even the most determined power-seeking men could not fail to be won over by the simple ease and acceptance of animals?'

Gisela looked sideways at Katharina.

'Come, Kätsche, you've seen the lions at their meat. They're vicious.'

'When hungry, yes, but not for the sake of it.'

'They would not kill another pride that encroached on their territory?'

'Well…'

'And the male would not fight a youngster who challenged his throne?'

Katharina sighed.

'I suppose he would.'

'Your precious chimps are the same, my sweet. You're being naive.'

'All the better for it,' came another voice.

Katharina spun round.

'Oskar!'

'I see the party is in the chimp house today.' She turned to let him in. 'You look thoughtful, meine kindl.'

'I sometimes feel thought is the only luxury left to us, O.'

He kissed her, making the monkey in her arms squeal in protest.

'You too?' he asked it, leaning in and laughing as the little creature puckered up her lips for him. 'Very well.'

He gave the chimp a quick kiss then looked to Gisela and Dieter.

'Are you all thoughtful today?'

'Lord no,' Gisela said. 'I do my best to avoid thinking these days. There is little else to focus on but war.'

'Oh, I don't know,' Oskar said. 'What about love, music, animals?'

Katharina smiled at him, her body warming instantly at the memory of the night she'd first met this man and he'd kindled previously unknown emotions within her clinical scientist's heart.

'You're as positive as Ursula, my love,' she said, kissing him.

'I wish I were. That woman is amazing.'

'Not so much at the moment. She says Pierre is hurting over the taking of Marcel and Victor.'

Gisela came over.

'Aren't we all. I fear for them – justice will be hard with the Führer baying for blood.'

'Perhaps,' Oskar said. 'We just have to hope the Amis reach Berlin before they go to trial.'

'What's that?' Someone peered into the cage, and to Katharina's horror she saw Dennis's thin face looking through the sparse greenery. 'You hope the Amis come, Herr Heinroth?'

Katharina's heart beat hard against her ribcage.

'Of course he doesn't, Dennis,' she snapped. 'That would mean defeat. How could we wish defeat for the Fatherland?'

Dennis's eyes narrowed dangerously and Katharina struggled to breathe. One word from the weasely driver and the Gestapo would take Oskar and probably her as well. They were finding any excuse to arrest people and this was one of the best. She looked anxiously to her husband but he was as calm as ever.

'Unless that is what *you* wish, Dennis?' he challenged.

The man withered instantly.

'Of course it isn't. Why would it be?' He looked around at them all, before adding, 'Anyway, it's not the Amis who are coming to take Berlin – it's the Reds.'

He looked almost gleeful and Katharina glanced at Oskar to see if he'd noticed this too.

'The Soviet advance is… worrying,' Oskar said carefully.

'Not if you're Soviet,' came the cheerful reply and, with a tip of his cap, Dennis was gone, leaving them all staring at each other in confusion.

'Do you think Dennis is a Red?' Katharina whispered.

'No idea,' Oskar said. 'I suppose he might be, though he's far too lazy to be a successful one.'

'Oskar!'

'It's true. I fear he might be right about the Soviets getting here first though. Rumour says the Eastern front is folding faster than a party newsletter, and the resistance rising in Warsaw will surely help the Reds.'

'We must pray not,' Dieter said, drawing them all deeper into the shade of the tropical plants. 'I saw what some of our men did to Russian women. It was ugly. Barbaric. I was ashamed of them. We were trained to go in fast, secure an area and then protect the citizens but so many of our men…' He shuddered. 'They treated the women like spoils of conquest. You should have heard them talk – it was as if the poor things were honoured to be "filled up" by good German stock.'

Katharina shivered and looked over to Adelaide, still engrossed in her baby chimp. She had blossomed further across the summer, her breasts growing and hips widening. Katharina made a note that she must talk to her of women's matters in Sasha's stead; she did not want those matters to include rape.

Gisela followed her gaze.

'Hush, Dieter,' she said, nodding at the girl.

Dieter closed his eyes against something only he could see, and when he opened them again they were full of sadness.

'She will not be safe if they come. None of you will. The Russians do not just want conquest – they want revenge. If they reach the city it will be horrific.'

Gisela huddled closer to Katharina.

'So what do we do?' she asked her husband.

In reply Dieter looked to Oskar.

'The transports,' he said, 'are they still going on?'

'Oh yes,' Oskar assured him, 'where they can. It's tricky with so many of the roads and rail-lines bombed but we find ways eventually.'

'You're shipping out to other zoos?'

'Sometimes, but increasingly to private collectors. They tend to be in the countryside, where the danger is less. I've been speaking this week with a lovely lady in Saxony who is taking several of our rarer antelopes. And possibly some chimps too.' As if it had heard him, the chimp in Katharina's arms reached over and yanked suddenly at his hair. 'Ow!'

'She doesn't want to go,' Katharina said.

'She wants to stay here and be killed instead, does she?' Oskar snapped, and she jumped at the harshness of his tone. He grabbed at her hand. 'Sorry. I'm sorry, Katharina. It's just—'

'I know, O. I know. None of this is easy. The zoo is home and it's hard to believe we might have to abandon it.'

'Not all of us,' Dieter said gently. 'Just the more... vulnerable.'

'Women?'

'I'm afraid so. And children.' He looked to Adelaide, babbling away to the little chimp. 'And babies. Perhaps especially babies.'

He shivered and no one dared press him further. Katharina thought of the women shot dead in the bakery queue this morning and found it hard to believe that things could get worse, but from the look on Dieter's face that was naive. However much she hated it, she had to turn her mind to escape routes for all those – both animal and human – in her care here at the zoo.

Chapter Thirteen

'That was so good!' Bethan enthused, as the surging crowd almost bodily lifted her out of the Stadion An der Alten Försterei, home to FC Union.

'We were lucky with the third goal,' Max said. 'They were coming back at us before that.'

Bethan laughed.

'Positivity, Max?'

He put up his hands.

'You're right. Positivity. We were always going to win! Is that better?'

'Much. It felt that way to me.'

Her head was still buzzing from the chants of the happy fans, who had all seemed to know each other and had spent the half-hour before the game going around shaking hands and passing out an array of home-cooked snacks. Then the whole ground had rocked to an unashamedly punk tune that was apparently their theme song, a sea of giant red-and-white flags waving proudly. Someone, seeing that Bethan did not have one, had thrust his own into her hand and she'd waved it with the rest, feeling a surge of belonging that had surprised her.

'The singing was fantastic, wasn't it, Ella?' she said, turning to her friend.

'Not as fantastic as the thighs on that Number 16. I should have got into football years ago.'

Max laughed.

'As long as it's Union. I can't have you chasing after the Hertha lot – they're not a proper club.'

'You mean their fans didn't build their own stadium?'

Max waved proudly around the stand they were trying to leave. 'Exactly – slackers!'

Bethan dug him in the ribs, but she had to admit she'd been impressed when he'd told her that the renovation of the three older stands had been made possible by fans volunteering their time to help out. Max himself had apparently spent most of his weekends down here with his dad and brothers, ripping out old seats and helping carry in new ones. It was an impressive show of commitment, though perhaps not as impressive as five years before that when fans had collectively donated blood to give their payments for this precious fluid to their team. This really was a people's club.

'Well, I'm now officially a Union fan,' she declared.

'Delighted to hear it. You too, Ella?'

Ella wrinkled up her nose.

'Can't say I'm a football fan as such, but if I support any team it will be this lot – especially if I can track down the players.'

'You fancy life as a WAG then?' Bethan asked her.

'A what?'

'Sorry – English expression for "wives and girlfriends".'

'Spielerfrauen,' Max supplied.

Bethan thought about it – players' wives. Not as good a term as WAGs in her opinion, but she wasn't going to say so.

'I think you might be a bit too intelligent,' she told Ella instead. Ella pouted.

'Oh, I can pretend not to be for a few million euros a year.'

Bethan gave her a friendly nudge, sending them both toppling sideways as the crowd shifted. Max put out a hand to support her and Bethan froze at the feel of his arm around her waist. He snatched it away.

'Dad and Peter will be pleased that their season tickets have been put to such good use,' he said hastily. 'They were gutted to miss today for work, but if they've made new converts then all was not lost. Now – who's for a beer?'

'Me!' they both shouted, and gladly followed the crowd out of the stadium and into the big beer garden surrounding it.

Afternoon sank into evening. Max took them to the pretty area of Köpenick for dinner and, although they didn't find Ella any celebrating players, she flirted outrageously with the pianist in the lively restaurant. The poor man was so distracted by her crazy curls and infectious smile that in the end Max offered him his seat beside Ella and took his place at the piano. Bethan listened, open-mouthed, as he played a selection of tunes for the gathered fans to sing along to, and was sad when he ceded the seat back to the pro.

'That was amazing, Max.'

He flushed and ran a self-conscious hand through his dark hair.

'I got carried away.'

'You should do it more often. I loved it.'

'Then maybe I will, but for now, I'm worn out. Shall we head off?'

'No way!' Ella scoffed, promptly abandoning them to slink up to the pianist.

He reached out to pull her onto the stool at his side and she threw them a happy wink.

'She's a quick worker,' Bethan said to Max.

'She's outrageous,' he agreed easily. 'But fine without us, it seems. Home then?'

'If I say yes does it make me really old?'

'Only as old as me.' Looking up at him, his hair only slightly silvered around the temples and blue eyes alive with energy, she figured that wasn't so very old. 'Besides,' he added, 'Cindi in the office got me out those old files the other day, and I've found a list of keepers during the war that might interest you if you fancy a night cap?'

'Absolutely!'

*

An hour later and Bethan no longer felt so tired. Max was telling her more about his travels around Africa in the early years of being a vet, and he had the ability to describe the place in such detail that she could almost have been there. He spoke of his trips with honesty, rarely offering anything about his own activities, instead focusing on Detlev and the local gamekeepers and, of course, the chimps. Always the chimps.

It was clear that Max loved his charges almost as much as the family he frequently referred to. It turned out he was one of four children – three brothers and a treasured younger sister. All three of his siblings were married and he had an array of nephews and nieces who knew him as Uncle Zoo. Both his brothers were still, like him, in Berlin, but his sister had moved to the far reaches of Bavaria and he missed her.

'She's always asking me to visit,' he told Bethan, pouring more of a dangerously nice pear schnapps, 'but I never seem to have the time. Then, whenever I do go, she insists on having dinner parties and inviting *lovely single girls* and I can't be doing with it.'

'You don't want to meet someone?'

He coloured.

'I don't want to meet someone Greta chooses for me. She says if I'm not careful I'm going to end up married to a chimp.'

'So – have you proposed to Binky yet?'

He laughed.

'Many times. She won't have me.' He drank more of his schnapps then said, 'Callum seemed nice.'

'No, he didn't.' The words were out before she could stop them. She coughed. 'That is, he wasn't on great form when you met him. He'd got a bit of a hangover. We went to that champagne bar in the centre.'

'E. Coli City? That's what the locals call it cos God knows what you can catch there. It's just cheap wine, you know, stuck through a carbonator at the base of the fountain.'

'I bet. I can't say I was keen but Callum said it was romantic.'
Max sighed.

'I'm sure it is. That's something else I'm not good at. My family are all very down to earth. Science and sport, that's what I was brought up on. My mum would never let my dad buy her flowers on her birthday unless they were bulbs for the garden. They weren't big on surprises either. One year my mum bought tickets to Paris for my dad for their twentieth wedding anniversary, and he was furious because it meant he missed Union play Hertha. He got it in the neck for that.'

'Did he go to Paris?'

'Oh yes, he's not stupid. But she went round the Louvre alone while he sat in some back-street bar streaming the match on his phone.'

'Was your mum mad?'

'Nope. Said it was far more restful without Dad making sarcastic comments about the artwork and nagging to leave the moment they got there. They both had a lovely afternoon. Union won, the Mona Lisa smiled, and they met up afterwards ready to be together again.'

Bethan smiled.

'They sound like they've got life sorted.'

Max nodded.

'They're great together. Not romantic for sure, but solid, you know – and happy.'

'I do know,' Beth agreed. 'My parents were like that. Or at least what I remember of them. Dad's never met anyone else. I've tried to get him on a dating app, but he just says no other woman would match up to Mum and it's not fair to ask them to try.'

'Is he lonely?'

Bethan considered.

'I don't think so. He has lots of friends. He does carpentry at a community place, plays golf and goes to the footie.'

'Leicester?'

'Oh, no! He's a Notts Forest supporter. You wouldn't know them.'

'I do. Red. Much better colour than nasty blue Leicester.'

A laugh burst out of Bethan at the thought of the vibrant blue duvet cover Callum had subjected her to. The next minute, though, the thought made her feel awkward. What was she doing sitting sipping schnapps with Max? Callum would be furious.

'What about this list then?' she asked Max hastily.

He got up and went over to his bookcase to pull down a small box. Rifling inside, he took out a file marked simply 'keepers' and handed it to Bethan. She opened it and pulled out a neat set of lists. Each paper seemed to cover a different period and she leafed through the exotic-sounding names of the late 1800s when the zoo opened, past the First World War and the thin lists from the harsh years of the twenties, before she finally reached a set that started in 1938.

It made grim reading. At first it was a long list, bursting with names – three or four to every animal house – but as 1939 hit and the men were called up someone had edited it, crossing out multiple names, with the initials EB for Einberufen (called up) or, even more chillingly, G for Gefallen (dead) and V for Vermisst (missing). For the first time, Bethan confronted the reality of the war she'd only really studied in primary school – crawling under desks with homemade gas masks on, and eating corned beef out of the can. It had seemed little more than a game in that creative classroom, but looking down the list of keepers lost to the zoo was like seeing a live death count. She placed it slowly down on the table and looked at Max.

'We're very lucky, aren't we, not to have lived through such a war?'

He nodded.

'We'll never know what it was like. Look here – by 1943 they only had forty keepers in the zoo and most of those were old men.

Someone has added in some other names in a different pen.' He pointed to a number of green-ink names slotted between the official black ones and Bethan squinted at the writing, trying to make them out.

'Does that say Dubois?'

'Where?' Max leaned eagerly forward, his hand brushing Bethan's as he reached for the list. 'Ooh yes – Pierre Dubois, alongside these other French names: Marcel Laurent, Victor Rousseau. They must be the French exchange labourers.'

'Exchange?'

'The Nazis had a man called Fritz Sauckel in charge of labour deployment. Lovely chap. Known as the Slave-Trader of Europe to everyone but Hitler, who presumably had nothing but praise for his lively efforts to bring most of Europe's non-combatant young men to the Fatherland to work for us. He did a deal with the Vichy government – 150,000 French workers in their early twenties in exchange for 50,000 prisoners of war. A pretty rough deal if you ask me, but made even worse by us only ever sending 1,200 back. But hey, that's Nazis for you.'

Bethan shifted.

'Do you hate it that you have that in your history?' she asked. 'Not *your* history. I understand it's not *your* history but, you know—'

'The nation's history? Of course I do. Why do you think Germans work so hard, Beth? We always have something to prove. We don't want that to happen again. Not ever. Though, to be fair, a lot of Germans didn't want it at the time either, especially in Berlin. They voted against the party time and again – not that it did them any good.'

He looked down suddenly and Bethan felt mean.

'Our lot did some pretty rubbish things in their time too, Max. But it's in the past; it doesn't matter any more.'

'Except if you want to find someone.'

Her heart contracted.

'Except then.' She put her schnapps down and reached for the list, searching the names as Max sat in silence. She felt bad for introducing such a tricky subject and fought for something kind to say, but all her personal positives about Germans – how kind and friendly and funny she found them – sounded patronising. She focused on the list but could find no Franke and no Schultz. Then suddenly she saw something.

'Look, Max – Robert Eberhard. Here.' Max leaped up and came round to her side. Relieved they were back on comfortable ground, she pointed, trying not to be too aware of his body. 'He's listed as zebra, deer and dog keeper. Oh, and look what else – someone's added "Sasha Eberhard" in green and someone else – a child, do you think? – has added two more names. Can you read them?'

Max stepped in, so close she felt his breath warm on her ear and had to concentrate to stop her hands shaking the list. He smelled so good – of soap and beer and fresh air, with a sweet hint of pear.

'Is it Adelaide?' he suggested. 'And Hanna. Yes, that's it – Adelaide and Hanna. They must have been Robert and Sasha's daughters. Perhaps we can pull up their birth certificates online?' He crossed to his computer and Bethan instantly missed the feel of him at her back, but he was already tapping at the keys. 'Yes! Here. Adelaide Eberhard – born in Berlin Zoo August 1933. And Hanna Eberhard quite a lot later – July 1944. And here, on the certificate, next to Sasha's name it says Verstorbene – deceased.'

Bethan looked at the screen and sure enough there, captured online forever, was little Hanna's birth certificate, listing her arrival in the world alongside her mother's departure.

'Sasha must have died in childbirth.'

'I'm afraid so.'

'So Hanna might have been "gifted" to someone better able to cope with her?'

'Maybe.' They both stared at the screen. 'What about Robert? He's not listed as deceased. And Adelaide.'

'Adelaide.' Bethan stared at the name. 'When was she born, Max?'

'1933.'

She leaped up from the chair, pacing as she did the maths in her head.

'If she was alive today that would make her eighty-six.'

Max grabbed her hands to keep her still. 'What are you thinking, Beth?'

'What's short for Adelaide, Max?'

'No?! You mean…'

'Ada.'

'It can't be.'

'Why not? She's always here, always talking to that bust of Katharina Heinroth. She told us she had to hide underground from bombs with her "Zoofamilie" so it all fits. What if she was here, in the zoo, when my mum was gifted to Oma Erika? What if she knows who the real mother was? God, Max, what if she's just been sitting there all along, able to tell us exactly what happened?'

She felt herself start to shake with the possibilities of it all and was glad of Max's hands to steady her.

'Don't get carried away, Beth. Ada isn't very…'

'Lucid?' As he nodded, she felt her excitement fade. He was right – Ada rarely spoke sense. But maybe that was just because no one asked her the right questions. 'We can try, right?'

He smiled at her.

'We can try. We can buy her cake and make sure she's relaxed, and we can try.'

Bethan did an involuntary skip and then felt foolish.

'Sorry. I'm like a little kid, aren't I?'

'What's wrong with that? Little kids are great.'

Bethan laughed.

'They are. Thanks, Max.'

'For what?'

'For everything. I couldn't do this without you.'

'Oh, I'm sure you could.'

He flushed and looked down and that's when they both noticed their hands, still linked together. Max let go of her and stepped back, clearing his throat.

'How about tomorrow,' she suggested. 'If you're free?'

'I'll make sure I am.'

Max looked so self-conscious that she longed to hug him, but it was late and she'd had rather a lot of schnapps and she wasn't sure she trusted herself to stop there. Her body, reawakened by Callum's attentions last weekend, was humming outrageously, and suddenly she knew it was time to go home.

'Night then,' she said, making for his door.

'Night, Beth.'

She paused on the threshold.

'Tomorrow, yes?'

'I'll look forward to it.'

'Me too,' she agreed, and then she fled before her demanding body made her do something very, very stupid.

She tumbled back into her flat, her heart thumping and her skin tingling as if she were a teenager. This was so unlike her. She made herself a cup of tea and stood at the window, looking out over the zoo, seeking sense. It was hard to find but one thing was abundantly clear: whatever had happened with Max just then, things were not right between her and Callum. They had been once, back when all had been giddy fun, but those days were gone and now, hard as it felt, she owed it to herself to decide if they still had a future together.

Chapter Fourteen

November 1944

'Heil Hitler!'

The voice of Joseph Goebbels screeched out of the microphone and echoed imperiously around Wilhelmplatz, but the reply from the gathered crowd was muted. You could blame the rain which was drizzling determinedly on the grand ceremony, but no Berliner was fazed by a little water and the mumbled response was a symptom of a far deeper depression, especially with the Führer himself standing tightly at Goebbels's side.

Katharina, dipping her head to 're-clip her brooch' and avoid the salute, saw hundreds of others with the same apparent problem and exchanged a daring look with another woman.

'Katharina, be careful.'

Oskar pulled her close against himself.

'Don't fret, O, even the Gestapo are giving up.'

He pressed his face against hers.

'That's not true, meine kindl,' he hissed. 'The Gestapo will never give up. For them it is not about the war but their own petty power, and they will cling on to that with everything they have. It would give them great pleasure to arrest a pretty woman like you.'

'Pretty, O? Has love blinded you?'

Katharina had never been pretty. Striking perhaps, in her younger days when her hair was still flame-red, but never pretty like luscious Ursula or slender Gisela.

'Love blinded me a long time ago, Kätsche. I do not want it to break me as well. Do not give those wolves the chance to bite you. *Please.*'

His words were so urgent and his face so pained that she kissed him contritely.

'I won't, O.'

'We know how we feel about all this, don't we? We needn't say it out loud.'

She nodded and looked back to the current show being played out at the heart of what had once been Berlin, and was now a sad sort of reverse building site. Today, 8 November, was the anniversary of the 'glorious' Beer Hall Putsch when Hitler had seized power, and the Nazis were using it to swear in 100,000 of the city's remaining men to the newly proclaimed Volkssturm, or Army of the People. It was a farce. The men standing in shabby lines across the Wilhelmplatz were, without wanting to be rude to them, the dregs of Germany's fighting force. With every fit male between sixteen and sixty long since called up, this 'salvation force' was made of up of those who had been deemed unfit years ago.

Goebbels was singing their praises to the sodden skies as if they were an elite troupe, finally released to wreak havoc on the millions of Russians advancing from the east and Amis from the west, but standing before him was a bunch of white-haired grandpas, frightened fourteen- and fifteen-year-olds, and broken soldiers, dragged out of the city's hospitals. They were, at best, cannon fodder, and it broke Katharina's heart that the Führer, standing safely on his flag-draped platform, was allowed to do this to them.

She looked sadly to her left, where the little zoo troop were gathered behind their leader. Only Oskar, at over seventy, had been spared the call-up. The rest were lined up behind Lutz Heck, who had been made a lieutenant and their personal commander. He had been given a smart uniform and a gun, but the rest had simply been issued their papers, given four days of nominal training over in the Sportplatz, and dispatched to find themselves both uniform and weapon before they faced the highly trained troops heading their way.

Gustav and Walter were standing together in their uniforms from the first war, a little tight and very shabby, though they wore them with their shoulders high. Both had ancient pistols that they had polished to a high shine, though as far as Katharina knew no one had issued them with any bullets, so they were as much use as a child's toy. The rest of the zoo troop were in their dark green keeper uniforms and had an assortment of weapons, from the two rifles the zoo kept for euthanising suffering animals to the damned rakes used for cleaning out bedding.

What use would they be against a Soviet tank? Katharina wondered, and hated Hitler all over again for sanctioning this madness. Why did no one rise up against him? Why did none of these poor men just lift their makeshift guns and shoot him? Katharina would do it herself if she thought she had the accuracy to achieve it, and she'd happily die in whatever cruel agony the party chose to inflict on her if it meant the rest of the country would be spared the inevitable slaughter ahead. Her eyes roamed the crowd, willing someone to act, but they had all been pounded into obedience by the party, whose flags and salutes had once been the call to freedom and were now surely just reckless condemnation of the people they were supposedly saving. She buried her head in Oskar's coat.

'I can't bear it, O.'

He stroked her hair.

'You can, meine kindl. And you will – for the children, yes? For the future.'

She looked up at him and shook her head.

'Such optimism, O.'

'It is all we have left. And it is important.'

He glanced sideways to Adelaide, and Katharina drew in a deep breath and reached out an arm to pull the girl in against her, noticing as she did so that she now matched her in height. She was growing up fast and starting to look so like her mother that the other day

Katharina had almost called her Sasha. Poor Robert was standing stony-faced behind Lutz. He had cared so well for his girls, but now that Hitler had pointed his scrawny finger at him, Katharina had to take on his precious charges. She felt both the honour and the responsibility of her role keenly. God had not granted her and Oskar children of their own, but during this horrible war she had become mother to so many orphaned animals, and now she must step up and look after the precious children of the zoo as well.

She looked to the grey skies, her heart bursting with sorrow.

I'll look after them, Sasha, she promised her departed friend. *I'll look after them with everything I have.*

It was not how it should be, but it was how it was and they must make the very best of it. She looked round for Gisela, clutching Hanna in her arms, and saw that tears were streaming down her friend's cheeks as the men raised their arms to swear the oath of allegiance to a party that was sucking their souls. Dieter had been called up, despite his missing leg, and was beside lopsided Robert. He had refused to put his army uniform back on, preferring to wear the keeper's uniform Lutz had given him, but he was a soldier again all the same and it was breaking Gisela's heart, especially as she was now four months pregnant. Her baby was due next spring, three months after Ursula's, and it was impossible to imagine what sort of world either child would be born into – or indeed if there would be a world left.

As Katharina watched, Dieter turned and blew his wife a kiss. It was a swift, stolen gesture, but one of moving tenderness amongst the storm of hate-filled rhetoric spewing out of the microphone, and it warmed her heart. Dieter's arms were firmly around the shoulders of two lads either side of him – Hans and Mark. Nominally they were helping to support his bad leg, but Katharina could see them trembling and knew that the support went the other way too.

The boys were stationed at the flak tower permanently now, not just carrying the ammunition to the men but actually firing the guns as their older compatriots were shot down or redeployed to the ever-closer front. Their once wide eyes were weary, clouded with sights that no child should have to see, and – whenever they could – they escaped their duties to help out at the zoo. Katharina always welcomed them into the chimp house and watched them play with their primate friends with a sort of furious intensity – as if they knew that this was the only chance at childhood they had left. Now, they stood with the men, swearing their young lives to a lost cause, and yet again Katharina found herself wondering why this crowd did not just open fire on the leaders who so clearly cared nothing for them.

She reached out and squeezed Gisela's shoulders. Her slim friend felt even more fragile than usual, so she took Hanna from her and bounced her on her hip. If the little girl survived, she would hopefully grow up never remembering any of this. Ursula, on Gisela's far side, added her now considerable bulk to their group and Katharina sucked in the support of her female friends. It was so good to have them with her, but she worried about them constantly.

Ursula was due not long after Christmas and Berlin was no place to give birth, as poor Sasha had proven. Paris had been liberated three months ago and Pierre was keen to take his secret wife to France, but trying to get out of Germany was almost impossible. There were guards everywhere ready to shoot 'deserters' at the slightest provocation and Pierre, as a foreign labourer, had no status to draw on. Now he, too, had been called up. Katharina had to question the wisdom of asking the Frenchmen to fight against what they surely considered their own side, but no decisions the Führer made seemed to be rooted in any grasp of reality.

The only good bit of news in the otherwise bleak arrival of winter was that Marcel and Victor had been deemed more use to the party on the frontline than in their dungeons and released. They stood alongside Pierre in the zoo troop, pretending ignorance of the German they were being asked to recite, even though they were now all but fluent in the language of their reluctantly adopted country.

'Kämpfer! Verteidiger des Vaterlands!' Goebbels cried over the crackling microphone and the new 'defenders of the Fatherland' shuffled to attention, old hips creaking and wooden limbs grating on the pavement.

Lutz glanced back at his troop and gave them a quick nod of approval. Katharina ground her teeth. How could he stand for this charade?

'He's done all he can,' Oskar would say, and to some extent she had to admit that was true.

Originally the men of the zoo had been assigned to various units across the city, including the poor buggers ordered to march out to the city's eastern limits to 'cut off the Red Army' – more of Hitler's sadistic fantasy-making. Lutz had insisted that his keepers were needed to protect the animals as a symbol of hope for the people, and had argued that they would be more effective defending the area they knew best from the zoo flak tower. After several agonising days of negotiation, he had won. Their men were part of the Volkssturm, but were stationed at the zoo and could continue their duties until such point as they were required to turn back the enemy tide that the full might of the Wehrmacht had failed to block. It was a nonsense but for now, at least, they were as safe as it was possible to be in beleaguered Berlin. And they were together. The Zoofamilie – depleted, scared and hungry but together.

Finally, the farce of a ceremony was over and they were free to return to the zoo. They walked together, a bizarre parody of the happy Sunday strolls of the pre-war years that now felt less like history and more like a time they must have collectively imagined. On the surface, parts of the city were maintaining a sense of prosperity, but it was all smoke and mirrors. Shops had windows full of produce, but a step inside showed empty boxes and thin bags of beans and rice taped to the front of jars to give an illusion of plenty. The same was happening in the bars, who lined their walls with a beautiful array of rainbow bottles that were filled not with whiskies and schnapps but coloured water. Life in Berlin was a carefully constructed and painfully empty illusion.

Only the children had any spring in their step. Katharina watched as Hans and Mark led Adelaide up a pile of rubble as if it were a shiny climbing frame, and tried to take a little of their spirit into her own heart. Then suddenly Hans reached for Adelaide's hand; something in his bearing made him look more man than boy and Katharina was chillingly reminded of how womanly her charge was becoming. She leaned over to Ursula, waddling along on Pierre's arm.

'How is your cousin, Ursula?'

Ursula shivered and put a hand to her belly.

'She's not good, Kätsche, not good at all.'

Katharina dug her nails into her palms as if that might somehow dig this curse out of their days, but there was nothing she could do. Ursula's cousin had fled with thousands of others from East Prussia, which the Red Army were now taking with the violence of a thunderstorm. When Katharina had first heard that they'd invaded the area her thoughts had leaped to Reike the giraffe, supposedly safe in Mülhausen zoo, but as the first refugees had begun pouring into Berlin, it had become apparent that a giraffe was one of the safest things to be in the battered area.

'Mutti says she just lies and cries half the time, and the other half she is trying to wash. They didn't just rape her, they destroyed her.'

Ursula's seventeen-year-old cousin, Martha, had arrived at her mother's house two weeks ago, half starved, half frozen and still bleeding from between her legs. She had so far been unable to form any coherent words of her own, but the kindly older woman who'd escorted her had shakily reported that a platoon of fifteen Russian soldiers had, in turn, violently raped her. Not only that but they had made her mother watch before turning on her as well. They'd shot the mother when they were finally sated but left Martha to live, telling her in broken German that if she was lucky she would bear a Red baby. Worryingly, it looked as if they might be right, and Hetti was searching for a doctor kind enough to perform an abortion.

'Have you found help?' Katharina asked discreetly.

'Sort of. The party in its great kindness have decreed that any woman who can convince an official that they were raped by a Russian—'

'Or fifteen.'

'Indeed. Can have a sanctioned abortion.'

'That's something.'

'It would be if poor Martha could find any words to speak to the dammed official. The woman who brought her from Prussia went with her to the interview but they are insisting that Martha must give her own testimony – as if her descent into madness and the bloody bruising all the way up her inner thighs is not evidence enough. Bastards.'

She spat into the rubble and Pierre ran a hand up and down her back.

'There's no point working yourself up about it, ma chérie.'

She turned on him.

'There is, Pierre. If we don't get worked up then it will just go on and on and on. No one is stopping this, so where on earth will it end?'

Pierre looked down at her and nodded slowly.

'You are right. Of course, you are right. I sometimes think you women are braver than us men, standing before the Führer, swearing allegiance to his crazy plans.'

'Pierre – hush!'

They all looked around, terrified, but people had peeled off for their own homes and no one was paying them any attention.

Lutz, walking ahead with Rita, cleared his throat but did not look round. It angered Katharina.

'What think you, Lutz?' she called out as they turned into the battered Elephant Gate. 'Will the Volkssturm save us?'

She saw Lutz's back stiffen.

'It's the only thing that can,' he said, turning.

'Then we are surely doomed?'

He looked anxiously around.

'You cannot say that, Katharina.'

'Why not, Lutz?'

'You do not know who might be listening.'

'It is forbidden, now, to speak the truth?'

Lutz ran a weary hand over his face, then looked her straight in the eyes.

'You know it is.'

It was the closest he would get to an admission and Katharina looked back at him, stunned.

'Then…?'

'Then we look after our animals, Katharina, as we always have. It is what we are here for. It is what we do best. It is the only thing still in our power.' They all stood there, drawing in the truth of this dark statement before Lutz spoke again: 'Feeding time, let's go. Their lives are in our hands.'

He clapped brusquely and they scattered to their various animal houses. Katharina made for the chimps, Oskar at her side and Hanna still in her arms. The baby had fallen asleep, worn out by all the noise and movement, and at four months old she was heavy against her, but Katharina held her tight, cherishing her warmth. Lutz was right about the animals, but he was wrong that they were the only thing in their power. Katharina had other charges too – women and children and yet-to-be-born children – and she was going to do all she could to help them. She looked to Oskar.

'It's time to step up the transports, O. There are... creatures that need to be got away.'

He nodded grimly and drew his little red notebook from his breast pocket.

'I'll sort it, meine kindl. Somehow I'll sort it.'

Chapter Fifteen

Bethan woke up the next morning feeling fuggy and out of sorts. She wasn't sure if it was last night's schnapps, or the churning awareness that she had to make a decision about Callum, but for the first time since she'd got to Berlin Zoo, she wasn't keen on getting out of bed. It was only the thought of going to talk to Ada that persuaded her to push back the covers and make for the shower, turning the water temperature down to try and drum some sense into her fuddled brain.

It worked. Or, at least, it persuaded her that talking to Ada was her first priority – a decision that was swiftly overturned when her phone buzzed out a cheery notification that Callum was FaceTiming. With an eye roll to whatever fates had chosen to do this to her, she pressed 'accept'.

'Bethan, babe. Looks like I caught you at just the right moment.'

'In what way, Callum?'

'The best possible way. Drop the towel hey, gorgeous.'

'What? Don't be ridiculous.'

He looked stung.

'What's ridiculous about wanting to see my sexy girlfriend in all her glory?'

It was a fair point, she supposed, but she didn't feel in the slightest bit sexy standing in front of the screen.

'I've, er, got to get on, I'm afraid,' she said, scrambling into her jeans. 'I might have a lead on Mum's real mum.'

He snorted, clearly cross at her refusing to play along.

'A "lead", Beth? You're not a detective.'

'I am, sort of.'

'Right. Well then, Sherlock, can you work out when you might come home?'

She jumped.

'Home?'

'Yes, home – to me.'

'It's a year contract, Callum, you know that.'

He rolled his eyes.

'Course I do. I mean for a visit. For a weekend. I came to you, right, so surely next time you have to come to me?'

She pulled her T-shirt on, cursing as the cotton stuck to her damp back.

'I suppose so, but it's not quite that easy. I'm on shift or on call six days a week. It's part of my contract. Anyway, I thought you liked Berlin.'

'Well, yeah, but it doesn't seem fair that it's always on me to travel. Flights are expensive, you know, and those rugby tickets cost a fortune.'

'Whose choice was that?'

He glared at her.

'Oh, so just because you chose to fly off halfway round Europe, I have to sit at home like a monk, is that it?'

'No! And you've hardly been a monk. You're in clubs every second night as far as I can see.'

'From where?'

'From your wretched Instagram.'

'You're spying on me?'

'Spying? It's out there for everyone to see – look at poor Callum Markeson, pining for his girlfriend knee-deep in foam and other women.'

'You're jealous!'

His brown eyes glowed delightedly. Bethan ground her teeth. She hadn't wanted to have it out with her boyfriend this morning, but it seemed he was forcing the issue.

'I'm just saying, Callum, that it might not be a Ryanair flight to Berlin that's emptying your pockets.'

He backtracked a little.

'You're right. I think it's all the takeaways I'm buying now you're not here to cook tea with.'

She frowned at him.

'You can cook by yourself, Callum.'

'I can. But it's no fun.'

'It's just tea. It doesn't have to be fun.' She ran a hand over her forehead, feeling her rare temper rising. 'It's not like you're paying much rent, is it?'

Now it was Callum's turn to frown.

'I'm looking after the place for you, Beth. People pay for that.'

'Or they rent their flat out and make a profit.'

'I see. You're begrudging me my place in your flat, are you? Your flat that you asked me to move into?'

Bethan drew in a deep breath. She *had* asked Callum to move in and it had been wonderful at first. She'd felt so relieved that she'd found someone to share her life with, though, looking back, relief probably wasn't the strongest emotion to build a future on. Her head throbbed again and she went to the window, looking into the zoo for the strength to speak out.

'I'm sorry, Callum.'

His eyes narrowed suspiciously.

'For what?'

She watched the baboons chasing each other happily around their rock and gritted her teeth.

'I don't think it's working between us.'

He stared at her, clearly astonished.

'You can't say that, Beth. You can't mean it. You're just feeling strange because you're away and we don't see each other every day.'

'And you won't come and see me.'

'Or you me,' he shot back.

It was a fair point. Bethan pictured herself flying back to her once-treasured flat and felt instantly tense. That wasn't right.

'What does that say, Callum? I think maybe we're... we're over.'

It sounded strange out loud but right too – a release. Callum, however, had gone very red and was spluttering like a child.

'Rubbish, Beth. You've just forgotten what we're like together. How good we are. Remember that time we went to Brighton for the weekend? And when we climbed Snowdon in fog so thick we couldn't even see our own hands by the time we got back down? Remember how much we laughed then? And when we got lost in that maze as the sun was going down and, in the end, we just found a dark corner and—'

'I remember, Callum.'

'Weren't those good times? Weren't we happy?'

He'd picked well, but those lone days weren't the point.

'We were,' she agreed. 'But what about all those other times you left me to come home alone from a night out because you wanted to party?'

'Is it my fault if you're a bit boring sometimes?'

She sucked in her breath.

'Or when I don't see you most of the weekend because you're at the footie?'

'You could come with me. A good girlfriend would want to support her boyfriend's team now and again.'

'My point exactly, Cal. I'm not a good girlfriend to you and maybe it's time to face up to it.'

He looked panicked.

'I don't want to "face up to it". There's nothing *to* face up to. We're fine.' He fidgeted on her sofa. 'Is this about that champagne bar? I'm sorry, Bethan. It was a stupid idea. I thought it would be romantic. I wanted to give you a good time, for us to party together. But you were right – we should have just stayed in and cuddled. We like cuddling, don't we?'

'We do. Or at least we did.'

'Is there someone else?'

'No!' That was true; she'd never cheat on him. Yet the fact she'd been tempted at all had shown her that things weren't right. 'Callum—'

'Is it the German thing? Is it because I can't speak the language? I could learn. I mean, I'm not the best at that sort of stuff. My French teacher told me I spoke French like a sheep with its head up another sheep's bum.'

'What? That's horrible.'

'It was a bit. She was right though – I was awful at it. Couldn't wait to drop it. But German might be different. It sounds more like English, right? The words don't all do that weird running into each other thing that the French have going on, so—'

'Callum, it's not about the German.'

'Then what can I do?'

He sounded so plaintive, so forlorn, and she looked at him sitting in her flat. She remembered the day he'd moved in, how exciting it had been, how grown-up they'd felt. She remembered clearing a space in the wardrobe for his clothes and a drawer in the bathroom for his toiletries, and loving the fact he was there when she came in at the end of the day. When had all that faded? She couldn't pinpoint the moment exactly but now she'd stepped away, it was abundantly clear that things had been going wrong between them way before she came to Berlin.

'It's not about having to *do* anything, Callum.'

'Well, of course it is. I love you, Bethie. I'm not letting you go, not like this. I'll come out again. Soon. We can talk properly. I won't make you go dancing in stupid loud bars, and I'll come round the zoo and listen to what you're doing with the animals, and—'

'Callum, don't.' It was heartbreaking listening to him quietly putting his finger on exactly what was wrong between them.

'Please just let me come and see you.'

'Are you sure you can afford the flight?' she snapped, but he looked so upset that she felt instantly bad. 'OK, maybe. But not quite yet. Let's take a little time to think about what we want in life, hey?'

'I know what I want,' he shot back. 'I want you. You're mine, Bethan. Everyone knows it.'

His ferocity stung.

'I'm not a possession, Callum.'

He rolled his eyes.

'Don't go all feminist on me. You know what I mean.'

Sadly, she thought that she did know and she didn't much like it, but her head was pounding again and she was too weary to push it further.

'Let's just take a few days to think things over, shall we? Then we can talk again.'

'Fine. But I'm not taking this lying down, Beth. You're mine and you know it.'

Then, suddenly, he was gone. She sank onto the bed, staring at her phone. Her screensaver came up – a picture of her and Callum, taken at a friend's wedding last summer. They looked great together, happy. She'd thought perhaps they'd be next up the aisle – now she could see that was just the way she'd longed for the story to go. She was annoyed at herself for not having the courage to finish it once and for all, and vowed to be firm next time. She was moving on and, although she didn't want to hurt him, she had to admit that ending it with him felt like a weight off her shoulders.

Flicking to her photos, she found a picture of herself and Ella standing with the Knautschke statue, laughing into the spring sunshine. Perfect. With one click of a button she'd replaced her screensaver so it no longer reproached her with what might have been, but celebrated what was. Her job at the zoo and her pursuit of her mother's lost history were what mattered to her now, and this morning she had a lady to talk to about some babies…

*

Ada settled into her chair in the canteen like a queen, folding her blanket neatly away and smoothing down her silver hair which, to Bethan's surprise, looked as straight and well-tended as her teeth. Max had been quick to join her when she'd texted that Ada was on her bench and now, as she queued up to get them all cakes, she watched him putting the old lady at her ease and even making her laugh.

The tension of her conversation with Callum eased a little, only to be replaced by nerves. Ada might have the answer to the mystery of her mother's list and the excitement of that felt all-consuming. Bethan almost willed the queue to slow down and prolong this moment of possibility, but that was ridiculous. Soon, tray laden with frothy coffees and slabs of carrot, coffee and chocolate cake, she joined the other two at the table.

'Which cake would you like, Adelaide?'

Ada looked up, startled by the name, but then gave a funny little smile and said, 'No one's called me that for years. It's a girl's name, isn't it? A pretty name. Not right for an old hag like me.'

'You're not a "hag", Ada.'

She chuckled.

'I'm old though. Too old for Adelaide.'

'But you *were* Adelaide?' Bethan pushed, handing her the chocolate cake she was pointing out. 'And you had a sister, yes – Hanna.'

Ada froze, cake halfway to her mouth. Her cloudy eyes locked onto Bethan's and for a moment she thought she was going to speak, but then she started shaking her head violently from side to side.

'No sister. No. No Hanna.'

Her voice was rising and Bethan looked nervously around the canteen, but Max was already leaning towards the old lady.

'No Hanna. Of course not, Ada. Don't worry about it. Here, try your cake. It's delicious. And so's mine. Would you like some of mine as well?' It worked. Ada zoned in on Max's coffee cake and calmed. Bethan took a deep breath and for a little time they all just ate their cake and sipped their coffee and talked of nothing. Then Max put a hand over Ada's and said, 'You lived here, didn't you, Ada? You lived here during the war?' Ada's fingers picked at the crumbs on her plate, darting out at them like a hen pecking in the dirt, and dabbing them onto her tongue. She gave a sharp nod. 'It must have been hard, then?'

'Hard?' She glared at him. 'You have no idea, young man.'

'I don't,' he agreed meekly. 'You must have had to take great care of the animals?'

'Great care,' Ada agreed. 'Very great care. I looked after them. I gave them their milk. I held them when they cried.'

Max glanced at Bethan.

'Who, Ada? Who did you hold?'

Ada banged her hand down on the table suddenly.

'The babies.' She looked from Max to Bethan and back to Max. 'I looked after the babies. Someone had to, didn't they? Someone had to keep them safe.'

'That was you? That's amazing, Ada.'

She softened.

'I was good with them. That's what Kätsche said. I was a "natural".' Her voice had taken on an almost childish lilt, as if she were back there. Bethan forced herself to breathe slowly and not to push her but the truth felt tantalisingly close.

'These babies, Ada, were they were with you here, in Berlin?'

'Here, yes. At first.'

'And then?'

'Then they had to go, didn't they? It wasn't safe, whatever we did. It wasn't my fault. Kätsche said it wasn't my fault. It was the Russians. It was their fault – the Red Army. They did bad things to babies, everyone knew that, so we had to get them out.'

'Out to where?' Max asked, but Ada shook her head fiercely.

'I can't tell you that, can I? Then they wouldn't be safe.'

She crossed her arms and kicked at the table leg with her purple boot, making the remaining cake crumbs shake on their plates. She was working herself up and people were looking over.

'Of course you can't,' Bethan agreed swiftly. 'Well done, Ada. Of course you can't.' The old woman seemed to relax a little and, fingers crossed in her lap, she asked her softly, 'Whose babies were they, Ada?'

'Whose?' The woman stared at her as if she was stupid. 'What do you mean whose?'

'Who were the mothers?' Max weighed in.

Ada spun round to him, tutting crossly.

'Stupid question, young man. You should know that.'

'I should? Why? Why should I know that, Ada?'

But Ada's face had gone dark red and she pointed a bony finger accusingly at him.

'Because, you fool, they're your babies now.'

Max stared at her.

'The babies were… were chimps?'

Ada tutted again.

'Well, of course they were. My lovely hairy little babies. They loved me. They all loved me. They'd jump into my arms. They'd play with my hair. They'd give me great big kisses with their great big lips. And they had to go. The Russians made them go. The Russians made us all go!'

Her voice had risen again and her words morphed into incoherence. Max battled to keep her quiet as Bethan ran for more cake, her heart pounding harder than it had before. They'd upset poor Ada and all for the sake of some chimp babies. Max had been right when he'd told her not to get her hopes up, but she'd done it anyway and the fall back down to earth was horribly painful.

She'd dumped her boyfriend, buoyed up by this quest, and now it had popped, the reality of her situation threatened to drown her weary mind. Her mother's precious list seemed as unfathomable as it had back when she'd first found it hidden beneath her jewellery all those years ago, and Bethan couldn't help but wonder if she would ever find the answers she was looking for.

'Sorry, Mum,' she whispered, not for the first time.

You'll do it, sweetheart, Jana's voice seemed to say back. Bethan shook her head – her mother had always had more faith in her than she deserved. She just prayed she was right.

Chapter Sixteen

January 1945

'How do I look?'

Lutz, resplendent in full dinner jacket, stepped into the kitchens where the Zoofamilie were cobbling together an evening meal. They all turned and he plucked slightly self-consciously at his bow-tie.

'Very smart,' Oskar said.

'Like a Golden Pheasant,' Katharina muttered.

'Sorry, Katharina?'

'Nothing, Lutz. I hope you have a lovely time at Goebbels's lovely film. How much did it cost to make again?'

'Nearly eight million Reichsmarks,' Ursula supplied, shuffling on her chair to try and get comfy. She was due at any moment and enormous. Katharina had battled throughout January to persuade her to leave Berlin on one of Oskar's transports, but she would have none of it.

'Pierre cannot leave, so I cannot leave,' was all she would say. 'Besides, what's the point? This could go on for years. We can't just put our lives on hold whilst those in power sort themselves out.'

It was a fair point, but there came a time when the risk was just too high and Katharina was pretty sure they'd reached it. She'd hoped that the war might be over by Christmas but the snows had come, digging both the attacking and defending armies into entrenched positions, and they all seemed to be in limbo. For a brief moment in the middle of December there had been a flurry of genuine excitement as Hitler's generals had launched a surprise attack on the Americans in the Ardennes, but it had lasted all of a week before the Amis had regrouped. Now the poor brigades were back where they'd started minus 80,000 men, myriad planes and most of their fuel reserves.

Here in the capital, the air raids, which had dropped off at the darkest point of the winter, were back with a vengeance. The planes came earlier than ever and sometimes twice a night so that it was impossible to rest. Katharina didn't think that Ursula was right about it dragging on. The spring of 1945 would bring not new life, but her country's final death, and yet here were the architects of their downfall heading off to the cinema for the launch of Goebbels's stupid film.

Kolberg was the tale of a plucky Prussian village holding out against their enemies in the Napoleonic wars and was being trumpeted to the skies by Goebbels, as if this one pathetic film would give everyone the courage for a glorious reversal. It was a nonsense. Defence took more than courage; it took troops and supplies and weapons, none of which they had any more.

'Which cinema is it being shown in again?' Katharina asked, all innocence.

Lutz glared at her.

'You know very well that it's at the Lichtspiele on Alexanderplatz, Katharina.'

'Ah, of course. Because the glorious Palast am Zoo is blown to bits – much like the glorious zoo itself.'

'Katharina, you do yourself a disservice,' Lutz said stiffly. 'The film is made and made well, I am told, so why not show it to the people?'

'Why not indeed? But the "people" aren't going to see it, are they? Because there's only one cinema still standing in Berlin and because, unless they are Golden Pheasants with vast, well-appointed bunkers beneath their enormous homes, they are far too busy mounting their own "plucky defence" to go and watch someone else do it.'

'Katharina, enough!' Lutz glared at her. 'There is no point in sniping negativity.'

'And no point in senseless positivity either,' she shot back, but Oskar was going scarlet at her side so she reined herself in. 'No matter, Lutz. Go, enjoy your shiny film with your shiny friends.'

'My "shiny friends" who are ensuring this zoo is provided with just about enough food to keep what animals we have left alive. That does not happen without the greatest cajoling, Katharina. Perhaps you should think about climbing down off your naive high horse and seeing how vital it is that we keep in favour with those who hold power of life and death over the creatures you claim to care for.'

Katharina flushed; he had a point.

'I'm sorry, Lutz. It's not easy, I know. It's just that a grand premiere seems a strange thing to be having at the moment.'

Lutz sighed.

'It does,' he conceded, 'but what can we do? A word of praise to the Reich Minister could mean enough meat to keep the lion cubs alive for another month.'

'Then good luck.'

Luckily at that moment Rita arrived, beautiful in a sequined gown that was only a little loose on her war-trimmed frame, and Lutz was able to take her arm and leave. Katharina watched him go, unsure what to think.

'I bet he loves hobnobbing with them all, however he dresses it up.'

'Of course he does,' Gisela agreed, shelling snow peas.

She and Dieter had sealed up what they could of the blasted aquarium and were growing early vegetables in its relative heat. The snow peas were the first of their crop but they had radishes, broccoli and kale on the way, and the taste of fresh veg was very welcome after a winter of dried-up stores.

'Whilst the party are still in charge, someone has to keep them on our side,' Robert put in.

He was sitting at Gisela's side feeding barley porridge to Hanna, now six months old and sitting up in her high chair, looking happily from adult to adult as if it was perfectly normal for various households to all be eating together in a half-bombed canteen. Which for her, of course, it was.

'Do they though?' Katharina challenged.

Robert looked at her.

'What would you rather?'

Katharina lifted her knife and brought it down, hard, on the rabbit she was chopping for the pot. The zoo, like many others in the city, had taken to breeding the prolific creatures to supplement their increasingly meagre rations. Adelaide loved them, and had learned the trick of sitting so silent and still beneath the trees that they would come right up and take bread from her hand – when they had bread, of course. No one had yet told her where her dinner came from and Katharina prayed that no one ever would, for she would certainly refuse it and she needed all the nourishment she could get.

'Surely,' she said carefully, 'if we all just bow down and do as we're told, they will continue with their orders until they grind us into oblivion.'

'Oblivion?' Adelaide queried.

Oskar gave Katharina a stern look and she bit her lip.

'I just mean, sweetheart, that sometimes it is a good idea to question what you are being asked to do. Not rudely but assertively.'

'Sometimes,' Pierre said, 'it is. But it very much depends on whether the person you are questioning is reasonable or not.'

At his side Ursula let out a guttural noise that made them all jump.

'Sorry, Ursula?' Gisela asked. Her friend wasn't usually given to political protest.

'Oooww!' Ursula said in reply.

For a moment they all stared at her, then everyone leaped up at once.

'The baby!' Pierre cried. 'The baby is coming.'

*

Ursula's birthing, thank the Lord, was nothing like Sasha's. They hustled her into the bunker and Katharina tried to block out the images of her dear friend's blood across those same sheets six months ago. She clearly failed miserably for Ursula looked at her and said, 'Cheer up, Kätsche. I promise I'm not going to die.'

'Of course you're not,' she agreed crisply, not quite daring to believe it, but Ursula was amazing.

She paced the little bunker room between contractions, up and down, up and down, and when they came, she braced herself against the wall and panted like a dog until they subsided. The labour moved fast – 'That's me,' Ursula joked through gritted teeth, 'always in a hurry' – and in the pause between raids, she pragmatically announced, 'It's coming now,' and kneeled up on the bed.

'Don't you want to lie down?' Gisela asked.

'Lord, no! You've seen how the monkeys do it.'

Katharina thought of the chimps and baboons she'd seen giving birth. Ursula was right – they crouched down, often on a precariously high rock, and pushed the baby out, usually reaching round to ease it out themselves, though sometimes one of the other females assisted.

'But they're monkeys, Ursula.'

'So they don't have bossy midwives telling them what to do just because someone's decided it's more decorous. I've thought about it a lot and if it works for them, it'll work for me.'

'Very well,' Katharina said, hands up, and it certainly did work for Ursula. The contractions came fast and hard, and she pushed down with all her might. After only three such pushes, Katharina could see the baby crowning.

'You're doing it, Ursula!' she cried. 'One more push.'

Ursula nodded, braced herself up against the bedstead, and when the next contraction came, bore down hard, filling the bunker with her determined roar. The baby's head emerged and, like a seal diving, the rest of the body slipped easily out onto the sheets between her knees. They all stared as the baby opened its mouth, drew in a deep breath and wailed, pure and true. Ursula swept it up into her arms and covered it in kisses.

'A girl,' she said, drawing back to look down at her baby. 'We have a little girl. Where's Pierre?'

'Don't you want to clean up?' Gisela suggested, looking at her friend's bloody shift and damp face. But Ursula just laughed.

'Come now, Gigi, he saw me all sweaty when he put her inside me, so he can surely cope now that she's out?'

Gisela threw her hands up and Katharina, smiling, went round the curtain to fetch Pierre. He was already hovering and rushed to her, kissing each cheek, as she told him he had a daughter.

'A daughter! God be praised, a daughter. Let me in – let me at them.' He bundled Katharina aside like a man in a rugby match and made a dive for the bed. 'Oh, my beautiful girl,' he said, clasping Ursula tight. 'My beautiful *girls*. We will call her Beatrice, yes, my love?' Ursula nodded, and Pierre beamed and looked around at the others. 'It means bringer of joy – something we all need in these dark times. Truly, I am truly the luckiest man alive.'

Katharina looked around the dirty bunker, crammed with the few things any of them had left in their possession, and blessed him for his happiness. He was right, this new life had brought joy, although there were still things to fight for, and she had to curb her rising cynicism and remember this moment to carry her through the weeks ahead.

Just two days later, however, her briefly rejected cynicism was rewarded with a direct hit on the Lichtspiele cinema, blasting the midday showing of *Kolberg* into a million celluloid pieces. The same plane, continuing its run of deadly bullets, blew the roof off the Hecks' villa at the heart of the zoo. Lutz, luckily, was working with Robert in the zebra house at the time and Rita was queuing at the grocer's store two streets away, so they were safe but it felt like a sign all the same.

'God,' as Katharina could not resist saying to Oskar, 'clearly did not like *Kolberg*.'

To Rita she was kinder, offering to put the couple up in their own apartment whilst they looked for somewhere more permanent. Oskar looked at her wide-eyed, clearly anticipating friction, but Rita thankfully said that Lutz was talking to friends about finding them somewhere.

'Maybe,' Katharina said to her, 'you could go and stay with Göring up on Schorf Moor. You could look after the cattle.'

Rita looked at her sideways, clearly unsure what to say, but she must have reported the suggestion to Lutz who came to find her later in the chimp house.

'Why are you being mean to my wife, Katharina?'

'Good afternoon to you too, Lutz.'

'Why?'

She went across to him, a baby chimp on her shoulder.

'In what way "mean", Lutz?'

'Teasing her about living with the cattle.'

Katharina rolled her eyes.

'I suggested you move up to Schorf Moor with your great friend the Reichsmarschall, that's all.'

'He is not my "great friend", Katharina.'

'A friend all the same, surely? He must have lots of space up there. I hear that his house has twenty bedrooms so he could spare one for you and Rita.'

'What about the zoo?'

'We'll look after it.'

Lutz's eyes narrowed in his thin face, dingo-like.

'Is that what this is about, Katharina? Are you trying to get rid of me? Trying to seize the zoo for yourself?'

'No!' Katharina was genuinely shocked. 'Of course not, Lutz. There is precious little left to "seize" anyway.'

'And there will be precious little more very soon.'

'What do you mean?'

'I am going to ask Oskar to arrange to ship the chimps out.'

'What?' She stared at him, horrified. 'Lutz, no. The chimps are fine. Their house is solid and we've dug them out more space under the rocks so they can hide when the planes come. Not one has been injured in the last six months.'

'Things are getting worse, Katharina, you've said so yourself. You do not believe that our beloved Führer can keep the city safe, so why do you want your precious chimps to stay here?'

She stared at him and he smiled sweetly at her. He had turned the tables and suddenly the direct hit on *Kolberg* was looking like a direct hit on herself as well.

'Please, Lutz, don't.'

'It's the only responsible thing to do, Katharina.'

'Not all of them. Not the pregnant ones. We have even more babies due than last year and they'll need me.'

He looked her up and down.

'You and I know, Katharina, that monkeys need no one when they are birthing. They pop their little ones out as easily as Ursula did. This protest is not for their sakes but for your own.' He leaned in so close she could see the red veins in his eyes. 'They are not *your* babies, Katharina, and you cannot pretend that any longer.'

'Pretend?' she gasped, but Lutz was gone, striding out of the cage without a backward glance.

He let himself out and then turned back to look at her through the bars.

'Of course,' he said, 'if you care about them that much, Katharina, you can go with them yourself. Take all the women and children you profess to care for. I believe Oskar has found a lovely place in Torgau run by Countess Sylvie von Weichs. Very rural. Very peaceful. Perfect really, but it's quite a long trip. The chimps will need someone with them – why not you?'

'But the zoo...'

'Oh, don't worry, Katharina, we'll look after it.'

He gave her a sly smile and then marched off, leaving her stuck in the cage, glaring out of the bars as he rapped off down the avenue and was gone.

That night she lay in Oskar's arms thinking over Lutz's words. No planes had come at the usual 8 p.m. slot and perhaps for once they would have a night in their own bed. The Hecks had been given a nice house a few streets away and were probably being feted there with wine from some party official's personal cellar right now. And why not? Lutz was doing his best for his personal comfort and perhaps she should think about that more herself. 'Take all the women and children you profess to care for,' he had thrown at her, but she had to admit that he had a point – and not just about the women and children.

'Oskar,' she said into the darkness, 'where is Torgau?'

She felt him shift next to her and knew that, were it not for the blackout, he would be searching her face to try and gauge her thoughts.

'It's in Saxony, meine Kindl. On the banks of the Elbe. Why do you ask?'

'Lutz says you have found a house there that might take the chimps.'

'Aaah. And you do not like that idea?'

'I do not see the need for it,' she agreed stiffly. 'He also suggested that I go with them.'

'Did he?' She heard the surprise in his voice. 'Why did he suggest that?'

'I think he's probably fed up of me.'

Oskar gave a small chuckle.

'Who can blame him. You are forever needling him, Kätsche.'

'Because he is forever sucking up to the Golden Pheasants.'

'In order to keep the zoo open.'

'In order to further his own career! But that doesn't matter now, O. I've been thinking about the idea.'

'Of going to Saxony?'

Now Oskar sounded astounded. She reached over and turned on the bedside light, covered in red film to dim it, despite the blackout blinds at the window.

'He says it's very rural.'

'It is.'

'Very peaceful.'

'I imagine so.'

'Oskar...' She wasn't sure how to put this, but really there was no other way than straight out: 'Oskar, you will be seventy-four in two months' time. You are frail.'

'I am not!'

'Not in yourself, my gorgeous man, but your body is not as strong as it once was. I hear your breath rattling in your throat when you sleep and I see the way you hunch over your little notebook as if trying to shield your lungs. I worry about you.'

'You need not.'

'But I do. Life is hard here and it is only going to get harder. The Russians are coming and you have heard what Dieter says of them. You have heard what they did to Ursula's cousin and a thousand others like her.'

'I am not a woman.'

'No. But I am. And will you be able to defend me if they come?'

Oskar sucked in his breath.

'Katharina! That's not fair.'

'I know, O, but it's the truth and maybe it's time we faced it. I will not be able to defend you either, my love, and if anything happened to you it would break my heart. Then there's Adelaide to think about, and the babies, not to mention their mothers. Maybe we should give up on this damned war, take the Zoofamilie with the chimps to the countryside and wait for it all to be over?'

He looked at her and she could see in his eyes that he was tempted. She thought of rolling hills and green fields, of the rich River Elbe, of farmland full of fresh food, and skies empty of planes. It seemed impossibly idyllic.

'Give up on the war?' Oskar asked.

'Maybe.'

'And give up on the zoo?'

Those words hit her like a punch in the stomach. They sounded so stark, so cruel. She thought of Pongo the gorilla, who beat his chest at her whenever she went to see him. She thought of the lion cubs, Sultan and Bussy, tumbling around together as if beating each other was the only problem the world had to offer. She thought of Robert's zebras and Lutz's precious baboons and the chimps she had come to love as her own.

'We can't, can we, O?'

He kissed her.

'*I* can't. I've been here for forty-four years, meine kindl, and I must stay here. Until the end if that's what it takes. But you can go. Maybe you *should* go. The women all look to you as a mother, so perhaps we must now let you mother them.'

'And leave you?'

'If it's what it takes to keep them safe.'

Katharina's gut twisted. She felt her responsibilities to the women and children keenly, but how could she leave her beloved husband?

'Let's think on it more.' She turned off the red light, then reached for him in the dark. 'Hold me, Oskar,' she murmured, running a hand down his chest.

He clasped her to him and covered her lips with his own, and suddenly his body didn't feel so frail and she wanted him with an urgency that pounded through her. Raising herself up, she pushed him onto his back and straddled him.

And at that moment, the air-raid sirens screamed out.

Chapter Seventeen

Bethan paused for a moment, hands on her thighs as she caught her breath. She looked down the long avenue at the centre of the zoo, delighted to see that almost overnight the blossom had come out on the trees. It wasn't even May yet but it seemed that summer came earlier in Germany, and with the sun lifting over the horizon and tingeing the white flowers a glorious pink, the world felt like a blessed place.

She'd been running every morning for several weeks now, the warmer days making it seem slightly less difficult to force herself out of bed early, and she was getting quite into it. Treading the streets of the city just as everyone else was rising had enabled her to see far more of it than when it was heaving with life, and she was starting to feel more and more at home here. Plus, turning back into the zoo was still a thrill and she felt herself, as she so often did, wishing her mum were alive so she could tell her about it.

Jana would have loved that she was working here. She'd have been out to visit her and taken her to see places that had meant things to her in her childhood. She'd have shown her where she went to school, her sports fields, the bars she'd drunk in as a teenager. She'd have shown her where she bought her first make-up, where she kissed her first boyfriend, where she sat her exams. She'd have taken her to the bar Paul had walked into and asked her for the drink that would lead to them committing their lives to each other. And eventually she'd have talked to her about Oma Erika's revelation and they would have hunted down their shared DNA together.

Bethan straightened, telling herself not to dwell on what might have been. It invariably just made her sadder and what was the point in that? She glanced at her watch. If she hurried, there'd be time to call her dad before she went on duty and talk to him about her progress – or the lack of it.

Sometimes, especially if she couldn't sleep at night, she would try to picture what Paul and Jana had been like together. Her memories were hazy but specifics stuck out: coming downstairs to find them cuddling in the kitchen; lying in bed listening to them laughing; seeing them hold hands across the handbrake when they went on trips. She was fascinated by a partnership that had been so wonderful Paul had not been able to contemplate sharing his life with anyone else since. It hadn't been like that with Callum. She could see that now and was glad she'd finally had the courage to end it. Guiltily reminding herself that she hadn't fully drawn a line under her relationship, she resolved to call him later and picked up her feet to jog back to the apartment block.

The seals were chasing each other around their pool, scooting up and over their slippery little island for the pure joy of it, and she laughed to see them play. Next door the penguins were coming out for their morning waddle, bumping into each other comically, as half asleep as Bethan had been at the start of her run.

'Morning!' she called cheerily to them, and got a couple of laconic squawks in reply.

She turned down past the pandas, still apparently fast asleep, round the antelopes and giraffes, grazing in the early sun, and past the primate house. She couldn't help looking into the cage to see if Max was at work yet and, sure enough, there was his dark head in the middle of the chattering chimps.

'Morning, Max.'

'Morning, Beth. Putting us all to shame?'

'No way. Just trying to get even half as fit as the rest of you.'

He laughed.

'You can come in here and swing around the trees with Binky and her crew if you fancy it – that'll soon trim you up.' He flushed. 'Not that you're not trim already. You are. Very. That is...'

She spared him.

'Thanks, Max, but I'm definitely not up to the monkey bars yet. See you later.'

'Yep. I've got this afternoon off so I might go and dig the rest of those old files out of the office. Cindi texted me yesterday to say she'd found another box.'

That stopped her. She stared at him, her heart beating at the thought of another chance at digging out some clues.

'Give me a shout when you find them, and if I'm free I'll come and join you.'

'Will do. And Bethan – don't worry. We'll figure this out one way or another!'

He gave her a wink and, spirits lifting instantly, she nodded her thanks and made for the apartment block, determined to get on with her work as fast as possible so she could join Max later.

As usual, however, the zoo threw a curveball at her, in the shape of Reina going into labour. The lioness had apparently sneaked away into her specially prepared den at about the time Bethan was jogging around the zoo. The keepers had been keeping an eye on her via a hidden camera, and at around four in the afternoon the first cub appeared. Tanya called Bethan in to watch and she was utterly rapt at seeing the tiny, blind thing stagger over to suckle from its mother – until she noticed the dark spots across its back.

'Oh my god, it's a leopard!' She looked to Tanya, already wondering how on earth the zoo could have made such a blatant breeding error, but her boss was doubled over with helpless laughter. 'It's not funny, Tanya. What will management say?'

Tanya flapped at her with a hand but still seemed too convulsed with mirth to speak, and it was one of the lion keepers who told her: 'Baby lions are always born with spots. Don't worry, they fade after a few months.'

Bethan was mortified. Staring at the cub, she dredged her memory for a point when she might have learned that but could come up with nothing. All the same, having known Reina was pregnant, it would have been sensible to do a bit of research and she felt a total fool.

'Tanya, I'm so sorry. I should have known. I—'

Tanya flapped her hand again and this time found the breath to reply.

'Don't worry about it, Beth. I made the same mistake myself when I was first here. I happened to see the camera when I was on my own one evening and had all the keepers out of bed in a total panic. I wasn't popular, I can tell you. Ooh, look – here comes number two.'

A little consoled, Bethan moved next to her boss to watch as a second cub was birthed. Reina seemed calm and the baby dropped easily into the hay – and did not move. Bethan stared, but didn't dare say anything after her last mistake. It was clear, however, from how everyone else in the room froze that this was far from normal, and she found herself crossing her fingers behind her back to will the fragile creature into life.

'It's not breathing,' Clara, the head keeper, choked out.

'What can we do?' Bethan asked, looking around for her bag, but Tanya gave a shake of her head, all laughter drained out of her now.

'There's nothing we can do.'

'But—'

'We can't go into the cage. Reina would rip us apart. And we can't tranquilise her because it will be terrible for any cubs she may still have to birth. We just have to watch and pray, and let nature take its course.'

Bethan bit her lip. She wasn't religious but she prayed now, as she'd only ever prayed for her dying mum. Reina licked at her baby but still it did not move. Time seemed to tick by with a dark, slow beat, and then suddenly the cub twitched. Its tiny pink mouth opened and with a squeak it sniffed at the air. Reina was swift to act, moving in to lick it again, and the small group on the other side of the camera watched with bated breath as the baby stuck out its paws and shuffled round to find a teat.

'She did it!' Bethan cried.

She felt instantly uncool, but it didn't matter because everyone else was cheering and hugging and Clara was crying and she knew, more than ever before, that she was in exactly the right place, doing exactly the right work – and that she never wanted to leave. She shivered and backed off from the others, suddenly feeling an outsider to their joy. She was only here for a year, she reminded herself, and then she was going home. It wouldn't do to get too attached, to—

'Look!' Tanya squealed. 'She's having a third.'

And that was that – Bethan was lost again. And why not? She was watching a lioness give birth and it would be wrong not to make the most of this precious moment.

She staggered out of the observation room at around 11 p.m., tired but invigorated, and looked down at her phone – three missed calls from Max and a text saying, *Call me*. She was instantly wide awake and, pulling up his number, she pressed dial. Only on the third ring did she realise quite how late it was, and she was about to hang up when he answered.

'Beth?'

'Sorry, Max. I didn't realise—'

'Don't worry, don't worry. I'm awake anyway. I've found a notebook with records of shipments into and out of the zoo during the war. It's fascinating. Do you want to see it?'

'Yes! Let me just grab a sandwich and I'll be straight over.'

'You've not eaten?'

'No. Reina gave birth.'

'Amazing! How many?'

'Four in the end. All gorgeous. And all healthy – though it was touch and go with one for a while.'

'Sorry. You must be worn out. This can wait.'

'But *I* can't. I'll come, honestly.'

'Great, but don't worry about the sandwich. I made a curry earlier and there's loads left.'

'Curry?' Bethan's stomach sang. 'I'm there!'

By the time she knocked on Max's door, a delicious scent of Indian cooking was wafting out of it.

'That is perhaps the most divine thing I've smelled in ages,' she said.

'What about this?' he countered, wafting a glass of fruity Shiraz under her nose. She snatched at it.

'That is the second most divine thing I've smelled in ages. Thanks, Max.'

She took a deep drink, feeling the alcohol hit the back of her throat and head straight into her brain. Max stirred the curry and she leaned back against the units and took another sip. It was slowly sinking in just how privileged she'd been to witness the birth today and she felt almost tearfully appreciative – probably not helped by the glass of wine she seemed to have almost drunk already.

'Did you need that?' Max asked, topping her up.

'I guess so. Sorry, I haven't brought anything with me.'

'No problem. You're my guest.'

'Thanks. I'll cook next time.'

There was a moment's pause between them, then Max chinked his glass against hers and said, 'Great,' and it passed.

'So,' she asked, 'where are these files?'

'In here.'

Max dished curry into a bowl then led her through into his living room. Papers were laid out all across his coffee table and in the centre was a small red leather notebook. Max waved her to the sofa then took a seat next to her. The cushions were squishy and tipped the pair of them close against each other.

'Sorry.'

'It's fine.'

It was. Max's leg was long and she could see the definition of his thigh muscles beneath his trackies. She was grateful her mornings of jogging had tightened her own a little, and tried to ignore the warmth that the proximity of his body sent rushing through her. It was probably just the wine. And the curry.

'This is excellent,' she said, focusing on spooning food into her happy stomach. 'What's in it?'

'Sweet potato, mushroom and chickpea. Oh, and quite a lot of chillies,' he added, as she bit into one and her eyes watered.

'So I see,' she spluttered.

'I hope you like it hot?'

'I do.' She took another glug of her wine to chase the spice down and turned to the notebook. 'Can I look at it?'

'Of course!'

Carefully she set her bowl down amongst the papers and picked up the notebook. The first page was headed: 'Zoo shipments, January 1944'. The writing was clear and precise and beneath it was a name: 'Oskar Heinroth'. Bethan gasped.

'Katharina's husband?'

'I believe so. He was the aquarium manager until it was bombed into non-existence in November 1943. Katharina came to the zoo when she married him.'

'And she ended up running it?'

'Yep. She must have been quite a woman. By all accounts she was tiny – not much over five foot and with fiery red hair.'

Bethan's hands went to her own strawberry blonde locks. Not exactly ginger, but not far off in the right light.

'Did she have any children?'

'Not that Google knows of. And she lived for a long time after the war, so why would she give them away if she did?'

'Good point. Her name's on the list though.'

'So we can't rule her out, no. Now, look – this is the detail of every animal who went out of the zoo from January 1944. It was quite an enterprise, by the looks of it. Sometimes just one or two animals to a private house, sometimes a whole group of them. There were animals coming into the zoo as well – usually parrots and other house-birds made homeless by the bombing.'

'Any mention of people travelling?'

He screwed up his nose, looking dangerously cute, and Bethan shifted on the sofa. It would be madness to rush from one relationship straight into another; she needed a little time for herself right now.

'Oskar, sadly, doesn't seem to have been that stupid. Occasionally a keeper is listed but there's certainly nothing in here that says, "plus one human baby, female".'

She nudged him.

'OK, OK. I guess that would have been too much to hope for.'

'The only thing we can do is note where the shipments went to towards the end of the war, and then try to research those places in case we can turn up any stories.'

'Right.'

Bethan tried to sound enthusiastic but her head swam suddenly at the enormity of the task. Her fingers went to her hippo brooch – the one concrete link between her mum and Berlin Zoo – but it felt cold and hard and stubbornly unfathomable.

'Bethan? Bethan, are you OK?'

Max's fingers gently grasped her chin and he turned her face to look at him.

'I'm OK. It just seems… so difficult. Is it worth it, do you think, Max?'

His blue eyes shone.

'Of course it is, Beth. We've got time, haven't we? There's no rush. Your grandmother has been hiding in the past for years. She's not going anywhere, so we can just work our way through all this and eventually something will come up.'

'We?'

'If you want me to, of course. You can just take the notebook, if you'd rather.'

'No! God no, Max. I'm so grateful that you're happy to help.'

'Of course I am.'

'Why?'

Max bit his lip. His eyes were bluer than ever as he looked into hers, and then his head was dipping towards her and she felt herself lean in towards him. Every fibre of her being was tuned into the feel of his leg against hers, his fingers gently clasping her chin, his lips dipping close to her own.

'Max,' she murmured, and then her phone bleeped and, remembering she was meant to be taking time for herself, she yanked back.

'Sorry,' he said straight away. 'Oh God, sorry, Bethan. That was wrong of me. You're tired. You've had a lot of wine. I didn't mean to, to take advantage.'

He looked stricken and she put out a hand to him.

'You didn't, Max. I wanted… Oh… Look, I better go, yeah? Thanks for the curry and the wine and the notebook. It's amazing, really. But it's, you know, late and, and…'

'I know,' he said gently. 'Shall I see you home?'

'Down the corridor?' They both smiled and the tension eased. 'I think I'll manage.'

'Right. Good. Gute Nacht then, Beth.'

She looked at him, standing there so tall and handsome and vulnerable-looking, and nearly stepped back into his arms, but that wasn't right. She had to tell Callum it was definitely over before she went rushing into a late-night kiss with a colleague.

'Gute Nacht, Max. And thank you again.'

'My pleasure.'

He gave her a little wave as she escaped out of his door and then, as she steadied herself in the corridor, she heard him groan on the other side and a soft thud as he, presumably, battered himself over the head with a cushion. She pressed her head against the smooth coolness of the wall, dizzy with all the changes in her normally steady life. But then she thought of the women on her list, battling for their lives as the enemy closed in around them. Really, her problems were nothing in comparison.

Chapter Eighteen

25 April 1945

'It's a girl! Oh Gisela, it's a beautiful girl.'

Katharina watched in awe as Ursula lifted the tiny newborn from between Gisela's legs, carefully cut the cord, and handed her to her mother. Gisela held her close, pressing her up against her face to kiss her.

'She's here. She's really here.' She looked tired but ecstatic. It had been a long labour but smooth enough, and already the colour was returning to Gisela's cheeks. 'Thank you, ladies. What would I have done without you?'

'Exactly the same,' Katharina said with a laugh, but she knew what Gisela meant.

This felt like a blessed female moment and she looked around the little circle, honoured to have been a part of it. Ursula was at Gisela's side, resting her three-month-old daughter Beatrice on the bed to say hello to the younger baby. Adelaide was next to Katharina, nine-month-old Hanna on her hip, and Katharina put an arm around them both.

'Three daughters for the Zoofamilie,' she said softly. 'We are blessed.'

'I wish Mutti was here to see,' Adelaide said, scrubbing tears from her eyes.

Katharina bent down and stilled her hand.

'It's all right to cry, Addie. It means you care and it's good to care. I wish Sasha was here too, truly I do, but she is looking over us and smiling at all these pretty girls.'

'Perhaps it is Sash who told them not to come out male,' Ursula said. 'And very wise too. The city belongs to women at the moment.'

Katharina shivered at the truth of that, though they saw precious little beyond this bunker now. The Russians had exploded into the suburbs three days ago and the final, bitter battle was being fought all around them. Shells and bombs tore up the streets of Germany's once elegant capital at all hours, carelessly snatching away the lives of any citizens foolish enough to venture out. The women of the zoo, plus a large number of others who had lost their homes in the streets nearby, were living permanently underground, and dirty days leached into over-lit nights so that no one ever truly slept.

The only man in the bunker was Oskar and he was scarcely awake enough to count. Katharina's dear husband had taken a piece of shell in his calf when crossing the zoo to feed Pongo, and it was festering. His temperature had risen alarmingly and she could only pray that his body was fighting the infection, for she had little more than some aloe lotion and a few bandages stripped off the bottom of her dress to help him. She had begged him to let her get him across to the flak tower hospital, but he'd insisted that there were more important patients than him.

'Not to me,' she'd snapped.

Yesterday she'd braved the shells to go and ask for help, but the tower had been crammed with people so that even getting up the stairs to the hospital floor had seemed impossible. Men had been coming in on stretchers all the time, limbs blown off and faces torn to pieces, and she'd seen the truth of what Oskar had said – not that her precious husband was less important, but that he wouldn't stand a chance of being seen. It was then, standing amidst the screaming hubbub of a pointless war, that she'd made a decision – she had to get the Zoofamilie out, all of them.

Before his injury Oskar had organised a transport to take the chimps to Torgau, and there had been heated debate about who should go with them. Ursula had insisted she was up to managing the escape party, but Beatrice was only three months old and, with so little food, even rumbustious Ursula had struggled to regain full health. How could she cope with her own baby, plus lively Hanna, fast-growing Adelaide and heavily pregnant Gisela? Pierre would gladly have gone, but men always attracted the attention of the guards and it was a risk too far for them all.

'You will have to go,' Oskar had told Katharina.

'But the animals…'

'Are surely not more important than the people?'

Katharina had known he was right, but there had still been the matter of the one person who was the most important to her in the whole world – Oskar himself. She'd been secretly glad when the truck had not turned up, sparing her a terrible decision, but now that the Red Army were upon them, she cursed her foolishness. She had to find a transport, but how? What fool would drive into the mouth of Hades?

The only vehicles that had made it through in the last week had been those of the party officials, who'd all fled the city that they had ordered everyone else to defend to their last breath. Three days ago – the day Lutz had finally closed the zoo to visitors – Katharina had seen a parade of fine vehicles heading down Hardenbergstrasse towards the south, and known that the Pheasants were leaving the sinking ship. The transport lorry the zoo had been relying on had been requisitioned to have an anti-aircraft gun mounted on its flimsy roof, whilst those in charge of this disaster drove smoothly away in Mercedes luxury.

She'd have yanked them out of one and driven it herself if she could have done, but at the time she'd been caught up in a scrum around the market, where it had been rumoured that a supply of butter had come in. She'd stood there, closed in by desperately hungry people fighting over pats of butter, and watched the men who'd done this to them glide past behind their tinted windows. For perhaps the first time in her life she'd known hate. True hate.

'She's feeding!'

Gisela's happy cry brought Katharina back to the present, and she watched the baby suckle and tried to lose herself in the simple bliss of the start of life.

'What will you call her, Gigi?' she asked.

Gisela looked up at her.

'Dieter and I decided that when we first knew I was pregnant. She'll be Olivia – bringer of peace.'

Katharina smiled.

'A good choice. I hope she succeeds.'

'She has as good a chance as anyone. Is Dieter not here yet?'

'Soon,' Katharina soothed. 'Very soon, I'm sure.'

She wasn't sure at all. With the Russians overwhelming the city, Lutz's zoo troop had been ordered to the flak tower, coming back to help with feeding times if they could get away. Katharina had sent little Mark off to fetch Dieter to his wife's side hours ago, but with raids coming at any time of the day and night, who knew when he would make it.

At her side, Hanna gave a tired cry and, hearing Adelaide sigh, Katharina reached out to take the baby from her. Adelaide resisted at first but then her eyes lit up, and she happily shoved her little sister at her.

'Daddy!'

They all spun to see Robert coming into the bunker and, just behind him, Dieter. The younger man, spotting his wife and brand-new daughter, broke into a limping sprint, ducking round the myriad people crammed into the small space to pounce on them.

'Daddy,' Gisela echoed Adelaide, looking up at Dieter with sparkling tears in her eyes.

'Daddy!' he breathed, awed. 'Is it…?'

'A girl,' Gisela told him.

'Good. That's good. We don't need more men in the world – they just tear it apart.' His voice was harsh, but then he shook away his anger and sank onto the bed next to his wife. 'She's beautiful, Gigi. You're both so, so beautiful.'

Gisela looked up at him and Katharina saw Ursula turn away, ostensibly to adjust the stylish turban she was wearing over her dirty hair, but in truth to give the couple a little time alone. Katharina quietly turned her own back to speak to Robert. Hanna was drifting off and she hitched her up onto her shoulder, feeling the little girl's weight heavy against her.

'Did Mark ask you to come?'

Robert nodded.

'That lad's doing an amazing job. He's the same age as Addie here, but as soon as he'd found me, he was off up to the top of the flak tower to shoot at the Reds.'

'I could shoot at the Reds if Hitler would let me,' Adelaide said hotly.

Robert patted her head.

'I don't doubt it, Liebchen, and you'd do a fine job but, believe me, you are better down here. There's no way we can win now, and continuing to fight is only going to cost us lives as well as the war.'

Katharina frowned.

'Are we not, though, fighting to keep the Russians at bay until the Amis come?'

Robert looked down and Katharina squinted at him. Last week, when everyone with an ounce of strength had been coerced into digging anti-tank trenches in the pockmarked streets of the city, she had worked to that one end. The British and the Americans, for all their smug piousness, were at least known to be honourable. They would secure the city peacefully and take care of her citizens. The battle for Berlin, now, was not to win but to secure the best possible defeat.

'Robert? Is that not the plan?'

'It *was* the plan,' he agreed heavily. 'It still is *our* plan.'

'But?'

He looked left and right, then moved close to Katharina's ear so he could whisper: 'I overheard the officers talking in the tower yesterday. The word is that the Americans have stopped the other side of the Elbe.'

'What?!'

'Hush, Kätsche – you will cause panic.'

Katharina swallowed hard. Robert was right; already she could feel fear spreading through her, as sharp and painful as Oskar's fever. She looked over to her husband, tucked into a nearby bunk. He was frighteningly weak and would be unable to defend her if the Soviets came looking for the spoils of war. Suddenly Ursula's comment about Berlin being a city of women took on a darker turn.

'So the Russians will take us?'

'If we wait for them. We need that transport.'

'Gisela has just given birth.'

'Even more reason.'

His eyes moved to Adelaide, standing trustingly at his side, and Katharina did not need him to speak his fears for his eldest daughter. Adelaide would surely be among the first to be seized and they could not allow that.

The other day she had come across a small group of women, seemingly fighting amongst themselves. As she'd watched, one had run off at speed down the street, clutching something to her chest. Another had given chase, but she was an ageing lady and had soon run out of breath. She'd stopped near Katharina, leaning over with her hands on her knees to try and pull oxygen into her lungs.

'Did she rob you?' Katharina had asked. The woman had nodded grimly, though she'd still had a handbag looped over her large chest. 'What of?'

'Cyanide. The bitch took my cyanide.'

Katharina swallowed, remembering it now. The women of the city were more prepared to face eternal damnation than the Red Army; she had to get those in her care out.

'What's wrong, Daddy?' Adelaide asked, peering up at him in the gloom.

'Nothing, sweetheart. Well, nothing more than the usual.'

'The war!' she said, rolling her eyes with a child's carelessness. Robert managed a smile.

'Exactly. Now – it sounds quiet out there at the moment so I'm going to grab the chance to feed the zebras. Want to come?'

Adelaide's eyes lit up.

'Yes, please!'

Katharina stared at him.

'Are you sure that's a good idea, Robert?'

He shrugged.

'Is anything a good idea, any more? Can I leave Hanna with you?' She nodded and he pulled her into a swift hug, dropping a kiss onto Hanna's soft forehead. 'Thank you, Kätsche. From me, from the girls, and from Sasha. You've taken such good care of us for her. Now, come on, Addie.'

He took Adelaide's hand, and together they traced their way back up the bunker and pushed open the door. Katharina stood there, rubbing Hanna's soft little back as they disappeared into the night, then moved over to sit at Oskar's feet. She checked his ragged breathing and smoothed his white hair tenderly back off his dear face, desperate to soothe him back to health somehow. This man had helped her see past the intellectual challenge of science, deep into why it was so very important. He had shown her not just the biological mechanics of life but all that made it matter, and she could not bear to lose him.

Closing her eyes, she imagined for a moment that she and Oskar were cuddled up together, this baby their own and no shadow of war upon them. It was so unbearably sweet that she lost herself dizzyingly in the dream and was almost relieved to force her eyes open to the cramped bunker once more. Such simple happiness was not theirs to have, but they had each other and they had the Zoofamilie, and now she must fight for their very survival.

They'd had to move the hippos into the lavatory building, the one place still with walls intact enough to heat effectively. The storks, too, were living in any bathroom still with water, though they had long since run out of fish to feed them and the poor birds looked dangerously thin. They'd had to shoot the adult lions last week, afraid that with all the keepers in the flak tower, they might escape their cages unseen and take their own grisly meals across the city. It had broken Katharina's heart to see the magnificent beasts fall to the ground, but they had at least managed to save the two cubs, Sultan and Bussy, who were being housed under the baboon rock.

Somehow, the primates were still largely safe, including Lutz's favourite baboon, Kalifa, and Pongo the silverback gorilla. A number of Katharina's chimps had given birth but the Frenchmen had dug the community their own bunker, and they had the sense to hide in it when the planes came so the losses had been few. The other day two of the more adventurous juveniles had made a bid for freedom into the city but yesterday they'd shown up again, heads down like naughty toddlers, begging for food. Katharina had swept them up in her arms and given them all the scraps of fruit she could find, and they'd cuddled her just as Hanna might, threading their fingers into her rapidly silvering hair. It was time to save them all. At first light she would head out and requisition a van, even if she had to steal it herself. Her Zoofamilie were going to be safe, whatever it took.

A sudden run of shells overhead punctuated her thoughts, as if the enemy was mocking her determination to escape. There had been no siren but, really, what was the point when the attacks could come at any time? Katharina lay down next to Oskar, feeling his frail body radiating heat. Little Hanna snuffled crossly but then snuggled into the tiny gap between them, apparently oblivious to the bombs that now fell so close that the whole bunker shuddered. Katharina hated the fact that these would be baby Olivia's first sounds, and prayed that the loving murmurings of her happy parents were loud enough to drown out the noise of destruction overhead.

She let her eyes close. God, she was tired. She was sure there were other things she should be doing for Gisela, but she looked content and Katharina needed a little time to herself too. Perhaps, if she was lucky, she could just go to sleep now and not wake up until it was all over. She felt herself start to drift on a wave of baby-soft love and her exhausted mind saw Gisela's tiny daughter dance before her, olive branch in hand, green and fresh across the blood-red city. She smiled and let herself go.

'Candles!' someone suddenly shouted, and instantly all was pandemonium.

Katharina was jerked back to wakefulness as everyone leaped up and began handing children onto the top bunks. The foot-height candles had all guttered, indicating foul air, so she forced her eyes open and staggered out of her bunk, Hanna wailing furiously. Katharina knew how she felt.

'Hush, sweetheart,' she begged her, 'hush,' but really, why shouldn't she shout her complaints to what was left of the rooftops?

'Up here, Kätsche.'

She looked up to see Ursula on a top bunk with Beatrice and gladly handed Hanna to her. She looked anxiously at Oskar, whose wheezing lungs would surely not cope with the thinning air, but he was too heavy to lift any higher. The best thing she could do to help him was to man the pumps, so, rubbing gritty exhaustion from her eyes, she fought her way through to where several women were doing battle with the air pump. It was rasping more than Oskar and even as they poked at it, it gave a metallic sigh and stopped altogether.

'It must be blocked on the surface,' Katharina said. 'We need to work it manually until someone can get up there to clear it.'

The hand pump was a primitive device, with a see-saw handle that could be worked by two people. Katharina took one end, a sturdy hausfrau the other. They looked grimly at each other and then began to pump. Within minutes the air cleared slightly and someone bent to relight the nearest of the floor-level candles. The flame held.

'It's working!'

That was good news, but it would only remain so for as long as they kept pumping and, with the bombs falling hard overhead, there would be no way to get out there and clear it until dawn brought a few hours' respite. Katharina tried to look at her watch but it was impossible unless she stopped working.

'It's 5 a.m.,' her companion said. 'We've got an hour of this at least.'

'We'll have to take turns,' Katharina panted. 'You,' she said to another woman standing to one side, 'organise a rota of pairs. We can do ten minutes each until it's safe to open the door.'

The woman nodded and those unencumbered by children sorted themselves into a rough crocodile, like a parody of a school trip, to line up for the duty of keeping everyone in the bunker alive. Katharina's short arms ached but there wasn't long to go in her own stint and she gave it all she had. It felt like an apt metaphor for their days at the moment – working hard for the privilege of just keeping breathing – but at least it was something to do. Fixing her eyes on the ground, she pictured Hitler's weasely little face and pumped the handle hard down into it again and again and again.

Suddenly, just as her arms felt aflame with the effort, the door flew open and there, framed against the flak-lit sky, was Adelaide.

'Addie! Come in quick, child, close the door.'

But Adelaide seemed frozen, her eyes hazed and wild, and Katharina's heart plummeted. She pushed the next woman in the line towards the pump handle and ran up the steps to grab the girl, but she would not be moved.

'Come inside, Addie.'

'No.' The single syllable fell cold and hard from her young mouth and then, as if released by it, she said, '*You* come, Katharina.'

'Not out there. The bombs…'

'Have hit Vati.'

Katharina's dark world stood still.

'Robert? Where is he? Is he still alive?'

It seemed Adelaide could say no more. She just grabbed at Katharina's hand and tugged. Katharina looked back down into the bunker, over the heads of the two women pumping fresh air, across to Ursula, huddled with Beatrice and Hanna, past Oskar, his lungs rattling in sleep, and on to Gisela and Dieter, cradling Olivia. She wanted nothing more than to pull Adelaide bodily inside and shut the door on whatever horror was in the zoo, but then she heard a cry of pain, half shriek, half roar, and knew she had to face it. She reached for the rifle they kept by the door, though Lord knows what use it would be against a Soviet plane.

'Where's Vati, Adelaide?' she asked.

'Follow me.'

Together they headed into the zoo. The first tinges of dawn were coming up over the broken eastern edges of the city where the Russians lay, and it seemed, thank God, that the planes were concluding their attack. A lone fighter screamed overhead but its bomb dropped at least a mile away and then it was gone. The high-pitched roar, however, came again. It could not be Robert; it was far too bestial. Katharina scoured her mind for what creature might be making this otherworldly sound, but then they turned the corner and she saw Goliath, the Kodiak bear, writhing in his pit. The magnificent brown bear was wrenching at the chain that held him, shouting in pain and fury at the bloody wound on his side. As Katharina stared at this symbol of Berlin, it felt as if she were watching the city itself in its death throes.

'Goliath!' she cried out.

The bear seemed to hear her. He paused in his writhing and fixed her with a pain-filled look of such pleading that it tore Katharina in two. *Make this stop*, he was begging her. She looked to the rifle, then to Adelaide.

'Don't look, Addie,' she begged, but the girl did not seem to hear her and, as Goliath let out another desperate roar, there was nothing for it but to raise the rifle to her shoulder, aim as carefully as she could at his giant head, and pull the trigger.

Her aim, at least, was true. The bear's head jerked back, he tottered for a moment, and then fell slowly, almost gracefully sideways, curling into the bottom of his pit like a foetus returned to the earth. Katharina lowered the rifle to the floor and put her head in her hands. It was such a waste; such a senseless, purposeless waste. Then Adelaide made a choking sound in her slim throat and she remembered the other terrible task ahead of her. She picked up the rifle again and nodded her on. The girl looked darkly at the gun, and Katharina prayed that she would not have to offer Robert the same service as she had just performed for Goliath.

When they rounded the corner to the zebra enclosure, however, it was clear that there would be no such need. Robert lay in a circle of zebras, all nudging at his body – or what was left of it. His legs were blown off, exposing the grim red twists of his innards, and Katharina had to turn aside to retch into the spring grass. She grabbed Adelaide, pushing her head against her shoulder to try and save her the gruesome image, but knew already that it was a useless move. Adelaide must have seen the bomb fall, seen it cut her father in two and send his legs flying across the enclosure. She must have seen him drop the pail of oats that was still lying just a step from his hand, ignored by the apparently grieving zebra. She must even have seen his blood leach into the ground as the war devoured her only remaining parent, and Katharina doubted anything that anyone could ever do would now wipe that from her poor young mind.

'It would have been instant,' was all she could think to say. 'He wouldn't have suffered, Addie. He wouldn't even have known.' She prayed that was true, but it made Robert no less dead. Adelaide and Hanna were orphans now. 'I'll look after you,' she promised. 'I'll do everything I can to look after you.'

She meant it with all her heart, but as the sun came up over the ruins of Adelaide's childhood, she feared that everything she could do just wasn't going to be enough. Somehow, she had to find a transport out of here – and fast.

Chapter Nineteen

Bethan put the last stitch into Bruce the dingo's leg, tied off the thread and sat back, wiping sweat from her brow. May had launched itself on Berlin in a blaze of sunshine and she'd been embarrassingly sweaty all day. Right now, she was hoping to get called out to the bats – it was lovely and cool in the nocturnal animal house.

Thinking about it reminded her of the trip to the underground bunker with Max. It had been amazing down there, literally like stepping into history. She thought about all the people who'd been forced to sleep crammed under the earth as enemy planes chucked bombs onto their homes and their schools and the places they loved. If she'd been through all that, was it any wonder that poor Ada was only just clinging on to her wits with the tips of her bony fingers?

'Right – that looks good now,' she told the keeper, 'though the poor thing will have to wear the collar. Keep an eye on him and hopefully it'll heal quickly.'

'Thanks, Beth.'

'No problem.' She snapped her bag shut and made for the door. Bruce was just starting to come round; she'd judged it perfectly. She was definitely getting the hang of this job. A month ago she'd have freaked out at removing an abscess from a wild dog, but now she just got on with it. 'I'll be back later to check up on him.'

She left the enclosure and turned back towards the vet centre, looking enviously at the polar bears in their ice-cold water. She'd love to dive in and join them – save, of course, that despite them looking as cute as teddies, they'd tear her to bits instantly. These were wild animals and the zoo worked hard to keep it that way.

She sighed and looked at her watch. Not even 3 p.m. yet – still two hours to go.

'Hey, Beth. You OK?'

She jumped and looked up into a pair of enticing blue eyes.

'Max! I'm fine, thanks. Just a bit hot.'

'Not surprised. It's boiling. How about an ice cream?'

He indicated the van parked up a few metres away. Bethan looked at it as if it were an oasis in the desert.

'Yes, please! Oh, but look at the queue. I've got to get to the elephants. Bobo's foot is playing up again.'

'No problem.' Max marched up to the van, heading straight for the hatch with a charming smile at the queuing families. 'Emergency – zoo vet needing sustenance.' He pointed at Bethan. 'She's been in a long operation on one of the pandas, bless her. I'm sure you don't mind if she gets her cone first?'

They all hastened to agree and Bethan stood by, mortified, as Max procured two vanilla ices and brought them across.

'It wasn't a long operation,' she hissed. 'And it wasn't a panda, it was a dingo.'

'People love the pandas more. Not fair on dingos, I know, but there you go.' He winked. 'Now eat up or they'll be cross.'

She shook her head at him but smiled and licked her ice cream. It was deliciously cold and she felt it slip like nectar down her parched throat.

'Oh Max, that's just what I needed.'

'Good. Bethan, about the other night…' She looked nervously at him. 'I'm sorry. I was out of order. You're just very attractive and very interesting and, and…'

'I get it, Max. And if you were out of order, then I was too. Very much so.' She flushed and turned her attention to her ice cream. 'I just have some stuff I need to work out.'

'Course. No problem. I get it. You've got a boyfriend.'

'Well, actually—' she started, but he put a hand up to stop her.

'You don't have to explain to me, Bethan, really.' They both licked at their ice creams, then he added, 'Hey – I've been going through the notebook.'

'The transports one?' she asked, thankful for the change of subject.

'Yep. They really stepped up in 1945, plus they kept getting cancelled and rescheduled.'

'No surprise there. I've been reading up on it and it sounds as if it was hell in Berlin back then.'

'So we were always taught in history. Hitler was here, of course, hiding like a coward in his fancy bunker, making Berlin the big prize. The roads must have been filled with soldiers, so getting lorries full of chimps away can't have been easy.'

'Or of humans?'

'No. Hitler didn't want any Berliners leaving. Pronounced it treason not to stand up and fight.'

'Not babies though, surely?'

He grimaced.

'Who knows. I reckon the man had lost his mind by the end. That caretaker I told you about, Hans – from what he told me, he was only fifteen at the end of the war and they had him fighting. And his younger brother too. Hard to imagine, isn't it?'

'Impossible.'

'Perhaps we should go to the underground bunker again?'

He looked at her and the world seemed to fade away around them. Perhaps it was the heat, or perhaps it was the look in his bright blue eyes, but for a moment it was as if there was no one else in the zoo but them.

'Bethan!' someone cried. 'Bethan, my beautiful girl – there you are.'

She sprang back, noticing simultaneously the confusion in Max's eyes, the ice cream dripping down her hand and Callum running towards her in, incongruously, a full suit. She stood up as he skidded to a halt in front of her. He was red-faced and panting, and she felt a sudden rush of panic.

'Has something happened? Is it Dad?'

'Dad?' A frown crossed his face. 'God no, Bethan. It's not about your precious bloody father.'

'Callum!'

She put up a hand, wanting him to be quiet, but he grabbed it and pressed it dramatically to his chest.

'It's about us. *Us*, Bethie.'

She swallowed and looked awkwardly around, very aware of the entire ice cream queue gawking at them. Pulling him close, she hissed, 'I told you we needed time.'

But now Callum was gathering himself. His breath had steadied and he smiled confidently.

'I don't. No way. In fact, I've taken far too much time already, which is why I decided not to waste a moment more.'

'What?'

The ice cream was now a river across her free hand and she blinked as a young mother stepped out of the queue and kindly took it from her, passing her a baby wipe in its place.

'Thank you.'

'No problem.'

She pulled away from Callum and hastily wiped her hand, focusing harder than needed on the job. She had a horrible feeling she knew what he was up to and glanced desperately around for a way out, but still he stood there. In the end, she had to shove the sticky wipe in the pocket of her zoo shorts and look at him. He beamed.

'Bethan Taylor,' he said, obligingly loud for the ogling queue, 'I have been an idiot and a fool. I have taken you for granted and kept you waiting. Well, no more. You are the most beautiful girl in the whole wide world, and the most caring and the most fun and the most special. I love you and I want to spend the rest of my life with you.' Someone in the crowd gave a little squeal and his smile widened, but he kept his eyes focused on Bethan as he smoothly dropped to one knee and pulled a small box from his pocket. 'Please, my darling Beth, will you do me the honour of becoming my wife?'

Bethan stared as he flipped open the box to reveal a stunning solitaire diamond. A crowd had gathered and, for a moment, she thought that this must be how it felt to be the animals in their cages, but this was no time for reflection. Callum was looking up at her with his chocolatey eyes and the crowd were holding their collective breath.

'Callum…' she started, but he took this as a cue to sweep her into his arms, smoothly slotting the ring onto her finger as he did so.

Had she said yes? she wondered dazedly. Certainly, everyone in the zoo seemed to be laughing and cheering and snapping pictures of the happy couple; of *them*. If she'd ever dreamed of a proposal (something she'd tried very hard not to do, even when her friends had started popping out wedding invitations like, well, like confetti), it would have been exactly like this. She buried her head in Callum's shoulder, overcome, and he stroked her hair over and over until, eventually, he asked, 'Can I have a kiss?'

It was such a simple, uncharacteristically humble request. Slowly she pulled back. Over his shoulder she saw Max turning to leave, his ice cream splattered onto the ground.

'Max,' she cried, but the word was lost as Callum's lips closed on hers and the crowd whooped.

The announcer had got wind of something going on for his voice came over the tannoy: 'Looks like there's the best show of all going on down near the ice cream van, folks! Spring is in the air for one special couple today. Congratulations to our very own vet, Bethan Taylor, and her brand-new fiancé!'

'Fiancé,' Callum said against her lips. 'How good does that sound?!'

Bethan looked self-consciously around. The crowds were pressing in close, making her feel more like one of the animals than ever. Some were taking photographs and her shoulder wrenched as Callum pulled her proudly into a pose, putting her hand on his chest to display the ring like some sort of celeb. She pulled it away.

'Don't, Callum.'

He frowned.

'Why not? Its's our big moment.'

'*Our* big moment, exactly – not theirs.'

'It's nice to share.'

He looked hurt and he had a point, but still she felt hemmed in.

'You certainly know how to make an entrance, Callum Markeson.'

'You deserve it – Bethan Markeson.' The name shuddered through her. 'If you want to be called that,' he said hastily. 'It's not, you know, compulsory. We could double-barrel: Markeson-Taylor. How flash is that?'

'Too flash,' Bethan said firmly, fighting to collect herself. If she thought she'd been hot before, it was nothing compared to now. 'Oh God, Bobo!'

'Bobo?'

'The elephant. I'm meant to be checking her foot.'

A shadow passed over Callum's face, but was gone almost instantly.

'Perfect – I'll get to see you work. Lead on!'

Bethan pushed through the crowd to grab her bag. It was sitting next to Max's discarded ice cream and, as she reached out to pick it up, the diamond on her finger flashed in the sunlight like the flare of a gun. She froze and looked back to Callum, still drinking in the crowd's adulation. Then, leaving the bag on the floor, she reached instead for the ring and slowly pulled it off.

'Callum – we need to talk.'

Chapter Twenty

29 April 1945

Katharina paced nervously up and down outside the Elephant Gate at the back of the zoo, scanning the broken street for the promised transport lorry. She'd been working with Oskar's book of contacts, desperately sending messages via the primitive radio system he'd rigged up some time ago, and had finally secured a driver. If it arrived, the lorry would be driven by Margret Enger, an ageing but formidable ornithologist Oskar had worked with many years ago, and Katharina could only pray that the brave woman made it through the city.

So far there was no sign and, as the sun began to rise in the sky, the chance of attack only increased. The Russians, they had learned in the last few hellish days, liked to rest for a few hours in the early morning, worn out from a hard day's fighting and a hard night assaulting Berlin's terrified citizens. The area around the zoo, at the heart of the city, was still being fiercely defended, so the soldiers were more occupied with the fighting than the assaulting, but the tales coming in from the suburbs were chilling and it could only be a matter of time before they had the leisure for rape.

Katharina shuddered, not the least at the dispassionate way she had started thinking about her impending doom. But then, the moment she pictured a Red soldier attacking young Adelaide – and hundreds of others her age – her blood boiled. The poor girl had been through enough. She had stopped talking in anything other than monosyllabic grunts since her father had been killed four nights ago, and her remaining sanity hung precariously in the balance. Katharina peered up the road again, willing the lorry to arrive.

'Please come,' she muttered to Margret, wherever she was. 'Please, please come.'

The Zoofamilie was on its last legs and she had to get them out. It wasn't just Adelaide who was worrying her. Oskar's fever still raged and it was Katharina's secret hope that she could get him out of Berlin with the rest, but now Gisela was hot too. A midwife had made it to the bunker late on the day after Olivia's birth and, when checking her over, had expressed some concern about the afterbirth. In all the confusion of the raids and Robert's tragic death, no one had thought to check it had come out intact, and Katharina was cursing herself for the omission. She'd birthed enough chimps by now to know the importance of getting the placenta out whole and had stood at the midwife's side, cheeks burning, as they had turned it over and over in an old mixing bowl, looking at the ragged edges where it seemed some of the dark flesh might still be inside.

'What does that mean?' Katharina had asked the midwife in a hushed whisper, though Gisela had been fitfully sleeping and Dieter had been forced back to the flak tower so no one could hear her concerns.

'It may rot inside her,' had been the tart reply.

'What can we do to get it out?'

The midwife had put a hand on Katharina's arm.

'That would take surgery and…'

She'd glanced to the bunker door, and outside that the wreckage of the zoo and the flak tower beyond. There was still a functioning hospital in the tower but it was rammed with the wounded and short on supplies. Limbs were being amputated without anaesthetic, and cutting into fragile Gisela when she was awake would surely kill her more readily than the tiny bits of her own flesh.

'Might it come out unaided?' Katharina had asked desperately, and the midwife had offered her a weak smile.

'It might. The body is a wonderful thing and she's a fit young woman. Keep up her fluids, make sure she suckles the child, and pray.'

So, for the last two nights that's exactly what Katharina had been trying to do, but Gisela's fever was getting worse and last night she'd had to hold the baby to the breast for her. She was still bleeding, which they could only hope was a good thing as it might expel the poisons, but it was weakening her too and Katharina feared for her life. She couldn't bear to lose another friend.

'Please come, Margret.'

The sun was doing its best to wash Berlin with cheer, sending pastel light across the carnage, but a rose-pink corpse was still a corpse and Katharina had to swallow down bile as a young woman trudged past with a body curled like a foetus in a wheelbarrow. Tears were streaming down the girl's face and she stumbled, catching the wheel on a large piece of rubble and jerking the body so that for a moment it looked as if it were leaping back to life.

'Mutti!' the girl cried, then realised her mistake and burst into renewed tears.

Katharina rushed to help her, curling her mother's arm back into the barrow and pulling the girl into a hug. She crumpled against her chest, clutching at her as if she were the mother she'd lost.

'We were so close to the end,' she wept. 'We were so, so close.'

Katharina stroked her back.

'You need to get out of here, child.'

'I can't leave Mother.'

'But—'

'I can't. I can't leave her to rot in a barrow. I can't, I…'

She was getting hysterical, and with the lorry still not in sight Katharina had time to help.

'Come – we'll bury her here, just inside the zoo. The elephants will guard her.'

'Elephants?' The girl looked over to the two statues, still in place without their gate on their backs, and almost smiled. Katharina realised just how young she was.

'The elephants,' she repeated soothingly. 'Here – lay her here and we can cover her in rubble and she will be safe for all eternity.'

'With the elephants?'

'Exactly. Then you can get out of Berlin. Trust me, it's what she'd want for you.'

The girl seemed relieved to be given instruction, and together she and Katharina worked to cover the poor corpse with rubble until finally the pale limbs were obscured in a rough cairn. Katharina stood at the girl's side as she said a quiet prayer over the cairn, and then she took her arms.

'Now – go! You're young and fit. Head out of Berlin to the west and avoid the checkpoints if you possibly can. Do you have anyone you can go to?'

'I have an aunt in Potsdam.'

'Good. Get to her. Fast. Yes?'

She nodded.

'Yes. Yes, I will. Thank you. And you?'

'We're out of here too,' Katharina assured her grimly. 'Any minute now.'

They embraced again then she was gone, running off down the quiet street. Katharina prayed she escaped but she had more pressing concerns. The lorry still wasn't here and the day was marching on. A few streets away she heard the howling wail of 'Stalin's organ' – the Katyusha, a horrifying Soviet rocket that they fired down the streets from mounted launchers – and knew that the fighting would soon be starting up again. God, where was that lorry?

'Katharina!'

She spun round hopefully but it was just Lutz coming out of the zoo. He was staggering almost drunkenly and his eyes were bloodshot with what might be tears. She ran to him.

'Lutz! Are you hurt?' He gave a small nod and looked down at the rifle he was clutching, so tight that his knuckles were white around the handle. 'What happened?'

He answered with just one word: 'Kalifa.' His favourite baboon.

'He's dead?'

Lutz fixed her with a stark stare.

'I killed him.'

'Oh, Lutz.'

'I had to. The cage was damaged beyond repair and he was poised for escape. He is – was – an alpha male. He would have killed. If we'd got lucky, he might have savaged a Red, but I don't think he had the means of identifying friend from foe, do you?' His voice cracked on the attempt at a joke, and he dropped the rifle and buried his head in his hands. 'This is hell, Katharina. He has put us through hell.'

'Who has, Lutz?'

'Who do you think? Hitler – *the bastard*.' She gasped and he gave a dark laugh. 'The man is a megalomaniac, a fool, a murderer of his own people. You were right about him, Katharina, and I was wrong. I was so wrong. That must please you.'

She took his hands and pulled them gently from his face.

'Of course it doesn't please me, Lutz. I didn't want any of this. I believed in Hitler too, at first. He seemed to be taking us back to prosperity. He *was* taking us back to prosperity – he just went too far.'

'Too far!' Lutz laughed again, high-pitched and manic. 'That's an understatement, Katharina. You are too generous. You knew this war was wrong from the start and were brave enough to say so, but I wouldn't listen. I thought the party knew what they were doing. And maybe they did, at one point, but they sure as hell don't now. Look at us!'

He gestured down the street as a woman trudged past, leading a bleeding donkey with two corpses over its bent back. It was a sick tableau, but had become so commonplace now that it barely drew attention. Katharina and Lutz stood together and watched as she moved off down the empty street.

'You're waiting for a lorry?' Lutz asked, sounding slightly more composed.

Katharina nodded.

'Oskar's friend procured one big enough to take the chimps.'

'And others besides?'

Katharina glanced up and down the street, but there were few people to hear them and none that cared.

'That is my hope. We've listed Ursula and me as chimp keepers and Gisela as our assistant. The babies and Adelaide will have to hide behind the cages.'

'And Oskar?'

Katharina longed to confide her hope of getting her husband away but could not risk it.

'Oskar is a man so he must stay.'

Lutz took her hand. 'Nonsense. Get him out, Katharina, get them all out.' She stared at him but he was looking from the rising sun to his watch. 'I have to go. I'm meant to be leading a sortie against the Russians.'

'A sortie? Lutz, is that not madness?' He nodded bleakly and she pressed his hand. 'Then do not do it. Please. Why get killed now?'

'My feelings exactly, which is precisely why I have to do it.'

Katharina frowned.

'I don't understand.'

'My commanding officer is cut from Hitler's delightful cloth. He will shoot me if I do not.'

'So why go back?'

'And all my men besides. I must go back and lead them out, for we have a better chance against Stalin's bloody organ than we do defying our own high command. Don't fret, I will take them no further than a building we can hide in for long enough to claim to have done our duty.'

Katharina shook her head.

'This is a farce.'

'A hellish farce, yes, but one we are doomed to play out to the very end.' He pressed her hands. 'Take care, Katharina. I hope the lorry comes, and I hope you all get in it and get away from here. And, Kätsche, if you get out of this and back to peace, take care of her, will you – take care of the zoo.'

'Lutz, you can...'

He shook his head fiercely.

'I'm a party member. They'll kill me if they find me. Rita too. It's down to you now, Katharina. The zoo could not be in better hands.'

He gave her fingers a final squeeze and then, before she could say anything more, he was gone, up the road to the flak tower, to pretend to do his duty until he could find space to flee.

'Take care,' she called after him.

He raised a hand in acknowledgement but did not turn back, and she was left with nothing more to do but pray for his safety and look, again, for the lorry.

'Please come, Margret. Please, please come.'

It was two agonising hours later when the lorry miraculously pulled up alongside the marble elephants. Katharina had given up pacing the entrance and was watching from the door of the bunker, where she could alternate her job as lookout with dipping in to keep an eye on those she hoped to ship away. Gisela was scarcely conscious and earlier Ursula had fed little Olivia as well as her own daughter. The baby had spluttered in surprise at the richness of the milk but had drunk eagerly and was now asleep. Adelaide was in a corner cuddling Hanna. Her sister seemed to like her incoherent babbling and was content enough. Katharina was sure that if she could just get them all away, they could heal.

'Margret!' She went flying across the zoo, waving at the bold driver.

Margret waved back and swung herself down from the cab. She was a stout woman and Katharina remembered her from dinner parties before the war, always looking uncomfortable in formal dresses. Now, in dark trousers and shirt, she was bristling with purpose and she came forward to shake Katharina's hand with a firm grasp.

'Sorry I'm late. Bastard Reds were blocking all the best routes but I found a way through.'

'Thank you so much.'

'No, thank *you*. Your chimps are my pass out of this hole of a city, so let's get them loaded up and fast. The Reds are shaking off their hangovers and I want out of here as soon as possible.'

Katharina nodded.

'If you drive in through here, we can get right up to the primate cages and hopefully transfer the chimps direct.'

'No problem.' Margret looked around and then stepped closer to add, 'And the others?'

'I'll sort them.'

'Good. Hide them well. There should be nothing stopping the poor innocents leaving this city after their cowardly commanders, but the Gestapo are still under orders to release only those with a pass, and you know the Gestapo – they love any excuse to shoot their own.'

Katharina shivered, and thought of Lutz and his condemnation of the party that he had cleaved to for so long. If only he and those like him had come to this realisation earlier, then perhaps this could all have been stopped. If only Stauffenberg's bomb had taken out the Führer last July, they might be living in peace now and not shipping babies out in chimp cages. But there was no point in dwelling – they had to get everyone out. She watched as Margret began manoeuvring the truck between the elephants, trying to work out how many of them they could fit inside, but it was impossible to tell until they got it open, so she ran back to the bunker to prepare the precious additional cargo.

'Oskar.' She shook him gently where he slept, curled up his bunk. 'Oskar – we are going on a trip.'

'A trip?'

His fever was muddling him and Katharina prayed that it would make him more accepting of her little deceit. It was for the best. The battle was reaching its climax and, if they could just escape for a few weeks, things would be very different. The Russians would surely take care of the remaining animals and once peace was properly established, she and Oskar could come back and restore the zoo. For a year now they had been shipping animals out to save them, but what use was that if they lost their own lives? She did not like it, but they had to go.

'A trip, Oskar,' she said firmly. 'It's time to get up.'

She was delighted to see that Pierre had arrived and was holding Ursula and Beatrice tight in his arms. He was part of Lutz's zoo troop so this must mean that their ridiculous sortie had been safely concluded. She moved to welcome him but saw tears running down Ursula's pretty face, and her blood ran cold.

'What is it, Pierre? Who's dead?'

He drew in a deep breath.

'Dieter.'

'No!' Katharina's hands flew to her mouth and she looked to Gisela, lying semi-conscious on the bed with her baby asleep on her burning body. 'No, Pierre.'

'I'm so sorry. We had to go out. They made us. We were to "stop the Russians coming down Charlottenburger Strasse" – as if ten men armed with brooms were ever going to halt the Red Army. Lutz found us a house to hide in and we cowered there for as long as we dared, but we had to get back. We made a dash for it in a lull but then a tank came round the corner. We ran for our lives, Katharina, but Dieter…'

'Dieter couldn't run with only one leg.'

Pierre shook his head.

'I realised too late. I turned back to help, truly I did, but I was only in time to see him blown sky high.'

'Who?' The voice was high-pitched but dangerously alert. They all looked over to see Gisela sitting up in bed, Olivia clutched tightly to her chest, and her eyes fixed on Pierre. 'Who was blown sky high, Pierre?'

'Someone in our troop,' he stuttered, but she knew.

'It was Dieter, wasn't it? Dieter is dead?' Pierre just hung his head and Gisela let out a long, keening wail. She leaped out of bed and stormed over to them, holding Olivia before her.

'Take her,' she said to Ursula.

Her friend backed away.

'Gisela, no.'

'Please, Ursula. Take her with you to Torgau.'

Ursula drew in a deep breath, and gathered Gisela and her daughter into her arms.

'We will do, Gigi. We will take her, and you besides.'

Gisela shook her head.

'I'm too weak. I'll be sick. I'll die. It will endanger all of you. Please, Ursula, Kätsche, take Olivia.' She pushed her into Ursula's arms and backed off. 'Take her to safety. I will stay here, in the bunker. I will get better, and then I will find Dieter's body and bury him and come to find you.'

'The Russians…' Katharina started.

'Will not want this.'

Gisela gestured to her wasted frame, angular beneath the bloody white nightgown, and the high colour in her pale cheeks.

'She has a point,' Pierre said softly.

Ursula swung round and glared at him.

'I can't leave Gigi.'

'You can't take me,' Gisela said firmly. 'Not this time. But I will come, I promise. Soon. Very soon.' She staggered a little and looked to Katharina. 'Where's Dieter, Kätsche? Why doesn't he come?'

She'd forgotten already. Katharina wasn't sure if it was a blessing or a new curse but the poor woman was right about one thing – she'd be a danger to the rest. She guided her back to her bed and pulled Ursula aside.

'What do we do? We cannot leave her here like this.'

Ursula shook her head.

'It would be certain death. But the journey will surely kill her too.'

Katharina looked around the bunker. She could hear fighting starting up again, just streets away, and knew the Russians would be upon them at any time. She looked from tiny Olivia in Ursula's arms to Beatrice in Pierre's, and Adelaide clutching sunny Hanna. Then she looked to Gisela, curled up around her own desperate misery, and Oskar sitting on the side of his bed, his head in his hands. Her heart turned over.

'I'll stay.'

'Kätsche, no.'

She folded her arms.

'I have to, Ursula. I can look after Gisela and I can look after Oskar and if – *when* – they are better, I will bring them on. Can you do it, Ursula – can you manage the children alone?'

'Of course, but—'

'Then that is what we must do.'

Ursula looked distraught but now Margret burst in.

'This lorry leaves in twenty minutes – who's going to be on it?'

'Ursula is,' Pierre said, ushering her forward. 'With Beatrice. And…' He looked to the baby in her arms. 'And Olivia.'

'Come then.' Margret ushered them forward.

Ursula grabbed Katharina in a hug, and for a moment Katharina longed to just hold on to her all the way into the lorry and get away, but that could not be. Not now. She forced herself to drop a light kiss on her friend's cheek and step away, turning determinedly to her charges.

'And Adelaide and Hanna,' she said, but Adelaide clung to her leg, so tightly that she feared she might squeeze the blood from it. She looked down at her. 'You must go with Ursula, Addie.'

'And you, Kätsche. We're going with you.'

'Not this time, sweetheart. I have to stay to bring Aunty Gisela and Uncle Oskar as soon as they're better.'

'Then I'm staying too.'

'No, Addie. You must go with Ursula and the chimps. You like the chimps, don't you? You like the babies?' Adelaide was shaking her head furiously, banging it against Katharina's side. Katharina swallowed. The poor girl was working herself into a frenzy and needed calming down. 'Very well then,' she said easily, 'but let's help the others load up.'

Adelaide looked at her suspiciously but when she made for the primates' cage, she followed, and Katharina could only pray that once she saw that the lorry was safe, she would agree to climb into it. Fifteen minutes later, however, with the chimps screeching from their cages, Katharina turned around and found the girl gone.

'Where's Addie? Hanna?'

They all looked frantically around, but neither the girl nor her nine-month-old sister were anywhere to be seen.

'She was here a moment ago,' Pierre said. 'She helped me load two of the baby chimps.'

'Well, she's not here now,' Ursula said. 'We'll have to hunt for her.'

But at that Margret put her foot down.

'This lorry is leaving in five minutes, no more. Those who are on it then are coming with me; those who are not…'

'Addie's only twelve.'

'I'm sorry, Katharina, but the Russians are coming. Listen.' She gestured to the west where the shelling was starting up again, breaking the brief peace. 'If I don't go now, I won't get the lorry out and then we are all lost.'

Katharina nodded grimly, cursing Adelaide for her foolishness. The miracle of the transport arriving was fast dissipating, but she had to stay strong to get those she could out of this hell.

'You should go, Ursula,' she said.

Ursula crushed a kiss onto Pierre's lips, then turned and stepped determinedly up into the lorry. There was a space behind one line of the chimp cages into which they had put Beatrice's carry-cot, well-padded and secured to the edge of the van, and now she laid her daughter into it before turning back to take Olivia from Pierre and lay her alongside. She tucked the two little girls up together, then stepped away to let Pierre place the last chimp cage across in front of them.

No border guard, surely, would prevent babies from leaving Berlin, but it wasn't worth the risk, and the way the chimps were leaping and screeching, Katharina doubted they would hang around to check too carefully. It would take several hours to get to Torgau but once Margret was clear of the city, Ursula could bring the babies out and at least, for now, they were in there together.

The lorry, however, looked horribly empty. Katharina looked desperately around for Adelaide and Hanna but they were still nowhere to be seen, and now Margret was climbing into the cab and starting up the engine.

'Paperwork,' she called.

Katharina grabbed the forms and crossed out her own and Gisela's names. She stared at them for a moment, then around the bomb-torn zoo.

'Katharina?'

'Here!' She shoved it at her and stepped away.

'Take care,' Pierre urged Ursula as he went to close the doors.

'Of course.'

She managed a smile, though Katharina could see even her usual buoyancy struggling as the door began to close.

'I will come to you as soon as I can,' Pierre promised. 'I will come to you and I will bring the others and we will be happy. It will be soon. Very, very soon.'

Ursula nodded and gave a frightened little wave, but Margret was revving the engine and Pierre had no choice but to close the door on his wife and child. Slowly the lorry pulled away. Katharina looked to Pierre who reached out and drew her close.

'They'll be fine,' he said. 'Ursula is tough and Margret seems even tougher. No one will stop those two, and by nightfall they will be unloading in a beautiful chateau in the countryside.'

'Under American protection.'

'Lucky them. Now, Katharina, I must get back to the tower before I'm missed. Will you be all right?'

'Of course,' she said, more bravely than she felt. 'Addie will come out now the lorry has gone, and we can get back to the bunker with Oskar and Gisela.'

Pierre shook his head sadly.

'I don't know which of us has the worse job. Take care, Kätsche. The end is coming, I know it is. All we have to do is hold out.'

'Hold out,' Katharina agreed faintly as the truck bounced out of the zoo, taking her chance of escape with it. It sounded simple, but the terrifying question was what they were going to have to hold out against?

Chapter Twenty-One

Bethan crept into the vet centre the next morning feeling raw, tired and very self-conscious. She made straight for the coffee machine but before she could even get close, Ella pounced.

'Woo-hoo, it's Bethan Taylor – fiancée extraordinaire! Let's see the ring then.' Bethan flushed furiously as Ella grabbed her empty hand, then did a double-take. 'Where is it, Beth? Where's the big flash diamond I've heard all about?' Bethan grimaced and Ella gave her a wry smile. 'Ah! You weren't so keen on the grand proposal?'

'Let's just say, it clarified things in my mind. Things I should have realised ages ago.'

'Been there, babe, definitely been there. Tanya – we need your strongest coffee and urgent pastries.'

Tanya came across and took in the situation in an instant.

'I'm on it. You look like a train crash, Beth.'

'Cheers.'

Tanya grinned then drew her into a hugely welcome hug.

'Don't fret, we're your rescue party.'

Tears sprang to Bethan's eyes, and she gratefully let herself be guided to a chair and brought breakfast. It had been a long night and the sweetness of both the excellent pastries and her new friends' kindness was oh so welcome.

Callum had not been happy when, finally hidden away in her flat yesterday, she'd handed him back the ring.

'Don't you like it? The man in the shop said everyone liked diamonds, but if you—'

'It's not the diamond, Callum. It's you. That is, it's *us*. I just don't want to be us any more.'

'You don't mean that,' he'd snapped. Then, more uncertainly, 'You can't mean it.'

'I'm sorry, Cal.'

'I thought you were just, you know, giving me a nudge. I've told everyone I was coming out here to propose. All my friends. They're all made up for me. Charlie's been planning the stag do already.'

'Well, my apologies to Charlie.'

He'd caught himself.

'Sod Charlie. I didn't mean that. That's not the important thing. You, Bethan – you're the important thing. You and me.'

He'd tried to take her hands but she'd ducked away, feeling as trapped as she had amidst the crowds in the zoo.

'I told you – I don't want "you and me" any more. I'm sorry.'

'Why?'

'I don't think we've been right for a while, Cal. It's just taken this time apart for it to become clear. You did say it would be a test.'

'And I failed it?'

'Or *I* did.' He'd looked up at that. 'I'm too boring for you, Callum.'

'What?'

'Think about it. You've got a cool job, you like to party, you drink champagne from fountains.'

'Not the bloody fountain again.'

'There was nothing wrong with the fountain, Callum. It's just not my sort of thing.'

'You're not boring,' he'd said stoutly, though he'd sounded a little less sure.

'I like animals, Cal. I like country walks and tiny pubs and camping.'

'That's true. I never understood what you had against a luxury hotel.'

She'd given him a small smile.

'You're a wonderful man, Callum. Your proposal was gorgeous.'

He'd pouted.

'Not if you don't love me, it wasn't.'

'True. That's so true. You deserve a woman who's swept off her feet by such a wonderfully romantic gesture. You deserve a woman who will wear your amazing ring with pride.'

'You don't like the ring?'

She'd sighed.

'I love the ring, Callum.'

'You just don't love me?'

His voice had been so small suddenly, so lost. It had stabbed at her like a knife, but it had been true and she couldn't dodge it any longer.

'I don't love you *enough*, no. I don't love you as much as I should, as much as you deserve.'

There'd been a long pause. He'd gone to the window, but somewhere below a kookaburra had let out a sharp laugh and he'd flinched and turned back in, pushing his hands through his dark hair.

'Does this mean I have to move out of your flat?'

Bethan had blinked.

'Of course not. At least, not yet. Take your time.'

'I don't need charity.'

'It's not charity, Cal. It's friendship.'

He'd shaken his head, pink patches rising on both cheeks.

'I don't believe in all that let's-still-be-friends crap, Beth.'

'OK. Sorry. I just meant I won't kick you out on the street. Take all the time you need.'

She'd stepped towards him but he'd thrown up his hands, warding her off.

'I don't need time actually. Charlie's mate, Dom, is looking for a housemate. Got a great place in Marylebone. Only ten minutes from Soho.'

'Right. Sounds good.'

'Yeah, well, I'll need a few bars, won't I, if I'm out on my ear.'

'You're not—'

'No point sugar-coating it, Beth.'

'No.'

'Right, I'll be off then.'

'Off?'

'Well I'm hardly going to hang around here, am I? Have a nice cup of tea together, listen to whatever that stupid bird is down there.'

'It's a kookaburra.'

'Do I look like I give a—'

'Sorry, no.'

There'd been an awkward pause while Callum pushed the ring box fiercely back into his suit pocket. Then he gave a funny little shrug of his shoulders and said: 'Thinking about it, you've done me a favour actually.'

'What?'

'You are a bit boring, you know.'

'Callum?'

'This is a mutual decision, really. A parting of the ways. Different goals in life and all that.'

Bethan had stared at him in disbelief as he'd busily rearranged the break-up into something he could present to his friends. Thank God she'd worked this out in time. Thank God she'd come to Berlin and found out who she really wanted to be.

'Is this goodbye then, Callum?'

'Seems that way.' His voice had wobbled a little. 'Bit weird.'

'It is. I wish it could have worked out better.'

'No, no, no – mutual decision. Best thing for us both.'

'I'm still sorry.'

'Yeah.' She'd heard him choke. 'Me too. See you around, Bethan Taylor.'

Then he'd been gone, taking his fancy diamond and two years of her life with him. It had been kind of hard to sleep after that.

'For what it's worth,' Tanya said, pouring her a second premium-strength espresso, 'I think you made the right decision.'

'Me too,' Ella said promptly. 'He was a nice enough bloke and pretty good-looking, but he didn't seem very... very you.'

It wasn't exactly insightful but it didn't need to be. It seemed her new friends here in Berlin could see the real her more clearly than she had done herself.

'No more men,' she said, knocking back the espresso and feeling it zing through her tired brain.

'None?' Ella looked horrified.

'None.' She touched her hippo brooch. 'This is all the jewellery I need right now. I'm going to dedicate myself to the animals for a while.'

'But—'

'Quite right,' Tanya said briskly. 'And on that note, here's today's job list. Beth, you need to check up on Bruce, then see if Bobo's pedicure sorted her out. After that, I've got you down to help me with the meerkat inoculations if that's OK?'

'That's more than OK.'

Bethan stood up, glad to have something practical to focus on.

'Great. Ella, can you head over to the primate house? Max says Binky's been off her food so it would be good to take a look at her.'

Bethan jumped.

'Binky? Oh no. Max would be heartbroken if anything happened to Binky.'

Tanya looked at her curiously.

'He would, but I'm sure it's something simple. She's probably been eating blossom again. She got herself into all sorts of bother with that last year. Silly thing seems to think it's pretty enough to eat.'

'Poor Binky.'

'Silly Binky.'

'Do you want to take that one then, Beth?' Ella offered. 'I can do the inoculations with Tanya if—'

'No, no, no. It's fine, thank you, Ella. Meerkats are good. Really.'

'OK then,' Tanya said. 'Off you both go.'

They picked up their bags and headed out together. The sunlight was dazzling for Bethan, even after Tanya's best coffee, and she scrabbled for her sunglasses as they came up to the monkey house.

'Max!' Ella cried. 'Guten Tag. I'll let myself in.'

She slipped round to the side gate, leaving Bethan facing him through the bars.

'Congratulations,' he said gruffly.

She shuffled her feet.

'I'm not engaged, Max.'

'What? But I was there. I saw him propose.'

'Did you hear me say yes?'

He frowned.

'I'm not sure, but I saw him kiss you. I saw the crowd all whoop.'

'So you assumed I had done?'

'It seemed logical.'

Bethan closed her eyes. Already the effects of the espresso seemed to be receding, leaving her weary and sad once more. She knew she'd made the right decision but that didn't make it easy.

'Not everything is logical, Max.' She ached for another of Tanya's big hugs or, even better, one from her dad, but Paul was on the other side of Europe and she had to deal with this herself. Max was still staring at her and she turned uncomfortably away. 'I'd best get to the dingos.'

'Bethan!' She glanced back, and he gave her a small smile and said, 'I found an entry in the transport notebook for April 29th 1945.'

She shot back to the bars.

'You did? When?'

'Last night. It was scrawled in amongst some notes on chimp illnesses so I missed it at first.'

Suddenly all awkwardness was gone.

'Weren't the Russians in the city by April 29th?'

'I believe so, yes. Hitler killed himself on the 30th so things must have been getting pretty rough. I don't know how they managed to get out but it looks like they did, or at least they left Berlin.'

He'd moved closer up to the bars as he talked and Bethan took a step in too, desperate to know more.

'Where was it going, Max?'

'The notes said Torgau.'

'Where's that?'

'Saxony. As it happens, it's the place where the Russian and American forces met up. Must have been about the same time, though I assume that's just coincidence. The important thing is that the Americans were holding it, so it would have been safe for, for…'

'Babies?' she yelped, feeling instantly better about life.

'Maybe. You see, the thing is, Bethan' – he put up a hand to the bar and leaned in to half whisper – 'the keeper is listed as…'

'As what?'

He grinned at her, all tension forgotten in the excitement of whatever he had to reveal.

'As Ursula Franke.'

'No way!'

'Interesting, isn't it? Looks like someone else was written in too, maybe two people, but they've been crossed out.'

'Ursula! But why Franke? Surely she was married by then?'

'Well, yes, but illegally as far as the authorities were concerned, so I assume her official papers were never changed. Guess where she was headed?'

'Torgau. You said.'

'I did – but I didn't say who was there waiting for her.'

'Who?' He grinned again and she looked to the skies for patience. 'Don't tease me, Max. I didn't get much sleep.'

'Sorry. It must have been hard to—'

'It doesn't matter, really. Who was at Torgau?'

'The person listed as due to receive the shipment of chimps, with "keeper" Ursula Franke, is down as Countess Sylvie von Weichs.'

'Countess Sylvie!' Bethan grabbed her phone and pulled up the photo of her mother's list. Sure enough, there, second from the bottom, was Countess Sylvie. It was exactly the news she needed to distract her from the mess with Callum, and she grabbed the bars excitedly from the other side. 'It's working, Max. The pieces are coming together!'

'I hope so. I hope we can find your grandmother, Beth.'

'We will! We just have to go to the Torgau place and find someone who knew Countess Sylvie and ask if, if…'

'If she smuggled any babies out to anyone?'

Bethan grimaced.

'It might not be easy, but it's got to be worth a try, right?'

'Right.'

'So when can we go?'

'We?'

She froze. Suddenly she realised that Max's face was just centimetres from her own, albeit separated by bars.

'You don't want to come?'

'Do you want me to?'

It was a fair question, she supposed, after all that had happened, but this wasn't some romantic day trip, this was a fact-finding mission for her mother.

'I'm sure, Max. You've helped me so much getting this far. I'd really like to have you there if we get to the end of the trail.'

'We might not, you know. It might be a dead end.'

'It might, but I'd like you there anyway.'

'Saturday then?'

She swallowed.

'Saturday. Thanks, Max.' His hand moved on the bar and for a moment it touched hers. The warmth shot across her skin and she leaped back. 'I'd better go – Bruce is waiting!'

With that she fled. She'd told Tanya and Ella that she was going to dedicate herself to the animals and she'd meant it. Well, the animals and the list. Her weary body thrilled at the thought of finally getting to the bottom of her mum's origins. Who'd left Berlin with Ursula Franke and the chimps – and what had become of them when they got to Torgau? She could hardly wait for Saturday.

Chapter Twenty-Two

1 May 1945

'He's dead!'

Katharina looked up at Gisela, crouching in the doorway to the bunker with her ear pressed to a small radio. Outside the noise of artillery fire filled the air of this, the least blessed May Day ever, but they had all got so used to it now that they largely ignored it.

'Who's dead, Gisela?'

'Hitler.'

Everyone in the bunker sat up. Even Oskar pushed himself up on his pillows next to Katharina.

'How do you know?' he croaked.

Gisela waved the radio.

'It's on the BBC. They're saying he committed suicide yesterday.'

'Too scared to face his enemies,' someone growled.

'Don't blame him,' someone else put in. 'They'd tear him to pieces.'

'If we didn't do it first.'

Katharina looked around the faces of her fellows, and saw the anger and fear of what had now been over a week cowering underground bubbling up into a dangerous stew of emotion. They slept little with the constant bombardments, and were always on the alert for the door to burst open and Red hell to arrive in their hiding place. Whenever they could, the remnants of the Zoofamilie went out to check on the remaining animals.

Pongo the gorilla was still beating his increasingly skinny chest with pride, and Siam the bull elephant was stubbornly alive if increasingly grumpy at his harem-less state. A number of Robert's zebras clung on to life, as did those of Katharina's chimps not out in Torgau. The lion cubs grew strong on the carcasses of their bombed neighbours, and various birds had made roosts wherever they could, including in those houses still standing. Katharina marvelled every day at the precious creatures' continued resilience, but it was too precarious to be outside now, and two days ago they'd had to toss all the remaining food supplies into the enclosures and pray the creatures could fend for themselves.

They had little left to eat either, and water was scarce for the hundred women and children still trapped in the bunker. The zoo, thankfully, had its own pump not far from the safety of the bunker, and every so often someone would dash to fetch as much water as they dared before a sniper found them. Katharina could only begin to imagine how dangerous it must be at the street pumps and feared that, whenever this horror finally ended, they would find many of Berlin's poor citizens parched to death beneath ground.

She looked to Adelaide, cowering at the end of Oskar's bunk with Hanna sleeping in her arms. She'd come crawling back to Katharina hours after Margret had driven the lorry away from the zoo and had followed her like a shadow ever since. She had said one word – 'sorry' – and then nothing more, save to babble to little Hanna. The infant was, thank the Lord, an amazingly sunny child, guzzling down any food they could find for her and crawling around the bunker chattering in mysterious baby talk to anyone who would bend to engage with her. Many would, for she was the only happy distraction in a dark, dark world.

'There's more,' Gisela said, putting up her hand to silence the angry murmurings.

She, at least, had brightened, though she seemed wired and excitable, forever pacing the bunk. Katharina supposed it must be the only way she could keep her mind off her newborn child, sent across Germany behind cagefuls of chimps, not to mention her lost husband, saved once from the mutilations of war only to be sent back into its merciless clutches at the final hour.

'What, Gigi?' she asked her.

Gisela gave a strange smile.

'Hitler didn't die alone.'

'Goebbels, I suppose,' someone said bitterly.

Gisela shook her head.

'Himmler?'

'Nope.'

'Bormann?'

''Fraid not. Someone much more interesting than all of those.'

'Who then?' Katharina demanded; she hadn't the patience for games.

'Fine, fine – Hitler died with his wife.'

'His what?!'

The bunker exploded, as Gisela had clearly known it would. The Führer, they'd all been led to believe, had stayed single, devoted only to the Fatherland.

'Who is she?' Katharina asked.

'Someone called Eva. Eva Hitler, I suppose, though they're calling her Eva Braun. They say they only married a day or two before they died. Not the most romantic honeymoon ever, is it – marry me, honey, and come with me into hell for all eternity.'

She gave a high-pitched laugh, and Katharina eased away from her beloved Oskar and went to put an arm around her friend. She was hot again and her frame felt dangerously slight, though her breasts were large and leaking pitifully, and her stomach sagged. There were signs that she might have thrown the poison from her womb, but she needed weeks of peace and rest to recover fully and there was precious little chance of that here.

'Poor woman,' she said simply.

'Poor?' Gisela turned on her, cheeks flaring instantly. 'Even if this Eva wasn't his wife, she must surely have been his mistress. I doubt even Hitler would pick some girl up off the street to marry before he shot himself, so that makes her complicit, Katharina. That woman must have slept in Hitler's bed night after night. She must have kissed him and stroked him and pandered to him. She must have listened to his sick ideologies and told him what a clever man he was. It's because of her and her ilk that I have lost my husband – and millions of other women besides. She deserves to be dead.'

With that she burst into choking tears and all Katharina could do was hold her and let her cry, as everyone else looked on in a stunned silence broken only by the arrival of Hans and Mark.

'Katharina! Gisela! The flak tower has surrendered.'

That stopped Gisela's tears mid-track.

'When?'

'Now. Just now. They sent in German prisoners last night to negotiate. They promised that if we surrendered no one would be hurt and now – now we have.'

Hans spread his hands wide, looking down at them as if astonished by the simplicity of the final surrender. Behind them Adelaide crept from the bunk and reached out to touch his shoulder, as if to check he was real.

'The Russians have taken the tower?' Katharina stuttered. She wasn't sure why this was such a surprise but, much like sitting by the bedside of a dying relative, the moment of death itself was still a shock. She glanced nervously to Oskar, who'd roused himself again. 'And have they kept their promise?'

'So far,' Mark said. 'They let us go.'

'What about Walter and Gustav? What about Pierre and the other Frenchmen?'

Mark and Hans exchanged a worried look. Mark edged behind his brother, leaving Hans to face the bunker.

'They have marched them away,' he admitted.

'Away where?'

'I'm not sure. The Russians were detaining everyone in a military uniform.'

'But they don't have a military uniform.'

'I think their keepers' ones confused them.'

He looked torn apart by his news and Katharina forced herself to smile at him.

'Let us hope that justice prevails once someone realises the mistake,' she said as confidently as she could manage, though she feared that their poor men might be corpses in some dark clearing by the time that happened. She looked again to Oskar and his fever-red eyes met hers in shared pain. Had the smart zoo clothing condemned their men? Katharina thought of Ursula in Torgau, waiting for Pierre to come to her, and her heart wrenched.

Don't think of it, she told herself urgently. There was nothing she could do to help the men, but everything she could do right here.

'What are the Russians doing now?' she asked the boys, but at that moment a fierce volley of shots sounded out across the front of the bunker door and suddenly it filled with Soviet soldiers.

'You will all stand!' the lead soldier commanded, levelling his gun.

Katharina's heart battered against her chest as she stood before him. All around her nervous women followed suit, clutching on to each other and holding children tight behind their legs as if that might somehow protect them from the enemy crowding into their safe haven. Katharina thought of Ursula's cousin, raped over and over by just such men, and felt fear freeze every inch of blood in her veins. She pressed an arm tight around Adelaide and prayed desperately for mercy. Why hadn't she forced her into Margret's truck? Why hadn't she forced them *all* in?

The lead soldier, an officer judging by the stripes on his shoulders, paced up and down between them, checking bunks. He reached Katharina and pushed her roughly aside.

'You!' He levelled his gun at Oskar. 'Get up!'

'He's ill,' Katharina said, fear for her husband giving her strength. 'Feel him – he burns up.'

The soldier stepped hurriedly back.

'What is wrong with him?' he asked in rough German.

Katharina remembered another thing Ursula's cousin had said – the Russians hated disease.

'Typhoid. Look, this woman may have it too.'

She pointed at Gisela, whose pale face was highlighted by sharp scarlet cheekbones and slicked with a sheen of sweat. The soldier took more steps backwards.

'Scum,' he spat. 'Filthy German scum. Get out of here.' The people in the bunker looked at each other, confused. 'I said, get out! Now. All of you.'

They needed no second asking and began scrambling for the door, desperate to escape. The Russians stopped them to strip them of valuables as they went, snatching watches off wrists like magpies, despite already having three or four strapped up their arms. Thankfully, however, that was as close as they got.

'And you,' the officer rapped at Katharina, grabbing her wrist and grinning at her beautiful silver watch. 'I'll have that.'

A lump rose in her throat at the thought of losing Oskar's gift, but she told herself sternly that it was only an object and fumbled it off.

'Good. Now – out of here.'

'But my husband.'

'Take him or leave him. I don't care, just do it fast.'

'We must go, Kätsche.' They were the first words she'd heard Adelaide speak in days and they galvanised her into action. The girl picked up a now screaming Hanna and made for the bunker door, Gisela in her wake like a bloodied ghost. Katharina looked to Oskar.

'You need to get up, my love.'

She saw pain cross his face but he nodded and pushed back the covers. She reached down to take him under the armpits and help him to standing.

'Not fast enough!' the Russian snapped.

Katharina felt his gaze boring into her back, as if lining up his rifle sight. She forced herself to speak calmly.

'Just a few steps, O. Just a few steps out of here and we'll find somewhere to rest.'

Oskar nodded and forced himself to walk. His small frame was like an inferno against her own and, as they passed the officer, she braced to feel a bullet in her back, but it did not come, and finally they were up the steps and out into the smoke-filled air of the city. Katharina looked around her. Few buildings were still standing and those that were tottered precariously. Just outside the Elephant Gate, a gas pipe had burst and was spewing flames across the street like an apocalyptic dragon. Five tanks were sunk into the road and Russian soldiers were dancing on them, throwing a bottle of something around with shouts of laughter. One was pulling blossom off the trees and scattering it over his fellows, like a dark parody of a wedding, and in that moment, Katharina saw that Berlin had truly been taken from them.

'This way,' she urged Oskar, turning into the zoo. Gisela stood shivering with Adelaide and Hanna beside the miraculously still standing antelope house, and Katharina looked up at it as if at a mirage in the desert.

'We can hide in there,' she said, hope flaring within her, but the soldiers had followed her out and she felt the butt of a rifle glance across her shoulder.

'Go! Out of here.'

'But the zoo—'

'Is *our* zoo now. Don't worry, we will take care of the animals. We like animals.' He leaned in so that his next words hit Katharina's face in a shower of spittle: 'Very tasty.'

'Bastard!'

Gisela gasped but the Russian just laughed and hit Katharina again.

'It was good of you to save them for us. Now – go!'

There was no choice but to flee, past the antelope house, past the few remaining wild dogs and round to the hippo house. A roar greeted them and Katharina looked over to see Knautschke, dear little Knautschke, bellowing a desperate appeal. His skin was parched and cracked and he was standing over the body of his mother, sprawled across the near-empty pond with a gaping wound in her side. Katharina longed to run to him, but the Russians fired a warning shot over their heads and she had no choice but to give the hippo a helpless wave and lead her loved ones onwards, out of the Lion Gate. To their right, she could see the Red Army celebrating in front of the flak tower, so she turned to the left but already Oskar was struggling.

'Leave me,' he croaked.

'No! I'm not giving up on you.'

'You're mad,' he muttered, and sank to the ground.

She crouched next to him.

'I'm not mad, Oskar. I love you.'

His pain-filled eyes softened.

'And I you, meine kindl, truly. You are the best thing that ever happened to me.'

'I am happening still,' she said stoutly.

She looked desperately around, but there were few buildings intact nearby and even if they found one, the sheer concentration of Russians made the odds of survival far too small. She turned to Gisela.

'We need transport.' Gisela let out a manic laugh but Adelaide tugged on Katharina's skirts and, pushing Hanna into her arms, ran back into the zoo. 'Addie, no! Come back.'

The girl didn't listen and, with Hanna on her hip and a now barely conscious Oskar propped up against her legs, there was no way Katharina could follow. Thankfully, Adelaide came running back almost immediately, pushing a rusty old wheelbarrow.

'Oh, Addie – well done!'

Katharina helped Oskar as gently as she could into the barrow, trying to shake away the picture of the corpse she'd seen that poor girl pushing as she'd waited for Margret just a few days ago. Behind her was the cairn that hid her mother's body, but Oskar wasn't dead. Not yet. If they could just find somewhere to stay, he might yet recover. He *would* recover. Surely they had not gone through all this suffering to lose him at the final hurdle? She set Hanna on top of Oskar and looked down incredulously as the beautiful little girl gave a happy giggle at her new transport.

'Quite right, Hanna.' She took the handles with new determination and looked to the rest of her rag-tag group. 'Come on, let's get out of here!'

It nearly broke her heart to walk away from the zoo, but what choice did she have? The Red Army had taken her baby from her, and all she could do now was try her best to keep those in her protection alive.

Chapter Twenty-Three

Torgau. Bethan looked around her, stunned by the prettiness of the place. If someone had asked her to draw a German town (and if she'd been vaguely able to draw), this is what she would have come up with. There were elegant red-roofed buildings set around a quaint market square, the spire of a graceful church and, beyond, a lazily meandering river and rolling green fields. She couldn't imagine anything more different to Berlin, and prayed that those caring for her mother had escaped here at the end of the war for it must have felt like a haven indeed.

She drank it all in as Max drove her down the high street. She couldn't believe she was finally here. She'd had to work the morning shift, so they hadn't got away until after lunch and then the traffic had been frustratingly slow, but at last she spotted a sign to their destination – Schloss Ermau. The grand house was a luxury hotel and spa now, with no countess in sight, but a Monica von Weichs was listed as living in the grounds and Bethan prayed she might have some answers.

She'd brought Jana's list with her, feeling somehow that the original was required, and now she felt in her pocket and drew it out, stroking her finger down the names her mother had written so long ago. Might she finally be close to finding out which of these women was her real grandmother? It was an exciting prospect.

'We're here.'

Max turned the car up a long, elegant driveway towards the fairytale Schloss and she stared out of the windscreen in disbelief.

'It's huge.'

He chuckled.

'What did you expect, Beth? Anywhere that had its own private zoo was going to be pretty grand.'

'True,' she admitted. 'Even so…'

'It is pretty flash. My poor little car is going to look rather out of place in the car park.'

Max indicated the run of gleaming Mercedes and BMWs as he turned his battered Polo into a space in the far corner. Bethan smiled.

'I'm very grateful to your little car, Max. And to you. Thank you for bringing me.'

'My pleasure. Shall we head in?'

'I guess so.'

'Beth?'

'I'm just a bit nervous, I guess. Silly, hey? I've waited all these years for answers and now that I'm close, it feels sort of scary.' He reached out and gave her hand a quick squeeze. The touch of him shot through her, doing little to settle her nerves, but she smiled gratefully. 'Let's go.'

He nodded, and they climbed out of the car and made for the grand entrance. Bethan glanced ruefully down at the summer dress that had looked so right in the mirror this morning but now felt embarrassingly unsophisticated. Max, she noticed, was dressed perfectly in a faded linen jacket and smart shorts. His clothes weren't expensive, but they sat very well on his tall frame and he walked with a purpose that made him fit right in. Bethan saw a suited woman look him discreetly up and down, and hurried to catch up.

'What are we going to say?' she asked.

'We're going to say hello. Don't worry, Beth – they're expecting us, remember?'

'You're right.'

Bethan had called yesterday and spoken to Frau Schneider, the manager, who had seemed very interested in her story. She'd said that she would inform Monica von Weichs of their arrival, but had made no promises about whether the eighty-year-old would be able to meet them. Bethan had googled the family and knew that Monica was the youngest of the Count Albrecht and Countess Sylvie von Weichs's four children, but Google had not been able to tell her how fit Monica was, and Bethan could only pray that she was well and lucid – not to mention prepared to talk to her. Her heart fluttered in her chest again and she pressed her hand to it. Her fingers met the brooch she'd pinned onto her dress just before they left this morning, and the feel of the chubby silver hippo gave her strength.

'This is for you, Mum,' she whispered, and stepped firmly inside.

The entrance hall was stunning. White marble tiles glistened on the floor and above them was arching space all the way up to a cupola window several storeys above. The corridors on each storey were balconied onto this grand space and a red-carpeted staircase curved up at every corner. Bethan couldn't help picturing herself sweeping down one in a wedding dress and for a moment saw Callum at the bottom, waiting for her. She blinked furiously. She didn't regret her decision at all but it was still taking some getting used to.

'Fräulein Taylor?'

An immaculate woman in a discreetly logoed suit came up to them and Bethan forced herself to focus.

'Bethan, please. This is Max.'

'Welcome to you both. I'm Lena Schneider, manager of Schloss Ermau, and I'm so pleased to meet you. Your story intrigues me, Bethan. It's so romantic – and I can well believe it of the Countess.'

'You knew her?'

Lena smiled.

'A little. I came to the hotel as a receptionist when it was first converted back in 1991. Countess Sylvie lived in one of the suites on the top floor and took a great interest in the running of the hotel. I imagine it drove the manager mad as she was very particular about the way she wanted the place to be run, but I found her fascinating.'

'What was she like?' Bethan asked eagerly.

'She had that natural charm that seems to come from high birth. She'd come and chat to me on reception if I wasn't busy and tell me all sorts of stories about her antics as a young woman. Of course, during the war people got away with all sorts.'

'Not in Berlin,' Max said.

Lena looked across at him.

'No. They had it hard in Berlin.'

'Which is why the zoo sent animals out here?'

She smiled again.

'You're impatient to get to the matter in hand.' Max coloured but she put up a hand. 'I don't blame you. Since I spoke to you yesterday, Bethan, I've done a little digging. There are photos on the bar wall of the zoo back in the forties, but I'd never looked into where the animals came from. It seems that the chimps did indeed come from Berlin Zoo.'

Bethan felt her heart start to beat harder.

'And the babies?'

Lena shook her head.

'No evidence of babies in the records – but then, there wouldn't be, would there?'

'I guess not. The Countess never mentioned it to you in your chats?'

Lena gave her an apologetic smile.

'I'm afraid not, but don't fret, Fräulein. I've spoken to Monica and she's keen to meet you.'

Bethan's head snapped up.

'Monica von Weichs?'

'The very same. She has a house in the grounds. It was an old folly, but she had it extended and made habitable when she came back here a few years ago. I can take you down when you're ready.'

'I'm ready now, thank you. And she's, er…' How to put it?

'With it?' Lena supplied easily. 'Oh, yes. Monica is one of the sharpest tools in the box. If there's anything to know, she's the one who'll know it. Shall we go?'

Bethan nodded eagerly.

'Yes please.'

Monica von Weichs was not just with it, but very much on top of it. She walked with a stick but exuded energy, and her eyes sparkled with intelligence as she shook Bethan and Max's hands and ushered them into her beautiful home. It was a three-storey hexagonal building, covered with painted frescoes. On the ground floor was a dining room and galley kitchen, on the upper floor Monica's bedroom, and in between a beautiful sitting room with 360-degree views of the parkland. Bethan was enchanted.

'This is so beautiful,' she said, peering around her like a child.

'It's quite fun, isn't it?' Monica agreed. 'Cost a fortune to renovate, but the alternative was the poor building falling into rubble and I couldn't have that. I call it my Rapunzel tower. Mad, I know, with this thinning top.' She pulled unselfconsciously at her short white hair. 'But I have a plaited rope I can throw from my bedroom if I ever want handsome princes to climb up. They don't, of course – not any more.'

'I'm sure they would, given half a chance.'

Monica threw back her head and laughed.

'I like you, Bethan Taylor. Maybe you're right – though I doubt there are any men my age who could climb it.'

'Why stick to ones your age?'

Again the laugh.

'Why indeed. I certainly never used to. I've lived a chequered life, I'm afraid. My siblings all despaired of me. I wouldn't "settle down" and marry but I couldn't really see why I should. Marrying, it seems to me, is rather like only having one chocolate out of the box.'

'Maybe you just didn't find a delicious enough chocolate?' Max suggested.

Monica looked between him and Bethan.

'Clearly not,' she said lightly.

'It's not what you—' Bethan started self-consciously, but Monica waved her quiet.

'Ignore me. I'm a foolish old woman who enjoys scandalising people. No man would have been able to put up with me for long enough to marry me, and I never stayed still long enough either. I worked all over the place until finally age caught up with me five years ago, and I moved into this little Rapunzel tower. It's the longest I've lived anywhere since I was a child, which, of course, was here too – well, in the big house.'

Bethan leaned forward.

'During the war?'

Monica looked at her, her eyes sparkling.

'During the war, yes. Which is what you've come to ask me about, right?'

'If you don't mind.'

'Of course not but, remember, I was born in 1939 so I was pretty young, and it wasn't the same here as elsewhere. There might as well not have been a war, save that most of our men had to go off and fight. For the first five years of my life I barely knew I had a father, let alone brothers. It was just me, Mother and my sister Barbara. Oh, and Anke of course.'

Bethan looked at Max and saw that he, too, had jumped: Anke – the last name on Jana's list.

'Who was Anke?' she asked, hearing her own voice squeak on the key name.

'Anke Meyer, our housekeeper. Oh, she was a gem. A great big lady, which was good news for us kids as she couldn't catch you if you nicked something from the kitchen. She had a sharp tongue but the biggest heart and she cooked like a dream. She was from Freiburg and made the most delicious Schwarzwälder Kirschtorte you ever tasted.'

Monica licked her lips at the mere memory of the treat.

'She looked after you?'

'Unofficially, yes. Mother was always busy running the estate, especially when Father was away. We had acres of farmland back then and she had to keep it all working. Food was vital so we couldn't afford to let the crops ruin.'

'How did she manage it?'

'Land girls mainly. We had all sorts of young women come out to live with us. They were housed up in the maids' rooms on the top floor, and in the evenings I'd hear them all laughing and talking and trying on each other's clothes. If we were lucky, Babs and I would sneak up there, and they'd make up our faces and dress us in their clothes and let us parade the corridors in their heeled shoes. The poor lasses had no one to party with but us, but they seemed happy enough. They worked hard too.'

Bethan swallowed. Was this the link they'd been looking for?

'Do you, by any chance, remember a girl called Erika?'

'Erika?' Monica looked to the ceiling as if seeking inspiration, but eventually she shook her head. 'I don't remember an Erika, I'm afraid, but there were so many of them and I was so young. They all rather melded into one.'

Bethan looked down, trying to hide her disappointment, and Max leaned forward.

'Did Lena explain what we were looking for?' he asked.

'Babies,' Monica said straight away.

'That's right. Do you remember any babies, Monica?'

Bethan dared to look up again, holding her breath as she watched the sprightly old lady, who swung her eyes from Max over to Bethan and smiled.

'Babies? As a matter of fact, I do.'

Chapter Twenty-Four

8 May 1945

Katharina crept out of the coal bunker like a mole braving daylight for the first time. For seven long days and nights she, Oskar, Gisela and the girls had huddled down there in the dirt and the dust, only daring to venture out at dawn to find what food and water they could to survive another twenty-four hours of discomfort and fear. Thankfully, the bunker was beneath a partially standing house whose inhabitants must be either dead or fled, and Katharina had been able to drag blankets, pillows and even two mattresses down into the substantial space. Gisela slept on one with Adelaide and Hanna, whilst Katharina took the other with Oskar.

Her dear husband was still fevered and coughed a great deal from the coal dust, but he had at least been able to rest and seemed calmer. He was not alone, for this morning, they had been woken from fitful sleep to the sound of loudspeakers in the streets above announcing peace.

'Frieden!' the voice had blared. Peace, freedom, an end to war. Rarely had a word sounded sweeter. They had made it. Somehow, they had made it through the bitter battle for Berlin. More information had followed. Generalfeldmarschall Keitel had signed the official surrender and the war was over. They had lost, of course, and there were still their Russian conquerors to worry about, but the whispered messages that passed amongst the rubble had it that the Red Army were usually asleep at dawn, so Katharina had decided to risk it.

She looked nervously around but it was quiet in the city. Orderly. Even the piles of rubble were being arranged in neat heaps by the

Trümmerfrauen, stoically passing their buckets down long lines to get the streets clear for traffic. Katharina felt her heart lift just a little and turned to Gisela.

'If we can find another van, we can get you to Torgau. You will be with Olivia, Gigi. You will be safe.'

'And you, Kätsche.'

'Maybe.'

'What's stopping you?'

'I want to see the zoo before I decide.'

Gisela raised her eyes to the blue skies.

'Always the zoo, sweet one!'

Katharina smiled shyly.

'She means a lot to me. But let's see – there may be nothing left.'

Her heart contracted again as she remembered poor Knautschke bellowing for help the day the Russians had taken the flak tower. That had been a week ago. If no one had given him food or, even more importantly, water, he would be as dead as his mother. And he would have died thinking she had abandoned him.

She shook herself crossly. Hippos did not think that way and, besides, what choice had she had? She'd have been no good to Knautschke or any of the animals with a Red bullet in her back. She turned to the girls. Adelaide was struggling to hold Hanna, who had miraculously found her walking legs in the coal bunker and was keen to use them out in the open. Katharina smiled and reached for the little girl, offering her hands to help her walk, though she knew her back would pay for it later.

'Come on,' she said, as if this were any family outing, 'let's go to the zoo.'

They reached the Elephant Gate some time later, after a very welcome pause at a Russian street kitchen set up beneath the battered Brandenburg Gate. Katharina had scarcely been able to believe her eyes, but there before them had been long trestle tables laden with rough bread and cauldrons of stew set over fires on the broken pavement. Russian soldiers, some of them women in uniforms identical to their male compatriots, served food to the Berliners with efficiency and even, on occasion, smiles.

It was a far cry from the marauding bands of rumour, though the group of men loudly partying around the burned-out Reichstag just down the road was a reminder of the threat the Red Army brought to the German capital. Katharina had heard the cries at night, both the grunts of male triumph and the screams of female horror, and knew that this orderly feeding masked a darker reality. She would have her charges back in the bunker long before dark brought the violent side of conquest to Berlin, but the taste of warm, rich goulash was like the nectar of Elysium and she gulped their conqueror's dish down.

The rest of their walk had felt even more hopeful. Blossom was blooming on the trees and little shoots of new life were pushing up between the cracks in the road, determined to grow. She'd laughed out loud when they'd passed the sign for Charlottenburg and seen someone's rough correction, scrawled on it in black paint: Klamottenburg – heap of rubbish. The dark Berlin sense of humour was still, it seemed, intact, and for the first time in far too long she actually felt glad to be here. Then, at last, they were back at the zoo.

'The elephants are still here!' Gisela cried, going over to stroke one marble head.

Katharina watched her friend with concern. She moved well enough but hunched over her tender middle, and Katharina knew that she was still bleeding for she had seen the torn strips of reddened bedlinen in the corner of the bunker. Was that normal? Probably, but it needed keeping an eye on all the same. At that moment, however, she caught a sight that drove all worries briefly from her head.

'Pierre!'

The Frenchman was walking down the avenue, a bucket in each hand, but seeing her, he dropped them and ran. They clutched each other, laughing and crying and patting, as if to be sure they were both whole.

'You made it!' he cried. 'I've looked and looked for you but couldn't find a trace.'

'We hid well.'

'You needed to. But now we have the surrender, the officers are abroad and it seems perhaps the worst of it is over. Oh Kätsche, it is so good to see you. Gigi too! Ursula will be so, so happy.'

'Have you heard from her?'

He nodded, his eyes shining.

'A letter came to the zoo office. Lord knows how, but some brave soul got it through. She is safe, as are the babies.' Gisela gasped and fell to her knees, but Pierre swooped her up in his strong arms and held her close. 'It's over, Gigi. I'll get a van, I promise. I'll get a van and I'll take you to Torgau.' Gisela gave a small whimper and promptly fainted. Pierre held her tight against him and looked to Katharina. 'You've had a hard time?'

Katharina gave a shrug.

'We are here.'

'The girls?'

A little giggle was his answer and he turned to see Hanna walking proudly towards him, bottom lip held between her tiny teeth in concentration as she put one leg stoutly in front of the other. Adelaide hovered behind her, totally fixated on her baby sister, but looked up as Pierre let out a loud laugh.

'She's walking! Hanna is walking. If Hanna is walking, surely we all are?' His face clouded. 'Oskar?'

'Is alive,' Katharina assured him, bending to welcome a now tottering Hanna into her arms.

Gisela was coming round, though she looked pale and Katharina wished she had left her in the bunker.

'Katharina!'

She looked around to see Walter and Gustav come running down the avenue, and her heart swelled. She rushed to meet them, hugging them tightly. It was perhaps the first time she'd ever touched the two men, who were normally very formal in their dealings with her, but formality was gone, along with almost everything else, and she rejoiced at the feel of them, warm and whole.

'How did you all escape?' she asked, looking around at the men. 'Hans told us you'd been marched away.'

'We were,' Walter agreed. 'They took us to their HQ on the eastern edge of the city. People were talking about labour camps and bullets in the back. It was awful, Katharina, but then the next morning a senior officer turned up, walked down the line and yanked Gustav here out in front of him. He peered at the logo on his uniform.' He paused to point at the little embroidered gorilla on Gustav's old chest. 'Then he laughed and grabbed hold of the soldiers in charge of us, calling them all sorts of Russian insults. We understood none of them but we got the tone and the gestures. They were... animalistic!' He suddenly remembered who he was addressing and flushed. 'Apologies, Frau Heinroth.'

'Come, Walter – a few Russian obscenities is hardly the worst I have endured recently. So they released you?'

'Yep! They pulled us out and sent us on our way.'

'All of you?'

'All of us,' Pierre confirmed. 'Marcel, Victor, even Dennis and Kurt, though you should know—'

Walter seemed to kick Pierre and he cut himself off.

'We got a few kicks and a few, er, gestures of our own,' Walter said hastily, 'but who cares? We ran all the way back to the zoo and we've been here ever since.'

'Lutz?'

'Lutz is gone, melted into the night before they worked out who his high-placed friends had once been.'

Katharina sighed.

'It will have broken his heart to leave the zoo,' she said softly, remembering the dark morning of Kalifa's death when the former manager told her that the zoo was in her charge now. She squared her shoulders and dared to ask, 'How are the animals?'

Gustav gave a weary shrug.

'A few made it.'

Katharina swallowed.

'Knautschke?' she asked nervously, but a smile lifted Gustav's old lips. 'He's alive?'

'Alive and well and eating all we can find for him. Thank the Lord the grass is growing in Berlin, for he is one hungry kid.'

Tears burst from Katharina's eyes, and she fumbled for a small wall behind her and sank down onto it to absorb this little sign of hope. The keepers were alive, Knautschke was alive, she and Gisela and Ursula were alive – perhaps, therefore, the zoo could live again too. She looked up at the concerned men.

'Show me around,' she said. 'Show me everything.'

It was a long, hard tour. They sent Gisela to rest on a camp bed in the kitchens, under the watchful eye of Marcel who was cooking up something meaty, and took Adelaide and Hanna around with them. Katharina was nervous of what the girls might see, but Hanna was mainly absorbed in her own feet and Adelaide had seen too much already to have scruples now.

The clear-up had obviously begun but there was much to do and few people to do it. A troop of Russians had been assigned to the zoo, but they appeared to be concerning themselves more with the remains of the Heck wine store than the animals. They passed a group of them trying to coax an alpine ibex down from the balcony of the ruined concert house but they tired of the game and, as Katharina passed, one of them lifted his rifle and fired. It was a poor shot and merely grazed the creature's back. It bleated, staggered and then fell, hitting the avenue below with a crack that jolted through Katharina, but at least spared it any further misery. The soldiers cheered.

Everywhere there were corpses, both human and animal. Injured horses and deer staggered around. Goliath was still wedged in the crooked cage in which Katharina had dispatched him to the afterlife thirteen long days ago and men were tucking wood beneath his rotting flesh, preparing to cremate him where he had fallen. In the monkey house, poor Pongo the gorilla was dead, seemingly gashed repeatedly with a knife, though there were three SS corpses in there with him so it seemed he had not gone down without a fight.

'It's senseless,' Katharina wailed, stroking the beautiful beast's silver back. 'So very, very senseless.'

There were, thankfully, moments of relief too. She came across Father Jörg, supervising a quiet service for several people being buried in a bomb crater at the back of the zoo. As Katharina approached, the little group broke into a muted hymn, the music lilting poignantly across the broken landscape. Katharina paused to sing with them and the dignity of the ceremony soothed her soul. She bent to promise Adelaide that they would hold a similar service for her parents, and for Dieter. The girl said nothing but Katharina caught the ghost of a smile cross her drawn-in face, and vowed to arrange it with Father Jörg as soon as possible.

In the largely intact pheasant aviary, the remaining birds were gathered in an apparently contented cross-continental mix, the water for the storks and herons coming from a handily burst water main that one of the keepers had siphoned into the building by means of a length of hose. Their numbers were swollen by a mass of parrots that Katharina did not remember seeing before, and Walter told her that most had flown here of their own accord, apparently drawn by the squawks of their fellows.

'Can I see Knautschke?' she asked.

'Of course.'

The hippo was wallowing in ten centimetres of muddy water, turning over and over to rub it into his skin. Behind him, Katharina noticed men battling to cut up Rosa's enormous body with inadequate saws, and she wanted to rush in and protect her poor son from the sight but it was hard to cuddle a two-tonne animal.

'Look, Addie, how Knautschke turns,' she said, hoping to distract the girl, but Adelaide's wild eyes were fixed on the men hacking up the blubbery flesh and Katharina feared that she was seeing again the body of her father, blown in half, or that of her mother, bleeding out on the birthing table.

'Death might be a mercy for her,' Pierre whispered, looking at Adelaide in concern, but Katharina shook her head fiercely.

'There has been enough death. We are here, now, to preserve life.'

Knautschke looked up as if he had heard her voice, and gave her a wide-mouthed roar of greeting.

'You made it, boy!' she called. 'You made it and I made it and together we are going to build a future.'

'Are you sure about that?' a snide voice asked.

Katharina whipped around and saw Dennis standing before her, Kurt close at his left shoulder and, on his right, a highly decorated Russian officer. Fear shot through her and she found herself dropping into a clumsy curtsey. Dennis laughed but the officer reached out a hand and raised her.

'Frau Heinroth, I believe?' he asked in near-perfect German.

'Yes, sir.'

'Welcome. I am Marshal Vetrov and I am in charge of this segment of Berlin.'

Katharina stared at the smart, dark-skinned man before her, trying to process what that meant. Should she congratulate him? Bow down before him? Beg him for her job? If indeed she had a job for, despite all her work, she had never truly been anything at the zoo save for Oskar's wife and assistant.

'I am at your service,' she stuttered out.

'I know.' He looked her up and down for a moment. 'It is my job to resurrect the zoo. It will be like a, a…'

He looked to Dennis who leaped to attention.

'A phoenix, Marshal.'

'A phoenix, exactly. Apt, is it not?'

'It is very good news,' Katharina said cautiously. 'I would love to help. I know the zoo well and—'

'Excellent, excellent. This is what we need. Report to Dennis and he will tell you what to do.'

'Dennis?' Katharina looked from Vetrov to Lutz's lazy driver and suddenly noted his smart new clothes, his slicked-back hair, his smug look. She swung her eyes to Pierre who gave her a miserable shrug. 'Dennis is in charge?'

'Correct,' the officer said. 'He has been most helpful to us, and he will raise our phoenix as a symbol of Russian benevolence to the German people.'

'Benevolence?' Katharina gasped, but Pierre nudged her ribs in time to stop her saying more. This Russian had her life in his hands – and had apparently passed control of it to Dennis. Could there have been a worse choice?

'Very well,' she managed.

Dennis smirked.

'I will see you in my office later, Katharina.'

He lingered on her name. He had never dared call her by it before and it felt as insolent as if he had struck her, but what could she do? It was like watching a sewer rat carry away her baby – except that he had not carried it away yet and she would not let him. She would bend the knee, but only for the animals – and only for as long as it took to get him out. She turned wearily away as Dennis shuffled off after Marshal Vetrov, and took Pierre's arm.

'You started to tell me?'

'Walter stopped me and I can't blame him. It is too much to bear, truly.'

Katharina had learned over the last three years that there was little that was too much to bear when the survival of those you cared about most depended on it. She was glad, now, that she was still here in Berlin. She must get Gisela, Adelaide and Hanna to safety and then, somehow, she must save the zoo. Her enemies, it seemed, were not quite done with her yet.

Chapter Twenty-Five

'Babies? As a matter of fact, I do.'

Bethan felt her breath tighten in her throat at Monica's reply and found herself looking out to the skies, as if her mother might be there, peering desperately into the hexagonal house.

'Are you all right, my dear?' Monica asked.

'I think so. I just can't believe you might remember the babies.'

'Do I look so doddering?'

'No! Goodness no. I didn't mean that at all. More just that I can't believe *anyone* might remember them.'

Monica laughed.

'I'm teasing you. You're talking about the babies that came from Berlin?'

'I hope so. *Do* you remember?'

'Only just. Only because you reminded me. There were so many people coming and going at the time – babies included. Various of the land girls were pregnant, either from their husbands coming home on leave or from indiscretions with those men lucky enough to still be in the area. Mother never said anything on either count. She once told me that all new life was a blessing and we must cherish it. She said that what people did with their own bodies was their business and ours was simply to look after them. It stuck with me all my life – and gave me a hell of a lot of fun! But, listen to me drivelling on about myself. That's not what you're here for. You want to know about the Berlin babies. I'll do my best, but I warn you, my memories are sketchy.'

'Anything you can tell me would be wonderful,' Bethan assured her, glancing to Max who was as rapt as she was.

'Very well,' Monica said, settling in her chair and patting at her immaculate white hair. Outside the sun was already starting to dip towards the manicured horizon and Bethan felt strangely as if she were back with her mother, curled up for her bedtime story. 'If I recall correctly, they came in a lorry, driven by a fierce lady who only stayed a few days. I don't know where she went. She said something about following the birds, which I remember struck me as very odd because she wasn't the smallest of women and I had no idea how she thought she was going to fly.' She rolled her eyes at herself. 'I was a very literal child.'

'Who was in the lorry?' Bethan asked.

Monica narrowed her eyes, as if trying to look into the past.

'A lot of chimps. Noisy little buggers. It was the sound of them that woke Babs and me up. It was late when they arrived, you see. Dark. You could hear those monkeys shrieking from right up in our room. Well, we ran down straight away. The lorry was heading off to the zoo which was over there.'

She pointed out of the window to a large open area by the river that meandered along the bottom of the hotel grounds. Bethan peered out, as if the shadow of the enclosures might still be seen in the dusk, and Monica gave her a little grimace.

'I call it a zoo but it wasn't, not really – just a handful of cages with some curiosities from my father's travels. He'd bag an animal wherever he went and have it shipped back here. Terribly irresponsible, of course. It wouldn't be allowed now and quite right too, but plenty of people were at it back then. We were all fascinated by anything "exotic" and I was desperate to see the monkeys that night. Babs and I ran round through the trees and hid in the bushes where the lorry pulled up.'

Bethan turned round.

'Who got out?'

Monica frowned.

'Let me think about this carefully. It was over seventy years ago so it's a little hazy, but it was a striking night. There were the chimps of course, over the moon to get out of their tiny cages and flinging themselves around the enclosure Mother had prepared for them. I confess, I was so fascinated by them that I didn't pay much attention to the boring old humans.'

'But there were some – humans?'

'Oh yes. There were three, I think – a young woman and two babies.'

Bethan gasped.

'Two babies? Did you meet them? Do you remember them?'

'I do. They stayed for some time. Mother introduced Babs and me properly the next morning, and we smiled politely and never said that we'd watched them arrive.'

'Do you remember their names?'

'The woman was Ursula. I liked her. She was very talkative and very kind. She played with me when Babs was having lessons in the schoolroom.'

'And the babies? Do you remember their names?'

'One was Ursula's daughter. She had a French name – Belle? Bridget? Beatrice? Yes – I think perhaps it was Beatrice. I thought it was very pretty.'

'And the other one?'

'I don't honestly remember.'

'Was it Hanna?'

'Hanna? No, I don't think so. Not Hanna.' Monica frowned up at the ceiling. 'Let me think. It might come back to me. In time. And with some food maybe.' She pushed herself up and joined Bethan over near the window to look out on the sun, starting to kiss a blush across the river. 'Would you like some dinner?'

Bethan jumped.

'Oh no – we couldn't possibly put you to any trouble.'

Monica laughed and placed a slim hand on her arm.

'It's no trouble, my dear. I just call the hotel and ask them to send something down. It must be a real pain for them but they never complain. I think they like the PR of it – you know, mad old aristo living in the grounds. It's a nice quirk for the guests.'

Behind them Max burst out laughing.

'You're hardly a "mad old aristo", Monica.'

The older lady winked at him.

'Oh, but I can be if I want to. Lena and I, we have an arrangement – she lets me know if there are journalists in and I do something appropriately eccentric. Last time I went for a lovely naked swim in the river. Lapped that up, they did. Lena reckons foreign bookings went up by ten per cent after that article was published. It means I have to do it again every so often to keep up the "sightings", but it keeps my blood circulating.'

'You're better than the Loch Ness monster,' Bethan chuckled, but both Max and Monica stared at her in confusion. 'Never mind.'

'Dinner then?' Monica clapped her hands and moved across to unpin a cream menu from a noticeboard, then handed it to Max. 'Order whatever you want – they'll be on top form today because your story, my dear, will probably boost bookings by twenty per cent.'

'You think?'

'Of course. That's why Lena is being so lovely to you. Not that she isn't lovely anyway, but she's a sharp operator and she can see the headlines already: "Bombed-out Berlin babies rescued by Torgau hotel". Commercial gold dust.'

'I suppose so,' Bethan said, though it seemed a little callous. And there was another worry too. She coughed awkwardly. 'You do *really* remember this?'

Monica started to laugh and then caught herself. She reached out and took Bethan's hand.

'I do, Bethan. I promise. Taking a skinny dip for the press is one thing but I wouldn't make this up, not when it's clearly so important to you.'

'Thank you.'

'So, let's order dinner.'

She waved to the menu in Max's hands, and Bethan was left with little choice but to go over and perch on the arm of his chair to read it.

'Isn't this cosy?' Monica said happily.

Bethan could only agree.

Dinner was delicious, as was the very nice bottle of Riesling Monica opened. The old lady chatted away about her life, though she remembered little more of Ursula or the babies, and as the clock ticked on, she started nodding quietly in her chair.

Bethan looked to Max.

'We should go.' He nodded and checked his watch. It was already almost ten o'clock and they had a two-hour journey back to Berlin. Bethan realised guiltily that she'd been happily enjoying Monica's wine while poor Max had stuck to the water. 'Sorry, Max. I didn't realise it had got so late. You should have said.'

'I was enjoying it, and I'm off duty tomorrow so I can have a lie-in.'

'OK.' Bethan stood up, aware she felt a little unsteady. She looked down at Monica, snoozing in her chair. 'Do we wake her up?'

'I think we better. She's been so hospitable, we can't just sneak off. Besides, she should get into bed.'

Bethan leaned forward and gently touched Monica's arm. The old lady didn't move so she shook her a little harder and suddenly Monica sat bolt upright, with a strange snort.

'Who? What? Oh! Oh, Bethan, did I fall asleep? How terribly rude of me.'

'Not at all. It's very late and we've kept you talking for ages. We'll be off and thank you so much for everything.'

Monica snorted again.

'I've been next to useless. Goodness, look at the time. You must stay.'

'Oh no, we—'

'It's much too far to go back to Berlin now. I'll get you a room in the hotel.'

'There's no need.'

'Don't worry, they'll just put it on the family bill which goes who knows where. It'll come out of my estate when I finally pop my clogs, I suppose, so we might as well have some fun with it.'

'Really, Monica—'

'I insist.' She was up now and reaching for her phone to call reception. 'We need a room please, for Bethan and Max. Yes. A nice one. I know, I know, but a *really* nice one. The girl's grandmother was effectively born here so the least we can do is put her up in style. Which one? Oh yes – perfect. I'll send them up straight away.'

She clicked off her phone and beamed at Bethan.

'They're putting you in the Sylvie suite. Apt, don't you think?' She leaned in. 'It's very nice. Lovely big bed – make the most of it!'

Bethan felt herself flush lobster-red and didn't even dare look at Max.

'That's very kind of you,' she heard him say. 'We're honoured.'

'Nonsense,' Monica said. 'It's I who am honoured. Plus, this way we can have breakfast together and I might be less dopey.'

'Will you be OK to get to bed?' Max asked, and Monica giggled.

'Get away with you, young man, I'll be fine. You take your beautiful girl off to the Sylvie suite and I'll see you both tomorrow.'

'Thank you.'

'Yes, thank you,' Bethan echoed and then, somehow, they were leaving the hexagonal house and heading across the grounds towards the main hotel. They walked carefully apart and didn't quite look at each other.

'It's very kind of her,' Bethan said awkwardly.

'Yes.'

'But a little…'

'Yes.'

'We could just go.'

'It would look rather rude.'

'It would.'

They'd reached the back of the hotel and hesitated, but a waiter spotted them and flung open the doors, leaving them with little choice but to move inside. The receptionist was waiting with a key and, with all obsequiousness, showed them up to the fifth floor. As they walked down the corridor it was all Bethan could do not to lie down and stroke the super-plush carpet, and when the young man opened the door and ushered them into what was apparently their room for the night, she couldn't believe her eyes.

The suite was the ultimate in luxury. A huge living area, with gilt-backed chairs and a shiny cabinet packed with decanters, led through a high archway to an opulent king-sized bed beyond. To one side the door to the bathroom stood open, and Bethan glimpsed floor-to-ceiling marble and the biggest claw-footed bathtub she'd ever seen.

'Is all to your liking, madam?' the bellhop asked.

She turned to him.

'Oh yes! It's wonderful, thank you.'

'Here.'

He held something out to her and she looked down at it, puzzled.

'What's this?'

'Our comfort package, madam, for those guests who have, for whatever reason, come without all they need.'

Bethan flushed.

'Oh! Thank you.'

'My pleasure. Have a wonderful night.'

He bowed out and, rather than look at Max, Bethan opened up the 'comfort package' to find toothbrushes, toothpaste, his and hers undies, and a condom. Flushing again, she hastily put it down and made for the bathroom. Closing the door with a mumbled, 'Won't be a minute,' she sat on the edge of the gorgeous bath. Somehow she had sunk fully into the fairy tale of Schloss Ermau and it felt, well, fantastic actually.

No men, she reminded herself sternly. She could manage that, couldn't she? Just because Max was out there, and there was only a double bed and Monica had made all those assumptions, didn't mean that anything had to happen. They were just two mature, sensible colleagues sharing a room. Right?

'Right,' she told her reflection in the ornate mirror, and headed determinedly back out.

Max was at the cabinet pouring himself a large brandy.

'This seems to be included in the price,' he said, holding it up, 'so I thought why not.'

'Quite right. I'll join you. Sitting room or bedroom?' That came out all wrong and she put a hand to her lips. 'I just meant – there are so many places to enjoy yourself. I mean, your drink. *Our* drink. I… Thank you, Max.'

She accepted the brandy and sank into one of the gilt-backed chairs to take a large sip. She'd probably had enough to drink already, but it wasn't every Saturday you found yourself in a luxury suite in a German Schloss, so why not make the most of it? Plus, at least when she was drinking brandy, she wasn't talking tripe. She sipped again. She was tired, she realised, and the air suddenly felt heavy. She sought for a safe topic of conversation.

'Shall we review what we've learned?'

'Good idea,' Max agreed.

His eyes looked very blue in the low light and his smile very enticing. She shook herself.

'Right. So, we know that Ursula Franke – probably really Ursula Dubois – left Berlin at the end of April 1945 in a truck full of chimps, plus two babies. One was her own daughter, probably Beatrice – a French name, backing up the likelihood of her being married to Pierre, right?'

'Right,' Max agreed. 'But because there are so many Dubois in France we don't know if she survived.'

'Though if she got to Torgau the odds must have been good?'

'Better than in Berlin, where the mother of the other baby presumably either still was or had already died.'

'The other baby, who probably isn't Hanna – the only girl whose birth we know of in the zoo during the war.'

'And who Ada, probably her sister, won't talk about at all. Indeed, she got very upset at even the mention of her name, suggesting, suggesting…' Max ran out of steam.

'Suggesting she died,' Bethan finished dully, pushing herself out of her chair and going over to the window. This was surely hopeless.

Max stood up and came over to her.

'Even if all that's true, Beth, it still leaves the mystery baby.'

She turned to look at him.

'Great! A mystery baby – that's what I've had all along.'

'There's Gisela Schultz to look into, remember.'

'But I've had her name all along too, and I'm no further on with it than I was when I first found the list.'

She felt flat suddenly, worn out by the rise of excitement that seemed to have built and built to a great big nothing. A stupid tear pricked at her eye and she brushed it crossly away.

'Oh, Beth.' Max came closer and it was the most natural thing in the world to step into his arms. She closed her eyes and let herself rest against his broad chest. His hand stroked her hair and she drew in a shaky breath. 'We're close,' he said softly. 'We have to keep looking a little bit longer, but we're close.'

She pulled back to look up at him.

'Do you really think so?'

'Of course.'

His blue eyes shone with certainty. His arms were warm and strong around her. They were here, in the most beautiful room Bethan had ever seen, just the two of them, just…

'Callum!' She sprang back and Max flinched and backed off immediately, hands held up as if in self-defence. 'Sorry,' she stuttered. 'I don't know where that came from. Callum doesn't mean anything to me any more.'

'Are you sure?'

He turned away to snatch up his brandy glass and Bethan leaned against the wall, feeling suddenly unsteady. It had just been a moment, a flash of residual guilt that she was already regretting.

'Well of course it takes time to get used to not being with someone,' she said carefully, 'but that's not the same—'

'Because I'm not the sort of man who moves in on a girl who still has feelings for someone else.'

'I didn't think you were. Max—'

She tried to step towards him but he put a hand up to stop her.

'How long were you with Callum, Beth?'

She swallowed.

'Two years, more or less. We got together just before Leicester City won the league. I remember because it was mental in the city that night.'

'Mental?'

He frowned. Clearly the German word she'd chosen didn't have the same connotations as the English version.

'Crazy,' she tried. 'But in a good way. Loads of people, you know. Lots of singing and dancing and climbing lampposts.'

'Lampposts?'

Bethan shook her head crossly; the conversation had taken a very strange turn.

'It really doesn't matter, Max. It was a long time ago.'

He ran a hand through his curls and she longed to step across and do the same, but he'd folded his arms protectively across his broad chest and she didn't dare approach.

'It'll take time to get over him,' he said stiffly.

Bethan shook her head.

'I don't think it will. We'd been growing apart for ages, it just took me a while to realise it. Routines and all that.' She attempted a laugh but it came out rather hoarse and suddenly she felt stupid. 'Haven't you ever stuck with someone for longer than you should have done?'

Max's brow crinkled as he thought about it. He looked incredibly cute but his arms were still firmly crossed and his eyes fixed on the floor.

'No,' he said eventually. 'What's the point?'

Bethan sighed. He was right of course, but it was rarely as simple as he was making out.

'I guess we're not all as perfect as you,' she said tightly.

He looked up at that, his eyes blue in the soft light of the beautiful room.

'I'm not perfect, Beth. Not at all. I didn't mean—'

'It doesn't matter, Max,' she said wearily. And it didn't, did it? All along she'd told herself that this was a fact-finding mission not a romantic trip away and that was still true. She was surely so close, now, to finding out where her mum had come from but the final gap in her knowledge suddenly felt like a chasm. 'It's been a long day. We're tired. Let's go to bed.'

'Bed?' Max jumped as if scalded and darted through the alcove to point at the big double. 'This bed?'

'I guess so.'

'Together?'

She swallowed and looked around; it seemed to be the only option.

'It's very big.'

'Not big enough.'

'Max, please—'

'It could never be big enough.'

She stared at him, stung. 'To get away from me?'

He shook his head.

'No, Bethan, to stop me wanting you.' Her breath caught. The giant room felt impossibly tiny. 'It's not your fault,' he said softly, then, reaching out, he cupped her face for a brief, sad moment before pulling the decorative counterpane off the end of the bed. 'I'll sleep through there.'

'But—'

'Please, Bethan – allow me that.'

There was little more she could say. Somehow their happy day had turned sour and she had no idea how to claw it back. *No men*, she reminded herself fiercely, but as she crawled into the vast bed, all she could think about was Max curled up in a feather-patterned counterpane just through the alcove, and the Sylvie suite, for all its luxury, offered her no comfort that night.

Chapter Twenty-Six

31 May 1945

'It's working, Kätsche – it's working!'

Pierre came running into the battered kitchen of Katharina and Oskar's apartment, waving an oily rag like a victory flag.

'The truck?'

He nodded excitedly.

'Come and see.'

Katharina looked around for Hanna, scooping her up from her happy occupation drawing swirls in the dust that settled endlessly on the floors. She and Oskar had moved back into the zoo last week after Pierre and Marcel had battled to make their old house liveable, and it was impossibly exciting to be home again. It had raised even Oskar's spirits and, although he was still weak, he seemed to Katharina to be a little better with each day that passed. If he could only recover, he could surely challenge Dennis for the management of the zoo before the wretched man wrecked it even further than the Allied bombs.

Dennis and Kurt spent their days rolling from work party to work party, drinking their new bosses' vodka and sneeringly exhorting everyone to harder labour without ever raising a finger to help. The only time they leaped into action was if Marshal Vetrov or one of his aides arrived at the zoo, at which point they busied themselves sucking up to whoever had the most stripes. It was sickening.

'Adelaide?' Katharina called. 'Gisela?'

Gisela and the girls had moved in with them, and whilst it was a little tight for space, it was a palace compared to the coal bunker. Gisela was listless and quiet, barely eating and spending hours in bed, but she was happy to watch the girls which at least meant that Katharina could help out around the zoo. And now Pierre might have found a way to get her to Torgau where she could be reunited with Olivia.

She looked down the avenue to the truck. It was a battered green Kübelwagen, abandoned by whichever German soldiers had been meant to be fighting the Red Army from its flimsy safety. Pierre had found it and had it pulled back here by two zebras and a young bison three days ago. It had been a peculiar sight, even within a city full of peculiar sights, and the locals had come out to cheer them on. The burly Frenchman had waved proudly to them all and had been working on it ever since.

'Gisela!' Katharina called again. 'Come and see Pierre's truck!'

Her friend emerged from the house, frowning.

'It won't start,' she grumbled.

'It might. It just might. Addie! Where are you?'

Adelaide emerged out of the zebra enclosure, where she was often to be found since they had set up a memorial to her parents at its edge. Katharina had polished up a piece of marble from the once-exotic ostrich house, Gustav had carved Sasha and Robert's names, and Father Jörg had presided over a small service to bless it. Adelaide had come with armfuls of flowers she must have gathered from all over the city and seemed to find the grave a comfort.

'Look,' she urged her, pointing as Pierre swung himself into the cab, holding the key up as if he were in a magic show.

Adelaide rolled her eyes but Hanna tottered eagerly towards the vehicle, only to jump back, landing on her nappy-clad bottom, as the engine leaped into life. She sent up a shocked wail but for once Katharina didn't care, for the metallic roar was the sweetest sound she'd heard in ages.

'It works, Hanna,' she said, picking her up and dancing her around as Pierre revved the engine again. 'It works. Isn't Uncle Pierre clever?'

Pierre beamed down at them from the cab.

'Uncle Pierre is a miracle worker – or he will be if he gets this beauty to Torgau. Gisela, look, the Olivia-mobile is in action!'

For a moment Gisela just stared at her best friend's husband, but then she burst into tears and picked up her listless feet into a run. Reaching the truck, she ran a hand tenderly along its side, as if it were the softest of animals, then, just as suddenly, she sprang across to Katharina, grabbing her in a big hug.

'I'm sorry, Kätsche.'

Katharina hugged her back.

'What on earth for?'

'For being so useless. For sitting around all day while you get on with all the work. For not helping with poor Oskar, who is truly sick.'

'You're truly sick too, Gisela – or you were. I hope and pray you are mending now and if we can get you to Olivia, I'm sure all will be well.'

Gisela sobered.

'Not all,' she said, 'for nothing can bring Dieter back. But it will be better. Much, much better. And it is all because of you.'

Katharina hugged her again.

'Nonsense, Gigi. You've been incredibly brave.'

'We all have.'

She looked around her at the few animal enclosures still occupied and Katharina nodded grimly. A grand total of ninety-one animals and birds had survived the six years of the war, out of well over three thousand back in the happy days of the 1930s, but she supposed it was better than none. Plus, Marshal Vetrov was insisting that the zoo would open to the public again on 1 July and was already planning a grand ceremony to mark the occasion, so he was keen to find more stock.

Already he had arranged a phone line for Katharina, who had managed to make contact with several other zoos to organise the return of their refugees. Sadly, many had suffered the same cruel bombings as they had, but just the other day Katharina had learned that Reike had somehow survived the carnage in East Prussia and might be able to return. The thought of the giraffe's calm face peeping over the wall at her every morning once more had given her cause for hope and, with the Red Army behind the project, transport should be possible.

Katharina had tried to convince Marshal Vetrov to find them a vehicle for the trip to Torgau, selling it as a way of getting the chimps back, but their cage was mangled beyond repair and Pierre hadn't been prepared to wait for it to be mended. Now, though, it seemed he wouldn't have to.

Little Hanna had recovered from her upset and was straining to be put down so that she could bang her hands on the big rubber tyres.

'She's testing it!' Gisela cried, bending to help her. 'How do they feel, Han-Han? Will they get us there, do you think?' Hanna let out what might have been an affirmative squeal and Gisela smiled. 'She says yes. So – when do we go?'

Pierre looked around the zoo.

'I see no point in hesitating. We have fuel and now we have a vehicle. We go tomorrow.'

Gisela gave a little skip, as if Pierre had reawakened her own engine along with the truck's.

'We must pack!' She grabbed Katharina's hand. 'Come, Kätsche, we must pack.'

Katharina swallowed.

'I'm not coming, Gigi.'

She had thought about this long and hard once Pierre had started work on the truck. She had thought, at the height of the battle for Berlin, that she had to choose between the animals and the people of the Zoofamilie, but now there was a glimmer of hope that she could save both and she had to take it.

'What?' Gisela cried. 'You must. You cannot stay here, not with all this.'

She cast a disparaging hand around the zoo, taking in two Russian soldiers riding a camel backwards down the avenue, and another two dangling what looked horribly like a finger into the lion cubs' cage on a makeshift fishing rod.

'Can't you see, Gigi – it's precisely because of "all this" that I *cannot* go.'

'But Kätsche, the Russians—'

'Will care little for me. And some of them are good. The vet they have sent us is a very caring man.'

That much was true. Yuri was a quiet, earnest young man who had clearly delighted in shedding his army uniform for a medical coat, and was working wonders with the injured animals. The other day Katharina had sat listening to him chatting soothingly away to Lotte, one of the four bears who had been kept in a pit in the Köllnischer Park to the east of the city, all the way until the final battle had cost the other three their lives. Lotte had been brought to the zoo to take up residence in Goliath's patched-up cage but was limping badly and clearly traumatised, at least until Yuri had started working his magic.

'What are you saying to her?' she'd asked him. He had little German and she no Russian but they managed with gestures.

'Pushkin,' he'd told her, and that at least she had understood – the vet was soothing the Berlin bear with Russian love poetry.

It had been a rare moment of happy collaboration and that night she had gone home, pulled down a dusty book of Goethe and read it to her husband. Oskar had slept with a smile on his face that night and now she reminded herself that, with the others gone, they would have a little peace together, just the two of them. Like old times. Or, at least, a fragment of old times – small but all the more valued. She feared her dear husband might not have long left and she wanted to cherish every precious moment with him.

'It's Oskar,' she said to Gisela now. 'He's not fit to travel and I cannot leave him here alone.'

'We can make him comfortable,' Gisela insisted, but it was a nonsense. A hundred metres in a wheelbarrow had nearly killed him, so a hundred kilometres in a battered van would be a direct route to hell.

'What will make him most comfortable,' Katharina told her calmly, 'will be to know that you and the girls are safe so that he can let himself rest properly.'

'Once he is rested you will join us?'

'Perhaps.'

'That means no.'

Katharina shook her head.

'It does not, Gigi. It means we shall have to see. If Dennis stays in charge of the zoo then, yes, we will come. We will come and we will take the chimps and we will make a new zoo far away from Berlin.'

'But…?'

'Dennis is drinking so much that it will be a miracle if he keeps himself alive, let alone in charge of the zoo. And if Oskar can recover…'

'He will be well placed to take over! Ah, Katharina – always you think further ahead than the rest of us.'

Katharina kissed her friend.

'I don't know about that but I can certainly see far enough ahead to know that you, my dear one, are leaving Berlin. First light?' she asked Pierre.

He nodded decisively.

'First light.'

They left the next day, as the first rays of the summer sun kissed Berlin's ragged edges. Pierre had padded the inside of the van with as many cushions and blankets as he could find, and he tucked his precious charges tenderly inside before assuming his position at the wheel. They had no papers granting them permission to leave the capital but the Russians did not seem to care who went and, besides, they would all be sleeping off their excesses at this time in the morning and would probably not even notice the truck slipping like a dirty shadow from Berlin.

'Take care,' Katharina said, over and over, kissing them all in turn. 'Take care of yourselves and take care of each other. And write.'

'We will,' Gisela promised her.

Hanna added a happy babble, but Adelaide said nothing. She was white-faced and hunched. She had not hidden away this time but, as Pierre revved the engine, she leaped up suddenly and flung herself into Katharina's arms, hugging her so tight that Gisela had to prise her young fingers from Katharina's back one by one. Still the girl said nothing but, as Gisela pulled her down into the cushions and the truck lurched forward, leaving Katharina standing alone in the middle of the zoo, there were tears streaming down her cheeks and for the first time Katharina felt guilty about not going with them.

'I will join you, Addie,' she called. 'I will join you or, when the zoo is prosperous once more, you can rejoin me.'

In reply Adelaide tossed a single flower out of the back of the truck, then it turned out of the zoo and was gone. Katharina ran forward and picked up the bloom. It was not for her, she understood, but for Robert and Sasha, and slowly she traced her way back to the zebra enclosure to lay it before their memorial.

'I *will* look after her,' she promised her lost friends. 'I will look after both of them. But for now, this is the best way of doing that.'

She knew she spoke the truth but felt a quiver of fear as she looked around at her beloved zoo, run now by reckless Russian soldiers and drunken German upstarts. The city was far from safe. Marcel was sleeping in the entrance hall of their apartment with a selection of kitchen knives to keep any randy Russians at bay, but a determined mob would still get through if they really wanted to and it was always hard to sleep. Was the zoo worth risking all that for? She wasn't sure, but one thing certainly was – Oskar. With a new spring in her step, she hurried back to his side.

Chapter Twenty-Seven

It was a relief when dawn finally broke between the brocade curtains of the Sylvie suite and Bethan could give up her pretence of sleep. Max was already up.

'Morning,' he said gruffly.

'Morning.'

She didn't ask how he'd slept; it was already clear from the dark shadows under his eyes.

'I've got to get back to the zoo,' he said. 'Trouble with the two new juveniles.'

'OK.' Bethan was pretty sure there was no trouble but it was an easy way out for them both. 'I can get a train back.'

He looked up in surprise.

'You're not coming?'

'We promised Monica we'd breakfast with her.'

'She'd understand.'

'Yes, but I'd like to talk to her again. I'm sure there's more in her memories if we can just ask the right questions.'

'I could…' He stopped himself; he'd already said he had to get back. 'Just make sure there are trains before I go.'

'Good idea.'

'I'm having a shower, if that's OK?'

'Of course. I'll call for coffee.'

He scurried into the bathroom and closed the door. Bethan looked at it with sadness, but what could she do? She dialled down for coffee then called up trains on her phone, but this was Germany and the Sunday service was almost as efficient as in the week; she could go back whenever she liked.

She heard the shower turn on and looked to the bathroom door, her lips suddenly dry. Max was in there, naked. The water would be running over his muscular shoulders, down his well-defined back, on to... She shook herself, but still her body tingled with the image she simply could not get out of her mind. Now another thought came to her – the bathroom door had no lock on it. She could just step up, turn the handle and—

A knock at the door broke her wanton thoughts and she leaped up to let the waiter in. He was bearing a tray with a coffee pot, milk jug, two pretty cups and two delicious-looking pastries. She could get used to living like this! She thanked him and reached for a pecan swirl, savouring the sweet kick through her weary body. Crossing to the window, she looked down across the elegant grounds and drew in a deep breath.

'You were here, Mum,' she said to the skies. 'I'm sure of it.'

Anke, the last woman on the list, had to be the key. Had Oma Erika not told Jana that she had been a gift from Anke? And now Bethan was here, in the beautiful house where Anke had been housekeeper and where two babies had arrived from Berlin at the back end of the war. She just had to keep looking and she'd surely get her answers.

She stared down the rolling green lawns to the river beyond and caught sight of Monica's quirky hexagonal house. Something snagged at the edges of her memory. She'd seen this view before. But that was surely impossible. She'd never been to Torgau. Unless, of course, her mum had brought her out here. But no, it wasn't that. The memory was flatter somehow.

Oma Erika's photo! Of course. Bethan cursed herself for not bringing the scrapbook with her, but she had at least taken a snap of the key photos on her phone. She turned back to the table to grab it but just then Max came out of the shower, a towel wrapped around his waist and his upper body bare. It was just as lean and muscular as she'd imagined. Her throat went dry and she stopped dead.

'Forgot the "comfort package",' he said awkwardly.

'Ah, right – yes.'

She snatched up the little pack, reaching inside to remove the simple pair of ladies' pants before handing him the matching briefs. It felt agonisingly intimate, especially when, in her embarrassment, she fumbled and dropped them. They both bent to pick them up and her arm brushed against his torso, making her skin tingle all over again.

'No men,' she muttered fiercely.

'Sorry?'

'Nothing! Nothing at all. I just, er, just had a thought.'

'A thought?'

Too many thoughts, frankly. She tried to regain her focus on history; it was far, far easier than the present.

'About that photo of my Oma's. I think it was taken here.'

'Really? Can I see?'

She fumbled for her phone but her fingers didn't seem to be working properly, and it took her three goes to unlock it. At last she got to her photos and scrolled through to find the relevant one. It was a little grainy, and a little shiny where the light had caught the original, but it was clear enough.

'Look.'

She held the phone as far across to Max as she could, but he still had to come close enough that she could smell shampoo in his wet hair and feel the warmth radiating from his skin. He didn't even seem to notice, so intent was he on the image on the screen.

'That's Monica's house.'

'Do you think so?'

'It's pretty distinctive.'

He was right. There was no doubting the presence of the hexagonal building in the background of the picture. She stared at it.

'It's proof, Max – proof that Oma Erika was here.'

'So, who are the other two women?'

Bethan looked at him and grinned.

'That's what I'm hoping Monica might be able to tell me.'

'Yes! Let's get dressed and see… Oh.'

'The juveniles?'

For a minute he seemed to wrestle with himself, then he looked down, as if only now aware of his semi-nakedness.

'You're right. I need to go. It's your mystery to solve anyway.'

He backed away.

'It is,' Bethan agreed, 'but you've helped so much, Max, that it feels like it's more ours now.'

His face hardened.

'Nothing is "ours", Bethan.'

Then he was gone, back into the bathroom, shutting the door firmly behind him and leaving Bethan with a grainy old photo, a cooling pecan swirl, and an uneasy sense that she was doing this all wrong.

Monica welcomed her into her house with a wide smile.

'Good morning, my dear. How was your room?'

'Beautiful,' Bethan said. 'Truly the nicest place I've ever stayed. Thank you so much.'

'My pleasure. Your visit means the world to me. To revisit a past I haven't thought about for decades has been wonderful, and if we can solve your mystery too then I will consider myself useful again. Where's your young man?'

Bethan flushed.

'He had to rush back to Berlin – trouble with the chimps.'

'What a shame. I hope he didn't go too early.' She gave a lewd wink. Bethan sought for words but could find none and Monica frowned. 'All well?'

'Oh yes,' Bethan tried, but it came out rather hoarse and she sighed. 'He's not my "young man", Monica. Max and I are just friends.'

'Didn't look like it to me.' Bethan gasped and Monica slapped her own hand. 'Oh, will you listen to me, causing trouble. Ignore what I say. I told you last night – I'm just a foolish old woman.'

'You are not!' Bethan said hotly. 'Quite the reverse.'

Monica patted her arm.

'Thank you, my dear. Come – breakfast.' Bethan followed her up to the sitting room to find a delicious spread of cold meats, breads and mini pastries. She'd not been able to face the rest of her pecan swirl up in the room and now her stomach grumbled. 'Tuck in, tuck in.'

Bethan did so gladly and, once they both had laden plates, she looked to her hostess.

'Will you tell me more about Anke, Monica?'

'Anke? Dear me, of course. What do you want to know?'

It was a good question. What she really wanted to know was if she'd been the sort of woman who would give babies as presents, but that didn't sound quite right.

'Was she kind?'

'Oh, very. That sort of gruff kindness you get from a busy person. She wasn't the gushing sort – you'd never have caught her telling you she loved you, but if you fell over and grazed your knee, you'd want no one more than Anke to sort it out for you. She had a… natural warmth.'

Definitely the sort to give people babies then. But why would she?

'Did she have children?'

'Several, though they were grown up by the time I came along. Both her sons fought in the war, and the only time I ever saw her cry was when I walked in on her reading a letter from one of them once.'

'Did they survive?'

'They did. In fact, I had a bit of a dalliance with the older one. Years later, of course. He was newly widowed and very sad. I soothed him.'

'I bet you did!'

'And scared him besides. He said that after three months with me, he was quite happy to be on his own again.'

'That's not very nice.'

She chuckled.

'Oh, he said it kindly.' She caught sight of Bethan's face and laughed. 'I was pretty scary back then. I lived life fast and liked it that way. I wasn't a settler like you.'

Bethan thought of her body's reaction to Max in the shower this morning and frowned.

'I'm not so sure that I'm a settler any more.'

Monica smiled at her.

'Oh, you are. You just need to be sure you're settling with the right person. But anyway – Anke.'

'Yes, Anke,' Bethan agreed quickly. 'If she had children of her own, she wouldn't want more?'

'I doubt it. I'm no expert, obviously, but I gather from friends that once your little darlings start to grow up and fly the nest, the last thing you want is more of them.'

'So, if there was a baby that fell, somehow, into her charge…'

'She'd look to find a happy home for it, yes.'

Bethan remembered the photo. She pulled her phone out and, finding the picture, passed it across to Monica.

'Do you know who these women are, Monica?'

Monica peered down.

'Goodness, that's small. I'll need my glasses.' Bethan hovered behind her shoulder as she reached for her specs and examined the three women staring out at them from the screen. 'Yes,' she said, pointing to the middle lady, 'that's Anke.'

Bethan's heart leaped.

'Then she did know my Oma. That's her there, on the left.'

Monica turned the screen from side to side, as if trying to find her way into the picture.

'She looks vaguely familiar but I don't remember her specifi-cally. Still, if that's her then she certainly knew Anke. They look very close.'

Bethan nodded, swallowed.

'And the third lady? Is that Ursula?'

Monica stared at the picture for a long time, but finally shook her head.

'I don't know. I'm sorry, but I honestly couldn't say for sure. It's not the best picture, is it? Do you have the original?'

Again Bethan regretted not bringing the scrapbook.

'I do, but not with me. I can bring it another time, if you'd be happy for me to visit again?'

'Oh, my dear, of course I would. I'm sorry – there seem to be more people that I don't remember than ones that I do. Oh!' She suddenly grabbed Bethan's hand. 'There is one thing that came to me in bed last night. You mentioned a Hanna.'

'Yes?'

'There *was* a Hanna. She came later, with the Frenchman.'

'The Frenchman?'

'Ursula's husband. Oh, he was a handsome one. I was only six but even I was caught by that man.'

'And he brought Hanna?'

'Yes, and her sister – Adelaide?'

Bethan clutched at Monica's hand.

'You knew Adelaide?'

'Oh yes. She was older than me, quite a bit older I think, but she didn't act it. She was a bit odd, especially at first. She wouldn't talk to anyone. Very shy, I suppose.'

'She'd lost both her parents in the war. Her mother died in childbirth and her father was blown up right in front of her.'

Monica put her hand to her mouth.

'The poor child. No wonder then.'

'No one told you that at the time?'

'We didn't speak of those things really. It wasn't like today. We weren't big on counselling or even just straightforward talking. It was more of an if-you-don't-mention-it-we-can-forget-it-happened approach. Didn't work, of course.'

Bethan thought of poor Ada, still babbling to herself eighty years later.

'No. But she came here?'

'She did, yes. We used to play together – climbing trees and running hoops and swimming in the river. Games that didn't need words. Her little sister was the cutest thing. I loved her to bits but Adelaide got jealous if I played with her too much.' She shook her head. 'Funny summer. I'd forgotten all about it until you came along.'

'So there were three babies here in 1945?'

'Three babies, yes. And only two mothers.'

'Two?' Bethan leaped on this. 'Who was the second?'

Monica looked out of the window, blinking her way back into the past.

'I think the second one came with the Frenchman and the two girls. In fact, yes, I'm almost sure of it. The second baby must have been hers because, now I think about it, she cried like a – well, like a baby – when she was reunited with it.'

'Does the name Gisela Schultz mean anything to you?' Bethan asked.

Monica thought about it but eventually wrinkled up her nose and said, 'Not that I can recall, but that doesn't mean it wasn't her. She just used to sit with the baby all the time so I didn't pay her much attention, not with trees to climb and rivers to swim in.'

'I don't blame you,' Bethan managed, but her mind was swirling.

If Ursula Franke had been here in Torgau with her daughter, Beatrice, and this other woman, possibly Gisela Schultz, with the second baby, that left only one child without a parent. What if Ada had got upset over the name Hanna not because her sister had died, but because she'd been given away – given away to Bethan's Oma Erika? What if Ada was, in fact, Bethan's great-aunt? The thought made her feel almost physically dizzy and she sank down onto a chair at Monica's side.

'I have to tell Max,' she said. 'This is amazing, Monica. I have to get back and tell Max.'

'Max?' Monica said, one eyebrow lifted, and Bethan smiled, feeling warmth radiate through her like the spring sun over the beautiful grounds of Schloss Ermau.

'Max,' she said firmly, picturing his dark curls and his blue eyes and his wry smile.

Her feelings for this man were too big to ignore, and there was no way she was risking losing him because of everything that had happened with Callum. If there was one thing her journey into the past had taught her, it was that life was too precious, too short, not to take every opportunity to hold the ones you love close. As for her mother's list – was it not Max who had helped her get this far? She had to be with him at the end. Actually, scratch that – she just had to be with him.

The journey back to Berlin felt endless, but finally she reached the welcome of the two ancient elephants at the entrance to the zoo.

'You OK, Beth?' Mikey asked her from his ticket booth.

'I'll let you know later.'

'What?'

'Things to do, Mikey. People to see.'

She waved and ran through, her heart pounding now that she was finally close. What if Max refused her? What if she'd read it all wrong? But then she thought of him standing at the foot of the beautiful bed in the Sylvie suite: 'It could never be big enough, Bethan, to stop me wanting you.' And she wanted him too, she knew that now. She wanted all of him, for always.

She shot past the pandas, lazily chewing their bamboo.

'Over-rated,' she shot at them, giggling wildly. A couple of visitors looked at her askance and she ran on, grateful for her early morning training. The monkeys were out, swinging around their cage, and she paused to check Max wasn't in there. There was no sign of him, but Binky flung herself at the cage in greeting and she reached up to touch hands with the cheeky chimp.

'Wish me luck, Binky.'

Binky peeled back her top lip and gave her an encouraging chatter, and she looked across to the apartment block. She'd made it at last and there was no point in hesitating further. What was the worst that could happen?

He could say no, her heart muttered treacherously, but she frowned it down. It was a risk she'd have to take. Running up the stairs, she banged on Max's door.

'Max! Max!'

It seemed to take forever but he finally appeared, sleepy-eyed and frowning and utterly gorgeous.

'What is it? What's up? Have you found something?'

'Found? Oh – about Mum?'

'Yes.'

'No. That is, I sort of have but it can wait. It's not important.'

'Not important?'

'Not compared to this.'

She put her hands on his chest and pushed him back inside his apartment, her whole body singing with his closeness.

'Bethan, please – you're not ready.'

'Oh, I am, Max. I truly am. I was confused yesterday, I know, but I'm not any more. I don't want—'

But whatever she didn't want was cut off by the press of Max's lips on hers. He gathered her in against him, his hands soft but firm in the small of her back, his kiss growing in insistence as he felt her response.

'Max,' she whispered against his lips, and then he was pulling her into his bedroom and there was no need to say anything more.

Chapter Twenty-Eight

1 July 1945

'Ladies and gentlemen, I am delighted to pronounce our beloved Berlin Zoo once again – open!'

Dennis flung his arms wide, flushed with pride – not to mention vodka – and the gold-trimmed crowd cheered wildly. Katharina, standing at the back with Marcel and Yuri, had to resist the urge to spit at the arrogant hypocrisy of it all. Her poor, dear zoo was beloved of no one here, Dennis included, and that had never been more apparent than at this supposed celebration of her reopening.

The ribbon was not being cut out in the zoo itself, in front of the loving locals who had given their crusts to keep the animals alive through the hardest days of the battle for Berlin. Oh no, it was shut away, in the patched-up concert hall before a clutch of specially selected Russian grandees. No one here cared about the animals, just about parading their fancy uniforms and their Bolshevik egos, drinking fine German wine and coarse Russian vodka, and shouting to be heard over the buzz of their own smug pride. After years of being run by a clutch of devoted women and invalids, Berlin Zoo was back in the hands of men of power, and they were rapidly stripping it of its very essence.

It had been the same for the painful weeks leading up to this empty ceremony. Katharina had had such high hopes when Vetrov had announced his plans to rehabilitate the zoo, but the Russian soldiers he'd assigned to it treated it as their personal playground. They had cleared several of the key avenues but only so that they could practise riding the bikes they had stolen from poor Berliners and seemed to find a great novelty. Katharina was forever having to leap aside as they came careering round corners, often two or three to a bike. She had even caught one trying to force a baboon to ride and had been glad to see the creature lash out in his own defence. His claws had been sharp and she hoped his tormentor would be scarred for life.

None of the animals were safe from the Soviets' reckless attentions, and Katharina was beginning to fear that her precious charges had been better off taking their chances with Allied bombs. The carnivores in particular fascinated the Red soldiers and, just a week or so into their takeover, she had caught two of them vaulting the fencing around the rapidly growing lion cubs with lumps of meat in their hands.

'No!' she'd shouted, starting forward, but Marcel had pulled her back.

'Leave them to it. They do it all the time. The fools think it's macho, but Sultan and Bussy must surely soon work out that the hand holding the meat is every bit as tasty as the meat itself. And fresher besides.'

'Marcel!'

'What? Those pair cavorting so cutely with the cubs right now probably raped twenty German girls apiece last night. Frankly, I hope they get torn to shreds.'

Katharina had closed her eyes, acknowledging the dark truth of what he said, but she'd still been glad when the fools had made it back out of the enclosure intact. She'd tried to talk to Dennis about it but he'd been far too busy creating himself a plush office in the antelope house to care.

'They can feed the animals with whatever they like, Katharina – including themselves. Why should I care?'

'Because you're the manager,' Katharina had fired furiously back at him. 'If the lions eat the Russians, they will shoot them, and then our battle to keep them alive will be for nothing.'

He'd just reclined in his leather-padded chair and snapped his fingers to Kurt for another bottle of Lutz's wine.

'I trust my workers, Katharina.'

'Then you're a fool.'

It was breaking her heart to see him ruin all that she and Oskar – and so many others – had worked so hard to keep intact, but they were powerless now. Oskar was little better. Tonight she'd had to leave him in bed in their apartment and was so afraid for his health that she'd paid Hans precious coins to watch over him. The lad and his brother had got themselves work at the zoo and were a great support. If she could have got Oskar well enough to mount a bid for the management, she would have promoted them both on the spot but, even if Oskar were fighting fit, the chances of them ousting Dennis whilst he was creeping up to Marshal Vetrov were non-existent.

Apart from the vet, Yuri, who stood quietly at her side as his countrymen partied, Katharina was learning to hate the Russians. The British weren't coming, she knew that now, or the Americans either. They had abandoned Berlin to its fate and she refused to be abandoned with it. Enough was finally enough. She had a bag of clothes hidden beneath her bed and had paid a man at the railway station to let her know when a train was scheduled towards Torgau. When the call came, she and Oskar would grab their things and go. It broke her heart to leave Siam and Reike and dear Knautschke, but they would survive. Pierre had written to say his truck had made it safely to Torgau and she ached to join her Zoofamilie. She had promised Sasha and Robert she would care for their girls and now she just wanted to get to them.

For tonight, though, she must endure this farce of an event. Marshal Vetrov was strutting around accepting the congratulations of various highly decorated Soviets as if it had been he, not Katharina, who had slaved to keep the remaining animals alive and to bring others back from safety elsewhere. If she'd dared, she would have stopped the transports once she realised how little the Russians truly cared. The poor creatures would have been better off in their provincial homes, but it was the one thing Dennis had taken any interest in and she'd been forced to keep bringing them back. It made her feel even worse about plotting to leave them, especially as Marcel, Victor and the others were due to return to France next month, but she had run out of energy to fight.

The large military band crammed into the corner struck up with gusto and the grandees burst into an energetic rendition of their new anthem – the so-called Hymn of the Soviet Union. The lyrics were in Russian but Katharina had had it rammed down her throat often enough now to understand it, and looked desperately to the door as they hit the chorus:

> *Long live our Soviet motherland,*
> *Built by the people's mighty hand.*

She listened in despair to the furiously bellowed lines and watched as the men, and occasional uniformed woman, punched the air to mark out the pounding rhymes. It was every bit as terrifying as watching Hitler's rallies had been just a few short months ago and she knew, deep in her battered heart, that Germany's beleaguered capital was in the hands not of liberators but of new despots. Yes, she had to escape – and fast.

Oskar was sleeping when she let herself back into their little house later. The Russians had reached the dancing-on-the-tables stage of their grand ceremony and thankfully stopped caring whether she and the other workers were there. She'd quietly done the rounds of the cages with Marcel and Victor, trying to enjoy the starlit night and ignore the raucous cries from the concert hall, and she came in a little calmer.

'Katharina? Is that you?'

'It's me, my love.'

'Are you safe?'

'Of course.'

'And the animals?'

'All fine, bar the Russian ones who are drunk enough for us to pray they might feed Dennis to the lions.'

He gave a soft chuckle and put out his arms to draw her in against him as she climbed into bed. He was hot but not, perhaps, as hot as he had been at the height of his fever when she had pushed him down a fire-ravaged street in a wheelbarrow, a baby on his heaving chest.

'I have been waiting for you to get back.'

'I'm sorry. It was hard to get away.'

'Was it awful?'

'Awful,' she confirmed. 'The Russians are eating our zoo alive, O, but they won't have us with it.' She stroked his hand where it curved around her. 'We have to get out. If a train isn't scheduled to Torgau soon, I think we should try and find a van. I have contacts now, with the transports.'

He held her tighter.

'It's a long way, Kätsche.'

'Not that far. I'll get you there.'

He kissed her neck, his lips dry against her skin and his breathing tight in her ear. For a while they lay there, wrapped quietly together, then he said, 'We thought the end of the war would bring peace, did we not?'

'It will,' she promised. 'Eventually. There are just a few battles yet to be fought.'

'And you are the woman to fight them.'

She turned in his arms, cradling his thin face in her hands.

'With you, O.'

A single tear rolled out of his eye.

'I don't know, Kätsche. I think, maybe, you are going to need enough strength for both of us.'

'No,' she said fiercely. 'You are going to get better.'

'One way or another,' he agreed, kissing her.

His lips were sure but she could feel his heartbeat fluttering alarmingly against her chest.

'Oskar?'

'I love you, meine kindl.'

'And I you, O.'

'If I had to choose, you know, between saving the zoo and saving you, it would be you every time. A thousand times over. I would shoot every beautiful animal in here if it kept you safe.'

'Oskar!'

Tears were in her eyes too now and only she, perhaps, understood the magnitude of what he was saying to her. This place had been their baby and it meant the world to them.

'I remember the first time I saw you,' he murmured, his voice thick. 'That conference room was full of stuffed suits. I was bored stiff and then suddenly there you were, all wide-eyed and youthful. And when I spoke to you – oh, you were so full of life, my sweet one, so full of enthusiasm. You made me fall in love with my subject all over again. And fall in love with you too.'

'I felt the same, O.'

'For a sagging, white-haired old man?'

'For a passionate, exciting, caring man who I've been privileged to share my life with.' She caught herself. '*Am* privileged to share my life with.'

His hand squeezed her side.

'You were right first time, meine kindl. I am fading.'

Her whole body juddered at the words. She stared at him in the darkness and saw his skin ghostly pale in the moonlight.

'No! Oskar, don't go, please. Don't leave me.'

'I'm not leaving you, sweet one just… going ahead.'

His grip was loosening and she felt as if her heart would tear into a million shreds. They'd come so far, been through so much; surely she couldn't lose him now that they were finally at peace?

'I'm sorry,' he murmured. 'My heart is yours but it has pumped out all the love it can manage on this broken earth. Look after yourself, Kätsche.'

'Oskar, no!' she cried.

She clasped him tight against her, trying to will her own life into his, but it was too late. His lips found hers, light as a feather, and then he drew in a shaky breath and went still.

Katharina stroked his hair gently, telling herself he was sleeping, telling herself it was good for him to rest, telling herself that this was the start of his recovery. But, finally, a kookaburra gave its harsh laugh outside, as if mocking her foolishness, and she had to face the fact that he was gone. Her husband had slipped unobtrusively out of life and she was alone. Truly alone.

She lay there, warm beneath the covers, in the arms of a dead man, listening to the romp of the invaders across the zoo and waiting for the grief to strike. It did not come the way she had expected. A slow sadness crept through her veins, as if they would never allow her blood to flow quite as freely again, but with it came peace. She had known, in her heart of hearts, that the trip to Torgau would be too much for her ailing husband. She had, perhaps, been dreading the call from the station and what it would mean. She could not subject her dear, dignified, intelligent Oskar to being transported anywhere in a wheelbarrow ever again.

His death, here in her arms, had at least been a quiet one – not a bomb ripping him in half, or a shell puncturing his lungs, or a building falling on his head. She had seen all of that in these last years, over and over and over, and his passing was, in contrast, a blessing. All those she loved had now escaped whatever horrors were left in Berlin, and that was in itself a form of peace.

And she? She would have to somehow escape, but for now she would have one last night in her beloved zoo with her beloved husband. War had robbed her of so much and her tears fell into the darkness as she clutched Oskar to her heart – battered and bruised but swollen with love. That, at least, war had never been able to take from her.

Chapter Twenty-Nine

Bethan blinked slowly awake, her body warm and deliciously weary, and every one of her senses alive to the man with his arms wrapped around her.

'Max,' she murmured.

He stirred slightly then settled back to sleep, and she was glad of it. She needed a little time to absorb the feeling of being with someone new. Not that it felt new; more as if she'd been with him forever. She groaned at herself. What sort of a soppy cow was she turning into?

'Beth? Are you OK?'

She turned to face him, taking in those amazing blue eyes looking sleepily into her own.

'More than OK.'

'You sounded like you were groaning.'

'Sorry. Just thinking what a shame it was we didn't manage this in the Sylvie suite.'

He grinned.

'I don't think it's the surroundings that matter. Other than the immediate ones, that is.' He ran a slow hand down the curve of her side, sending her whole body singing once more, but at that moment his alarm rang and now it was him who groaned. 'Work!'

Bethan looked at the clock. They were both due on duty in under an hour. Still…

'We could shower together to, you know, save time.'

'Genius!'

Then he was pulling her up and tugging her into his bathroom and, OK, so it wasn't marble tiles and a claw-footed bath, but Max was right – the immediate surroundings were beyond compare.

*

'What are you grinning about?' Ella demanded later that day, as Bethan approached her at the hippo house with a set of papers on an experiment they were preparing. 'This is hardly exciting stuff.'

'I think you'll find that the study of the diving habits of hippopotamuses in captivity is a fascinating subject, Ella.'

Ella looked her up and down, a grin spreading across her face, and then she suddenly cried, 'Monkey man!' and launched into a vivid chimp impression, leaping around Bethan with her hands tucked into her armpits, whooping and screeching most realistically.

'Ella – stop! People are staring.'

'So? They come to the zoo to stare.'

'Not at the vets! Stop it.'

Bethan tried to catch her friend but Ella whooped off round the back of the hippo house, pausing only to give a special little chatter to a delighted pair of children as she passed. Bethan rolled her eyes, but she couldn't stop her own smile all the same. For all her flighty ways, Ella had become a good friend and Bethan valued her opinion; if she was pleased about her getting together with Max then perhaps it was the right thing.

Who was she kidding? Of course it was the right thing. Every bit of her was alive with the joy of him. It had never, if she was honest, felt this way with Callum, even at the start. They'd got on really well and had plenty of fun but there hadn't been this spark, this breathless need to have him in her life. Despite herself, she gave a skip and ran off after Ella.

She let herself into the space-age hippo enclosure with her pass, remembering the very first time she'd come in here, nearly ten weeks ago, wide-eyed and naively excited at being allowed through the barriers. She'd learned so much since then, changed so much. She stood for a moment, watching Klumpig and his friends rolling and turning in the pool, marvelling as she always did at the grace of the lumbering creatures once they were in their natural environment. She knew how they felt. Coming to Berlin Zoo was the best decision she'd ever made, and she wanted to leap and turn and jump for joy.

'Aah!'

She leaped back as Klumpig rose from the water and gracefully blew two great plumes out of his giant nostrils at her. That was her told! The crowd laughed and, with a wry shake of her head, she edged round the pool to find Ella. But as she went, her phone rang with an unknown number. Intrigued, she let herself into the food store and answered.

'Hello? Is that Bethan?'

The voice was older, cultured.

'It is.'

'Excellent. Bethan, it's Monica von Weichs.'

'Monica! How lovely to hear from you.'

'You're too kind, dear, but I certainly hope what I have to say will be worthwhile. I've remembered something about the third baby – Hanna.'

'You have?' Bethan leaned back against the shelves of herbivore pellets and took a few deep breaths. 'What is it?'

'She married. I was thinking back over old times after your visit and suddenly remembered that Mother went to the wedding and was full of it. A very fancy do it was, to a rich barrister.'

'Really?' This was amazing. 'Can you remember his name, Monica? Or anything about him?'

Monica gave a little chuckle down the phone.

'I can do better than that, my dear. I've found the invitation. I'm sending a photo of it right now.'

Bethan pulled the phone from her ear and, sure enough, a message was coming through. She switched Monica to speaker and opened it up, and there on her screen was a beautiful wedding invitation, embossed with swirls of silver and announcing the impending union of Hanna Eberhard to William Fitzbrau at St Hedwig's Cathedral in Berlin on Saturday 11th July 1970. The invitation was issued by none other than Katharina Heinroth. Bethan stared at it, trying to take it all in.

'Bethan? Are you there? Can you see it?'

'I can, Monica, thank you so much. This is amazing.'

'Even better, Hanna Fitzbrau is all over the internet. I've been looking her up and she's done very well for herself. I might have to come to Berlin and say hello.'

'She's here?'

'It seems so. Take a look.'

'I will do.' Bethan looked around at the hippo feed, feeling suddenly ridiculous. 'I really will. Thank you so much, Monica. And do come to Berlin. We'd love to see you here. You could meet Adelaide too.'

'She's still there?'

'We think so. She's not exactly with it, but if we have the right person she's always in the zoo, sitting on the same bench in a tartan rug.'

Monica gave a wistful sigh.

'Little Adelaide – one minute climbing trees with me in Torgau, the next an old lady in a zoo.'

'She's not *in* the zoo,' Bethan said, suddenly fearing she'd given the wrong impression, but Monica just let out the bark of a laugh that she had already come to know.

'Of course not, dear. Lord help us when society starts exhibiting its old folk like monkeys! I'll let you go now, and I hope you find Hanna.'

'I hope so too,' Bethan agreed, and said her goodbyes.

She moved to the door, but paused a moment more to let the implications of the invitation sink in. This might be the key to finding Hanna, although it told her one thing for sure – if Hanna Eberhard had gone up the aisle to marry William Fitzbrau on the arm of Katharina Heinroth, she was unlikely to have been the baby given away to Erika. The search, it seemed, was still on.

Hanna Fitzbrau was indeed all over the internet, and Bethan pored over the information with Max when they met up for lunch in the canteen. The Kartoffelsuppe was delicious and Bethan took her first two mouthfuls eagerly, but soon became so engrossed in what her phone was telling her that she let it go cold without even noticing.

There were all sorts of images of Hanna and William, especially from the sixties and seventies when they seemed to have been part of Berlin's in-crowd. Hanna appeared in a succession of wonderful dresses at every party, wedding, film premiere and social occasion going. But it didn't stop there. With patience, Bethan was able to piece together a visual timeline of almost her entire adult life, tracing the silvering of her lustrous dark hair, the appearance of lines on her attractive face, the growth of three neat pregnancy bumps and, after that, of three neat children turned teenagers turned adults, all seemingly in their parents' sophisticated mould. Most recently of all, she found a picture of Hanna and William celebrating their golden wedding anniversary outside their beautiful townhouse on Thrasoltstrasse in the smart area of Charlottenburg, barely streets away from the zoo.

'Look!' Max said, leaning in so that she felt his touch quiver through her entire body.

She turned to steal a kiss and he gave way easily, but then pointed to the screen again and there, when she enlarged the photo, was a plaque on the wall bearing the number 117.

'Not very privacy savvy, is it?' Bethan said.

'Nope,' Max agreed happily. 'Shall we go and visit?'

'Tonight?'

'Absolutely.'

*

All afternoon Bethan was excited by the idea of tracking down Hanna but, when she and Max finally stood outside her imposing house at seven o'clock that evening, she felt nerves bite.

'What if she doesn't want to see us, Max?'

He gripped her hand tightly and she felt a rush of gratitude at having this caring man at her side.

'Then she'll say so and we'll go away. Once we explain I'm sure she'll be interested.'

'She's very posh.'

'So? Monica von Weichs is very posh and she was lovely.'

'True.'

'Shall we knock?'

'In a minute.' He laughed and started to head up the well-groomed path, but she tugged him back. 'There's just one thing bothering me, Max.'

'Which is?'

'Ada. If we're right about Hanna then Ada is surely her sister? But she's in none of the pictures. Not even the family ones. What sort of woman abandons a sister like that? What sort of woman just lets her wander the zoo in a blanket?'

He shrugged.

'I don't know, Beth, but we're not going to find out staring at her front door.'

That much was true, so Bethan let Max lead her up the path and knock on the shiny red door. Her heart pounded harder as she heard footsteps approaching on the other side, but when the door swung open, she reeled back, stunned.

'Ada?!'

The old woman stood before them, purple boots firm on the black-and-white tiles of the long hallway, tartan blanket around her shoulders, and her eyes wide with horror.

'No,' she whispered, just about coherent. Then she started babbling, the noise getting louder and louder with every second.

Max darted forward.

'Ada, it's OK. It's just us, Max and Bethan from the zoo. You're quite safe.'

It had little effect. Ada sank against the wall, curling her arms protectively around herself and backing sideways along the hallway. Now more footsteps sounded out and an elegant woman appeared from a side doorway and ran to her.

'Addie, it's OK. You're OK.'

She put her arms around her, stroking her hair with the utmost tenderness. Ada curled in against her and slowly her noises dropped to a low crooning. The woman fixed them with a fierce stare.

'What did you say to my sister?'

This, then, was Hanna Fitzbrau and she had not, it seemed, abandoned Ada at all. Suddenly the well-kept hair and teeth made perfect sense. Bethan swallowed guiltily.

'I'm so sorry. We didn't say anything at all, not a word, save her name of course. We know Ada, from the zoo. She comes every day.'

'She does,' Hanna agreed, looking a little less hostile. 'But why are you here? Is there a problem?'

'No, no,' Max assured her. 'No problem.'

'Then?'

Bethan drew in a deep breath.

'I'm looking for my grandmother. I believe she was shipped out to Countess Sylvie von Weichs in Torgau by Katharina Heinroth at the end of the war. And I believe you were with her.'

Hanna gave a low whistle.

'Well I never,' she said. 'You'd better come in.'

She ushered them into the house, prised Ada from the wall and led her gently through to a beautiful living room, settling her in an armchair. When Ada was finally more relaxed, Hanna took a seat on a white leather sofa and indicated another opposite.

'I'm so sorry we upset Ada,' Bethan said. 'It wasn't our intention. In fact, we didn't even know she was here. When we asked her about Hanna – about *you* – a few weeks ago she just kept shaking her head and, well, wailing, like she did just now.'

Hanna sighed.

'That's my fault. When I was first dating William, Addie got into a habit of talking to everyone about me. I was pleased at first because she was finally using proper sentences again but, well, she didn't know how to regulate what she said and journalists were onto her like sharks. It was quite embarrassing, not just for me but for William too, so I had to have words. I told Addie never to talk to anyone about either of us, and she took it rather literally – has done ever since.' She looked sadly at her sister, who had pulled her omnipresent blanket from round her shoulders and covered herself with it, right up to just below her eyes. Hanna turned back to them. 'But please, let me offer you a drink.'

'Oh no—' Bethan started, but their hostess cut her off.

'Really. William's out at some worthy bash so I was feeling terribly guilty drinking alone. You'll be doing me a favour.'

'Well, put like that how can we complain?'

'Lovely. Wine? It's quite a nice Grauburgunder, if that suits?'

They rushed to assure her that it would suit beautifully and she disappeared, returning with a slim bottle sparkling with moisture. Pulling two crystal glasses from a cabinet, she poured them both a generous measure and raised her glass.

'Prost!' She leaned back in her chair, crossing one slim leg over the other, and eyed Bethan curiously. 'So, you're looking for your grandmother?'

Bethan did her best to explain the situation, from Jana's list to their discovery of the chimp shipment to Torgau, to the information Monica had given them. Hanna listened very carefully and, when Bethan finally ran dry, she nodded thoughtfully into her wine.

'I'm afraid I don't remember Torgau from that time, though I was often out there later. Katharina stayed in touch with Sylvie and we visited for several summers when I was a teen. I liked her.'

'She came to your wedding.'

Hanna blinked.

'She did. How do you know?'

'Monica found a copy of the invitation. That's how we tracked you down.'

'Just a few hundred metres from the zoo?'

Bethan nodded sheepishly.

'I feel a little foolish about that, especially with Ada there so often, but as I said...'

They both looked to Ada, who had unrolled her blanket to just below her nose.

'Don't worry about it. I'm glad you've found me now, though I'm not sure what I can do to help. I believe I had my first birthday at Torgau, but soon after that we went home.'

'To Berlin?'

'That's right. To the zoo. To Katharina.'

'You lived with her?'

'All the way through our schooldays. Well, *my* schooldays. Poor Ada never really recovered from what she'd been put through in the war and it was agreed by all that school would be of little help. She was happiest with the animals, and very good with them too, so she worked around the zoo while I went to school. Once she was eighteen, she had a little apartment of her own near the chimps and she was happy there for years, but when Katharina died she went to pieces. That's when I brought her to live with us. She has the basement to herself and I think she likes it, but she'll always go back to the zoo.'

'She seems happy there.'

Hanna smiled.

'That's good. She deserves to be happy because no one has ever loved me more fiercely than Ada, not even William or the children. And if her happiness doesn't look quite like other people's, well…'

'So what?' Max said stoutly.

She smiled at him.

'Well said, young man.'

Bethan shifted on the sofa.

'You said you kept in touch with those you were with at Torgau, Frau Fitzbrau?'

'Hanna, please. And yes, I did.'

'Did that include Ursula Franke?'

Hanna laughed.

'Ursula Dubois, you mean? It did. A lovely woman, Ursula was – so lively and positive and energetic. And her handsome Pierre, of course, and all their lovely daughters.'

'All?'

'Four in total. I think Pierre was hoping for a son but he got a fine clutch of womenfolk instead. They married and scattered across France. I used to talk to Beatrice regularly – it was good for my French.'

'Are you still in touch?' Max asked eagerly, but at that Hanna shook her head.

'Bea died three or four years ago. I'm so sorry.'

'No, no, it's we who are sorry for your loss,' Max said graciously.

Bethan hurried to echo him, though to her shame she felt her heart sink at this loss of a lead. If Ursula had been such a force of nature she must surely have spoken to her girls about her daring escape from Berlin. Then again, if Beatrice had such a tight family, she was not the child they sought.

'What about the third baby?' she asked. 'Do you, by any chance, keep in touch with the third baby?'

But at that Hanna just stared.

'Third baby?' she asked eventually.

Bethan gaped at her.

'We believe there was a third baby at Torgau,' Max said. 'She travelled in the first shipment with Ursula and Beatrice.'

Hanna gave a small shake of her head.

'I'm sorry, I don't know anything about that.'

'Gisela Schultz?' Bethan hazarded.

'The name means nothing, I'm afraid. Was she there, in Torgau?'

'We think so.'

'Then that's odd, isn't it?' She looked at Bethan, her eyes sharp with understanding. 'You think this third baby was your mother?'

Bethan took a careful sip of her wine, composing herself.

'I think she must be,' she said, 'for if you were brought up by Katharina, and Beatrice was brought up by Ursula, she's the only option left. The question is – who on earth was she?'

Ada made a strange little sound and Bethan looked across. The old lady's eyes met hers and she unrolled her blanket to below her mouth. Her lips worked and Bethan willed her to speak, but no sound came out and after a while she rolled the blanket back up again.

Chapter Thirty

6 July 1945

'The British!' Marcel shouted, running out of the kitchen waving a cleaver. 'The British are here.'

Katharina didn't even look up from the two newborn otters she was watching play with their mother. They were the first babies since the war and mattered far more than Marcel's daydreams. Every day since Oskar's death she had paced the streets of the city looking for a vehicle she could commandeer to follow the rest of the Zoofamilie out west, but every day she had failed. She was beginning to think she would have to walk to Torgau.

'I mean it, Katharina, the British are coming.'

She forced her eyes up from the baby otters.

'When, Marcel?' she asked wearily, for these shouts had gone up too many times. 'Before the autumn? Before Christmas? Before Armageddon?'

Marcel, however, was not to be cowed. He folded his arms and a smile crept across his face.

'Before teatime,' he said, and nodded towards the Elephant Gate.

Katharina pushed herself to her feet and took a few steps forward.

'Is that…?'

'A parade of Tommies! It truly is, Kätsche. They have come. They have *finally* come.'

Katharina huffed, refusing to be impressed.

'They're too late to be of any use.'

'I disagree, if they can get rid of the Reds. Come, my lady.' He held out an arm. 'Let's go and see these famed Brits, shall we?'

Katharina shook her head, but she took his arm all the same and let him lead her down the largely repaired central avenue to the Elephant Gate where, from behind the stone elephants, they watched the brown-uniformed British soldiers marching in quiet and orderly fashion down the street. One officer gave them a salute before turning to hush the young men pointing and nudging each other behind him. He was too late though and their words drifted across to Katharina: 'A zoo! Look, lads, it's a zoo. How marvellous.'

Her heart swelled. She did not know the last word but she could hear the wonder in the young man's tone and it steeled her resolve. Perhaps her bag would have to wait under her bed just a little longer.

'Shall we venture out?' Marcel suggested, and she nodded.

She hated the city now but something in the air felt different today – fresher, safer. Was that madness? These men were soldiers too, after all, but as they marched, they doffed their caps to the rapidly gathering citizens along the way. The parade was in no hurry and, although the officers kept rough order, they didn't stop the men from bending to talk to children, or handing out sweets and cigarettes to their gaping audience.

'They look… human,' Katharina stuttered.

She waited for Marcel to laugh at her but he did not. For this city full of women, these were some of the first men they had seen in a long time who were not here simply to take from them, and many were weeping with relief. Katharina felt her step pick up a little and began to look around the city with hope. She noticed fruit budding on the trees and vegetables in abundance in the many plots around the city. The main roads were cleared, many shops had reopened, and people were even drinking in bars and cafes, as if life might be there to be celebrated again. On one corner an abandoned tank had been plastered with fliers for a beginner's dance class and Katharina paused to stroke her hand over it. They were all having to learn to dance again, but for the first time today she felt that it might actually be possible.

'It feels different,' Marcel said. 'Is it the Tommies?'

'If it is,' Katharina snapped, not yet disposed to forgiveness, 'then their tardiness is unforgivable.'

'They did not necessarily know what the Red Army would be like, Kätsche.'

Katharina sniffed.

'If the stories from East Prussia made it to us, they most certainly made it to the British troops. They knew how violent the Soviets were, Marcel. They knew and they left us to their mercies.'

He patted her hand.

'That may be true but they are here now. And it was, after all, the German leaders who condemned Berlin, not the British ones.' Katharina bit back bile at the sour truth of that one simple statement, but then Marcel bent down and, to her surprise, dropped a soft kiss on her forehead. 'All nations, I think, have things to be ashamed of, but we cannot let them get in the way of moving forward. Together.'

'You are more forgiving than me, Marcel.'

He shrugged.

'I have less to lose.'

She looked at him in surprise.

'I have lost everything, Marcel. My friends are killed or have fled, the children in my charge are gone, my husband is dead.'

'But you have your zoo.'

She shook her head at him.

'You're such a romantic, Marcel.'

'As are you, madame, as are you.'

She disagreed, but all the same she was glad when they turned round to trace their way back towards home. The Russians seemed to have retreated into whatever holes they usually came out of, and there were British soldiers in their place. They were leaning on lampposts to chat in broken German to those curious enough to approach, distributing food and everywhere, it seemed, gathering in groups around portable stoves to brew up dark brown mugfuls of tea.

'Don't they have coffee?' Katharina asked, feeling sorry for them for the first time.

'They prefer that stuff,' Marcel said, nose wrinkled. 'They're a strange lot for sure, but harmless enough.'

Katharina was about to retort that they hadn't been harmless when they'd been dropping bombs on her animals, but what was the point? War made monsters of everyone and she should put it behind her.

They turned into the zoo to hear a loud bellowing and the sound of raised voices.

'Knautschke!' Katharina cried and, picking up her skirts, went running for the hippo house.

Inside, the hippo, now close to adult size, was throwing his considerable bulk around the poolside vegetation in quite a tantrum, and no wonder. Dennis was staggering in front of him, watched with clear incredulity by two British officers.

'Dennis!' Katharina cried. 'Get out of there. What on earth are you trying to do?'

'I'm talking to him,' Dennis said.

'He doesn't talk, you fool. And he doesn't like you standing there.'

Dennis frowned at her.

'Why on earth not?'

'It makes him nervous. You should never get between a hippo and water.'

'Or what?' Dennis sneered.

'Or he'll trample you to death.'

'Nonsense, woman. He's a herbivore. He doesn't attack humans.'

'It won't be an attack, Dennis, it will be blind panic. A hippo without water can die very quickly so he needs to always be able to get to it. Stand aside. Please.'

Dennis rolled his eyes but Knautschke was pawing the ground in a way that got through to even his vodka-addled mind, and he stepped aside just in time. The hippo, eyes rolling, made a leap for his pool and submerged himself with a giant splash that went all over the British officers. Katharina looked at them in horror.

'I'm so, so sorry.'

The most senior of the pair brushed himself down with commendable calm, straightened his moustache and came across to her.

'No need to apologise, my dear,' he said in clipped English. 'I'd rather take a small splattering than watch a man trampled to death. It's a good job you arrived.'

Katharina battled to understand him but her English was poor, and she could only hope that his tone indicated he was happy with her. Luckily the other officer came forward and offered a passable translation. She smiled.

'I know Knautschke well. He is a happy hippo but we all have our sticking points.'

The man translated for his senior, who nodded as if she had said something very wise and stuck out his hand.

'General Turner at your service.'

She shook it a little nervously.

'Katharina Heinroth.'

'This is Colonel Hardcastle. You know the zoo well?'

The translation came and she nodded.

'It is my life.'

'Then we should talk.'

He led her out of the hippo house, Dennis trailing unhappily in their wake, demanding to know where Marshal Vetrov was.

'The Russians have gone,' Colonel Hardcastle told him. 'This part of Berlin is ours now.'

'Just like that?' Dennis asked petulantly.

'Of course not. The division of a conquered Germany was decided a long time ago at Yalta, by Roosevelt, Churchill and Stalin themselves. It's just taken a while to put the relevant areas into place.'

Katharina looked at him.

'We didn't think you'd come.'

He gave her a little bow.

'For that we apologise, Frau Heinroth. Believe me, if it had been left up to us, we would have been here before the Russkies, but soldiers can only do as they are commanded.'

'What are you commanded to do now?'

'Restore Berlin to prosperity. Bring her men home, rebuild her houses and her public buildings, boost her productivity, and promote the happiness of her citizens.'

'Truly?'

He gave her a sideways smile.

'As best we can. It will take time. And we, er, we only have the west. The Russians will keep the east.'

'The city will be divided?'

'I'm afraid so, but hopefully not too badly. You, at least, are with us.'

With us – they were such simple words and so kindly said.

'And the zoo?'

Colonel Hardcastle grinned widely.

'Oh, we Brits love a zoo and I hear this was once a marvellous one. We will do all we can to help you bring it back to its former glory. We have access to materials and the Corps of Royal Engineers are on their way. They'll love getting stuck into some of these enclosures. That monkey rock of yours, for example – they'll soon have it safe again, and twice the size it is now if I know them.'

Katharina was unable to believe the blustering positivity of the man.

'Truly?' she asked again.

He smiled and clapped her on the back.

'Truly. But what we need is someone to manage it.'

Dennis rocked forward.

'I am the manager, sir.'

General Turner looked him up and down as if he were a maggot on his dinner.

'You, *sir*, could not manage a pliant prostitute. Get out of my sight.'

The translation came, a little red-faced, from Colonel Hardcastle.

'But… but Marshal Vetrov—'

'Is not here any more. I am in charge of this quarter now. I am in charge of the zoo and I need a competent manager. How long did you say you had been here, Frau Heinroth?'

Katharina glanced to the Colonel for the translation and swallowed.

'Twelve years, sir.'

'As a keeper?'

She looked down, but then remembered what was at stake for her and forced her chin high. Oskar had told her she could be strong enough for both of them and now was the time to prove it.

'I was not officially a keeper, sir, because I am a woman, but I did the job all through the war and would be honoured to do it again.'

General Turner smiled.

'We've taken many fine women into the British army in the last five years, my dear. In truth, I doubt we could have won it without them. My own daughter is a Wren and loves it – and why the hell not? The important thing is not your sex but your ability to do the job. Can you do the job, Frau Heinroth?'

The translation came and Katharina did not hesitate. She stood up straight, looked General Turner in the eye, and said: 'I can.'

He smiled.

'Then, my dear, it is yours. Now, tell me, do you have any elephants? I love an elephant.'

That word she knew and she smiled.

'Just one remaining, sir – our lonely bull, Siam. He is a little grumpy these days.'

'No wonder, poor old chap. We'll have to do our best to get him some company, hey? Lead on, Frau Heinroth, lead on.'

So, dazed and still unable to quite believe her luck, Katharina moved past a crumpled Dennis and, head held high, led the way on out across the zoo and into her future at last.

Chapter Thirty-One

Biting her lip in concentration, Bethan pushed her tweezers as gently as she could into the zebra's hoof and grasped the tiny stone bedded deep in the soft flesh. The animal gave a pained whinny and tried to kick away but Ruth, the keeper, held on tight to her leg and Bethan was able to pull the offending item out.

'Got it!'

She sat back triumphantly and held up the stone. Ruth smiled.

'Nice one!'

'I'll give it a quick swab but it doesn't look badly infected, so hopefully it will heal quickly.'

She took out her cleaning materials and efficiently swabbed the tender area where the stone had been niggling at the zebra's flesh. The animal gave another whinny but didn't try to pull away this time and, once Bethan was done, she went scampering off to join her fellows, kicking her hind legs up in joy.

'Thanks, Beth.'

'Just doing my job.'

Bethan smiled at the keeper and let herself out of the enclosure, the euphoria of this little success rapidly draining away. For the last three days she'd been working every moment she could to try and distract herself from the far harder task of finding her grandmother. Every time she thought she was getting to an answer, she hit a dead end and she had to admit that, despite the joy of being with Max, it was getting her down.

She was a fool, she told herself as she trudged back to the vet centre. She surely knew that Gisela Schultz, by default, had to be the mother of the mystery baby, and the absence of information around that child indicated that it was most likely the one gifted to Oma Erika to become her treasured Jana. But an absence of information didn't feel enough. Bethan wanted something more positive – someone who truly knew what had happened.

She glanced at her watch. She was supposedly only on shift until two and it was already two thirty. She should go home and get some lunch but she didn't feel hungry. She wandered down the avenue, looking at all the happy visitors and trying to feel her usual joy in her marvellous place of work, but it was hard. Perhaps she should go back to her dad for a weekend. She had to sort out her flat, after all, and it would be lovely to see him and talk some of this over face to face. But somehow she didn't want to do that until she had some definite answers.

'Wait for those and you'll never see Dad again,' she muttered to herself, then looked around self-consciously in case anyone had seen her babbling like poor Ada.

The thought of the old lady, at least, made her smile. She was glad Ada was living safely with her sister in her beautiful home, and wondered at how close she must have been to Katharina to still sit and chat to her every day. Then again, didn't Bethan talk to her own mum sometimes? It didn't make her mad, just connected. Desperately wishing that she could talk to Katharina Heinroth herself, Bethan found her footsteps turning down the avenue where the busts of the past managers stood in their unassuming line. For once Ada wasn't here and Bethan sank onto the bench opposite.

'What happened, Katharina?' she whispered.

The lady from the past stared impassively back. If the sculptor had captured her correctly, she'd had kindly but determined eyes, and Bethan couldn't even begin to imagine what the war years had demanded of her. Getting a mother for one little baby must have been the very least of it.

'Was it Gisela?' she whispered. 'Was it Gisela Schultz's baby?'

Katharina just gave her a marble stare and Bethan shook her head at herself, but suddenly Ada was before her, putting a proprietorial hand on the bust.

'She didn't look like this,' she burst out. 'She wasn't all pale. She was fire. Red hair. Like a fox. Lovely red hair. Green eyes. Not white. I don't like her white. It isn't right. She was fire.'

Bethan got up.

'It sounds like it, from what I've heard. It takes a lot of fire to rescue babies.'

Ada stroked the bust then suddenly spun round to Bethan. 'You look like her.'

Bethan jumped.

'Like who, Ada?'

'Like the other lady asking all these questions.'

'When?'

'A long time ago. Ages ago. I remember. I'm good at remembering.'

Bethan could feel her heart thudding in her chest.

'You are, Ada,' she assured her. 'Do you remember her name?'

Ada nodded.

'Jana. She was called Jana. It means "gift", you know, she told me that. But she didn't have a gift for Ada. Just questions. Lots of questions. Too many questions.'

'Did you give her any answers?'

Ada stamped her purple-booted foot.

'No. Not one. I told you – I wasn't to talk. No one was to talk.'

Bethan took a deep breath then retreated to the bench, patting the seat next to her. Ada took a cautious step forward.

'Back then that was right, Ada,' she told her, as softly as she could. 'Just like it was right not to talk about Hanna. But that's OK now, remember? Hanna said that was OK now. So perhaps it's OK to talk about Gisela too?'

Ada looked at her, her eyes for all the world like those of a nervous child, then took another step towards her.

'You're kind.'

'Thank you. I try to be.'

'The animals like you.'

'I like them. Very much.'

'Good. That's good.' Bethan patted the bench again and finally Ada sidled onto it. 'Animals deserve kindness.'

'As do people.'

Ada pursed her lips at that. 'Some people do.'

'Did Gisela Schultz?'

'Oh yes. She was so kind. So caring. She loved animals like you. Like me. I love animals. I always did. So did Gisela. She wanted to be a zoo keeper but her Vati wouldn't let her. Said it wasn't for girls. That's not fair, is it?'

Bethan shook her head vehemently.

'Girls make great keepers.'

'I was a keeper.'

'I heard.'

'I was a good keeper. I didn't go to normal school like Hanna. I went to animal school. That's what Kätsche said.'

'Kätsche?'

'Kätsche!' She nodded to the bust. 'Katharina.'

'Ah! Of course. She was a mother to you?' Ada nodded. 'What about Gisela's baby, Ada? What happened to Gisela's baby?'

Ada thought hard. Bethan held her breath and willed this curious old lady to speak, and with a sudden nod she reached a finger to her lips, as if giving herself permission, and spoke one word: 'Olivia.'

Bethan's heart squeezed.

'Olivia was Gisela's baby?'

'That's right. They all had babies. First my Mutti – she had Hanna but she had to trade her own life in. Then Ursula had Beatrice. That was an easy one. Ursula was good at babies, nearly as good as a chimp. Then Gisela – hers was hard because the Russians were coming. The Russians were coming and we were all hiding in the bunker. Not just night-times. All the time. They shot you if you went out. Or bombed you. They bombed my Vati. He was just going to feed the zebras. That should be allowed, shouldn't it, feeding zebras?'

Her voice was rising and Bethan put out a hand to her, amazed at how much she was saying.

'Of course that should be allowed, Ada, of course.'

She settled a little.

'Having babies should be allowed too, but it was hard for Gisela. There was a lot of blood.'

'But the baby was born safely?'

'Yes. Olivia was safe. Gisela was alive. Dieter came.'

'Dieter? Her husband?'

'Yes. He only had one leg, from the war. The Russians took it and then the Russians took the rest of him too.'

'At the birth?'

Ada frowned at her.

'No! Later. When the lorry came. The lorry for the chimps. I was meant to go in it, you know. I was meant to go with Ursula and the babies and the chimps. But I hid. I hid with Hanna. I wasn't going to leave Katharina to the Russians. She needed me.'

'That was very brave, Ada. Did Gisela go with Ursula?'

Ada shook her head.

'She was too ill. Too sad. She made Ursula take Olivia and she stayed in bed. And cried.'

This, then, was it.

'Gisela died in Berlin?' Bethan whispered.

'No, no, no,' Ada said crossly, as if this should be as vivid in Bethan's mind as in her own. 'Gisela got better. She was with us when we ran from the Russians in a wheelbarrow and hid in the coal bunker. She was with us when we came back to the zoo to find Pierre and all the dead animals. Only not Knautschke. Knautschke survived. And Siam and Reike.'

'That's good.'

'Very good. I looked after them. All of them. When Katharina was put in charge, I was too.'

'I'm sure you were brilliant at it.'

'I was.'

'But you went to Torgau first?'

'I did?' She considered. 'The fairytale house?'

'That's right.'

'Yes. With Hanna and Gisela in Pierre's van.'

'Gisela went to Torgau?'

'Yes.' Ada's voice was hoarse now but she pushed on. 'To find Olivia.'

This was getting Bethan nowhere. Was the whole list one giant, spiralling dead end?

'Did she find her?'

'She wasn't hidden. You don't hide babies. Well, except from Russians.'

'No. Silly me. Sorry. So, Gisela found her baby?'

'Yes.'

'And then?'

Ada looked at her.

'She died.'

Bethan sucked in her breath.

'Gisela died? At Torgau?'

'Yes. That wasn't fair either, was it? She got away and she still died. I knew it was going to happen. It was like with Mutti only much, much slower. She went paler and paler, like a ghost... Then she was gone. I was scared.'

'Scared that she'd died?'

'No! Scared that Katharina would die too. I wanted to get back to Berlin but no one would let me. They kept saying I had to stay "safe" but I didn't want to be safe; I wanted to be with Katharina.'

Bethan stared at Ada, taking it all in. What must this poor woman have been through as a child? No wonder her wits were shot – though it seemed that perhaps her memories were clearer than her understanding. Ada put out a finger suddenly and Bethan thought she was going to prod her, but she simply touched the tip to the hippo brooch on the lapel of her uniform.

'She had a brooch like that. Her husband bought it for her because she loved the zoo. She did love the zoo, you know, Gisela. Like me. I love the zoo.'

'And me,' Bethan said softly. She touched her own fingers to the brooch, pressing it gently as if it were the last piece in what had felt like a very complex jigsaw. 'Did you know a girl called Erika, Ada?' she dared to ask.

Ada tipped her head on one side again, then a smile spread across her face.

'Erika – yes. She had pretty dresses. She let us wear them. Me and Monica and Barbara. We wore her dresses.' She cut herself off. 'But she was sad too. Someone had died.' She gave a weary sigh. 'Someone had always died.'

'Who'd died for Erika, Ada – can you remember?'

'Her baby. Her baby had died.'

'So, she wanted another one?'

Ada beamed.

'She did. She did want another one. That's why she was perfect.'

'Perfect for what?'

Ada slapped her hand on her knee in triumph.

'For Olivia, of course. Anke saw it. Anke was kind too. Ursula was going to take the baby to France but Anke said no.'

Bethan sat upright at the mention of the housekeeper. Anke was the last name on her mum's list and, it seemed, the key to what had happened.

'What did Anke suggest instead, Ada?' she asked nervously.

'Anke said she knew a mother who would take her and care for her and love her like her own. Like *more than* her own. That's what Katharina did for me. I was more than her own. Because she chose me. And Hanna too. That's nice, isn't it?'

'That's very nice,' Bethan agreed, dazed.

Slowly she reached into her pocket and drew out her phone. Pulling up the picture from her grandma's scrapbook, she held it out to Ada.

'Do you know these people?'

Ada snatched at the phone, lifting it close to her face and peering at it from every angle.

'I do,' she said finally.

'Who are they, Ada?'

Ada pointed to the middle one. 'That's Anke. And that' – her finger moved left – 'is Erika. Erika with the pretty dresses. And that...' Now her finger went right. Bethan held her breath again. 'That's Gisela. See how pale she is? She was nearly a ghost then.' She looked at Bethan with sudden pride. 'I took that photo.'

'Really?'

'With Anke's husband's big camera. It was very smart, very heavy. I had to hold it very carefully. Anke said she wanted a photo of them all together. She said it was important.'

Bethan smiled and took her phone back, looking down into the eyes of the three women: one who had stood all these years as her devoted grandmother, one who was biologically so, and one who had brought the pair together at the tail end of a war that had already taken so much.

'She was right,' she told Ada, tears brimming. 'It *was* important. It was very important.'

A tear fell, then another and another, plopping onto the screen and blurring the three women captured deep in what had turned out to be her own past. She felt her body start to shake with the release of it all and looked apologetically to Ada but, without another word, the old woman threw her skinny arms around her and held her close.

'It's all right to cry,' she whispered. 'That's what Katharina used to tell me. It's all right to cry and to be sad because it means you care. It's good to care, isn't it?'

Bethan put her arms around Ada in return and, looking over her bony shoulder at Katharina Heinroth, she gave her a nod of thanks.

'It's very good to care.' She wiped her tears away. 'Now, Ada, I think we deserve cake. Lots and lots of cake.'

'Whooppeee!' Ada said.

Bethan put out a bleep call, summoning the chimp keeper and the two other vets of Berlin Zoo to an urgent meeting in the canteen. They came running to find her and Ada sitting either side of a giant cream-and-chocolate-laden cake and a large pot of coffee.

'What's all this?' Tanya asked. 'I thought it was an emergency?'

'It *is* – a cake emergency.'

'My favourite sort,' Ella said happily. 'Are we celebrating?'

Bethan nodded and looked to Max, who stepped up and took her hand.

'You found your grandmother?'

Bethan saw Tanya look to Ella at the sight of them together and Ella give Tanya a cheeky thumbs up, but she didn't care. She didn't care about anything right now.

'Ada remembers,' she told Max. 'Ada remembers it all.'

Max looked to Ada.

'Aren't you clever!'

Ada beamed.

'I am. Now – cake!' She lifted the knife and hovered it over the beautiful confectionery. 'Schwarzwälder Kirschtorte,' she said happily, 'just like Anke used to make.'

There seemed to Bethan to be no better way of celebrating.

Epilogue

July 2019

'Doesn't it look amazing in the summer?'

Bethan swept an arm around the zoo, trying her best to take in the joys of the whole place, from the baboons on their rock to the polar bear on his pseudo iceberg and the pandas in their bamboo hideout; from the families eating ice creams, to the keepers working with their animals, to her fellow vets keeping them all safe and well.

'Amazing,' Paul agreed. 'It suits you, Beth.'

She nodded and looked over at Max on her other side.

'It really does, Dad. I love the work, I love the people, I love the city.'

'That's great,' he said, 'your mum would be so pleased. She always missed Berlin.'

Bethan steered the three of them around the dome of the hippo house to come to a stop near the bronze statue of Knautschke. Two children were playing on the hippo's broad back, and Bethan touched her fingers to her grandmother's brooch as she watched them with a smile. That had been her once, sitting there while her mum tried to get the truth of her birth from Ada – the truth that was now, finally, out in the open.

She pictured her younger self hiding beneath the bed with her mother's jewellery box and finding the list, like a message from the grave. It had not been intended as such, she knew, but following its mystery had made her feel closer to her mother and brought her a peace she'd not even known was missing. The kids ran off after their parents and Bethan went up to Knautschke, throwing one leg over to sit astride him. A couple of children gave her a sideways look but she didn't care. Not now.

'Mum brought me here,' she said to Paul. 'I remember it vividly. I sat on this very hippo while she went off trying to talk to people. It's like I was on this quest right from when I was very young, though I didn't realise it for far too long.'

Paul sighed.

'I'm not sure I wanted you to realise it at all, sweetheart. It's been hard on you.'

'Briefly – but brilliant in the end. And look what it brought me.' She reached up to kiss Max, then turned back to her father. 'I just wish I could tell Mum what I've found out.'

Paul gave her a hug.

'She'd be very grateful. And very proud. Tenacious – that's how she used to describe you.'

'Tenacious?'

'Yep. Well, actually she usually used to say, "She's a little terrier, that one," but tenacious is what she meant. Even when you were tiny, you'd get hold of something and never give up until you'd sorted it to your satisfaction – from Play-Doh statues, to new wellies, to places you wanted to visit. And then, of course, being a vet.'

Bethan smiled.

'Apparently Gisela Schultz wanted to be a zoo keeper but her father wouldn't let her. Said it was too rough for a girl. Madness, isn't it, especially when those "girls" ended up running Berlin during the war. Gisela was learning right here in the zoo, from Katharina Heinroth herself, when the war struck. All through it too. She made it to the end, Dad. She even made it out of Berlin, but it seems all she'd been through was just too much for her poor body. If she'd only got well, she'd probably have come back and worked here with Katharina.'

'It was a terrible tragedy,' Paul agreed, stepping up to the hippo to hug her. 'But life works out in strange ways. It meant that Oma

Erika had the precious gift of Jana, and she and I, in turn, had the precious gift of you.'

Bethan squeezed him back.

'That *is* a blessing.'

Paul grinned.

'Everything works out if you hold tight to those you love.'

'It does. I'm so happy here, Dad.'

'I can see that.' He looked from her to Max and gave a wry smile. 'I guess I'd better brush up on my German – fast.'

Bethan laughed.

'Your German is fine, but I don't suppose a longer stay or two would hurt it.'

He looked sideways at her.

'What are you saying, Bethan?'

She coloured, but it was time to tell him.

'Tanya has asked me if I'd like to make my contract permanent,' she admitted. 'They want me to stay here, at the zoo, for good.'

'Wow.' Paul looked her up and down. 'So, you're telling me you're not coming home?'

Bethan thought about it. She thought about her flat, now vacated by Callum so he could live it up in Soho, and let to a delighted young couple. She thought about her old job in the surgery – gentle and enjoyable but all too predictable. She thought about pretty Leicestershire, but then about vibrant, exciting, challenging Berlin. She thought about the zoo and her friends, about the jazz bar and the canteen and Ada. She spoke to the old lady every day now and often Ada would chatter back, as if releasing her hard-held secrets had released something of her old self as well.

She looked to Max, who was waiting for her every evening when she came in, eager to hear about her day, and she smiled. She'd taken this contract to find out more about the zoo animals she'd always been drawn to, and more about the mystery that had haunted her mother in the weeks before she'd been taken from her.

She'd ended up finding out all of that and more besides – about the sort of person she wanted to be and the sort of life she wanted to lead. Coming to Berlin had been a far greater journey than she'd ever imagined, but it had taken her to places that felt both wonderfully comfortable and thrillingly exciting, and she couldn't wait to see where her life went next.

'I'm telling you, Dad,' she said softly, 'that I *am* home.'

A Letter from Anna

Dear Reader,

I want to say a huge thank you for choosing to read *The Berlin Zookeeper*. From the moment I first read about the fate of this amazing zoo during the Second World War, I was hooked and I really hope you were too. If you did enjoy it, and want to keep up to date with all my latest releases, just sign up at the following link. Your email address will never be shared and you can unsubscribe at any time.

www.bookouture.com/anna-stuart

I found it absolutely fascinating looking at the war from the perspective of the average German citizen and was horrified to find out just how much damage was done to Berlin in the final battles – all because of Hitler's maniacal refusal to submit. It was also a consolation, as I wrote this through the restrictions and privations of the horribly long first months of the Covid-19 pandemic, to think that at least I wasn't crouching underground, being bombed every night and awaiting the approach of the violent Red Army. In comparison, being stuck in my house with my family didn't seem so bad!

If you ever get the chance, do go and visit the zoo – and say hello to the statue of Knautschke from me! And if you enjoyed reading my story, I'd be very grateful if you could write a review. I'd love to hear what you think, and it makes such a difference helping new readers to discover one of my books for the first time.

I also love hearing from my readers – you can get in touch on my Facebook page, through Twitter, Goodreads or my website.

Thanks,
Anna Stuart

 annastuartauthor

 @annastuartbooks

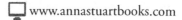 www.annastuartbooks.com

Acknowledgements

My very first thanks must go to Detmar, Penny and Sascha Owen – my utterly invaluable research assistants on the ground in Berlin. I wrote this novel in lockdown so was struggling, to my great disappointment, to get to Berlin Zoo myself. I'd been to the city before but never to the zoo and although Google is a wonderful resource, there is nothing like being physically in a place. I was incredibly lucky, therefore, to be introduced to the Owens by mutual friends (thank you, Brenda and Jamie) and, despite never having met me before, they threw themselves into my research like total heroes. They found out so many vital facts for me, visiting the zoo on my behalf and sending me all sorts of photos and answers to my myriad peculiar questions. They even recruited their neighbour Torsten, a lighting engineer doing some work in the zoo, to find out about staff homes on site for me, so thank you to him too. I honestly don't think I could have done this book without you, Detmar, Penny and Sasha – you have my undying gratitude.

Another really helpful researcher was Kevin Prenger, who wrote the excellent book *War Zone Zoo* (self-published 2018), originally in Dutch but thankfully recently translated into English. This was a brilliant resource for me, and Kevin was also kind enough to respond to my Twitter-pestering with great kindness and generosity, sharing all he knew to help me with the novel. Thank you, Kevin.

My next thank you must go to Natasha Harding. Natasha was my first ever editor back in 2013, and one of my fondest memories is of the aforementioned Brenda reading out Natasha's lovely first email to me on a windy, pebbly beach in Wales. Career turns for us both parted us for some years but it is wonderful to now be working together again and Natasha's input, expertise and enthusiasm have, as always, been invaluable to me. I'm delighted to be embarking on what I hope will be a long Bookouture journey with her.

Thank you, too, to the rest of the team at Bookouture – publishers and authors – who have been really welcoming, friendly and focused. I'm delighted to be a part of their world. On that note, another big thank you must go to my agent Kate for sorting all the tricky stuff and for being there for me as a wise sounding board and guide. And a shout out to her fabulous new assistant, Nell!

As always, I owe a debt of gratitude to my family, especially this year where we have all been in rather closer contact than would normally be natural for parents and teenagers – and have coped remarkably well. I'll never forget 'beach day' in the back garden, guess-the-intro games far too late into the night, and an amazing *MasterChef* Christmas Eve. Thank you all.

Historical Notes

I cannot honestly remember what idle half hour on Google took me to Berlin Zoo during the Second World War, but the moment I read the first words about the terrible time that the people and animals suffered, especially from 1943 onwards, I was horribly captivated and knew it was a story I wanted to tell. I did extensive further research and have done my very best to represent that terrible time as truthfully and honestly as I can in the novel, but I thought readers might enjoy some brief notes on points of detail here.

The Zoo in the War

Berlin Zoo is still located in the same place as it was during the war – right in the heart of the capital. These days there is a second zoo, established in the east when the city was divided by the wall, but at the time there was just the one near the Tiergarten and it was a key entertainment venue for Berliners. Established in 1844, it had about 100 visitors a day right from the start and was even more popular in the 1930s when zoos were in their heyday across Europe. Many exotic species were hunted down and brought to Europe for fascinated crowds and Berlin Zoo, at least, seems to have been at the forefront of establishing naturalistic habitats for the animals, especially under the Heck family. Those in charge certainly had a flare for exotic architecture, building an Arabian-style antelope house, an Indian-style elephant house and an Egyptian-style ostrich house – all of which can be seen on the internet.

In 1888 Dr Ludwig Heck was made zoo director and he brought up his two sons, Lutz and Heinz, on site. Lutz became director after him in 1932 and Heinz went on to run Hellabrunn Zoo in Munich and, with others, was a valuable contact for Lutz in his attempts to get some of his valuable animals out of Berlin once the bombs started. The idea of them also getting people out is all my own, but seems perfectly likely in a city in which, on the order of the Führer, citizens were considered traitors for not staying to defend the streets he did not dare to venture into.

Lutz Heck was, as shown, a Nazi sympathiser, at least before the war. He was quite close to Göring, a dedicated hunter and keen preserver of animals. They worked together, as briefly shown in the novel, to try and reverse engineer an aurochs, an extinct German bovine. This was part of the Blut und Bloden policy of elevating everything Aryan, so clearly had serious issues in the long term, but was still an interesting, if ultimately unsuccessful, scientific experiment at the time.

Heck joined the Nazi party as an affiliated member but seems to have turned against them when it came to the final days of the war. That was too late, however, and he fled the city once the Russians had taken it, knowing that he would be executed if caught. I found him a very interesting man, condemning his Nazi principals but admiring his compassionate and intelligent work with animals in the zoo he truly loved. I tried to show a little of the dichotomies in his personality through his sparring with Katharina.

The November 1943 raids, shown at the start of the novel, were truly horrific both for the city and for the zoo, and the opening scenes with the aquarium animals blasted all over the pavement are based on true accounts. It is also true that the zoo went from around three thousand animals when war broke out to just ninety-one by the end, although some others were safely brought back from evacuation after the German surrender. Those animals named – Reike the giraffe, Siam the bull elephant, Kalifa the baboon, Pongo the gorilla, Sultan and Bussy the lion cubs, Goliath the bear, and of course Rosa and Knautschke the hippos – are all real. The statue of Knautschke – who went on to live until the grand old age of forty-six and father thirty-five hippopotamus calves – can be seen outside the hippo house if you visit the zoo today.

The horror of the Russian conquest of Berlin continued for the zoo in the immediate aftermath of peace when Lutz's one-time driver – named Dennis by me – was given control, presumably by sucking up to the Russians in command. It was a torrid time under his nominal command and the stories of the Russians shooting alpine ibis off a balcony and attempting ridiculous feats with the lion cubs are true. We do not know exactly why the British, when they finally took the sector of the city in which the zoo was located, chose to replace him with Katharina, but it is documented that he was drunken and uncommitted so presumably common sense prevailed. And thank heavens, as the dedicated and passionate Katharina Heinroth was instrumental in returning the zoo to past glories.

Katharina and Oskar Heinroth

Katharina Heinroth was an astonishing woman. Born in 1897 as Katharina Berger in Breslau – now Wroclaw in Poland but then part of East Prussia – she was one of four siblings in a home of open-minded intellectuals. An academic child with a fascination with nature, she was encouraged by her liberal parents to pursue her interests and studied zoology, botany and geology at Munich University.

She graduated in 1923 and worked on hearing in reptiles before being taken on as an assistant to renowned naturalist Karl Von Frisch, the first man to spot the 'waggle dance' in bees. She moved in with another of Frisch's assistants, Gustav Adolf Rösch, and then married him in 1928 but they divorced a few years later. Ever the academic, she moved to Halle and worked at the Leopoldina Academy library before she met and married Oskar and moved to Berlin Zoo where he had been working for the last nineteen years.

The story of this couple is a wonderfully romantic one. There was, as shown in the novel, a 26-year gap in their ages and both had already been married (he was widowed) but they seem to have genuinely fallen in love with each other. We know from private letters between them that he called her 'meine kindl' – my child – because of the age gap. We also know that she called him 'O' or 'kleine O', so I chose to use those pet names in the novel.

Katharina and Oskar were childless, something that was a source of sorrow to them both, but they are known to have fled the zoo with 'two children'. There is little to identify who those two were and in the chaos of that period in Berlin they could well have been unknowns that they rescued along the way, but I chose to match them up with the Eberhards' daughters. Robert Eberhard was the real zebra keeper during the war (Walter and Gustav were also real keepers) and is recorded as having been killed feeding his zebras during a raid. Details of his family are not known so I shamelessly made those up, and linked them into the Heinroths. There is no evidence that Katharina and Oskar continued to look after any children but, then again, there is no evidence that they did not…

I have also been a little creative with the death date of Oskar Heinroth. As shown, he somehow survived the horrors of the Battle of Berlin, despite having a raging fever. Katharina genuinely did have to flee the Russians in the zoo with him in a wheelbarrow and they also had to hide in some form of coal bunker, so how he made it back to their home in the zoo I do not know. He actually died on 31 May 1945 but in the novel I applied a little creative licence to the date, pushing it back to give them a final scene together once the others had left Berlin.

Katharina's work rebuilding the zoo after the war was tireless, earning her the nickname of 'Katharina die Einzige' ('the one and only Katharina'). She retired as Scientific Director in 1956, aged fifty-nine, but carried on her research, lecturing in zoology at Berlin Technical University and producing numerous scientific and popular publications, including a biography of Oskar in 1971 and an autobiography in 1979. She died in 1989, aged ninety-four. She was a genuinely brilliant, hard-working and passionate woman, devoted to the care and study of animals, and it has been an honour to write about her.

The flak tower and zoo bunker

I was astonished when I first saw pictures of the enormous 'flak tower' built just outside the zoo in 1941 and knew I had to include a scene there to show it to the readers, hence Katharina and Oskar's fictional expedition to find a doctor for Sasha. The zoo flak tower was one of three built in the city and was much like a vast, concrete medieval keep. It was actually one of two buildings, with the G-Tower as the main structure and a smaller L-Tower as a communications centre next door.

G-tower was 132 feet high and covered the area of a normal city block. Its reinforced concrete walls were eight feet thick, with deep-cut apertures shuttered by four-inch steel plates. It had a battery of eight five-inch guns on the roof and 'pom-pom cannons' on every corner. Shell elevators carried ammunition from the ground floor arsenal to each gun.

This was not just a fighting station, however, but a small town of facilities. The top floor housed a hundred-man military garrison and below that, on the fourth floor, was a ninety-five-bed Luftwaffe hospital complete with X-ray rooms and two fully equipped operating theatres. It was staffed by six doctors, twenty nurses and thirty orderlies. The third floor was made up of storerooms holding vast numbers of prize exhibits from Berlin's museums – notably the Pergamon sculptures; the Golden Treasure of Priam; the Gobelin tapestries; and the enormous Kaiser Wilhelm coin collection.

The two lower floors held emergency quarters for the German broadcasting station, Deutschlandsender, but other than that they were for the public. They formed a mammoth air-raid shelter for up to fifteen thousand people, with large kitchens and food storerooms. G-Tower had its own water and power and was believed to be so well stocked with supplies and ammunition that it could last out for a year, though in the event those holding it surrendered.

The bunker under the zoo was also a real structure, built to house at least a hundred people but often keeping around two hundred safe. It seems to have been where the underground nocturnal animals' house now is, which certainly makes sense. As far as I am aware it does not still exist, though I couldn't resist leaving a fictional portion of it for Max and Bethan to visit as part of the story.

Although some Germans must have had their own shelters, most opted for the public ones which were furnished with primitive bunk beds and basic facilities. It seems to have been because of these huge and efficient public shelters that, despite comparable bombing, the loss of life was significantly less in Berlin than in London. The use of candles to check the air purity – one at foot height, one at waist heigh and one at shoulder height – is well documented. The pumps used to keep out noxious fumes and gases often failed during bombings and people had to man handpumps as I show Katharine doing in the novel.

French workers

As soon as I read that there were French workers stationed at the zoo, I knew I had to include them in the story. Before researching this, I knew little about the Service du Travail Obligatoire that saw over 600,000 Frenchmen forcibly shipped to Germany to fill the labour gaps created by those enlisted into the Wehrmacht and sent to the concentration camps. Similar orders were enforced in Poland, Norway and other Nazi-conquered nations, all overseen by Fritz Sauckel, known as the 'Slavemaster of Europe'. Many German tanks and weapons were made by such workers and there are stories of clever attempts to undermine them, though clearly this was risky to closely supervised men.

Whilst for many life must have been miserable, others settled into work with the German civilians and got on well with them. It certainly appears to have been that way in Berlin Zoo. The romance between Pierre and Ursula is entirely my own creation but it is documented fact that six Frenchman were assigned to the zoo and also that after a short period, Heck moved them from their rough barracks across town into accommodation above the zebra house. It is also documented that one of them was a butcher, brought in to sort food for the carnivores, and he was the inspiration for the character of Marcel.

The Battle of Berlin

I, like most people in Britain, have long been aware of the terrible time that the people of London – and several other major English cities – suffered during the Second World War, and particularly during the Blitz. What I had not, naively, realised was quite how similar the experience was for the citizens of various German cities, most notably Berlin. Clearly, as Hitler's capital, it was a prime target for the Allied troops. It was also the place where he was hiding out in the spring of 1945, safe in his bunker and arrogantly refusing to surrender, condemning his population to terrible horrors as the liberators had to fight all the way to his doorstep. Some 20,000 citizens of the capital were killed and around 450,000 homes were destroyed, with large parts of central Berlin being reduced to rubble. What made it even worse was that not once had the Berliners actually voted Hitler in, so their city, their homes and their lives were ravaged by a man they never wanted in power.

Even so, as I've shown in the novel, Berliners were known for their dark humour which helped them to cope through all these horrors. There was much ironic graffiti in the city, especially towards the end of the war. Districts were renamed, with Charlottenburg being daubed Klamottenberg (heap of rubbish), Steglitz as Steht Nichts (nothing standing) and Lichterfelde as Trichterfelde (the field of craters). A favourite quip was to quote Hitler from 1933: 'Give me four years and you will not recognise Germany.' On a more poignant note, many people wrote, 'Unsere Mauern können brechen, unsere Herzen nicht' (Our walls may break but not our hearts) and '1918' was scrawled on buildings to mark the date when Germany lost the First World War as a protest at what the country was again being put through. Dark jokes abounded. A Christmas quip truly was 'Be practical: give a coffin', as shown in the novel, and a favourite subversive ditty ran:

> *Great are the times*
> *But the portions are small*
> *What good does it do us at all*
> *When Hitler's flags stand tall*
> *If under those flags*
> *There's no freedom at all!*

The brave humour is impressive, especially considering that anyone caught singing this song, or painting anti-Nazi slogans on walls, could be executed for treason. I cannot get over how galling it must have been to live in Berlin as an opponent of Hitler in this period and I commend all who got through it with their spirits intact.

But get through it most of them did, and with stoic practicality. Trümmerfrauen was a term coined for the many women – as shown in the novel – who would come out after air raids to help clear the roads and make the area safe. They would work in long lines, passing bricks along in buckets, both to get them out of the way so life could go on, and to preserve them, with commendable optimism, for repairs and rebuilding at a later date.

Also shown in the novel is the creation of the Volkssturm – the People's Storm – as the Allies advanced on Berlin from all sides and Hitler decided he would rather his people die than surrender. This 'elite force' was presented by the ever-resourceful (and shamelessly untruthful) Minister of Propaganda, Goebbels, as a wonderful chance to be the liberators of the Fatherland but was, in truth, a pitiful and cruel cobbling together of those men who had been deemed unfit to fight throughout the rest of the war. It was made up of the old, the very young and the injured and was never going to be anything more than cannon-fodder. Those recruited were expected to find their own uniform and often their own weapons. Men tried to fight with ancient pistols, handmade weapons and even garden tools.

Lutz Heck was put in charge of the Zoo troop and fought to keep them stationed at his beloved zoo. It is true that the keepers were initially taken prisoner by the Russians who believed their zoo uniforms to be military ones before, a day later, someone higher up worked out what the animal logo meant and released them, sparing them a forced march to a Russian gulag.

Many of the Hitler Youth were recruited into the Volkssturm and Hans and Mark in the novel are based on known boys who saved Knautschke from his burning hippo house (though the addition of Katharina to the scene was my own, for narrative purposes). These young lads were often given the primitive 'panzerfaust' handheld rocket launchers shown in the novel and for a fantastic look at this whole phenomenon I would encourage any reader to watch the amazing dark comedy film *JoJo Rabbit*.

Another horror that I did not know about before researching for this book, but which has been widely covered by historians recently, is the terrible conduct of many Russian soldiers in the first days of conquest in Berlin. Russians, coming from harsh communist conditions, were stunned (and to a large degree jealous) to see the decadence of the West and there was widespread looting, with watches being the primary treasure. Bicycles also seem to have fascinated them and many were taken and ridden precariously around the streets.

By far and away the worst element of Russian behaviour, however, was the rape of literally thousands of German women. This happened all the way along the advance on Berlin and then in huge numbers in the capital. The women there knew it was coming due to the terrible stories from the thousands of Prussian refugees fleeing west through the city and there was a huge demand for cyanide, with many women choosing to end their lives rather than face such a fate.

The terrible crimes do not seem to have been committed by the first wave of professional soldiers, who were well-trained, disciplined and focused on conquest, but by the enlisted men who followed behind. They had been fed a lifelong diet of anti-Western propaganda and were also furious at Hitler's invasion of their own country when they were meant to be allies. There was a more personal element as well. It seems that many of the German troops had raped Russian women so these soldiers were out to take their revenge in the worst possible way. I could argue that only deluded men would choose to avenge the horrible fate their innocent wives, sisters and mothers suffered by forcing that same fate on other innocents, but choose it they did.

There are horrific tales of women of all ages, from very young to very old, being raped, sometimes by many men in a row, and left horribly scarred both physically and mentally. Thousands of these poor women fell pregnant and there was a huge demand on abortion clinics in the following months. The authorities, as shown in the novel, did allow these abortions but only as long as the poor victims could, somehow, prove they were carrying a 'Red bastard'. The further trauma this must have caused is unimaginable. According to my research Katharina herself was raped but it was a fact that she, understandably, kept very secret so I chose to respect that and leave it out of my novel.

The orgy of stealing and assaulting only lasted a week or so before the senior officers clamped down on discipline, but that was more than enough to make the poor Berliners hate their conquerors. It was General Eisenhower, US commander of the advancing Allied forces, who made the decision to hold their lines to the west of Berlin and let the Russian troops take the capital. It was, no doubt, a sound military tactic but it exposed the largely female civilians to great horrors from a force that was far less civilised than the one coming from the west.

Eva Braun

For many of us these days, the name Eva Braun is synonymous with Hitler. I was certainly aware that she was his mistress for several years and that he married her the day before they committed suicide together on 30 April 1945. What I did not know until researching this novel, however, is that she was kept a total secret from the vast majority of the German public. Hitler was presented as a single man, married to his country – almost a form of secular Christ figure – and having a real partner did not fit with that image. So, whilst Hitler's death was probably little surprise to the weary Berliners as the Russians began rolling their tanks down the main streets, the presence of a bride at his side was quite a shock. It must have been yet more proof of the way he had lied to them and played God with their lives.

In truth, Eva Braun is something of a tragic figure. She met Hitler in 1929 when she was just seventeen and he already forty, began seeing more of him when the half-niece he lived with committed suicide two years later, and was definitely his lover by 1933. She seems to have been quite naive, and was apparently a cheerful soul, charming to everyone around her. She was also a talented photographer and many of the photos we have of Hitler were taken by her.

Amazingly, she largely avoided politics, being kept away from all meetings and not even being a member of the Nazi party. She was devoted to Hitler, attempting suicide twice during their relationship to attract his attention and cleaving to his side throughout the war. In spring 1945 she refused to stay safely in the country, insisting instead on coming into Berlin to be with him in his – and her – final days. There is, of course, no excusing her close association with the Hitler and his Nazis, but she is a curious sweetness at the heart of all that evil and one day I would like to write about her…

FC Union

Having chosen to make Callum a Leicester City fan (well, actually he sort of chose that himself), I decided it would be good if Max could take Bethan to a German football match as a form of contrast and I couldn't have been more delighted than when I found FC Union – a truly historic club and one with a devoted, loyal and even friendly fan base.

The stories I touch upon in the novel are all true. In 2008 the club desperately needed to renovate the stadium but money was tight. The loyal fans mucked in and helped with the build, with more than 2000 supporters investing a total of around 140,000 working hours. It wasn't the first time they'd helped out, either. Back in 2004, with the club struggling to raise the 1.5 million euro guarantee required by the German FA, the fans set up a campaign called 'Bluten für Union' (bleed for Union). This involved them literally donating blood (for which you are paid in Germany) and giving the money to the club to make up the shortfall in funds.

The club is also famous for its unusual inclusive events. In 2014 they invited fans to take their own sofas to the ground for the whole of the World Cup to watch televised matches with their fellow

Union supporters. More than eight hundred sofas were placed on the pitch in rows and the event won the European 'Fan Experience Award'. This came off the back of a now traditional carol service held at the stadium each year. It started in 2003 when eighty-nine people climbed over the gates to sing carols together because they were missing each other through a winter break in fixtures. It was so popular that more people came the following year and it rapidly snowballed until around twenty thousand now attend to sing carols together for ninety minutes by candlelight. FC Union is a club that is still 51 per cent owned by the fans and they genuinely seem to love it in a refreshingly non-commercialised, honest way that seemed to me to fit Max exactly.

World War 2 was a terrible time for so many people across the world and I am glad that we are now enlightened enough to be able to consider the plight of many normal Germans caught, like the rest of us, in Hitler's vice. I hope this novel has interested readers in Berlin Zoo and its fate in the final period of the Second World War, and if anyone wishes to know more about it, I highly recommend Kevin Prenger's excellent self-published novel *War Zone Zoo: The Berlin Zoo and World War 2*. For more on the wider Battle of Berlin, three books I found especially helpful were Cornelius Ryan's *The Last Battle* (Simon & Schuster, 1966), Roger Moorhouse's *Berlin at War* (Vintage Books, 2011), and Antony's Beevor's *Berlin, The Downfall: 1945* (Penguin, 2002).

Made in United States
North Haven, CT
12 July 2024

54682381R00196